Dov Alfon

A LONG NIGHT IN PARIS

Translated from the Hebrew by
Daniella Zamir

MACLEHOSE PRESS
QUERCUS · LONDON

First published in the Hebrew language as לילה ארוך בפריז (Laila Aroch b'Paris)
by Kinneret in 2016

First published in Great Britain in 2019 by

MacLehose Press
An imprint of Quercus Publishing Ltd
Carmelite House
50 Victoria Embankment
London EC4Y 0DZ

An Hachette UK company

A CIP catalogue record for this book is available
from the British Library.

ISBN (HB) 978 0 85705 879 9
ISBN (TPB) 978 0 85705 880 5
ISBN (Ebook) 978 0 85705 882 9

10 9 8 7 6 5 4 3 2

Designed and typeset in Minion by Libanus Press Ltd, Marlborough
Printed and bound in Great Britain by Clays Ltd, Elcograf S.p.A

To Adam Vital, Yigal Palmor and the rest of the soldiers in the Apocalypse Department at the Yarkon Base.

"A long night in Paris will cure us of all this"

Napoleon Bonaparte, after the retreat from Moscow,
in response to an officer asking how they could recover
from the loss of eighteen thousand soldiers.

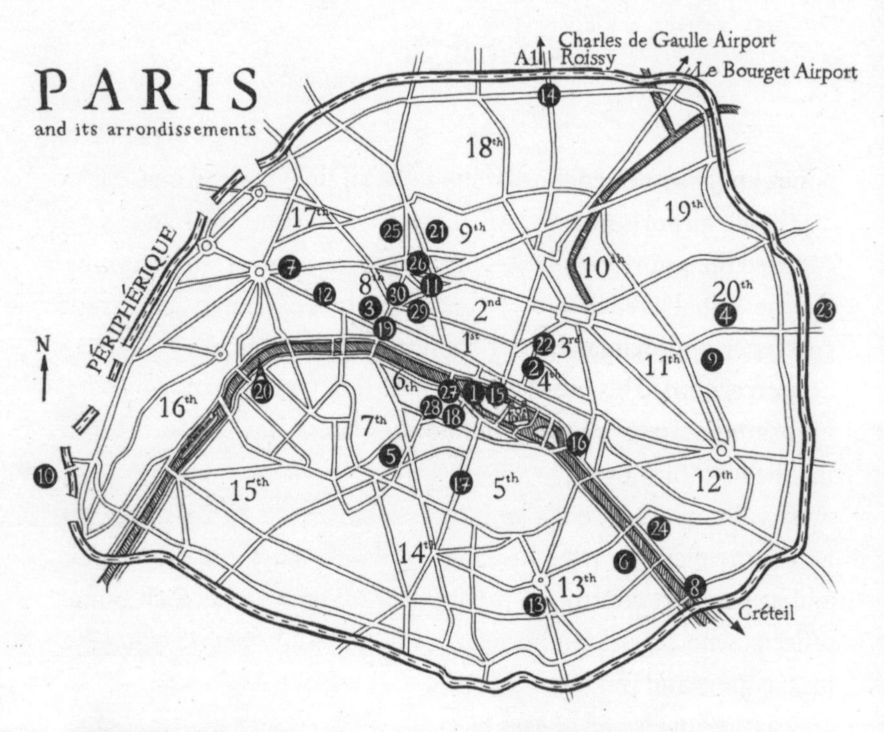

1. Police Headquarters
2. Pompidou Centre
3. Israeli Embassy
4. Belleville police station
5. Prime Minister's Office
6. Bibliothèque Nationale de France
7. Boulevard Haussmann
8. Porte de Bercy, Avenue d'Ivry
9. Père Lachaise Cemetery
10. Hôtel Molitor
11. Opéra
12. Le Président
13. Tolbiac Métro
14. Porte de la Chapelle, Saint-Ouen
15. Sainte-Chapelle
16. Paris morgue
17. Boulevard St Michel
18. Boulevard St Germain
19. Place de la Concorde
20. Eiffel Tower
21. Le Flamboire
22. Breizh Café
23. Bagnolet
24. Jardin Yitzhak Rabin
25. Gare St Lazare
26. Printemps Haussmann
27. Cour de Rohan
28. Le Danton
29. Le Grand Hôtel
30. Église de la Madeleine

Chapter 1

Nine people witnessed the abduction of Yaniv Meidan from Charles de Gaulle airport, not including the hundreds of thousands who watched the security camera footage once it had been posted online.

The initial French police report described him as "an Israeli passenger, approximately twenty years old", although a week earlier he had celebrated his twenty-fifth birthday. His colleagues described him as "mischievous", some calling him "childish". They all agreed that he was "fun-loving".

He disembarked, noticeably cheerful, from El Al flight 319. As he left the plane he tried his luck again with the flight attendants, and at passport control he played the fool with the French police officers, who regarded him with blatant hostility before stamping his passport and waving him on.

That is how it had always been. Ever since kindergarten, everyone had forgiven Meidan for everything. He had an exuberant, partly juvenile spontaneity about him which succeeded in charming every employer he had ever worked for, as well as winning over quite a few women, if only for a while. "It's easy to forgive Yaniv," a teacher once said to his mother.

Nothing else distinguished him from the other two hundred Israelis who had come to Paris to participate in the CeBit Europe Expo. With a buzz cut and matching stubble, wearing jeans and a T-shirt with the logo of a previous year's computer fair, he wore the uniform of all young men in a country self-described as a "start-up nation". In the footage he was seen forever fiddling with his mobile.

He was in his second year as marketing manager of the software company B.O.R., and that made him the most senior member of the team sent to the event. There were six of them, including him – a small team compared to the other, larger companies. "What we lack in money, we make up for in talent," he called out to his colleagues, who viewed him with a mixture of amusement and affection.

The baggage claim was in a dimly lit, cramped hall. Meidan picked up the pace of his jokes. The longer they had to wait, the more bored he became, and he ambled to and fro, chatting, drumming against the motionless conveyor belt. He hated waiting. He hated being bored. His success as a marketing manager was directly linked to this quality, his need to inject interest into any given moment.

There was no sign of the suitcases. At one point he began photographing himself in different poses, and uploaded a picture of himself next to the billboard of the Galeries Lafayette department store sticking his tongue out at the nude model, having no thought that the photograph would appear the next day on the front page of the most popular Israeli newspaper, *Yedioth Ahronoth.*

The marketing managers of the rival companies sat down with their laptops and made use of the time to work, rehearsing their presentations for the fair. "It's all about connecting," Meidan told his team, and whipped out a Visa card to pull a funny face in front of an American Express billboard.

Suddenly suitcases were shuffling onto the conveyor belt, and their luggage was among the first to appear. "Don't worry, guys, the fair will be there tomorrow too," Meidan jeered at the other passengers, and led his team towards the exit with a triumphant swagger.

They passed through the green customs line, he in the lead, his five colleagues in his wake. The automatic exit doors opened at once, and he was met with a row of a dozen greeters bearing signs, chauffeurs waiting for this or that passenger. Half of them looked like gangsters, but among them stood a breathtaking blonde in a red hotel uniform holding up her sign. Meidan at once approached her, sure that there was time for one last horsing around in front of the guys, just one more opportunity for tomfoolery, and that would be it.

It was 10.40 a.m., Monday, April 16.

Chapter 2

Meanwhile, in Tel Aviv, Segen* Oriana Talmor was being rushed into the special meeting.

It was the first time she had been asked to represent her unit at Camp Rabin, Tzahal's headquarters in HaKirya. She looked around in wonder at the huge Israeli Defence Forces compound, while the athletic military policeman who had been assigned as her escort walked briskly ahead. Segen Talmor followed him through a labyrinth of brutalist concrete barracks and futurist glass towers, along roads bearing incongruous names like "Iris Walk" or "Greenfields Lane", towards their destination.

It took twenty minutes and several security checks for them to reach the floor that houses the executive offices of Tzahal's Chief of Intelligence. The lobby was already full of people. They spilled out into the corridor, and a heavy-set rav seren bearing a pile of folders sat himself on the receptionist's desk, all the while ignoring her angry glares.

Oriana found a seat by a window overlooking Tel Aviv. In front of her, a mass of low-rise buildings, occasionally dotted with green, spilled towards the pale Mediterranean coast. The sea was nowhere to be seen, bleached by the sun and eclipsed by residential towers and hotel blocks.

Across the street from the huge military compound people were lining up at gourmet restaurants, riding stylish electric bikes, and exchanging greetings, confidential addresses, family news and vegan recipes. Closer to the gates, a few women dressed in black called

* A Glossary of ranks and their equivalents can be found on p.427

for the end of military occupation in Palestinian territories and were politely ignored by the American tourists and Israeli generals disappearing into the shopping mall ahead. By the car park, dozens of stray cats hovered around the dustbins, waiting for the duty soldier to dump the military food waste.

Although she was so high up, Oriana could sense the intensity of it all. Tel Aviv was celebrated now as the coolest city on earth. It was also the only place in Israel she had never really liked.

She moved away from the window and lingered in front of the strange objects displayed on the walls: a cowboy hat, a gift from the then head of the C.I.A.; a sword of pure silver, a present from Zimbabwe's head of security services; a vintage Toblerone poster from the head of Swiss counter-intelligence. She tried to guess what gifts the Israeli Chief of Intelligence had given in return.

At 12 p.m. on the dot, the heavy wooden door opened and everyone filed into the conference room, where the air-conditioning unit was on full blast. Oriana took a seat at the corner of the table close to the door.

A commotion erupted when representatives of intelligence-gathering units moved to take the chairs at the head of the table, while the research department staff loudly exclaimed that seating was pre-assigned. In his early twenties, Oren was the ambitious adjutant to the Chief of Intelligence. Clearly under pressure, he reprimanded both sides indiscriminately. The representative of the naval intelligence division, the only other woman in the room, casually sat down next to the seat reserved for the chairman of the meeting, her white uniform lending her the appearance of a bride on her wedding day. Slipping in through a side door, the head of research, less than impressed, demanded she move aside. From their row of portraits on the walls, the intelligence chiefs of generations past gazed down at the ruckus, secure in their black and white stateliness.

When everyone was finally seated, the adjutant opened with a roll call, a classroom ritual that only added to the childish atmosphere.

"Information security?"

"Here."

"Air intelligence group?"

"Here."

"Naval intelligence department?"

"Here."

The research divisions were called out by number, followed by the intelligence-gathering units, including two that Oriana had not even known existed. No fewer than three representatives from the Mossad were in attendance.

"504?"

"Here."

"8200?"

He pronounced the name of the unit like a rookie: "eight thousand two hundred" instead of "eight two hundred".

"Here."

All eyes turned to her with what felt like overly appreciative glances, some ogling unabashedly. Oren had a different problem.

"This is a meeting summoned by the Chief of Military Intelligence, Aluf Rotelmann. He explicitly asked that the head of 8200's Special Section be here today."

"There is no head of section at the moment, Seren. I am the deputy and acting head," Oriana said. The general's adjutant was a seren, only one rank above her, but his position conferred on him much more power. Running through her mind was the advice she gave herself at moments like these: "Do not smile apologetically. Do not repeat what you have already said. If they are waiting for you to elaborate, let them wait."

The adjutant was the first to break. "Sgan Aluf Shlomo Tiriani is head of Unit 8200's Special Section," Oren said, his eyes scanning the room for the sgan aluf. "Are you saying he's on leave?"

"He was released from duty yesterday," Oriana said. "His replacement is currently on a training tour abroad. He is expected to take up his duties when he returns," she said.

"We understood that Tiriani was coming," the young man said. He had big eyes and lips that formed the shape of an "O" even when they weren't moving, as if still hungry for the maternal breast. The paratrooper's wings on his chest completed the image of a child in fancy dress for Purim.

"I regret the disappointment my presence has caused you," Oriana said. Laughter erupted across the room, but Oren was quick to silence it. He completed the roll call, got up to open an inner door, and called out, "We're ready."

Chapter 3

The scene at Charles de Gaulle Terminal 2 was becoming unmanageable, and Commissaire Jules Léger of the Police Judiciaire wanted the day to be over and done.

His head hurt. Not a muffled headache, not the kind that stays politely in the background; not a hangover type of headache, the kind that's accompanied by comforting memories of the previous night. Not a headache that derives from hunger, heralding hope for a heartening and healing meal. And certainly not a headache that disappears of its own accord within a short while, like after drinking a granita in the summer. No, this was a genuine headache, verging on a migraine, and there were many reasons for it, which Commissaire Léger now tried to articulate to himself.

First, there was the simple and indisputable fact that a passenger had disappeared from one of the most secure locations in France, not half an hour after his flight had landed.

Second, and this was sheer injustice, the scene of the event had fallen under his domain completely by chance. The airport's chief of police was on a week's holiday, and Commissaire Léger had received an order that in the chief's absence he was to preside over investigations at the airport as well. He did not know the investigators around him, and he was not familiar with the scene either. His attempts to organise a semblance of police activity exacerbated his headache: the wail of police sirens outside competed with the noise of the radios inside, and together they pounded mercilessly against his aching temples.

Third, and high on the list of reasons for his headache, two

Israeli officials, who without warning had appeared on the scene, were now demanding to be allowed to participate in questioning the witnesses.

Léger vaguely recognised the one named Chico, an older man with a mop of red hair, not necessarily natural, who was the representative of the Israeli police in Europe. Léger had met him in meetings to discuss the security of Israeli institutions in Paris, but to the best of his recollection he had never requested to be involved in an investigation before.

The other Israeli did not look like a policeman at all. He was tall, in tight black jeans and a white shirt whose price Léger estimated to be more than his monthly salary. Blue eyes gazed out beneath a shock of black hair dashed with white, offset by a horizontal scar on his chin which prevented his face from appearing altogether too gentle for a man. He stared straight past Léger. The commissaire had encountered several of his kind throughout his career, usually in fraud investigations. He was familiar with the Israeli's obscure I.D., a laminated card with a photograph that looked too recent, this one bearing a foreign name and military rank. If Léger chose to believe the card, he was Colonel Zeev Abadi. Léger's urologist was named Abadi too, a fact that did not alleviate his concerns. The emblem of the state of Israel was proudly displayed on the back of the card, with the request, in English and French, that all law authorities across the globe "aid in any way the carrier of this card", whom it defined simply as "Investigator".

"Anyone could make a card like this at home," Léger said, looking up to meet Abadi's eyes. Military, he thought. *Intelligence?*

"I'm in Paris partly by chance," said the mysterious Israeli, and put the card back in his wallet, as if by doing so he had replied to Léger's comment.

His French was slow but precise, almost poetic. "*Un peu par hasard*," Léger thought, and it was only his headache that prevented him from remembering if it was borrowed from a poem. He wanted to ask Colonel Abadi – if that was indeed his name – how an investigator could stumble *partly by chance* upon a crime scene thousands of miles from his office, but instead he turned to the airport inspector. "Let's get them over to their witnesses."

Chapter 4

It was soon after midday in Tel Aviv, but you would not have guessed it from inside. There were no windows in the giant hall, which was illuminated day and night by white neon bulbs. The hands of a dozen conflicting clocks, each bearing the name of a distant city, advanced on the main wall. It was seriously cold. Even at the height of summer the soldiers sat huddled in coats, and spent entire shifts rubbing each other's shoulders. Over the years, numerous complaints had been submitted to the ombudsman, but the air-conditioning units kept rattling on: in the central nervous system of Israeli military intelligence, the welfare of the computers came before the welfare of people.

The reports poured in at a dizzying pace, dozens every minute, from every military intelligence unit. In 99 per cent of the cases, the algorithms distributed the reports to the relevant sections without the need for human intervention. In other cases the report appeared on one of the screens, and the soldier had to decide within seconds whether it warranted the shift manager's attention.

The volume of data was enormous. The computers were capable not only of screening the reports but also of determining their level of importance according to the credibility of the source and sensitivity to keywords. They also identified similar reports and linked them, so that at 12.14 p.m., the screens lit up in concert in front of the soldier at Station 23.

To: CENTRAL
From: HATZAV OSINT Europe
Priority: Very Urgent/Unclassified

Passengers at Charles de Gaulle airport currently reporting on social media police forces sweeping Terminal 2A (*El Al terminal*, duty officer's comment).

To: CENTRAL
From: El Al/Security/Chief Security Office
Priority: Immediate/Restricted
El Al chief security officer Paris reports possible abduction of Israeli citizen from Charles de Gaulle airport. Further details tk.

To: CENTRAL
From: Police/National Headquarters/Foreign Intelligence
Priority: Immediate/Secret
Israeli police representative in Europe reports Israeli citizen described as missing person by Paris police. Circumstances unclear. Police representative at location with military attaché's representative. Further information as available.

To: CENTRAL
From: Aman/Central Intelligence-Gathering Unit/U.S. Intelligence Liaison Unit
Priority: Immediate/Top Secret
Clearance level: Code Black
French Police canvassing Terminal 2A Charles de Gaulle airport in search of Israeli passenger Yaniv Meidan, approx. 20 y/o, visiting Paris to attend CeBit Expo. Disappeared disembarking El Al flight 319. (*Initial lead is criminal*, duty officer's note.)

The soldier in front of the screen did not take unnecessary risks, and pressed the forward button. Ten feet behind him, on an elevated podium, the shift manager sat in front of a giant screen that covered the entire wall. That day it happened to be a sergeant only days from her release date whose thoughts were fixed on her upcoming trip to the beaches of Sri Lanka.

"It seems criminal to me," she said.

"Why would a techie be involved in criminal activity?" the soldier said. "The U.S. liaison guys automatically label as 'criminal' any event that isn't Palestinian-related. Does their source even exist, and at that clearance level?"

Most of the reports from the U.S. intelligence liaison unit arrived from American listening posts, usually managed by the N.S.A. How could their duty officer even know whether it was a criminal or security event? The soldier's question was certainly apt, even if the sergeant would gladly have done without apt questions at that moment. The only questions she longed to hear were: "Would you like a special meal on your flight?" or "Would you like anything from the duty-free cart?"

"What do I need this shit for, forty-eight hours before my discharge?" she said to the soldier, who was sweet and understanding. She smiled at him and pressed the button.

"Executive office, this is Central," she said into the microphone. "We have a Code Black report for the chief, immediate urgency." On the top floor of the general headquarters building next door, two soldiers sprang up from their bench and raced downstairs.

Chapter 5

"Did you notice him on the flight?" Chico said to Abadi. "Is this Meidan guy the reason you're here?" The two men had detached themselves from the investigation team at Charles de Gaulle and were walking through the arrivals hall of Terminal 2.

"I'm not here," Abadi said, turning to face the Israeli police representative, who stopped in his tracks.

Unsure how to react, Chico ran his hand through his red hair. "Of course, of course," he apologised. "I completely understand if you prefer not to talk about your mission. In fact, I wish you wouldn't."

"I'm not," Abadi said.

"This kidnapping is just so strange," Chico said. He continued in a whisper, "France has the highest rate of unsolved crimes in the Western world. This investigation isn't looking too good. We may have to intervene."

Abadi did not bother to answer, instead turning and walking back towards Léger. What missing persons investigation did look good in the first few hours? The facts were unclear, there was no apparent motive, the witnesses contradicted themselves, and any shred of evidence had disappeared. The Israeli police probably would not have done a better job.

Which is why he was not surprised by the results, as presented by the airport police inspector, when they reached him. The bottom line was clear. Clear – and completely bewildering.

"We have a missing Israeli passenger, Yaniv Meidan, twenty-five years old, a marketing manager, who disappeared from the terminal as if he'd vanished off the face of the earth. The witnesses claim he was abducted in the arrivals hall by a woman he could not possibly have known, a tall blonde in a red hotel uniform."

"What do you mean when you say she abducted him? By force?" Chico said.

Léger motioned towards the airport inspector with a large, circular gesture that probably meant, "Explain it to them again, more slowly." Abadi had yet to decide whether the commissaire was ill or if his sombre silence was his way of expressing dissatisfaction.

"As far as we're concerned, this is for now a missing persons case," the airport police inspector said. "The woman was captured by the security cameras entering the terminal in a hotel uniform, and was here waiting for the passengers to arrive, standing next to the chauffeurs and greeters, all holding signs with the names of passengers. She waited for about half an hour with a sign. We couldn't read the name on it, but when the doors opened and the passengers started coming out, the missing person, and this is a fact, approached her. He is seen on camera accompanying her quite willingly to the lifts leading to the underground car park."

"So why are you searching the terminal?" Abadi said. "What makes you think he may have been abducted?"

"First of all, we're on alert because of intelligence reports about the possible abduction of an Israeli citizen in France. I mean, you're here, aren't you?" he said, looking at Chico for confirmation, before continuing. "And the second reason …"

"The second reason?" Abadi said, because the inspector had paused and seemed to be struggling to find the right words.

"The second reason is because they disappeared," he said at last. "They *disappeared.* I wanted to check if this guy walked out with the blonde of his own free will, so I asked for the footage from the surveillance cameras. They can be seen entering the lift together, but there's no sight of them exiting. That's why I said it was as if they'd vanished off the face of the earth. Given the situation, I updated Commissaire Léger, and we decided to launch an investigation."

Chico cleared his throat dramatically and asked, "Commissaire Léger, could you perhaps clarify this for Colonel Abadi, who as a military man and not a police investigator is perhaps finding it difficult to comprehend these findings?"

Abadi did not have a chance to intervene before Léger said, "I don't know in what capacity Colonel Abadi is here. I assume the witnesses called the Israeli embassy, which is their right. I'm co-operating with you as a matter of courtesy. If you don't like what you're hearing, you are welcome to return to the Israeli embassy and wait for our report through the customary channels."

"I meant no offence," Abadi said. "We just want to understand what evidence made you suspect he didn't leave the airport of his own volition."

Once again Léger motioned towards his deputy, who said: "There are three lifts that lead to the underground car park. There are no cameras inside the lifts, but we have one on each door, one on the ground floor and one at car park level. We cross-referenced the footage, ten minutes back and ten minutes forward. They entered the lift together on the ground floor, but they did not take the exit on the parking level. Both Yaniv Meidan and the hotel greeter disappeared as if they'd been swallowed up by the lift."

Commissaire Léger shot Abadi a questioning, almost defiant look. "I understand you're here to interrogate the witnesses. I'm willing to permit that, and perhaps you'll be able to draw information that will contradict the footage." He gestured magnanimously towards the other room, in which voices shouting angrily in Hebrew could be heard.

It was 11.30 a.m., Monday, April 16.

Chapter 6

As far as the adjutant was concerned, the report could not have come at a less convenient time.

Oren kept flipping the envelope between his fingers. It was marked and sealed in accordance with protocol. "Clearance Black," the stamp cautioned. Black was the only colour on the intelligence security scale that did not indicate the sensitivity of the source but of the report itself. It might contain information obtained by illegal means or with a direct connection to a specific Israeli citizen. In any case, it was too sensitive to be widely distributed. Since the days of telex and fax machines, intelligence reports had been transferred electronically; only reports with black clearance were delivered to the Chief of Intelligence in a secure envelope with a wax seal, by hand, as in the Middle Ages.

The special meeting had begun half an hour ago, which meant that Rotelmann was about to get to the heart of the presentation. On the one hand, the instructions were "do not disturb". But on the other hand . . . On the other hand, the report from Charles de Gaulle was connected to the alert that had triggered the meeting in the first place, in a direct, odd and almost prophetic way. Oren bounced the envelope between his hands like a hot potato. He asked the secretary again, "Are we sure he didn't serve in Unit 8200?"

"Yaniv Meidan, personnel number 8531272, enlisted in the armoured corps and was discharged with the rank of samal four years ago, after which he had his medical profile lowered due to back pain. He has since been serving his reserve duty in the food supply centre. He has not served a single day in the Intelligence Corps, let alone in Unit 8200."

She spoke to him in her habitual, almost insolent tone, pronouncing the sergeant's rank with contempt, but it was not the right day for a confrontation. He glanced at the clock. The meeting would be over in half an hour, and the temptation to wait until its end to present Aluf Rotelmann with the envelope was overwhelming.

"I'm going back into the meeting, slip me a note if there's any development," he said in the most authoritative voice he could muster. In the hallway between the chambers and the conference room, he placed his mobile in the secure box, straightened out his shirt in front of the mirror, and considered for a moment kissing the *mezuzah* for divine protection. He entered with rapid steps and sat back in his chair. His absence had not excited any particular attention. All eyes were on the presentation. All eyes – except for the beautiful eyes of the new 8200 officer, which lit upon the envelope he was holding. Her gaze lingered upon the black seal and then settled on him with quizzical suspicion.

Everything was going according to plan, he reassured himself, all in all. Everything, that is, apart from the unexplained disappearance of a citizen at the centre of the scene, and the simultaneously unexplained replacement of the head of the relevant section by an overly inquisitive officer. The sweat on his forehead was not part of the plan either.

Chapter 7

The police post at the terminal was larger than one would imagine from the outside, its narrow door leading to an entire suite of offices. In the first, technicians were busy printing photographs of Meidan from the security footage. They would not at this stage be distributed to every office in the port, and certainly not to the border police, the inspector explained to them. This was an investigation of a passenger who had gone missing under unclear circumstances – circumstances that included the possibility that the passenger had disappeared of his own volition.

The group was invited to watch clips of footage from the security cameras. Abadi did so merely out of courtesy, then asked to speak to the missing person's travel companions.

"The answer will not come from the witnesses either," Léger said, offended, but he led them back to the adjacent hall.

There were in fact two groups of witnesses: in addition to Meidan's frantic travelling companions, the French police had identified three of the drivers who had been waiting at the arrivals gate. All three, Léger informed his guests, were former Israelis without proper French work permits. As unlicensed taxi drivers hoping to attract tourists to their unmarked vehicles, they were paying more attention to the arriving passengers than to what was happening around them in the hall.

But all three remembered the girl. Long blonde hair, tall, red uniform – those were the descriptions that kept resurfacing in the witness statements. Like them, she was apparently waiting for passengers, and they had assumed she was working for one of the big hotel chains. They remembered Meidan, too, because he was among the first to emerge from the customs area. One of the drivers testified that he had said in a low voice, in Hebrew, "Want a cheap ride to Paris?" But Meidan had immediately approached the blonde, apparently trying to make out the sign she was holding, and the driver abandoned his efforts. None of the three knew what happened afterwards.

The interrogation proceeded in some disorder, without note-taking. Chico asked his questions in Hebrew and then translated the answers into English. Léger's deputy followed suit in French. It was a circus, but it hardly mattered; their testimonies were of no value.

"*Alors*, Colonel Abadi?" the commissaire asked in a tone that could have been patronising but verged on empathic. The room fell quiet.

"I don't like blondes," Abadi said at last.

"I believe you're in the minority there," Léger said, struggling to follow his guest's train of thought.

"And in a short red uniform, no less. That's all the witnesses are going to remember."

"She's a hotel greeter. Most of them are blonde, and all have some sort of uniform. We are questioning all the major hotels in Paris about her. I could share your opinion of blondes with them."

"Don't waste your time, no hotel will have heard of her," Abadi said, and turned to the second group of witnesses.

There were five of them, all members of Meidan's delegation, waiting impatiently for their interrogation and not without anger. "How long are these bastards going to keep us here?" one of them said after being introduced to the Israeli investigators. They looked tired and nervous, turning over in their minds the main question: where to go from here? Some wanted to stay in the airport until their colleague turned up; others wanted to leave for the fair without further delay.

A bald man named Assaf spoke on behalf of the group, since they had all had the same vantage point: they had seen Meidan leaving the baggage hall with his suitcase. Several greeters had been standing in front of him, some holding signs. Meidan had gone straight to the blonde in the red uniform.

"He was trying to flirt with her," Assaf said, at which Dubi, the oldest in the group, corrected him: "He was just trying to give us a laugh. It wasn't as if he thought he had a chance with her."

They agreed that he had gone straight to her, on the pretence of trying to read the name on her sign. Assaf said that Meidan "just wanted to get a look at her boobs". He saw them exchanging some words, then Meidan turned round and called out to them, "Guys, don't wait, I've found me a better ride!" He laughed and followed the blonde to the lifts to the underground car park. That was the last they had seen of him.

All eyes turned to Abadi, who chose to ask in French, if only to try out the simultaneous interpreting in the opposite direction, "*Est-ce que l'ascenseur montait ou descendait?*"

Chico, at first surprised by the switch of language, translated for the five members of the group. "He wants to know if the lift went up or down."

"Why would it go up?" Assaf said. "They were going to the car park." But then a scrawny, bespectacled man who said his name was Uri, and who turned out to be the company's security manager, said, "From what I saw, the lift did go up. The girl led him towards the lift, they went in, the doors shut. No floor number lit up, but I definitely saw a flashing arrow pointing upwards."

Commissaire Léger looked like someone who was enjoying a particularly refined moment in a concert. "This is, of course, an interesting turn of events," he said. "Unfortunately, it makes no sense at all."

"What's on the upper levels?" Abadi said. But what he really wanted to know was: since when did sense have anything to do with criminal activity, or with life in general for that matter? Familiar with the French, however, he stuck to the facts.

At that moment, Léger was a man losing his patience. "There is no upper level. That lift allows access to Terminal 2B, a level closed for the next five years for construction."

"Perhaps we could go up there?" Abadi suggested brightly, as if an unexpected idea had just crossed his mind.

"My officers have investigated that level. We found nothing there."

"We would nevertheless like to take a look," Abadi said, like a man used to apologising for his whims. "As an investigator I may not like blondes," he said, looking Léger's way, "but I love deserted construction sites."

Chapter 8

In the conference room above Tel Aviv, Aluf Rotelmann finished his introductory remarks. His deputy and head of intelligence-gathering, a brigadier general whose name Oriana did not know but whom everyone called "Zorro", got up to give the main presentation. "First, let's give a warm thank you to our commander," the tat aluf said. When Rotelmann replied with a nod, Zorro went on. "No, I mean it, I want to thank Aluf Rotelmann. Really, thanks to your leadership we are prepared to face any intelligence challenge and deal with it quickly and efficiently," he added with ceremony, turning to face the room rather than the subject of his statement.

By any standard of organisational bootlicking it was embarrassing. Rotelmann nodded slightly. "Thank you, Zorro, you were the one who came up with the solution, so, right back at you," he said with a blank expression. The phrasing, like every part of his speech so far, could have been interpreted in two ways. Judging from the sparkle in his eyes, Zorro clearly took it as praise.

Oren gave the signal for a snack break, and Oriana made use of the time to go over her notes. Although Aluf Rotelmann had only spoken for ten minutes, and had mentioned all the intelligence-gathering units, most of his introductory statements had been about 8200. She divided them into three categories: Bad, Sad and Mad.

Under "Bad" went his commonplace complaint about intelligence-gathering: there was simply too much of it. It was on everyone's lips nowadays. "We have the most powerful intelligence-gathering organisation in the world," Rotelmann had said, "a combination of our own Unit 8200 and our agreement with the N.S.A. Yet for us to be able effectively to benefit from all this data, information gathering must cede to research, and not the other way round."

On the face of it, it was an empty, meaningless statement. But it had a sound, movement and colour that stood out against the general landscape, like a snake slithering across the autumn leaves in the kibbutz where, as a child, she had played outside before supper. The explicit reference to 8200, in such a general speech that was supposedly intended to bring everyone together, could not have been coincidental.

It had become worse later, in a statement she filed under "Sad", an enigmatic sentence, more threatening than the rest: "As well as increasing collaboration between all branches of intelligence, we will make a point of screening clearance holders in our intelligence-gathering units more strictly, especially in Unit 8200."

And then it happened. Rotelmann pointed to an organisational chart on the wall titled "The Israeli Intelligence Community", and spoke about the need for tighter security. Every player was placed according to hierarchy. At the top was the Chief of Defence Staff at Tzahal, the I.D.F.; beside him was his deputy, the Vice Chief of Defence Staff; and beside the Vice Chief of Defence was Rotelmann himself, the Chief of Intelligence.

The chart correctly showed that Rotelmann had three deputies, one for intelligence-gathering, one for operations, one for research. The head of intelligence-gathering was a brigadier general. Tat Aluf Zorro was responsible for eight units, including Unit 8200. But where Oriana expected to see her section within 8200, under the direct responsibility of the Chief of Defence Staff himself, there was a blank space.

She scanned the chart for Special Section, but couldn't find it. Security for Unit 8200 – the people looking for spies, protecting sources, investigating leaks, enforcing intelligence discipline, managing counter-intelligence operations – would, the chart indicated, now be handled outside the unit by Field Security, the Military Police and even the Shabak, none of them working independently from the intelligence hierarchy.

"The Shabak," Oriana thought. "Those guys have wanted to get their hands on internal security in 8200 for years." In fact, the organisation had been eager to get full control of internal security everywhere. Formerly known as the Shin-Beth, a diminutive considered too cute for its ambition, it was now referred to by its real acronym, Shabak, although in recent years its commanders had been strict about using the full name, which was as vague as its inherent menace: "Sherut Ha-Bitahon Ha-Klali" ("The General Security Service").

Security. Rabin had been assassinated right under the eyes of the Shabak agents supposed to protect him, and the unit had suffered. It had lost stature and been stripped of many of its prerogatives, including the surveillance of sensitive military units for spies. In 8200, probably the biggest and most important of these, Special Section was now managing all security matters. Oriana looked again at the writing on the wall.

So who was supposed to manage the stricter screening of Unit 8200 and the tighter security of N.S.A. intelligence? Who was supposed to be the special police in this most powerful intelligence-gathering organisation in the world? Was Aluf Rotelmann suggesting that he would curtail Special Section's autonomy, turning it into an internal, toothless and ultimately unimportant branch of his huge organisation?

There was no way of knowing from his expression. He was sitting at the head of the table now, looking on as the participants devoured the chocolate rugelach, waited for the sugar to be passed and exchanged verdicts on the quality of the coffee. He himself neither ate nor drank. The message broadcast by his body language was "I need none of you."

That was all too clear from his next announcement, which Oriana wrote down under the heading "Mad".

"I've asked Zorro here to give you all a refresher on The Most Wanted. We will not tolerate intelligence-gathering efforts in which the left hand does not know what the right is doing."

Oriana had looked at him with distrust. "The Most Wanted" was the common name given to the "The Most Wanted Priority Intelligence Requirements as of Today" – the agenda of each soldier in the corps. Even though every commander had his own intelligence requirement, and some units had requirements for each operation and each day of the week, when intelligence people used this particular phrase with its definite article – The Most Wanted – they meant the Intelligence Chief's requirement, written by him and forwarded every night on the dot of midnight to thousands and thousands of sources, agents, operators and commanders.

The Most Wanted was the most important priority in the military, top of the intelligence agenda; the idea that intelligence officers would need a refresher course on it was puzzling enough; summoning the heads of all departments for that purpose was extraordinary. Would the Chief of the Air Force call a meeting to explain how to intercept an aircraft? Even the participants who were busy foraging raised their eyes in wonder.

"People, we'd like to continue," the adjutant said, and as if by magic office assistants appeared to clear the trays from the table. Zorro sprang up and turned on his presentation. On the huge screen the corps insignia appeared, with the title "Top Secret – Internal" flashing below it.

As a security officer in one of the army's most sensitive units, Oriana was all too familiar with the security protocols for military documents. "Top Secret", for instance, was certainly a security classification. "Internal", on the other hand, was a meaningless administrative title. In theory, there was no point adding it to a document that was already classified. But in practice, the word indicated that the presentation was not actually top secret because there never was a presentation. Once it was finished it would never again be mentioned; it had taken place only for a split second, in the "internal" confines of this conference room.

"Can we kill the lights?" Zorro said.

Chapter 9

"*Non, non, non. Écoute moi,*" the P.R. manager said adamantly, pacing up and down her office, phone in hand, a habit that somehow helped her dictate the pace of the conversation. "Now you listen to me, more than five thousand people disappear in Paris each year. Five thousand. Are you going to write an article about each one of them? Everyone has the right to embark on a new life."

The ruling of her boss, the airport's publicity director, was both simple and intimidating: nothing bad happens in Charles de Gaulle, ever. The last thing he would want to see on the news was an item about the abduction of a passenger. So far she had managed to fend off two reporters and had ignored messages left by three others.

"The question is whether he disappeared of his own will," the reporter said. He was at his house, an hour and a half's drive from the airport, and was not thrilled about the inconclusive information the news desk had sent him, which so far had appeared only on social networks.

"Listen, there's nothing to come down here for," the P.R. manager said. "You'd be wasting your time. The passenger picked up his luggage, met a girl and decided to explore his options. We're in France, aren't we? It happens all the time – airports are romantic places. If you came here for the press conferences I keep inviting you to instead of calling me with this nonsense, you'd see for yourself. Just imagine that each time you stood me up I called the police to report you missing. *C'est fou.*"

"It might be madness, but someone did call the police. A lot of police. Passengers uploaded photographs of the terminal showing dogs and security barriers. My editor wants me to look into it."

The P.R. manager changed tactics. "Darling, just about everyone has already looked into it, you're terribly behind. I've had calls from Europe 1, France Info and *Le Parisien*, even papers from Israel. Everyone checked the story and decided to drop it. The fact that he changed his plans doesn't mean he doesn't have a right to privacy. We have laws. The police looked into it, that's true, but they have advised us they aren't launching an investigation. I'm not even allowed to talk to you about it. I'm only returning your call as a courtesy."

"The police informed you they're not launching an investigation?"

"I can tell you for certain there's no investigation. The police have decided not to investigate. Listen closely to what I'm telling you: there is no story."

He rapidly weighed the risks and benefits. So long as the item was not snatched up by their competitors, the news desk would probably leave him alone. "Fine, I'll try talking them out of it," he said. He did not relish wasting his morning on a drive to Roissy, as romantic a place as it might be.

The P.R. manager could not rest on her laurels just yet. "Put the next pest through," she said to her secretary and continued to pace back and forth, like a boxer waiting for his opponent to get up off the floor.

Chapter 10

The famous lift turned out to be very ordinary. It had three buttons, the lower button marked with the underground car park symbol. The middle button, leading to the ground floor from which Meidan and the kidnapper had disappeared, bore the symbol of an airplane. There was no symbol on the top button – it was covered with red duct tape; next to it, the word "transit" had been erased.

Commissaire Léger got into the lift with reluctance. It was obvious to him as well as to his guests that the securing of the site was partial at best. Police officers were guarding the lift with no concern for fingerprints. The brigadiers saluted him and after a pause he reciprocated, like a stranded tourist. He was not familiar with the airport, certainly not with its ins and outs, and this strange investigation felt like a conspiracy plotted by his adversaries in the Paris police with the sole purpose of embarrassing him.

The group was led by the inspector from the airport police accompanied by two officers. He also provided the narrative. Terminal 2 of Charles de Gaulle airport was not really a terminal, he said, pointing at the map in the lift. It was in fact a cluster of terminals, some quite a distance apart. Since the collapse of Terminal 2E in a horrifying accident, all the buildings were being reconstructed.

Now it was Terminal 2A's turn, which was why the upper floor had been blocked off. "As you can see," he said with an evident lack of conviction, "the top button has been decommissioned. The builders still use it because the lift is the only way to reach the upper floor. But the passengers never press it."

The button did not light up, but the lift started moving.

"Decommissioned" but in appearance alone. If the button did not light up, people would assume it wasn't working.

The lift doors opened onto a dimly lit construction site.

"Before the renovations, this level served as an overpass between two buildings," the inspector said, "and now it serves as a temporary storage area for construction materials." The floor was extensive, covered with piles of sand and gravel. To the right stood four neon-coloured containers. To the left Abadi could see a parked forklift next to a chemical toilet and a wheelbarrow. No other work tools were in sight.

"Any cameras here?"

"Of course not. Why would there be cameras here?" Léger said. "It's a construction site, there are no passengers here, only construction workers. Anyway, the labour laws prevent us from surveilling them, not that we have any reason to."

"So where are the workers?"

This time it was the inspector's turn to answer. He had presumably looked into these issues prior to their arrival.

"The renovations are being carried out according to an overarching strategy. For the past month the crew has been working on the adjacent building, and they're due back here in ten days' time."

It was, in short, a good place for a murder. Abadi walked towards the forklift and pointed at the furthermost concrete wall. "And what's that vent over there? Isn't that a cargo lift?"

"There is no cargo lift here, these regular lifts are the only way to get down," the airport inspector said in a tone that had become steadily less polite. "What you see there is the chemical toilet shaft. They can't use the lifts to lower the compartments because of the smell they leave, so the contractor dumps one in the shaft when it's full and they use the lift to carry up a new one."

Abadi peered down. The smell was indeed unbearable, and the depth was impressive. The French could call it a shaft, but it was a sewage pipe that descended vertically down at least three floors. It looked as if the plan had been drawn up by an architect who had heard about construction sites but had never actually visited one.

Léger intervened in an attempt to make peace, the concern in his voice noticeable. "We have already checked every angle, Colonel, they could not have got down to the car park from here."

Abadi took a torch from one of the officers and shone it down into the shaft, but it was too deep for the beam to reach the bottom. The shaft walls were indeed completely clean.

"It goes down into the airport's automated sewage system, and the waste from the whole airport is cleared from the system every hour," the inspector said with conspicuous pride. "We don't have security down there because the air is toxic, but anyhow, there's no way a person could get there through the shaft. Unless he was a lizard."

"And if he was a body?" Abadi said.

Léger intervened once more. "Colonel Abadi, why all the drama? What body? We are dealing with the prank of a passenger who's probably having a good time with that hotel greeter as we speak. I don't think the woman we saw in the footage could have lifted a large and able-bodied man and thrown him down this shaft. And even if she could, she would have had no way of getting herself back down without using the lifts."

"And what would have stopped her from summoning the lift and taking it down?"

"But then we would have caught her in the footage," Léger said with despair. "Think what you may about my men but, believe me, they would recognise a blonde in a red uniform. Unless she hurled herself down the shaft after him, Charles de Gaulle airport's very own Romeo and Juliet."

The forklift was small, its engine cold. The chemical toilet next to it looked brand new, and on its door hung a warning sign in three languages: DO NOT APPROACH. Léger's deputy crouched theatrically in order to peer through the lower vent, as if to make sure no-one was there.

"My men already checked, there's no-one here," he said, ostentatiously wiping his hands on his trousers, as if to make clear that, thanks to this exasperating colonel, he would now have to pay for dry cleaning.

Abadi stood in front of the toilet door and in one motion kicked the handle. The door flew open with a thud. By the time the French had reacted, he was already lighting up the interior with his torch. No-one was inside, but someone had been there not long before. A woman. The toilet was clogged, and in the bowl lay the strands of a blonde wig.

"Commissaire Léger, I hear the sniffer dogs barking in the underground car park. Maybe we should bring them up here," Abadi said. "And in the meantime, let's check those containers for ourselves."

Chapter 11

"The topic of the presentation is a refresher on The Most Wanted," Zorro began, "so I'm going to use last night's list to demonstrate what I'm talking about." He brought up a slide with the document they were all familiar with: "The Most Wanted Priority Intelligence Requirements by the Chief of Intelligence, as of Date of Publication".

The three items from the previous night's The Most Wanted now appeared on the screen.

1. Alerts: any information, as partial as it may be, regarding the intention to abduct soldiers via stolen military vehicles in the north of Samaria, as well as any information, as partial as it may be, regarding the possible abduction of an active or reserve Intelligence Corps soldier in Europe. Special attention to a possible abduction in Paris.

2. Syria: any information based on irregular activity of the Al-Nusra Front along the border, including troop movements.

3. Jordan: confirmation or refutation of rumours regarding King Abdullah's physical health.

Below them was a fourth item that, as far as Oriana could tell, had not been included in the previous night's document:

4. Iran: full or partial information regarding the Chinese government officials in charge of a possible sale of advanced nuclear equipment to Iran, including personal bribes or any other personal information.

"Right," Zorro continued energetically. "The first three items were sent to all agents, all operators and all departments in all our intelligence-gathering units, without exception." He scrolled the cursor from one item to the next. "And this fourth item you see here, with more specific information, was sent only to the relevant elements in the intelligence community. But from now on this kind of item will also appear on the general The Most Wanted. OK, let's have a quick brush-up on the protocols."

From that moment on, Zorro rapidly clicked from one slide to the next, like a bored weatherman in the middle of summer. Everyone feverishly took notes, like students in a dictation. On the screen appeared flow charts, organograms, command tree diagrams, info box templates and dozens of acronyms, as if the heads of Aman had been sent back to Intelligence Foundation Course 101. Zorro only stopped after thirty slides. "Any questions so far?" he said.

There were two ways to conceal information, Oriana's father had taught her. The first was to hide it, which was the usual approach. Locking drawers, encrypting files, using hidden safes – all these were ineffectual, because they exposed the very existence of concealed information. The other way was to present the information as if it was utterly unimportant, to bury it in a sea of additional information, the duller the better. Very few people can detect the problematic clause in a mortgage contract, or the crucial data in a corporation's quarterly report to the stock market. Zorro's presentation was suspiciously boring.

Concentrate. She went into focus mode.

2, 3, 5, 7, 11, 13, 17, 19, 23. Oriana counted in her head all the prime numbers up to her age on her next birthday before opting for a different exercise.

"A time to get, and a time to lose," Oriana heard her father's voice, not her own. "A time to keep, and a time to cast away; a time to rend, and a time to sew; a time to keep silence, and a time to speak . . . "

"Concentrate. Concentrate. Concentrate." She looked again at her screen, this time transferring to her notes each instance of trivial repetitions, false claims or red herrings. She looked incredulously at what little remained, and questions popped up in her mind at an alarming rate.

How could The Most Wanted, the official agenda of the Intelligence Corps, be distributed in several versions? Why would a possible abduction in a Palestinian territory be linked to a possible kidnapping in Paris, when evidently the relevant intelligence sources for each case would be different? Who received the fourth request and who didn't? Why all the fuss about Tiriani's presence at this meeting when Oriana couldn't see any reason Special Section should be involved? How long had this exclusion of certain areas of the Intelligence Corps been going on? Why convene a special meeting to stop it? Why today?

"If there are no questions, let's move on to the second part of the presentation," Rotelmann suggested.

Stay out of it. Stay out of it. Stay out of it. A time to love, and a time to hate; a time for war and a time for peace . . .

"I have a question," said a voice from across the room. Oriana was so surprised that it had not originated from her own throat that it took her a little time to turn towards the enquirer. It was the second-highest ranking officer at the table, the head of the operations division, a young tat aluf. The hostility between him and the head of intelligence-gathering was common knowledge.

"You can ask," Zorro said, smiling. "But you might not get an answer."

"The Most Wanted is the only work document shared by all our units. It has always had just one definitive version, written by the Chief of Intelligence himself. When and why did that change?" he asked.

Zorro shot Rotelmann a look Oriana could not decipher. Suddenly questions erupted from around the room.

"Who received the fourth item and who did not?" one of the Mossad representatives wanted to know, while the heads of research asked how Iranian nuclear information could be restricted while a Jordanian health bulletin was not. Zorro raised his hand for calm.

Rotelmann intervened with palpable reluctance. "All understandable questions. This item is based on highly sensitive material from Unit 8200, and it was therefore decided to restrict distribution. The truth is, Shlomo Tiriani, head of 8200's Special Section, was supposed to present this and tie up any loose ends, but I don't see him here."

All eyes turned to Oriana. Rotelmann noticed and his gaze travelled all the way to her, at the other end of the table. "Who is this young lady?" he asked without taking his eyes off her. "I'm pretty sure that's not Tiriani."

His adjutant flinched in panic. "Commander, I understand Tiriani was discharged yesterday quite unexpectedly. We were not consulted. This lady," he said, pointing at her, not unlike the telltale who had sat next to her in third grade, "was sent in his place to represent 8200 in this meeting. Perhaps, Segen –" and here he laced both syllables of Oriana's rank with scorn – "you could explain how something like this could have happened?" His voice rose suddenly in the second half of the sentence, as if the annoying classmate had turned into the self-righteous teacher.

"Seize the day, put very little trust in tomorrow" – her father used to quote the Romans to her. And she could recite much of Horace by heart as a result. Horace had been right, no-one was about to give her till tomorrow. She heard herself replying, "That I can explain, if necessary. What I can't explain is why, for the past twenty minutes, you have been holding a report sealed with a 'Top Secret Black' clearance instead of handing it immediately to its recipient, the Chief of Intelligence, Aluf Rotelmann, who is sitting right here in front of you."

Oriana heard whispers and the scraping of chairs. Zorro looked anxiously at Rotelmann, who, in turn, looked at Oriana, his face an unreadable mask. The adjutant began stammering an answer, but Oriana would not let him proceed.

"According to the instructions of Tzahal's Chief of Defence Staff, a security officer must intervene at once in severe offences regarding security information, whatever the offender's rank. I'm sorry, Seren, but if you don't hand Aluf Rotelmann that envelope immediately, I'll have to detain you on suspicion of gross negligence in securing a classified document."

The room became as silent as a graveyard. Oren looked at his commander and then approached him with the envelope in his hand, a scolded expression on his face, the very same expression the telltale used to have when she beat the shit out of him.

Chapter 12

The oddest thing, at least in Abadi's mind, was not that a passenger had disappeared soon after landing in Paris; the oddest thing was the fact that throughout the entire mess – while barriers were at last being erected around the terminal, while helicopters hovered above like mosquitos, and while at the scene itself three dogs barked incessantly as they tracked the scent of blood – an alluring female voice continued to invite passengers over the loudspeakers to smoke only in the designated areas.

Evidently, Commissaire Léger was hearing different voices. He lit another cigarette in front of the chemical toilet cabin from which the police officers had extracted not only a blonde wig but also a red hotel uniform and a matching bra and panties. The strong chemicals had coloured everything a single shade of blue, but on the blouse could be seen darker blotches that suggested blood.

"We've gone over the footage from the lifts a thousand times," the inspector said in despair. "Neither Yaniv Meidan nor your blonde kidnapper is to be seen in it."

Meidan, it was already pretty clear to Abadi, had indeed not come down in the lift. His body had in all likelihood been tossed into the shaft, God knows how. And only God knew where the body had ended up, along with the chemical waste from every building in the airport.

The abductor, on the other hand, could only have taken the lift. The officers who checked the video footage had been asked to locate a blonde in a red uniform, but by the time the woman had taken the lift down, she would have borne no resemblance to the hotel greeter who had taken it up.

Much to Abadi's surprise, Léger understood all this intuitively. "We need to analyse the footage again," he said to the inspector, and Abadi heard the suppressed rage in his voice. "We need photographs of every person who exited the lifts on the ground floor between 10.45 and 11.15. Women with heels are high priority. She left her wig and uniform here, but no shoes, so it's very possible she didn't change them."

"The camera angle doesn't show feet," the inspector said. "That's hundreds of women, hundreds. And we have no idea what she looks like. The dogs can't pick up her scent because of the chemical toxins that have penetrated her clothes."

"Let's try taking them back to the area with the containers," Abadi suggested for the second time, and this time, out of desperation, the French agreed.

The storage containers were sealed like vaults. It did not look as if anyone had tried breaking into them, and the sniffer dogs lost interest in them and started barking towards the shaft.

"Why are they even locked?" Abadi said. "Don't the workers need to go in and out all the time?"

"They belong to the airport, not to the contractor," the inspector said. "Airlines use the containers during periods of construction because their offices here are closed."

"So there's an El Al container here?" Abadi said, his gaze searching for identifying marks.

"I don't know. If they fly out of this terminal, then one of these could be El Al's, yes. But what does it matter now?"

"We don't discriminate against El Al," Léger said, trying to regain his composure. "We've been practising equal rights here since 1789."

Yeah, tell me about it, Abadi thought, but refrained from rising to the bait of the Frenchman's sarcasm. Instead, he turned to Chico and said in Hebrew, "Check as quickly as possible with El Al's security officer whether he installed a camera to monitor their container. If he did, get him to hand over to the police this morning's tapes right away."

"I know him," Chico said hesitantly. "He's a hard-ass. I'm sure that if he did install a camera, he'll refuse to co-operate with the French."

"They're going to find out, come what may, in the next few hours," Abadi said. "The problem is that I'm not sure we have a few hours."

Chapter 13

On the surface, Time had stopped doing what it was supposed to do, and just stood still. Everyone was waiting; no-one moved.

But in fact, everything advanced at blinding speed behind the fictitious display of a well-organised and managed reality, the one visible to the public from the windows of houses, the screens, the formal announcements, the sanitised reports.

From the windows of Meidan's parents' home in Ramat Gan, for instance, you could not see the press photographers who had politely settled in the café on the corner, waiting for a signal.

From the Military Censor's office windows on Kaplan Street in HaKirya, Tzahal headquarters appeared calm, almost sleepy. The duty officer stood firm in his refusal to lift the gag order, and his soldiers obsessively scanned the news sites to make sure no-one was sidestepping the injunction without his knowledge.

Within a half-mile radius, each of the four editors of the major news websites separately debated whether to direct readers to the rumour mill that had evolved on social networks and been spreading through online communities for a good hour. They eagerly checked each other's coverage, ready at the click of a button to announce the abduction of Meidan, if any one of the others made the first move.

In the U.S. embassy in Israel, the N.S.A.'s head of security looked at his screen with disbelief. He reread the audit report, then asked for a secure line to Washington.

In the room next to the Prime Minister's chambers, in the government compound in Jerusalem, the Military Secretary had finished his review. He did not present it to the Prime Minister himself, who had announced he would be late and they should start without him, but to four of his advisors, who, in spite of their different titles, were all communications advisors. He gave his presentation in English, because one of the four was an American strategic advisor who did not speak Hebrew.

The American advisor complained that he lacked sufficient data to reach a decision. But the Military Secretary had no more information. "It looks as though he was the victim of mistaken identity," he said patiently, not for the first time. "He has no connection to any state official in Israel. He's just an employee of a small start-up. It's possible that the kidnapper did not even know he was Israeli. The military intelligence liaison unit with the N.S.A. has even raised the possibility that this whole affair is criminal in nature, whether the abduction was linked to his Israeli nationality or not."

"But is he alive or dead?" said the youngest in the group, an advertising executive who was on loan to the office as a strategic advisor.

"We don't know."

"And what *do* we know?"

The Military Secretary shifted uneasily in his chair. "In the past few minutes it seems to have become more likely that he was murdered in the airport itself, and that his body was dumped there in a chemical toilet disposal pit."

The American advisor grimaced. "That's not good. That's not a good image at all."

"He may not have been murdered. We won't know for sure for a few hours, and there's no point waiting."

"I agree," said the advisor in charge of social media. "According to the latest report, the story's going viral. There are hundreds of questions surrounding the fate of Meidan, friends from the delegation are posting like crazy, people are sharing his photo, asking for help in finding out what happened to him. Right now, the Ministry of Foreign Affairs is prohibited from answering these questions, and if we wait another hour or two, they won't be able to suppress it anymore, it'll blow up."

"On the one hand, it could deflect from the usual trouble, get the security agenda back in focus," the American advisor said. The Prime Minister served as defence minister and minister of communications, and it was not always clear to which of the many troubles under his various jurisdictions his advisor was referring. "On the other hand, there are a lot of things here we don't know yet, and I don't like turning the spotlight on something I'm not sure about and then finding out the facts at the same time as the public at large."

The Prime Minister's political advisor, a former publicist now in charge of donor relations, added that he had received a telephone call from a senior official at El Al, asking them to cool the flames. "The company itself had nothing to do with the abduction, so it's not appropriate that El Al's image as a safe airline be libelled over such nonsense," he said. "But if we carry on with the gag order, the story will only gain momentum. The French are with us on this, they have no interest in letting their main airport take a bad rap. It's important that we put out this small fire before it spreads."

The Military Secretary was a veteran. He remembered different times and different offices. In the past he would have refused to present classified military information to publicists. But he had since learned – the hard way – that resistance was futile. He was three years from retirement; he preferred going with the flow.

The American advisor likewise had no intention of launching a revolution. Most of his political clients hired him close to election day, but in Israel that distinction was meaningless. It was always election season for his client, and a young Israeli dumped into a pit of shit on his way to a high-tech convention was sure as hell not a campaign booster.

"I suggest we play it down as much as we can," he said. "We lift the injunction but brief the media not to turn it into something more than it is. It's a criminal matter. The police are on it. If they come to us, we refer them to the Ministry of Foreign Affairs. If they go to the army, the military spokesperson refers them to the police. We'll call the senior editors and explain that it would be irresponsible to overplay it. It's not a significant event."

They picked up their mobiles and went to work.

It was 1.45 p.m., Monday, April 16.

Chapter 14

Scores of commuters got off the Réseau Express Régional at Châtelet station in the centre of Paris. The blonde was still a blonde, but her hair was now short and like a boy's. She wore a long beige raincoat that veered towards the masculine yet matched her red high heels. She took a hesitant step onto the platform, crowded with police officers, but no-one thought to stop her for a background check.

Leaving the station, she turned right and walked as quickly as possible along the neighbouring street, rue du Renard. Just short of the river was her next port of call, the art deco building that housed the municipal sports centre, where a change of clothing awaited her. She negotiated the slippery stone steps, took out a keycard and made her way to the pool's changing rooms. There she retrieved a nylon rucksack from her locker. She took off those damn heels and turned on her mobile.

It took forever to locate the network. Three new messages appeared, all sent by Wasim. First: "Corinne, did it go well?", then "Is everything O.K.?" and finally "Corinne, call me as soon as you can."

"*Putain*," she said in a whisper, and then again, like a mantra, "*putain, putain, putain.*" She wasn't sure if she used the obscenity in reference to him or whether she was describing herself. Her phone beeped again.

"Call me, I have a big, grade A gift for you."

"*Putain.*" This time the insult locked cleanly onto its target. She switched off the mobile and took toiletries and a towel from her locker. She removed her raincoat and, looking in the large mirror, remained naked for several minutes, tears running down her cheeks.

Under the shower nozzle she began to feel like herself again, her spirits slowly reviving under the stream of warm water. But when she saw her raincoat on the bench, she remembered everything and burst into tears once more. She left the building dressed in her own clothes: a pair of light-blue skinny jeans, a green nylon jacket and trainers. She hung the raincoat over a parking bollard, from where it would no doubt be snatched up by a beggar.

In the bustling square next to the Pompidou Centre she sat down by the fountain with its colourful, funny sculptures that she liked. She gazed at the painted figures spurting water at each other, lit up a fat joint and let her mind wander. By the time she was ready to move on, she knew she was going to demand that Wasim double her fee. She also knew there was only one thing she wanted right now – to forget everything that had happened.

Chapter 15

At first Léger struggled to accept the idea that a camera had been installed in a place prohibited by law. Once it sank in, he was uncertain if he required the investigating judge's legal clearance to watch the footage. He contacted the juge d'instruction, who contacted the justice department, who got back to the juge d'instruction with the vague instruction "to act in the best interests of the investigation according to your discretion, with the understanding that a human life might be at risk".

Abadi and Chico were waiting in the meantime at the police post, and nearly an hour went by before Léger returned to take them back up to the top floor. He seemed to be in worse physical shape than he had been earlier that morning. As they waited in silence for the lift, Léger fixed his eyes firmly on the ground, his jaw set firm.

The site was now illuminated by police spotlights, and technicians in white lab coats ambled to and fro, grumbling that the crime scene was contaminated and the set-up unprofessional. You could almost hear Léger grinding his teeth as they crossed the cordoned-off area on their way to the El Al container.

The door was open now. Posters from the Israeli Ministry of Tourism hung on the wall. "Jerusalem celebrates three thousand years"; "In Israel your roots will grow wings"; "Israel, your true home". A bulb dangling from the ceiling gave off a yellowish light which granted the sofa below it an almost cheerful appearance.

On the sofa, between two agitated French policemen, sat a man with blue eyes and white hair who was no youngster. He could have been a model in an advertisement for an executive car, someone who had done his homework and had assessed the competition before deciding on a Lexus. "Abadi, I'd like to introduce you to Ron Barak, El Al's security officer in Paris," Chico said.

Barak sat with a straight back, an air-gapped laptop on his knees, his gaze challenging everyone around him. It was impossible to tell whether the appearance of the Israelis was a relief or a disappointment. Léger's English, which up to now had been rather limited, improved miraculously thanks to the sudden rage that flared in him. Even his terrible French accent seemed less strong.

"Colonel Abadi, this man on the couch here, this man by the name of Ron Barak, has been brought in for questioning. He is an Israeli citizen residing in Paris on a special visa, and is obliged, among other things, to co-operate with the representative of the French Republic. But for nearly an hour now he has been sitting on the documentation of a kidnapping from an illegal camera he had installed in the airport, and he is refusing to hand over the footage to me. The juge d'instruction has just permitted me to arrest him for obstruction of justice, but I have decided to agree to his request to summon the Israeli investigators of the case, in a final, last-ditch attempt to persuade him to co-operate."

Not a muscle on Ron Barak's face moved. Abadi knew the type, and could read his thoughts: The French can drop dead, I'll never talk. Long live El Al's independence. Tell my mother I was a loyal soldier.

Abadi asked himself with whom he would rather be stuck on a desert island, the grumpy French commissaire or the cocky Israeli security officer. He might just let the raft sink.

In some ways the security officer's attitude was enviable. Most people, certainly in a city like Paris, are sensitive to what people around them think of them. Barak, and this was quite clear, was utterly indifferent to what anyone might think.

He spoke English with a heavy Israeli accent. "At 10.10 a.m. the passengers who disembarked from El Al flight 319 reported that one of the passengers, a young high-tech employee by the name of Meidan, had disappeared following an unsuccessful prank in the arrivals hall of Terminal 2A. It should be noted that the police here did not bother reporting this disappearance to El Al's security. I only found out about it from the passengers themselves."

Even Chico, who so far had seemed quite blasé, understood that this confrontation was not going to take the investigation anywhere. "Now that all this has been straightened out, the competent authorities of our two countries have approved the transfer of the security footage to the investigating officials," he said to Barak with the studied nuances of a politician. "I suggest that we look at the footage right away. Every minute counts."

But Barak was unimpressed. "I arrived at Terminal 2A, but the locals refused to let me approach the witnesses. Only after a lot of wasted time did it turn out that the missing passenger had gone to the top floor, where El Al's kosher food storage is currently located. I was requested to hand over to the police the security camera that was installed here for the duration of the construction work, and obviously I refused."

"The camera is unregistered, unauthorised and unreported, secretly documenting the workers and everything that happens on the floor, twenty-four hours a day, in violation of the privacy laws and the unequivocal instructions of the French police!" Léger yelled. He had finally lost it.

"God save us from the French police," Barak said, and Abadi wondered how long it would be before he mentioned the Holocaust. A minute? Half a minute?

"As I said, it's all been settled," Chico reminded them, the strain evident in his voice, "and you, Barak, are required to present the footage to the investigation team."

"But it doesn't work that way," Barak said. "I need the consent of El Al's chief security officer. I don't know you people, and this is El Al's property; it isn't personal."

"Let me explain to you why it *is* personal," Abadi said. He chose to speak Hebrew in a friendly tone, one that would keep their hosts in the dark. "It is personal, because if you don't give them the tape in the next minute, I will personally make sure your security clearance is knocked down to a minus. There will not be a single official job in Israel in which the person in charge will not get a phone call from me warning him about you. You'll find your name on suspect lists you didn't even know existed. Amira Hass and Gideon Levy will have a higher security clearance than you. This is my promise to you, and that makes it entirely personal. You have thirty seconds to make a decision."

Barak seemed surprised. You could almost hear the wheels of his mind turning while he tried to assess the odds that Abadi was bluffing.

"Fifteen seconds," Abadi said.

Just as he had been taught on his course, Barak was performing a damage control assessment. After twenty-five seconds of heavy silence, he switched on the laptop.

Chapter 16

In the waiting room of Aluf Rotelmann's chambers, the participants of the special meeting were taking advantage of the forced break. A string of notifications on their mobiles transmitted news alerts concerning the possible abduction of an Israeli in Paris.

The resemblance between this initial information and the alert that appeared on The Most Wanted list they had just discussed was clear, even suspicious. The senior officers had taken over the secure computers, and in no time agreed that, according to all indications, the missing Israeli, Yaniv Meidan, had no connection to the Intelligence Corps.

"I could have told you that at the outset, but instead you people had to make all this fuss," the secretary grumbled. One of the Mossad representatives sat beside Oriana and explained to her in a fatherly tone that he had never given any credence to the alert, so he was not one bit concerned by the news. They'll find him in some bar in Paris in no time, and we can all call it a day. Oriana nodded without interest. The Mossad representative asked if perhaps they could grab a coffee together after the meeting to get to know each other better. He suggested the McCafé in the nearby mall.

Finally rid of him, she was free to read her messages. Two urgent ones. The first an official letter from the head of Unit 8200, whom she had yet to meet.

"The Commander extends his gratitude to you for standing in for the head of Special Section following the unexpected release of Sgan Aluf Shlomo Tiriani. The Commander of 8200 has requested that the new head of Special Section, Colonel Zeev Abadi, assume his new role a.s.a.p. You will therefore cease serving as acting head at midnight."

The rest was the usual fluff. "The Commander is confident that you will aid the new head of Special Section's transition into the role in any way possible. The Commander has been very impressed with your ability to fill the role without prior warning or preparations, and has added his acknowledgement of these achievements to your personnel file."

Well, that was short-lived. She felt the pang of an insult, although of course it was unwarranted. She was out of her league by every known military standard, certainly in seniority and rank. She was surprised to feel so disappointed, and tried to find an explanation for it as she opened the second message.

It was a summons to a secure video call, today at 4.00 p.m., with the incoming head of Special Section, Colonel Zeev Abadi. This was plain weird. If he was still abroad, why was it so urgent for him to talk to her today? And if he had already returned to Israel, then why a video call and not a standard orientation meeting at the office?

She approved the summons and wrote down the details on her secure screen. The code number with which she was supposed to connect to the call in three hours did not appear in her unit's database, and she had to approach the chamber's obnoxious secretary and ask her to find out to which facility the number belonged.

The secretary ran the decryption with a minimum of enthusiasm, looked at the screen, ran it again, and then said with surprise: "Well, I'll be damned, it's the code room in the Israeli embassy in Paris. The adjutant asked me just a moment ago to find out how to contact them."

Oriana annotated her notes below the summons with an exclamation mark. After a moment, she scrawled another, much larger exclamation mark alongside it.

They were called back into the conference room, but this time there was no ceremony over the seating, and not even the ceremony of the commander's entrance. Zorro stood at the head of the table and did not bother waiting for everyone to enter before concluding the meeting.

"I'm sorry for the delay, we had something that needed looking into. As you may have read, an Israeli passenger seems to have been abducted from Charles de Gaulle airport. I'm happy to say that the classified information delivered to Aluf Rotelmann confirms that the news has nothing to do with The Most Wanted item. So we can put it behind us. Most of what I had to say to you has already been said, so I suggest we break. A summary will be sent to you before the end of the day."

The officers made for the door like children at the end of a long day at school. Oriana took her bag and stood in the line by the exit.

"Not you," Zorro called out to her, and, adopting a more formal tone, said, "The representative of 8200 is requested to stay a few moments longer."

Chapter 17

The juge d'instruction was young and very nervous. He consulted with his superiors in a loud voice, while his agitated pacing interrupted the efforts of Léger's technicians to connect Barak's laptop to the large screen. Abadi monitored the preparations with growing, if not entirely focused, concern.

When everything was eventually ready they still had to wait, because the juge d'instruction asked that the floodlights outside the container be turned off, and the forensic team objected on the grounds that they could not work in the dark. Throughout the furious argument Léger looked as if he was about to pass out. "This is how it is in France," he whispered with embarassment to Abadi, who smiled graciously without saying that it would have looked much worse in Israel.

At last the signal was given. Barak pressed the button, and Meidan was there on the giant screen.

The camera was sophisticated, perhaps too sophisticated. It pivoted every few seconds to encompass the area around El Al's container from every direction, rendering the documentation frustratingly fragmented. It had a very sensitive audio microphone, which created an odd soundtrack of background noises. Abadi felt as though he were watching a strange work of video art, an homage to a classic black and white film lacking only the narrating title cards: "The protagonist does not notice the trap", "The villains sneak up from behind", "The blonde undresses", "The protagonist begs for his life", "The End".

The flashing clock on the corner of the screen lent the drama its rhythm. It displayed 10:48 when the cheerful ring of the lift's arrival was heard and out stepped Meidan. "What's that?" he exclaimed with surprise in Hebrew. The honeytrap followed him out.

From this footage it was clear that she was not as tall nor as attractive as the witnesses had described her. She was also younger, perhaps not even twenty. She held his arm, both to steady herself in her high heels and to coax him out of the lift.

He still seemed amused, if somewhat bewildered, and his first steps were hesitant. He too looked very young, almost a child. He dragged his suitcase, whose wheels struggled to advance along the makeshift gravel path. She pointed to the dark construction site, signalling their destination. "Parking, parking," she repeated. He was heard translating the word to himself in Hebrew, and looked at the forklift with interest, as if he had just been considering buying one.

When the camera pivoted again, the lens locked on him; that was the frame they could use for the missing person notifications. Léger's men shot him questioning looks, and in reaction Léger turned his gaze to Abadi, who shrugged.

The camera continued to document the couple walking slowly, but at 10:49 it started pivoting again and they disappeared from the frame. He was heard joking with his kidnapper in English about the limo awaiting them and the champagne they would pop. She did not respond. His voice grew louder as they approached the container and its microphone. Moments later he was clearly heard saying, "It looks like you're leading me somewhere very romantic."

She apparently understood the word "romantic" because she burst into laughter. Encouraged by his success, he kept chatting away. The volume level of his voice remained the same for an entire minute, and when the camera returned to them, at 10:50, it became clear why: they were standing in the same spot, right in front of the container, while she leaned against him to remove her heels.

The sudden intimacy must have awoken the voice of reason

within him. The microphone picked up his apprehension as he tried explaining to her that it was a case of mistaken identity.

"It isn't me, I'm not that passenger, it was a joke ... " (10:50:15)

Was he starting to understand? Did he suspect that the joke might be on him? Run, you moron, run, Abadi thought. Had he broken into a run towards the lift at that moment, he would have had a chance of saving himself. But what man would leave a barefooted girl on a deserted construction site without attempting to explain his good intentions? And what Israeli would leave his suitcase behind unattended?

The camera began pivoting again, moving to the dark area of the site. On the screen two men appeared. They were unmistakably South East Asian. "*Des Chinois!*" the juge d'instruction called out, and they did indeed look Chinese. They stepped out of the dark in the couple's direction. With his back to them, Meidan failed to notice the danger. The blonde was now leaning into him with all her weight, while he tried again to explain his prank.

"It was just a joke, you see . . . " (10:50:22)

They advanced stealthily with hurried and silent steps. Both in black suits with dark shirts, they looked like a thousand other businessmen who land in Paris every day from South East Asia. But they crept ahead like commandos, and Barak's sensitive microphone did not pick up the slightest sound from their steps on the gravel. Meidan did not stand a chance.

"Well, I'm sorry, I have to go." (10:50:46)

When the Israeli finally gave up hope of finding an elegant way out of his altogether unamusing prank, the digital clock on the camera flashed 10:51:04. The camera caught him turning back in the direction of the lift, tugging his suitcase behind him. He was heard saying, in Hebrew, as if making one final joke, "O.K., enough, bye-bye." Those were his last words.

She understood the "bye-bye" perfectly well, and reached out to grab him. Turning towards her, he must at least have seen the

Chinese. The camera started pivoting again and caught them leaping on their prey like tigers in a nature film. The investigators ran the footage again and again, trying to freeze the moment. It was impossible to detect a knife or any other weapon, but professionals like that could presumably make do with their bare hands.

The audio tape did not provide conclusive information either. Did they stab him? Strangle him? Beat him? The microphone registered the echoes of the struggle, but the girl's shouts prevented any exact understanding of what transpired. When the camera was kind enough to move again, the two Chinese were seen carrying Meidan's body – dead? injured? unconscious? – over to the dark area, the shaft out of site just beyond the frame.

The camera came full-circle. The blonde was now standing with her back to the camera and although he could not see her face, it seemed to Abadi that she was crying. She took off her clothes. She seemed so fragile that, even with her back to the camera, watching her made Abadi feel guilty.

She stood naked, holding her clothes and staring at what from a distance looked like bloodstains on them. At first she tried putting on her skirt inside out, but then she noticed Meidan's suitcase and pried it wide open on the gravel floor. She pulled out a suit, jeans, a sweater, and finally chose the easy solution – a classic long raincoat that the victim had probably thrown into his suitcase at the last moment.

She tried it on, wrapping it around her naked body like a towel after a long swim. She pulled out of the suitcase a pair of trainers, but they were too big and masculine. She walked back along the gravel to her red heels near the lift. The camera started moving.

The lively ding of the lift was heard in the background, then the opening and closing of the doors. At 10:53, as the camera shifted back to the scene, the two men were alone. One of them was holding a blonde wig and a red uniform. The other was rolling Meidan's suitcase towards the shaft. At 10:54 the sound of the lift was heard again. When the camera pivoted, the area was empty – an abandoned, dreary construction site.

Six minutes. The entire event – from the victim's arrival on the scene to the abductors' organised retreat, including tidying the premises sufficiently to throw off the police – lasted just six minutes.

The first to break the silence was the juge d'instruction, still struggling to comprehend what he had just witnessed. "But if the passenger was murdered and not kidnapped, where's the body?" he asked – the elementary legal question. Léger was the one to reply, his answer no less elementary: "They threw him into the shit," he said. The juge d'instruction said nothing.

Next to speak was Chico. "All in all, this is good for us," he said in Hebrew.

Abadi did not reply, forced into thoughts about language and possession. "It's good for us." The Israeli police official clearly did not mean "us" in its characteristic, representative meaning, the one instilled in all Israelis. He did not mean "us" as in the State of Israel and certainly not as in the Israeli public; he was not thinking about Meidan's family or even "us" in the wider sense of solidarity. He simply meant "us", the skeleton crew of investigators. In fact, he meant only himself. "It's good for us."

"How is this good, exactly?" Barak asked. Abadi was curious too.

"It's obvious from the footage that they didn't kill him because he's Israeli, that they didn't even understand who they had killed. This has no connection to the high alert from military intelligence. They probably meant to kill someone else. So for us, it's good. Now I'll quickly write up a report that this was a regular criminal event involving a case of mistaken identity. Nothing happened."

Nothing happened. Every law enforcement officer's dream.

"How is it that nothing happened when we have an Israeli murdered in Paris? And can we be sure that it has no connection to the alert if they meant to murder another Israeli?" Abadi said.

"You heard it yourself, four flights landed in this terminal more or less at the same time. What do the Chinese have to do with us, what are the chances that this gang has anything to do with Israelis? To me it looks like some drug deal gone bust, probably with Moroccans. One of the flights that landed after El Al 319 was an Air Morocco flight. Nothing happened. I'm going to bid the French "*adieu*" and run to the office to report it."

Commissaire Léger received the news about his guests' departure with undisguised relief, and nodded distractedly while the representative of the Israeli police laid out his new theory. Abadi took advantage of all the parting handshakes to pull Barak aside.

"I need one more small favour. Just in case they really were targeting another Israeli, I'd like to have as soon as possible the list of passengers with Israeli passports who were on that flight."

"We're not allowed to keep the passenger list after the flight lands," Barak said with a blank expression.

"I know," Abadi replied indulgently, "but you're also not allowed to install secret cameras in a foreign airport, yet here we are."

Chapter 18

After all the other officers had left the meeting room in HaKirya and when the secretaries had finished clearing away the last of the food and coffee, Oriana stood looking at the long table. It appeared menacing.

Zorro was still at the head of the table, the adjutant Oren to his left. They were waiting for her to sit down, and the seat they meant her to sit in was on Zorro's right, facing the adjutant. So she chose the seat beside him. Zorro seemed to consider telling her to take the opposite chair, but decided against it.

"Aluf Rotelmann has asked me to apologise for the less than warm welcome you received here today," he said. "We were not updated and we did not know who you were."

And now you think you know who I am, she thought. On the table in front of him was a yellow folder with her name on it. She found it amusing that the head of the intelligence-gathering command, a man who controlled one of the world's most advanced and expensive technological infrastructures, was trying to threaten her with a folder.

"So you were Mikey Talmor's daughter," he said, opening the folder as if to refresh his memory.

"I'm still Mikey Talmor's daughter," she said.

"Yes, yes, of course, I meant . . . I mean, the daughter of Mikey Talmor, may he rest in peace."

She said nothing. What kind of nickname was "Zorro" anyway, she mused. True, her father's nickname was "Mikey", but at least his real name had been Michael. The head of the intelligence-gathering's real name, as she had found out during the break, was Moshe. Who would choose to exchange the name of the most important biblical prophet for a character from an American television series?

"I have nothing but appreciation for your father's work. He was a role model to every man in the intelligence community," Moshe-Zorro continued, again using the past tense.

"I'm happy to hear that."

"And I'm pleased to see that you're carrying on his legacy, so to speak."

She wondered why Aluf Rotelmann – by all accounts a man of superior intelligence – had chosen such an uninspiring man as his deputy, a head of intelligence-gathering who could not even track down the most basic information such as her father's identity.

Perhaps he wanted someone who would suck up to him. "Let's give a warm thank you to our commander", "Your guidance, leadership", "We don't say it enough", and all that rubbish? Could it be that these high-ranking officials, whose shoulders bore utterly formidable responsibilities, privately needed constant bootlicking, even if it came from an idiot? A type of lift music to accompany their rise to the top?

And would her new commander, the mysterious Aluf Mishne Zeev Abadi, also require doses of flattery from his deputy?

"Thank you," she said.

"And we could see for ourselves in the meeting, the moment you called out the adjutant for breaching protocol, that the apple has not fallen far from the tree," Zorro said, smiling, and he and Oren chuckled. She returned as wide a smile as she could muster.

"And rightfully so, rightfully so," Oren said. "You were doing your job, I get it. And in some ways I'm even happy you acted as you did. Luckily, the material in the envelope was nothing urgent, just more evidence pointing to the murder of the young Israeli at Charles de Gaulle airport as being criminal-related."

"He was murdered? I saw a report that he had been abducted," she said. She asked herself what the odds were that Abadi was in Paris purely by chance. Very low, she decided.

Zorro waved his hand in dismissal, a gesture meant to look confident and reassuring.

"The representative of the Israeli police just passed us a message on the matter. The murder victim had no connection to the intelligence units. Accordingly, this has nothing to do with The Most Wanted alert on the subject. It's coincidental, we checked the matter thoroughly."

Oriana said nothing.

Zorro gazed at the folder in front of him, appearing to have lost his train of thought. The silence stretched for long moments until the adjutant broke it.

"The fact is that we wanted to talk to you about the appointment of Aluf Mishne Zeev Abadi."

"I'm not sure I understand," she said.

"There's no doubt we were taken by surprise by the departure of the former head of Special Section, Sgan Aluf Shlomo Tiriani," Zorro said, evidently uncomfortable. "However, we are even more surprised by Zeev Abadi's appointment. He's a decorated officer, yes, but his loyalty to our values is unproven, and he is a man with very questionable people skills."

Oriana had heard enough about Abadi to agree, more or less, with that description, but she was surprised it was being communicated so openly to a junior officer, the direct subordinate of the man concerned. There were many other questions on her mind. For instance, the significance the executive office was placing on the subject of who was going to command a section that until very recently had not been a high priority even within Unit 8200 itself.

"I did not make the decision," she said mildly. "The section performed valuable work under the former commander, and I'm very sure it will continue to provide valuable results under Aluf

Mishne Abadi's command. But these are matters that ought to be directed to the commander of Unit 8200."

Again it was Oren who pushed ahead. "I've been trying to reach him for an hour. But he's on a flight from the States and there's no way of conducting a secure conversation with him. We have also been trying to reach Aluf Mishne Abadi to share our concerns with him before we go ahead, but he too is abroad and is not answering."

"We simply want to gain a better understanding of the considerations that led, within a single day, to the replacement of the head of Special Section without anyone updating the executive office," Zorro said. "Only last week Aluf Rotelmann briefed the former head of Special Section in person, and in light of the new head of section's particular record I find it difficult to see how Aluf Rotelmann will be able to trust him."

This was becoming more interesting by the moment. So Tiriani had been briefed directly by Rotelmann, probably behind the 8200 commander's back, and obviously without disclosing anything to his deputy. If memory served her correctly, she had never seen a summons from Aluf Rotelmann in Tiriani's appointment calendar.

"I'm not sure I'm the person you should be speaking to about this," she said.

"It's important to clarify that Aluf Rotelmann has nothing personal against Abadi. As far as he's concerned, Abadi simply isn't the right man. It isn't the right place, it isn't the right time," the adjutant said.

"Aluf Rotelmann wants to guide Special Section's activities in the manner he finds most practical and professional," Zorro said.

"It's entirely professional, not personal," Oren said.

Incredible, she thought, they're like scissors: snip snap, snip snap. Well, they could take their dog and pony show elsewhere.

Zorro cleared his throat and sat up straight in his chair, his voice taking on a new and portentious tone.

"And that's why, in the interest of all parties, we thought we would discuss with you the possibility of cancelling Abadi's appointment and appointing you as a stand-in."

"Obviously we'd want to expedite your promotion to the rank of seren, and you'd serve as an acting rav seren, with the special authorisation of Aluf Rotelmann," the adjutant said.

"For all intents and purposes, you'd be the head of Special Section," Zorro said. "For this to happen, we have to be sure you understand the implications. We want to run by you our conditions for this move, this office's need to receive regular, thorough updates and for Special Section to be led according to the interests of the State of Israel and its Directorate of Military Intelligence, not only those of Unit 8200."

"Or of some kind of angle the 8200 commander's working on with his friend Abadi," the adjutant said.

"So the ball's in your court," Zorro said, his voice losing all trace of the playful tone he had affected at the beginning of the meeting. "Are you interested, yes or no?"

So that's how it works, she thought, that's actually how it works. How was she supposed to react? Why did the Officers' Training School teach astronavigation and urban warfare and other nonsense that had no use later, in real life? And why did her father raise her with principles that had nothing to do with her reality, and probably nothing to do with his reality either?

She was currently making 6,000 shekels a month. They had just offered her a base salary of 9,400 shekels plus a special remuneration of 3,200 shekels – a rav seren's pay grade.

Zorro was impatient. "We're waiting."

"Sure, of course, it's a yes," she said, looking him straight in the eye. "We'll stall and then sideline, no problem. I'll bypass all of my unit's control channels and report to you, behind my commander's back, whatever you wish to know, which is anyone's guess. And in return I'll get the rank of seren with a rav seren's pay grade. Sure, why not? Where do I sign? You know what, Zorro, you can just go ahead and sign for me, I'm guessing you have more experience."

The adjutant was the first to come to his senses, and let fly. "You've got some nerve, you hear? You think you're somebody, but you're this small, a little *pisher*. Who do you think you are? Have you forgotten who you're talking to?"

Zorro raised his hand and Oren fell silent. The Deputy Chief of Intelligence looked at her intently before saying, "Get the hell out of here. Now."

She got up and walked towards the exit.

"Segen Talmor?" she heard him call out.

"Yes?"

"You're not that stupid, so you must be crazy. I want you to go straight from here to the mental health officer. That's an order, go get yourself examined. I think you must have suicidal tendencies."

Oriana nodded and closed the door behind her.

Chapter 19

To feel at home everywhere is the privilege of kings, thieves and good prostitutes, Honoré de Balzac wrote. As far as Abadi could tell, this was only one of the characteristics he shared with them.

Commissaire Léger, on the other hand, was struggling to breathe where they were standing – next to the world's biggest sewage treatment plant. The stench was unbearable. Boudin, the facility's deputy director, a tall, bespectacled man in an immaculate white coat, continued to explain why the chances of finding a body there were between slim and zero.

If the Inuit really have dozens of words for "snow", the French have more than a hundred words for "shit". Abadi, a regular user of the word "*merde*" since childhood, kept a running inventory of the many synonyms in Boudin's arsenal, ranging from "unpurified mud" and "natural returns" to "used water".

The "Acheres" purification plant ("nothing to do with Asher from the Old Testament," the deputy director said, at pains to explain the similar pronunciation, as if a biblical name might have damaged the sewage facility's fine reputation) was built long before the airport, in the late nineteenth century. More than 380 tonnes of raw sewage a day surged into the plant from Charles de Gaulle airport and the neighbouring communities.

"You have to understand the unique difficulty of the situation you're presenting," Boudin said in the tone of a schoolmaster, perhaps because of the professional challenge placed before him, or perhaps because of the lack of enthusiasm the two investigators displayed towards his lecture. "Usually, large objects thrown into the Seine get blocked many kilometres before they reach the plant.

If someone jumps off a bridge in Paris, the body does not end up here. If someone tosses an old carpet into Charles de Gaulle's sewage drain, the carpet will not reach the plant. There are wire fences to filter out those kinds of things and enable only the unpurified mud to flow into the plant."

Nearly knocked out by the smell, Léger was not up for an argument. Abadi tried to elicit some civil service solidarity from the deputy director: "You must understand the difficulty of our position too. We were assigned to investigate whether the victim of the abduction is alive or dead, in order to be able to notify his family. You're the only one who can help us verify whether there is a body."

"You don't have to locate the body to understand he's dead," Boudin admonished him. "The French mathematician Urbain Le Verrier discovered Neptune without seeing it, just from simple deductive reasoning. You're describing a situation in which a man was dropped from a great height into the shaft of a construction site, and landed in a container filled with neutralising chemicals. There's no need to put the work here on hold to make sure he's dead. It's elementary, deductive reasoning."

"So where's his body?" Abadi said.

"If it had been a regular sewer, the body would have ended up a few kilometres from the facility. But the chemical toilet disposal contractors have a special permit to pump their containers straight into the plant, because their materials have already been neutralised. So the body is probably here, in the primary settling tank."

"What's the primary settling tank? Is it this?" Abadi said, pointing to the vast areas below them.

"It's the building furthest to the left," Boudin said and indicated a structure the size of a stadium. "The used water there undergoes carbon filtering. Luckily, it's intended for agriculture purposes, so your body won't do much harm."

"It isn't such a big lake," Léger said, revived by the concrete information. "I can get a divers unit over here and they'll locate him within a couple of hours."

The deputy director grimaced. "You can't put divers in the primary tank. These are extremely powerful cleaning agents. You'd be jeopardising their health."

"Then drain the water from the tank," Léger said.

"You cannot shut down the facility. It services eight million people!"

"Then what do you suggest?" Léger asked in despair.

"You have to wait for the next stage. The used water passes into the next station, the open lake you see on your right, through a duct with dense wire nets throughout. Your body will stop at the first net, it'll trigger the sensors, and then I'll call you."

"When do you expect that to happen?" Abadi asked.

"In the next twenty-four hours. This time tomorrow at the latest," the deputy director said. "If there even is a body here. But if there are inaccuracies in your story, the water will continue to flow uninterrupted, and I won't call you."

"Elementary deductive reasoning," Abadi said.

"We need a body," Léger said as they walked back to the police car waiting in the car park. "His shit continuing to flow is no legal proof that the abductee is still alive."

"Don't worry, you'll have a body," Abadi comforted him. He glanced at his mobile, but there were no new messages. It seemed as though back in Israel they weren't too perturbed by what had happened in Charles de Gaulle. As someone who exercised great caution when it came to the press, he was usually reassured by media silence. But this time, the silence was foreboding.

"As a matter of fact, Commissaire Léger, I fear that if we don't get information quickly, you'll have to contend with more than one body."

Chapter 20

It was 3.50 p.m. in Jerusalem when the Prime Minister's Office received a request for comment on a report to be aired on the evening news.

Nearly all the radio stations were under the direct control of this office. Two T.V. channels were under its close supervision, and another channel was directly owned by the Prime Minister's biggest donor, a Swiss tycoon who reigned over casinos from the U.S. to Macau. The T.V. channels had websites and newspapers, and those also yielded to the pressures of this office.

But there were other media outlets that were not under their thumb, and the television reporter who had submitted the request to the Prime Minister's office for comment worked for one of them.

For the spokesperson, the mere fact that material of such nature had already been gathered, researched, verified and passed through the editing rooms without anyone from the channel's news department giving him a telephone call was troublesome enough. But the report itself was a blatant declaration of war.

Shortly after, they reconvened. The four advisors passed the reporter's questions round among them. The spokesperson did his best to translate for the American advisor.

"They're in possession of a report by the Ministry of Foreign Affairs stating that, on his last trip to Geneva, the Prime Minister applied pressure for an official visit to Monte Carlo to be arranged on his way back to Israel."

"Why Monte Carlo? For the casino? Sounds unlikely."

"There were no plausible grounds to pass through Monte Carlo at taxpayers' expense, but eventually they managed to pull off some kind of dinner with a few Jews who had arrived from France especially for the occasion, and they called it a 'fundraiser'."

"That's the story? An unnecessary trip? That won't grab headlines in any major outlet."

"When they arrived at the hotel in Monte Carlo, the Prime Minister's wife demanded that the head hairdresser from Alexandre de Paris – once Princess Grace's regular salon – be brought to their suite."

"No. No, no, no, please no," the American advisor said, rocking in his chair as if in prayer.

"The Israeli consul in Monaco tried to explain that it was out of the question, but, as expected, she was forced to surrender. The stylist was duly summoned and arrived with a team of eight; three hours later he was taking a selfie with the Prime Minister's wife. The channel claims to have the photograph."

"Please tell me she paid for it out of her own pocket," the American advisor said.

"The hairdresser asked the Prime Minister's wife where he should send the bill, and she told him she did not involve herself in such matters, and asked him to charge it to the room."

"Please tell me the hotel refused and that the story boils down to nothing more than some goy hairdresser who's owed money," the American advisor said.

"The hotel accepted. The receptionist added the bill to the room, including tax but not a tip."

"Which explains why the photograph ended up in the hands of some reporter," the political advisor said, and sighed.

"The next day, the consul was surprised by the expense, and asked the Prime Minister why this bill was included in the room's account."

"And the Prime Minister apologised and said it was a mistake," the American advisor said, trying to guess the turn of events.

"The Prime Minister yelled at the consul for pestering him with issues she was supposed to resolve herself. She consulted the Ministry of Foreign Affairs and it was decided that the hairstyling should be added to the trip's budget under the only available category."

"Please tell me it has a boring bureaucratic name."

"The category was 'unexpected security expenses.'"

The room fell silent.

"That's not good," the American advisor said.

"No, it's not," the spokesperson agreed. "The Prime Minister's wife's haircut cost the taxpayer 1,250 euros. A rinse and blow dry included."

They processed the information. In their profession, information was measured not by its importance or credibility, but by the potential for stories it might spawn. The more they mulled over the details, the less possibility they could find of anything good coming out of it, only snowballing damage.

"I'm not confident we can attack this head-on," the strategic advisor said at last. "It's a tiny corruption story, but easy to understand. It's not like interfering with the work of the investigation of the corporate bonds committee."

"Excuse me, but the Prime Minister did nothing wrong. It was clearly a mistake on the part of the Ministry of Foreign Affairs," the political advisor said.

"It doesn't matter," the American advisor said tersely. "It's his wife's hair, it's a capricious trip, it's a 1,250-euro haircut, it's an unexpected security expense. The jokes can practically write themselves."

"Then we'll deal with it indirectly," the spokesperson suggested. "Maybe drown it in a bigger story. Maybe a military threat."

"We can't drum up a military threat on such short notice," the strategic advisor said. "They won't actually wait for the evening edition, they'll start drip-feeding it in the show's promos. We have two hours, tops."

"Didn't we have a military story this morning? The Israeli who was abducted in Paris?" the political advisor said.

"He was probably murdered, but there's no body yet," the spokesman said.

"Wonderful!" the American advisor said. "Big drama, gag order has been lifted, an Israeli was kidnapped in Paris, officials suspect nationalistic motives, the Prime Minister has contacted his French counterpart and pressured him into action. Are there any pictures?"

"But I've since spoken to the Military Secretary, who said they're now certain the abduction had nothing to do with him being Israeli, it's a criminal case, a case of mistaken identity," the spokesman said.

"What is he, an Isis spokesman? How can he be certain of the motive?" the American lashed out. "It's *our* job to come up with ridiculous speculations, not his. I asked if we have photographs."

"We have more than photographs," the spokesperson said. "There's footage from El Al's security camera. You can see the woman who kidnapped him."

"The *woman*?"

"A real knockout, if I understand correctly."

"Well, what are we waiting for?" the strategic advisor said. "Pass the footage on to all the channels, breaking news, announce preparations, the Prime Minister is receiving regular updates from the Minister of Public Security, the Intelligence Corps is investigating, the rabbi of the Western Wall has said a special prayer, the Mossad is on alert, the Shabak is also in the picture."

"Wait, I need to co-ordinate this with the deputy minister of defence."

"Heaven forbid! You collaborate only with the police. I don't need the Military Secretary here getting in our way."

"Less than an hour ago we told all the channels that it was a trifling criminal event," the spokesperson reminded them.

"And in the meantime we've received new information," the American said calmly. "This security event is brought to you by Alexandre de Paris hair salon of Monaco. Let's go, the clock's ticking."

Chapter 21

Back when her father used to take her here, the ugly mall on the parallel road had yet to be built and no road signs mentioned Glilot, let alone the presence of a military base, and most cars in the vicinity were military vehicles anyway. They would drive from their suburban house in Ramat Hasharon along a half-concealed dirt road next to a strawberry field that today served as the officers' car park.

It was always after dark – on the way to her ballet class or a sleepover. After a few sharp turns, in which her head banged against the car roof from the potholes, suddenly there it was, the jungle: dozens and dozens of giant antennae of all kinds, a futuristic cluster of space spiders, as beautiful and blinding as the promise of love.

She could have gazed at them for hours, but usually he would leave her in the car in front of the illuminated jungle for fewer than ten minutes, returning after being briefed and giving orders, always without a briefcase or documents. When they arrived at the ballet class or sleepover, it was all she could do not to tell her friends about her father's secret, next to the strawberry fields north of Tel Aviv.

Where do these amazing feelings go when you're no longer a child? When she was in secondary school they took a trip to New York, and in the taxi from the airport she braced herself for the famous skyline of skyscrapers which had been mentioned so often in discussions of their upcoming holiday. And indeed, all of a sudden, as they were emerging from a boring tunnel, New York revealed itself to be everything she had been promised, beautiful and mysterious and frightening and blinding, and still she could not help feeling a little disappointed, because the skyline was not as breathtaking as that of the 8200 headquarters' jungle.

Back then no-one had dubbed the place 8200, least of all her father, who simply called it "the unit". In their neighbourhood, which was populated primarily by career soldiers and pilots, it was referred to as "the secret base" or "the headquarters". The day the retiring 8200 unit commander appeared on the cover of the weekend edition of *Yedioth Ahronoth*, her father refused to open the newspaper for the whole Sabbath, telling her, "You see this, Oriana, you see this? This is the beginning of the end for this country."

By then, she was already an expert in deception. My mother is upstairs. My mother will be back soon. My mum just left. My mum is visiting her own mum. Mum is dead. Mum is in the hospital. Mum is a speaker at an international conference. My mum will laugh at all these rumours when she gets back.

They left the kibbutz at night. Her father drove, her younger brother in tears in the back seat, and she naturally took the seat next to the driver. She remained at his side for years to come, because her father never remarried. Then the family moved closer to the antennae, into a villa which felt way too big and where all the furniture was new. Her mother stayed in the family unit in the kibbutz with her young Palestinian lover, a part-time Arabic teacher from one of the surrounding villages, straight from the Israeli leftist textbook.

When she visited her childhood home every second weekend he was never present, but it didn't take her long to find traces of him: a man's sandal under her mother's bed, strange scribblings on the telephone pad, an Aqua-Velva aftershave tucked under the bathroom shelves, to say nothing of her mother's browser history. He certainly was unavoidable everywhere outside the house – in all the kibbutz dinner halls, clubs and along the bike paths her mother's new love interest was on every member's disapproving lips.

She didn't care. She was happier in Ramat Hasharon, she could swim in the Mediterranean, buy cool outfits, go out. Her father appeared to be unaffected by the whole thing, and that was all that mattered to her.

It changed radically three years later. She was in her last year of secondary school, concentrating on her exams. Her father was the lead candidate to oversee the relocation of the Intelligence Corps to the Negev desert scheduled for 2022; it was an important promotion that, he reluctantly admitted, would force them to move yet again.

And that was when the Arabic teacher returned to their lives. Not in person – he was under house arrest – but in the form of a secret note sent from the internal security service to the nominating committee. The head of the Shabak respectfully notified the committee that the top contender for the post, Aluf Mishne Talmor, had shared his then-wife with a young Arab Israeli whose cousin was now suspected of belonging to a terror organisation.

Of course, the note went on, Aluf Mishne Talmor himself was not suspected of any wrongdoing, and his record as a brilliant intelligence officer stood; but the record showed that a possible terror suspect had had access to his home, to his private documents, to his landline, and possibly to any intelligence documents he might have taken home.

"The role of the counter-espionage unit is to collect information, and to distribute it to the relevant authorities at the right moment, but ultimately the decision is yours," ended the note, duly signed by the head of the Shabak, one Aluf Rotelmann, probably already working on his own nomination to head the Intelligence Corps.

Backstabbing in Tzahal, or in any huge organisation for that matter, was not a science, it was an art – it had to have an emotional impact. And so an incompetent from the Shabak got the job and her father got cancer. Oriana did not suspect Aluf Rotelmann of any wrongdoing either. All she knew was that one day her father was there, taking her to Tzahal's I.Q. tests before her enlistment, and three months later he was dead.

She had hoped never to return here as a soldier – on her

preference questionnaire at the induction centre she had written "anything but 8200", and when she arrived at the officers' intelligence course after serving in the information security department, her interview write-up stated: "Owing to personal circumstances, the officer has been exempt from being assigned to the unit in which her deceased father served."

But a series of upheavals shook Unit 8200, a flood of events that could all have been prevented if only someone had been awake to the incessant ringing of alarm bells. One paedophile officer, a sudden wave of conscientious objectors, and hundreds of news reports around the world following the leaking of classified information by their American counterpart: the National Security Agency. Suddenly Unit 8200 was in every newspaper, and not only in flattering articles in the technology sections.

The Commander in Chief of Tzahal decided to establish Special Section, and its recruiters immediately approached her – an outstanding cadet in the course, an outstanding researcher in the department, with a record of cracking cases other officers had long abandoned. "We have four branches here," her commander used to tell officials on V.I.P. tours, "security, research, teleprocessing and Oriana".

And yet, it felt a little strange coming back here, making her way on a new, well-marked asphalt road. The soldiers guarding the entrance to the base all recognised her car from a distance, and therefore adhered to the strict security protocols, including checking her I.D. cards and the boot of her car. It was the price she had to pay for her own stern approach to security, even if today it was just downright annoying: she had only ten minutes until the secure video conversation with Abadi, and she wanted to catch up on everything that had happened in the section during her absence.

The duty sergeant in Special Section was Rachel, the only person who could get a smile out of her even on a bad day. And indeed, Oriana had barely made it through the door when the samelet broke into one of her usual animated and incoherent monologues, which she called "the commander's update".

"Commander, commander, come quick, you have a summons for a secure conversation with the new head of section. Get to your room and your screen. The summons came from him, so he'll be the one making the call. You also need to approve three messages that have arrived for you. Should I read them to you in the order in which they came or by the sender's rank? Actually in this case it's the same thing. O.K., here I go. Are you sitting? Coffee first? No? Good, because I would not have time to make coffee *and* give you the commander's update. So should I begin? First, there's a message by the unit commander stating that you're no longer the head of Special Section, because the world-class silver fox, Aluf Mishne Zeev Abadi, decided to assume his position earlier."

"I know, Rachel, I was cc'd on that e-mail. I don't remember it mentioning that the new head of section was a world-class silver fox."

"It's obvious, it didn't need mentioning, his profile photograph is in the e-mail. As if it isn't enough that you're such eye candy, now a guy like that's joining. I'm going to be the section's ugly duckling. I'm seriously considering putting in a transfer request."

Rachel, who complained that she was short and fat owing to her mother's genes, had the guys on the base wrapped around her little finger as if she was a supermodel. Oriana spent a significant amount of her time in the office boosting the self-confidence of her favourite investigator, but now was not the time.

"Rachel, please don't call me, or any other woman, 'eye candy'. Can we get on with the update? We don't have much time."

"See how it affects everything? Me being ugly? I didn't mean to offend, it's just that, well, I anticipate a decline in my performance when he arrives, so I wanted to warn you in advance. I might get so flustered that I stutter and forget what I wanted to say."

"I doubt that'll ever happen," Oriana said and switched on her screen.

"Wait, don't read it yet, I'm the one who's supposed to update you, it's important."

"Go ahead. The first message was from the unit commander, announcing that Zeev Abadi is assuming his new position. What's the second one?"

"The second message is from Aluf Rotelmann, saying that you're not allowed to work with Zeev Abadi."

"What?"

"It's in your inbox, an official letter. He's suspending Zeev Abadi's appointment because the announcement was not released according to protocol, so Special Section is requested, in the meantime, not to co-operate with the new head of section until we receive word from Aluf Rotelmann that the appointment has been approved."

"You're kidding, right?"

"No. His adjutant even called to make sure I got the letter. He said he tried contacting you but you weren't answering. I explained that you turn off your devices when you drive, and that it drives me crazy too because sometimes I have an urgent message and I have to wait until you stop at a petrol station or something."

"Rachel?"

"Yes, Commander?"

"You said you're reading me the messages according to the order in which they came or by the sender's rank?"

"I told you, Commander, in this case it's the same thing."

"Rachel, the third message came from someone higher-ranking than the Rosh Aman?" Oriana knew the samelet was reliable, but someone higher than the head of Israeli Defence Intelligence? Higher than Rotelmann?

"Yes. The third message arrived fifteen minutes ago, from Tzahal's Vice Chief of Defence Staff."

"*What?*"

"Yes. He said that you do have to work with the silver fox and that you should ignore Aluf Rotelmann's letter because the Vice Chief of Defence Staff for the entire Tzahal is the man who decided to replace the head of Special Section and appoint Abadi, in accordance with standard General Staff orders or something like that, there was a whole list of detailed jurisdictions. In short, the appointment is on. By the way, Aluf Rotelmann is also cc'd on the letter, which is pretty embarrassing for him."

"Pretty embarrassing," Oriana repeated, partly because she was experiencing a temporary lack of focus in light of recent events, and partly because Rachel's remark was spot on.

"His order also came in an official letter, including the sender's secure seal. It really did come from the Vice Chief of Defence Staff's office. But it wasn't his adjutant who called."

"No?"

"No. The call came from him. Well, a secretary put him on."

"Are you serious?"

"Yeah. From Vice Chief of Defence Staff, Noam Zeel, himself. He asked who I was, and I told him I was the duty sergeant of Unit 8200's Special Section. He asked when you would be in the office, and I told him you had just left general headquarters and that you'd get in just before four, in time for a video call. He asked if I had received the e-mail and I said yes, and then he asked that I make sure to show it to you the moment you arrived. I told him, sure, Chief, you can count on me, Chief."

"Rachel?"

"Yes, Commander?"

"You spoke to Tzahal's Vice Chief of Defence Staff?"

"I know, isn't it insane? No telling what more the day will bring!"

"No telling what more the day will bring," Oriana absentmindedly repeated after her sergeant.

A secure call appeared on her screen. The caller was Aluf Mishne Zeev Abadi, the new head of section, a special appointment by

Tzahal's Vice Chief of Defence Staff, so it turned out, and, according to Rachel, a silver fox. "Do you accept the call?" the computer asked her.

Oriana now regretted not having asked for coffee. She sat up straight in her chair, looked into the camera lens and clicked 'YES'.

Chapter 22

The rue Rabelais is one of the smallest streets in Paris, containing only four buildings and located in one of Europe's most expensive real estate areas, close to the Champs-Élysées.

"The first building, 1 rue Rabelais, was once owned by Gustave Eiffel," the letting agent said to his visitors, aiming for name recognition but receiving none. He thought he understood, perhaps. "Eiffel did live there until the day he died, but, as you can see, the original structure was torn down, and the rather dull office building you passed took its place.

"However, the second building was one of those *hôtels particuliers* once owned by the Baroness Gérard," he said, the emphasis on "*particuliers*" and "Baroness". His visitors remained unimpressed and he hurried to supply more illustrious context. "She was the niece of François Gérard, the official painter of both Napoleon and King Louis XVIII." Silence again. The agent began to feel unnerved, but he rallied to fill the void – they were paying for every gem of historical knowledge that he had in his possession.

"With the death of the Baroness, her daughters discovered that she had bequeathed them the mansion and nothing more. Of course, they sold it," he told them, "and the current building was erected on the grounds. Due to its size, it is now listed as two buildings: 2–4 rue Rabelais." Not the slightest interest. He concluded nonetheless with his *pièce de résistance.* "Since 1925, it has housed the aristocratic 'Le Jockey Club', one of the hotbeds in France of nineteenth-century anti-Semitism. And opposite it, in number 3 – call it divine punishment – is the Israeli embassy." Had he discerned the slightest trace of a response to that?

Thoroughly unnerved at this point, the agent was not about to share the final detail that the owners of the last structure, 6 rue Rabelais, the glass office building in which they now stood, had a hell of a time renting out space here because, among other reasons, access to the street was blocked day and night by the Israeli embassy's security. From the window in front of him, the agent had a clear view of the embassy that caused him so much grief. But his attention was now on a detailed review of the contract in his hands.

He could not believe his good fortune.

The renters were the Chinese representatives of a major mobile network company from Hong Kong. Owing to the increase in Chinese tourists to Paris, they had to boost their network's coverage in the French capital. He had tried to interest them in additional assets in the 8th arrondissement, but they had wanted to start with the office on rue Rabelais.

In his profession, careful consideration of attire was critical. To work, he always wore inconspicuous grey suits – even if they were tailored to his form by an excellent man – so his clients would not feel outdressed. But with these clients, he ran no such risk.

The woman, maybe fifty, wore a vintage Chanel suit. She did not speak French; in fact, she did not speak at all. Even when she shook his hand, she did not bother to remove her giant sunglasses, and the gold logo twinkled at him each time she nodded.

The men were younger. One of them, head to toe in black Armani, did not take an interest in the negotiation, and remained by the open door throughout the conversation. The other two wore dark suits that accentuated the whiteness of their shirts. They were both relatively tall. The senior Chinese representative, who spoke excellent French, wore a rather conservative suit, black with thin white stripes. The other one wore a slim-fit double-breasted black suit, as in a gangster movie from the 1930s. Every few minutes he took a pack of cigarettes from his inside pocket with a theatrical gesture that suggested this time it was going to be a gun.

They were willing to pay the asking price, 2,000 euros per square metre, double what he had anticipated. They were planning to install only micro-antennae in the office, equipment that did not require him to obtain permits from the Ministry of Communications or city hall. And they had agreed to a year's rent up-front!

Their only requirement was that they be allowed to move in immediately. Installing the antennae, against the dark windows but without damaging the facade, was expected to take approximately four hours. He promised to speak with the concierge so the neighbours would not complain about the noise, but it hardly mattered, since at that hour no self-respecting Frenchman would still be in his office. After signing first, he offered them the fountain pen he used on special occasions, a Montblanc.

The woman glanced at his pen with disdain and took out of her purse a black Omas platinum pen. She used it also to fill out the cheque, drawn on a bank in Hong Kong. He looked at the sum before handing her the two sets of keys. She did not respond to his civilities, but the man who spoke French cordially accompanied him to the door.

As he left the building he remembered to talk to the concierge, and then found himself on the street. His commission from this last hour of work amounted to 100,000 euros. He passed in front of the Israeli embassy, for the first time without feeling vexed. The police officers at the entrance of rue Rabelais opened the gate for him, and he saluted cheerfully. Only out of fear that the Chinese might be watching from the window did he stop himself from bursting into a dance of pure delight.

Chapter 23

The coffee the secretary had brought him was too weak, but Aluf Rotelmann did not care. He was probably the only major general in Tzahal whose coffee preferences were unknown even within his own chambers.

In fact, he had no preferences. He could take it with sugar or without, he could work with his office door open or closed, he could drive his car himself or summon the driver; and even in the officers' dining hall, the duty soldiers knew there was no point asking him which dish he preferred that day. As an intelligence man, perhaps the best of his generation, he had trained himself to cope with shifting realities. He believed that a man with preferences was a man with weaknesses.

For instance, until that morning he had favoured his head of intelligence-gathering, Zorro, over his other deputies. And now, reading the reports on his screen and drinking coffee that was too weak, even that preference seemed worth reconsidering.

The enforced appointment of Abadi had been by far the most surprising event of the morning. The man was thought to be finished, his contract terminated, his honour tarnished forever. A year had gone by, and yet here he was again.

Elusiveness happened to be a subject about which Rotelmann knew a thing or two. He searched on his computer for the folder and located it in the archives. The scandal had broken out in 2014, an eternity ago in the world of intelligence. "We, officers and soldiers of Unit 8200, past and present, declare that we refuse to allow the use of the unit's technology and human resources in spying operations against the Palestinians, most of them illegal and all of them immoral," the open letter began.

Refuseniks in Tzahal were nothing new, but it was the first time that conscientious objectors had come from within Intelligence. For most international media who carried the news, it was also the first time they had heard about 8200, "a semi-clandestine organisation", "Israel's most secretive unit", "a very secretive Israeli military organisation", as they presented it. Wishful thinking, that.

The investigation had been swift, legal charges prepared, military trials held. Rotelmann had been out of the loop that year, commanding an infantry unit in the north.

Fast forward a few years, and everything had changed. The commander of Unit 8200 had been replaced, a new law forbidding the publication of his name had been ratified; the internal security section of the not-so-secretive unit had been placed under the direct command of the Vice Chief of Defence, with a vastly improved budget and a new, bombastic name, "Special Section"; and Tzahal's Rosh HaMateh HaKlalli, its Chief of Defence Staff, had officially announced that the new Rosh Aman, the new Chief of Intelligence, would be none other than Aluf Rotelmann himself, "a brilliant officer with an independent mind and a clear ethical voice".

Wishful thinking, that, too. He'd been too busy to notice and had been caught off-guard when Abadi, in his later capacity as head of 8200's Big Data project, had popped up to testify on behalf of the treacherous soldiers at their appeal. The man had talked about "mistakes", "honesty", "conscience" and other nonsense.

Rotelmann remembered signing the termination letter himself; it had been January. He found a copy in the archived folder and clicked. He regretted that Aluf Mishne Abadi had "chosen the wrong way" and "put himself above his unit".

For Rotelmann, having an enemy inside the corps was problematic; having an enemy working closely with the daughter of another man whose career he'd sidelined was dangerous. The thought that his own adjutant had summoned her to his chambers that morning, and that Zorro had let her humiliate them, vexed him.

But he could not hold Zorro alone responsible for today. There had to be another explanation. A rundown of recent events: his deputy had given a catastrophic presentation in his chambers before all the intelligence representatives, among them the daughter of one of the adversaries; a special investigator from the N.S.A. had arrived in Israel to audit a possible violation of the intelligence co-operation agreement between the two countries; the Prime Minister's office had decided to impose a security alert surrounding an event that Rotelmann decreed was unrelated to security matters; and Tzahal's Vice Chief of Defence had forced an appointment that Rotelmann had instructed Zorro to thwart.

And the day was far from over.

He called his wife to say he would not be able to join her at their son's school concert. She made him apologise to the boy right then on the telephone, and it was probably the only conversation in the world where he came close to fear. He had no choice, he said to his child, and as the screen in front of him confirmed.

The results of the disorder in the system were evident. Queries about the abduction in Paris came in from all units, seemingly without any co-ordination. The intelligence-gathering units had flooded Central with so many reports – from the Mossad's European informers, from Unit 504's Arab agents, from Hatzav Osint's ferretings, and inevitably from 8200's huge apparatus – that the computers were at risk of crashing.

The secretary had left his door open, and for the past fifteen minutes he had been able to hear the hysterical reports on television. "A clear oversight by the French security units . . . a remarkable kidnapping . . . special forces are now searching for the kidnapper . . . the Prime Minister has spoken to the Chief of Defence Intelligence, Aluf Rotelmann . . . the possibility the victim was selected at random has still not been ruled out . . . Israel, however, will have to investigate whether a higher state of alert should have been in order . . . prayers for the victim, and with us on the line we have one of the members of his delegation, who was witness to the abduction."

He got up to ask the secretaries to lower the volume, but once he reached the desk he changed his mind. "I need the code for secure contact with the Israeli embassy in Paris," he told the secretaries, who could barely drag their eyes away from the T.V. screen.

"It's 340-98 on the blue one." The swift response came from the secretary sitting to the left, who was usually the least efficient. His curiosity was piqued.

"You remember the codes of all the embassies by heart?"

"No, Commander, I have been asked for the code twice today. It started with your adjutant when the envelope with the black clearance material arrived."

"And then it was the adjutant again?"

"No, the second time it was for that female officer who was in the meeting earlier. When everyone went on their break she asked me to identify the number in the database."

"The one from the navy corps?" he said, although he had already guessed the answer.

"No, the one in the green uniform. From 8200."

He nodded, absorbing the information. The secretary waited several seconds, then said: "Should I get you the embassy in Paris?"

"No, no need," he said. "Bring Zorro to my office as soon as possible."

Chapter 24

For a long time, Yermi saw nothing but fields.

Half an hour later, the view expanded into dull office buildings and ugly shopping centres. It was only when the bus finally came off the *autoroute* that he saw residential *quartiers*; they were just as he had imagined them, beautiful and unvarying in their sophistication. Yermi guessed they had finally entered Paris.

It started to rain heavily. Real French people appeared on the pavements, men in long raincoats, slender girls in high heels, stylish elderly women, some with poodles, all with umbrellas, as if some divine order had ensured their protection even from the first drops of rain.

He had no idea where the bus was taking him. He had boarded it at the exit of Terminal 2A, instinctively putting a distance between himself and the police activity he had observed in the arrivals hall. The bus with the airport's logo was white. Many passengers boarded, and Yermi followed suit. It seemed that he was the only Israeli. He paid the driver like everyone else, lifted his suitcase onto the special rack like everyone else, and sat by the window like everyone else. The knot in his stomach was his alone.

The rain was now drilling against the bus windows. Pedestrians ran towards the cafés, which were large and well lit. Yermi started noticing tourists, singles and couples, looking as lost as he felt. The bus entered the small streets of the city, and he now saw businessmen as well, sporting light spring suits in cheerful colours. The taxis were white, the buses green, and the car lights spread a yellow glow. His thoughts remained grey.

The bus took a sharp turn into a very narrow street, managing to negotiate the puddles close to the passersby who huddled under the awnings. Yermi wiped the steam off the window again and perused the shop windows – luxury stores, that much was clear, with no end of lace, jewellery and designer brands, including a large Fabergé store, which would certainly have delighted his grandparents, who had an entire shelf of art books in their living room in Ashdod devoted to the Tsar's missing jewels.

Now the small street became a wide boulevard, teeming with more people than he had ever seen in his life, ambling this way and that. He guessed by the shopping bags that it was a street with large department stores, maybe the one his grandmother had told him so much about. Instinctively he checked the front pocket of his trousers in which he had secreted the money she had given him for the trip.

The bus turned slowly onto a small roundabout, and a moment later came to a quiet halt. The driver opened the rear door and the passengers pushed their way to the luggage compartment, apparently worried that, out of all the suitcases, theirs would be the one to go missing. The last to get off, Yermi clutched his suitcase in his right hand and, with his left, pushed back the fringe of the hood attached to his padded military coat.

He stood in a small square that, according to the plaque, was named after the Russian impresario Sergei Diaghilev. He tried to take this as a positive sign but had no idea where to go next. He estimated that he was beyond the department stores, which meant that the opera house should be in front of him. Crossing the street, he advanced several paces and glanced at the shop windows. George Clooney stared at him from a poster in one, recommending he drink coffee made from capsules.

There were hotels on all sides, but they seemed shabby, and he doubted that any of them were equipped with the technology he needed. He walked into a stiff breeze, and after a short while saw to his left a building that was monstrous in both size and ugliness.

He assumed that he had reached the rear facade of the opera house. The square in front of him was deserted in the rain. On either side of the street were hotels.

In the first, the receptionist stared at him and explained – with an almost convincing tone – that regrettably no rooms were available.

He crossed the street to a hotel whose lobby seemed much broader than the Opéra itself. He heard a melange of languages being spoken around him, a lot of Russian, and even Hebrew. There were only women in the reception area, a fact that increased his chances exponentially.

The receptionist looked at him quite eagerly as he explained that he had no credit card. After consulting the shift manager, she returned with a reasonable compromise: under the present circumstances and without a reservation, the hotel would be willing to host him against their regulations, but the payment – even for one night – must be up-front. She photocopied his passport and offered to help fill out the forms she had handed him. She copied his name from the passport, Vladislav Yerminski. Nationality: Israeli. Age: 21. He provided an address and postal code. Purpose of visit: Business? Holiday? Other? "Business." After depositing half his money into her hands, 250 euros, he received a key for room 5508. As he had hoped, the key was a 32-bit encoded card. A piece of cake.

The room was smaller than he had expected, considering the price, but the price included the option of connecting to the hotel's Ethernet network, and that was all that mattered. The curtains were wide open, revealing a view of the front of the opera house with all its gilded Greek deities. The T.V. was on, playing an annoying adaptation of Tchaikovsky by way of a commercial for the hotel. He searched for the remote and pressed the T.V. button in an attempt to change the soundtrack. The music switched immediately to a frenzied news report in French, and when the picture appeared on the screen, he saw an El Al plane underneath a giant headline: "*Le Kidnapping à Charles de Gaulle.*" Without taking his eyes off the screen, Yermi tried to sit down on the bed, feeling that his legs had ceased to obey him. He slid down until he found himself on the carpet, staring at the footage of the Chinese and the blonde, his brain slowly processing the images.

Chapter 25

Every car park along the Champs-Élysées announced in neon letters that it was full. The avenue projected cheerfulness and pride, glittering in the sun after the squalls that had washed the city only moments before. Abadi tried his luck in the nearby streets. Thanks to the long and blundering security checks at the Israeli embassy, he was at risk of running late for the secure conversation, and for a moment considered driving up to the embassy's barrier and taking a chance on parking there. But it was a rental car, and he was in for enough confrontations as it was.

He noticed a valet parking service at the entrance of an expensive restaurant, Le Boeuf sur le Toit, and casually handed over his keys along with a generous tip. Immediately upon entering the restaurant he apologised to the hostess, saying he had forgotten something which he would collect and then return, and was gone before she could protest. He cut left onto avenue Matignon. Of all the monuments in Paris, he had a strong aversion to the Arc de Triomphe. The mere sight of it depressed him. His last school trip as a French pupil had been here. For the briefest of seconds, Abadi remembered standing on the roof, his beloved teacher M. Lefebvre gesticulating into the wind towards the Place de l'Étoile while glorifying the military achievements of Napoleon. Two weeks later, his parents made their *aliyah* to Israel, and he had never forgiven either them or the monument that presaged his exile.

He hastened towards the embassy. The police officers behind the barrier noticed him from a distance. Abadi had years of experience visiting Israel's embassies around the world, and it always seemed as though the guards disliked him on a personal level, always having difficulty understanding the nature of his role and taking offence at his refusal to elaborate. The ordeal generally involved twenty minutes of questioning, X-ray security scanners, physical searches, and then a humiliating wait. The security business was a circus and every circus allows time for clowns to express themselves. Inhaling, he stepped into the ring.

At the first barrier, the one under French jurisdiction, everything went rather quickly. The officers asked to see his passport and reported his name on the radio. Abadi noticed tiny cameras fixed to their uniforms. No doubt in his mind that the personal details of every visitor to the Israeli embassy were stored somewhere in French counter-intelligence's database. He was the last person who could protest.

To his surprise, the officers almost instantly received authorisation to let him in. There were no delays at the second barrier either. The X-ray scanning was straightforward, almost careless, and the physical search was cursory. The security guard said, "You can go ahead," and handed him his passport. He did not request instructions over the radio or ask Abadi the purpose of his visit.

At the third barrier, he was asked the purpose of his visit. "I need to use your code room," Abadi said, and pulled out his security officer I.D. card, which had expired some time ago. The guard did not seem too bothered. He searched for his name on the printed list of names hanging on the wall of his booth, spoke to someone on the intercom, and returned the card to Abadi without comment, possibly even with a smile.

"Third floor, all the way to the right. The embassy's head security officer is waiting for you."

Now this was just plain science fiction. The embassy's head security officer had abused Abadi many times in the past, stalling his entrance each and every time, interrogating him about his job, trying to deny him access to the secure wing. This time he was indeed waiting for him upstairs, promptly opening the code room for Abadi and wishing him good luck.

On the wall in front of him hung six clocks set to the time in cities around the world – an old-fashioned yet endearing practice. He punched in his code and typed the access number to Special Section of Unit 8200. According to the wall clock, it was 15:59 in Israel – time to call the one person in 8200 whom he could trust, a young officer whom he had never met.

Chapter 26

They proceeded towards the *Quartier Asiatique* on foot.

Like all *xiake* in the organisation, the warriors were named after dragons in Chinese mythology. The senior of the two, the *xiake* Zhulong, was named after the dragon with the human face, and like him preferred to keep his secrets to himself. He did not bother explaining to his young partner why he had decided they should get off the métro at Tolbiac instead of staying on the train to the last station.

He simply assumed the chances for random security checks by the French police would be higher at the end of the line – certainly considering the number of illegal immigrants that passed through the station. He had no reason to suppose there would be any police checks at all; until now, everything had gone smoothly.

That was thanks largely to his young partner, who would certainly be promoted to senior dragon after this mission. He had chosen the optimal location for execution, had done an excellent job guiding the girl they had used as bait, had helped his commander carry out the operation and had also proven himself in planning the retreat, in which they blended into a group of Chinese tourists leaving Charles de Gaulle airport.

So far, the tally of unexpected obstacles had been nil, a rare achievement even for more experienced soldiers. Now they had only to get to the safe house in the 13th arrondissement, in the heart of Chinatown, and wait for the briefing before being shipped back to the homeland.

They took the escalator up to the avenue d'Ivry exit, where the torrential rain caught them by surprise. Their matching suits, which had given them cover in the airport, stood out on this street, right next to Buttes-aux-Cailles, Paris' historic left-wing stronghold. They started along the avenue towards Chinatown, but the rain was relentless and after a few minutes Zhulong said that they would take shelter.

In front of them was a supermarket, its bright sign boasting "The Largest Chinese Supermarket West of Beijing!" He decided to purchase umbrellas and light raincoats before continuing on their way.

Apart from one or two Frenchmen, the customers inside were all Vietnamese. The only Chinese were the employees. He felt uneasy glances directed at them as they followed the signs to the clothing aisle. He bought two rolled-up nylon raincoats for two euros each, cheaper than in the homeland. Then he added two black umbrellas, though he was not sure they would survive in this wind.

They got lost on the way to the cash registers. The supermarket was huge – the fish section alone was bigger than any Chinese supermarket he knew. Having tried to retrace their steps, they found themselves in the electronics department, in front of a wall covered with dozens of cutting-edge T.V. screens, all silently broadcasting the same news channel. A French anchorwoman with big beautiful eyes spoke animatedly, the image of an airplane behind her.

Suddenly the image changed, and he saw himself.

He ducked instinctively, as if under fire, then cautiously stood back up, his gaze fixed on the wall. The video was in black and white, but the picture was sharp and his image stared back at him, multiplied on dozens of screens, mocking him – mocking the precautions he had taken, his premature confidence in the mission's success, all his past achievements. The past was dead.

The video was edited oddly; at any rate, it did not capture the event from beginning to end. The *xiake* had been filmed sneaking up from behind, lunging at the victim, then collecting his belongings. Maybe the camera had not caught everything, but what it did catch was too much.

When the newscast cut back to the presenter, her blue eyes turned to the viewers in a plea for help, and the image switched to a screenshot of the two of them. A telephone number appeared underneath, and, even without knowing French, Zhulong understood the text. Have you seen these people? If so, call the police immediately.

Slowly he looked around, trying not to attract attention. The shoppers were absorbed in their own affairs, but one or two were following the report. Despite the enlarged images from the security camera – sophisticated as it might be – Zhulong knew that under different conditions they would have had a decent chance of escaping. All South East Asians look alike, after all.

But here, in this supermarket, people could tell each other apart, and anyone might quietly take out his mobile and call the police. They had gone to the *Quartier Asiatique* assuming it would be easier to blend in, but, like their previous paths of action, this plan was flawed: it had led them to the one spot in Paris where they might be identified.

His partner stood beside him frozen in his tracks, still glued to the screens, which were now reporting on the violence in the Middle East. He looked very young, almost a child. But he understood only too well the significance of what he had seen. His first task for the mission had been to choose a location in the airport where there were no security guards or cameras. He had interviewed more than twenty employees in the terminal, had grilled the constructions contractor for an hour, had toured the place himself three times.

He did not understand where he had gone wrong. But there was one thing he understood for sure – that it did not matter. He had failed, and that was doubling the odds that his commander would get caught. He tried to think of something to say, if he could still right his wrong and be useful. His mind refused to comply.

The nylon raincoats and umbrellas in their hands suddenly

weighed a ton. Any interaction with another person in the quarter, let alone paying at the cash register which probably had a surveillance camera above it, posed a risk. They abandoned their items on one of the shelves and went in search of the exit. The danger must have sharpened their sense of direction, because this time they made it out of the maze in less than a minute.

The rain had stopped. Looming in front of them were the towers of the *Quartier Asiatique*. There the safe house waited. As things stood, the apartment owners – not to mention the neighbours or the thousands of passersby they would encounter along the way – might very well turn them in.

Zhulong looked to his right. Judging by the flight of seagulls and the sound of the wind, the river was nearby. He hoped it was deep enough to accept the body of his young and promising partner, whose luck had betrayed him in, of all places, the most beautiful city in the world.

Chapter 27

The encryption system started running its usual complex algorithms. Her interlocutor, Aluf Mishne Zeev Abadi, had already appeared on the screen and was staring into the camera without moving a muscle. They were not allowed to speak until the installation of the encryption was complete, which took about a minute. Oriana always felt uncomfortable during this suspension, as if on a silent lift ride with a stranger. She took advantage of the wait to ask Rachel to make coffee.

So that's what her future commander looked like. While he certainly resembled the user photograph she had lingered over since his appointment, there were a few stark differences. First, he was in civilian clothing – an elegant white shirt, the two top buttons open against a tanned and hairy chest. His skin tone was darker than it appeared in the photographs, perhaps because her gaze immediately fell on his light eyes, which even a low-resolution encrypted communication could not dim. Seconds before the voice joined the picture, she spotted the difference between him and his frozen head shots: his gaze was soft and distant. It reminded her of her nephew watching his beloved birds on the kibbutz.

"Hello, Commander," Oriana said. She was aware that the smile in her voice sounded somewhat ironic, but she had no intention of changing just because some thug with swagger had suddenly entered her life, a man who knew how to terrorise even Aluf Rotelmann.

Chapter 28

Yermi took the box out of his suitcase. The tin foil he had wrapped it in was unwrinkled. As he expected, no-one had tried to open it. First he removed the audio reel, the reason for his journey, and put it on the narrow dressing table. What he needed now was the second piece of military property in the box: a hacking scanner, black and shiny, proudly displaying the Tzahal emblem. The standard warning for intelligence equipment was etched on the front of the device, detailing the punishment awaiting anyone who attempted to remove it from the premises of Unit 8200. Yermi placed it next to the T.V. set.

The hotel's cable box was unencrypted, not that it would have taken him long to crack the code. He located the cable at the bottom of the suitcase and connected the scanner to the box.

On the floor around him were all the tiny bottles he had found in the minibar – a little pick-me-up. There was no Irish whiskey, only three very mediocre brands of Scotch. Yermi mixed the three bottles in the elegant glass provided by the hotel, hoping that blending them might improve the quality of the drink.

He sat on the bed in front of the screen, picked up the remote and flipped back to the hotel's home channel. The appalling soundtrack had changed to Vivaldi's "Spring". A narrator with a soothing voice sang the praises of the hotel, built by the Pereire brothers in the 1800s, and in which Émile Zola had set the death of the heroine in his novel *Nana*. Yermi liked that. The narrator explained that today the hotel featured 470 rooms, a fact he liked even more, since the number of rooms increased his chances of finding what he was looking for.

The scanner started running. One after another, every connection from the building's network appeared on the screen, beginning with the adjacent rooms. In the first three rooms the guests were surfing Facebook, which did not help him. In the next two rooms, the guests had their Gmail accounts open, and drafts of personal letters appeared on his screen – an option that gave him some leeway if he did not locate something better.

On the tenth scan, the guest in room number 5348 appeared, checking his account balance in a London bank. Big mistake. An app which saved all the user's passwords appeared on the screen. Yermi did not need much more than that. He began recording the screen and raised his glass of mixed Scotch to salute the generous guest.

Chapter 29

Rachel knocked on her commander's door and entered, as usual, without waiting. "Did the conversation get disconnected, Commander? Would you like me to reconnect you two?"

"No, Rachel," Oriana said pensively. She looked at the screen with a mixture of surprise and distrust. "The conversation was not disconnected, the conversation ended."

"What? How long was it, a minute? I didn't even have time to make you coffee."

"According to the system, forty-eight seconds."

"But don't you have a million things to talk about?" Rachel said with genuine concern. "How are we going to issue the reports, and what about his weird appointment, and when is he coming back to Israel, and, like, a million other questions?"

"Absolutely, we have a lot of things to discuss," Oriana said, still lost in thought. "But he had one urgent request. I guess that's why the conversation was so brief."

"What was the urgent request? Does it have to do with the meeting you went to this morning instead of him?"

"No, nothing to do with that. He needed to ask me to urgently pick up his laundry."

Rachel sat in front of her favourite commander, plopping her body down in the office chair with a dramatic flair that was not the least bit feigned. "Say that last part again, more slowly?"

"He said that prior to his trip he sent his uniforms to the laundry service and they're supposed to be ready today, and could I go and pick them up and put them in his office, because otherwise they'll get lost in the base's laundry facility."

"I don't understand, he scheduled a secure conversation for *that*? He opened with that?"

"No. I introduced myself. 'Nice to meet you. Segen Oriana Talmor, deputy head of Special Section.' And he introduced himself. 'Nice to meet you too. Abadi.'"

"That's it? Abadi?"

"Yes. I asked him whether I should call him 'Commander' or 'Zeev' and he said, 'I prefer Abadi.' So I said, 'No problem, Abadi it is.' I started reporting all the complications with his appointment and the Vice Chief of Defence Staff's meddling, but he interrupted me and said we'd talk about all that some other time, and that he called because he needed some help. And then he asked me to run to the laundry service before it closes."

"And what did you say?"

"I told him to go fuck himself."

"You did not."

"I did. I told him: 'Go fuck yourself, Abadi.'"

"You shouldn't have, Commander. You could have just let me go there, I really don't mind. How did he react?"

"O.K., actually. He apologised and said he doesn't usually do such things, but this time he had no choice."

"That sucks."

"It sucks," Oriana said, nodding in agreement. "But he asked nicely, so I'll go." She got up and stretched. Rachel whistled admiringly.

"I'm not in the mood for your nonsense, Rachel," Oriana said. "Where is the laundry facility, anyway? I didn't even know we had one on base."

"We don't really have a laundry facility. It's more of a shed where officers bring their laundry which then gets sent out to the Central laundry services on the Tel HaShomer Base," Rachel said. "It's the shed next to the vehicle section, you can see where it is on the 'hot spots' map."

“Why is it a hot spot?” Oriana asked, still not altogether focused. The map of hot spots marked every place on the 8200 base subjected to regular check-ups by Special Section.

“There’s an insecure civilian telephone line over there. In fact it’s the only place on the base with a telephone line that’s both non-Tzahal and unencrypted,” Rachel said. “It’s in the security information file. I think they receive calls from civilian laundry services every now and then. Or something like that. I don’t really remember. Anyway, they have a permit for a regular civilian line. Our people inspect the location with detectors every Sunday.”

“Strength and blessing, Rachel.”

“Oh my God, where did that come from? It’s totally unlike you to use that expression.”

“That’s how Abadi ended our conversation. He asked if I understood what I needed to do now, and I replied, ‘Go to the laundry place.’ And he said, ‘Strength and blessing, Oriana,’ and hung up. What does it mean?”

“It basically means ‘may the force be with you’. It’s what the Mizrahis say in synagogue after reading the Torah. Strength and blessing.”

“So why did you say it’s unlike me to say that?”

“It would be pretty complicated for me to explain, Commander,” Rachel said cautiously.

“The shed by the vehicle section?”

“The shed by the vehicle section,” Rachel confirmed.

“Strength and blessing, Rachel,” Oriana said again, opening the office door with a swift motion, as if to surprise a burglar. The base seemed as sleepy as usual, but the footpaths leading to the parking garage were already filled with reserve men rushing to their cars to beat the traffic awaiting them at the Glilot intersection.

“You are all blessed,” Oriana heard Rachel whispering behind her. Oriana turned back.

“What?”

"That's the traditional reply, Commander. That's how you were supposed to answer Abadi. 'You are all blessed,' or 'We are all blessed.'"

"We are all blessed," Oriana mumbled to herself, although she did not feel that way at all.

Chapter 30

Getting away from the embassy took him longer than getting into it. Everyone involved tried to stall him with questions, and the French sentry was the only one who opened the barrier gate for him without a word.

He started searching.

On the nearby street he found only Japanese restaurants, branches of espresso bar chains, clubs and other pseudo-hip places which had no chance of meeting his needs. He found what he was looking for on the parallel street – an old-fashioned café, a kind of miracle in that area. It had probably received its name, Le Président, many presidential terms ago in the nearby Palais de l'Élysée. The sign declared it was a brasserie, not simply a café, but Abadi had no intention of trying out the food.

The place was almost empty, as could be expected at that time of day. A few tourists were sitting under canopies outside, arguing with a waiter who seemed properly hostile and condescending. Five elderly Parisian men sat inside on the red leather banquettes sipping early aperitifs. The bar was deserted. As Abadi had hoped, a small, outdated sign above the counter announced: "Toilets – Coat check – Telephones" with an arrow pointing downstairs.

He sat in front of the bartender, who was probably the owner, and who greeted him with an almost imperceptible nod. He was old, past the age of retirement, certainly, and the bags under his eyes were so swollen that it was difficult to meet his gaze. Abadi ordered a glass of white wine, and the bartender reached inside the small fridge and took out an open bottle of Graves, an unexpected choice. The wine was good. He hesitated whether to initiate a conversation by complimenting him on the wine, but decided it would seem insincere, even ingratiating.

"*Dîtes moi, patron, vous avez l'international au téléphone ici?*"

The bartender blinked and poured himself a glass from the bottle. A good sign. "I haven't been asked that question in a long time," he said. "You're trying to play Commissaire Maigret? You're too young and too skinny."

"No, just forgot my mobile," Abadi said, trying to bring the conversation back on track.

"Maigret used to sit right there, on the same stool you're sitting on," the bartender said. "The actor who played him, that is. Jean Gabin. Every now and then Marlene Dietrich would join him. They knew they could keep to themselves here and no-one would talk."

"I always say that discretion is the better part of valour," Abadi said. He even meant it, which was quite dishonest for a spy.

"Mme Pompidou, the President's wife, used my phone to make long-distance calls," the bartender carried on with his musings, sipping his wine. "She used to sneak in here every evening to talk to the President's American doctor. She explained that she could not speak freely in the Élysée because the D.G.S.E., the secret service, tapped the telephones."

"The conversation I need to have will not be as tragic," Abadi lied. "In any event, I hope it'll be less expensive."

The bartender poured them both more wine.

"The telephone for regular customers is in the booth to the right, here, by the kitchen. You need to dial nine first. I hope it still works."

Abadi took his glass with him. It was not so much a booth as a private room, complete with leather couches, a cigar humidor and a mahogany desk on which sat a telephone that could easily have found itself in a museum. Abadi pressed nine and got a dial tone. No choice now but to check whether his prickly deputy had been kind enough to comply with his plea. He took out his notebook and dialled the number.

She picked up on the first ring.

"Go fuck yourself, Abadi," Segen Talmor said. "What took you so long?"

Abadi tried to stifle a laugh. Relief.

"I had to listen to reminiscences about Marlene Dietrich in order to get a line."

"I'm sitting here surrounded by the affection of five bored quartermasters who made me coffee. I'm considering filing for a transfer to head of the laundry service, seems easier than being your deputy."

"No-one gets rid of me that fast," Abadi said. He felt a sudden pang. Ego or heart, he could not tell.

"That's not what I heard," she said. She had a warm voice, soothing and sarcastic at the same time. His gaze wandered across the room as if searching for an anchor, and fixed itself on a bust of Marianne, the symbolic freedom fighter of the Republic, perched by the door. He spoke to Marianne, and heard Oriana.

"How was the meeting?"

"Very strange," Marianne-Oriana said. "It started with some mix-up. They were sure Shlomo Tiriani was still the head of section, and for some reason it was very important to them that he be the representative." Special Section would not be investigating the kidnapping at Charles de Gaulle if Tiriani had still been in charge this morning.

Abadi said nothing, however, preferring to wait for the penny to drop. If Oriana heard it, and saw its tarnish, she did not skip a beat. "Afterwards they squirmed around for about an hour trying to explain that the daily list, the one sent to everyone, you know ... "

"I understand," Abadi said. Her voice now had a musical quality to it, as if she were confiding a secret.

"... that it's sent in different versions, and some of Zorro's guys got the full one and others did not. And then there was the whole business of the city you're in."

"I'm happy to hear someone other than me is taking this thing seriously."

"They're actually not. The big boss kept repeating that it has nothing to do with us, that it was just a case of mistaken identity."

"I understand."

"Understand what?" Her voice took on that mocking edge again.

"You'll see in a moment. I need you to write down a list of names. Do you have a writing implement?"

"A writing *implement*? Charcoal? A quill? Or would a regular pen be O.K. with you?" she said.

"A regular pen would be just fine." He might just get used to this.

"Then yes, I do."

"I'm going to read you thirty-three names. I only have the foreign spelling, so for some you'll need to guess how to write the names in Hebrew. These were the passengers on the El Al flight this morning. I need you to check the database to see if they had anything to do with the unit, whether in their regular service or in the reserve."

"There were only thirty-three passengers on the flight?"

"No. The passenger list is very long, the plane was nearly full. I ruled out all the women, the non-Israelis, those who pre-ordered kosher meals, and passengers who boarded with their spouse or kids. I also ruled out passengers who did not check in luggage, because they probably left before Yaniv Meidan collected his luggage and went off with the blonde."

"Now I understand."

"This is a covert investigation, without informing the base or reporting to Central."

"But checking, on our own, thirty-three names in various versions in Hebrew in such a huge database, that could take me two, even three hours."

"Let's settle for one," Abadi said.

It was 3.12 p.m., Monday, April 16.

Chapter 31

In the park, *xiake* Erlang Shen strolled along the riverbank. Dressed in rags and dragging behind him a heavy market cart, he looked like one of the many Chinese pedlars scattered across Parisian tourist sites. And indeed, should the need arise, he could pull out the usual ware: folding umbrellas, bottles of mineral water, selfie sticks, flying laser butterflies and postcards of the Eiffel Tower, the same tower that now gleamed at him from the other side of the city.

His name, Erlang Shen, had been chosen for him by the ultimate dragon himself, and it indicated the heavy responsibility the organisation had placed upon him. The original Erlang Shen had saved the Chinese people from deadly floods thanks to his ability to see into the future. According to the legend, this ability had been granted to him in the form of a third eye, smack in the middle of his forehead.

He too had a third eye – not on his forehead but in a concealed pocket of the cart. The device looked like one of the new-generation mobiles, at least in routine checks at airports. Two red pips moved across the satellite map on his screen. According to the device – a state-of-the-art tracker from the People's Republic of China's military industry – the two dots were now crossing Bercy's commercial zone on the opposite bank of the river. Miniature transmitters had been sewn into the collars of the suits the *xiake* had worn to their botched mission earlier that morning.

Erlang Shen still did not know why they had decided not to continue to the safe house. Obviously it was just another of the mishaps the two had committed. Killing the wrong Israeli was a failure in itself, but choosing to do it at a site surveilled by sophisticated security cameras – that was a colossal lapse.

Erlang Shen's job was to enable the organisation to erase failures and quash embarrassments. Commercial companies could always issue an apology, hire a publicist, rebrand. But the Ming empire employed other methods. Ming did not suffer fools.

And now these two fools had complicated things further. The arena was not some sealed apartment in an immigrant neighbourhood, a well-planned trap, but the very heart of the most tourist-invaded city in the world. Children frolicked around him on the bank; tourists clicked their cameras from every possible angle; hordes of Parisians took advantage of the scattering clouds to have picnics, and on two separate occasions he saw policemen patrolling on their bicycles.

He picked up his pace slightly, all the while watching the two dots on the screen, until he reached the bridge. It was a pedestrian bridge, new and shiny with an expensive wooden deck and a lower ramp that offered children ample opportunities for hide-and-seek; the place was crowded with parents and their young. The bridge led to a large park, which, according to the map on the device, was named – a sign from above – after the Israeli leader Yitzhak Rabin.

Towering across the river, on the left bank, were four eccentric buildings that the map recognised as the Bibliothèque Nationale de France, the national library complex. Next to them was a large shopping centre and a sculpture garden next to the river. The two dots had just descended the stairs of the complex.

The bridge itself was named after Simone de Beauvoir. Erlang Shen knew who she was, and had even read some of her writings. He liked what she had written about the great Chairman Mao, the birth of communism, the plight of women in the West, and he certainly liked what she had written about the fear of death. "All men are mortal, but for each man death is an accident, an undue violence," his psychological warfare instructor had summarised.

Erlang Shen understood this perfectly. He sat on the wooden deck in the middle of the bridge and leaned against the railing. All around him, the French carried on with their business, avoiding his gaze. He took out the device and tuned the signal. It was the moment to request the commander's final approval.

The two dots advanced towards him.

Chapter 32

Oren pressed the buzzer and waited. He had no reason to rush; at a time of impending chaos, a little bad news could always wait.

Zorro always had his door closed; he often let people wait on the other side for long moments, but this time he called him in straight away. Everyone was too wound up for games. The adjutant shut the door behind him and waited.

"Yes, what can I do for you on this fine day?" Zorro said without glancing up from his papers. It was his usual opening. It served as a substitute for actual humour.

"I've done what you asked. We have nothing."

"I don't understand," Zorro said, looking up at the adjutant. He hoped his gaze would be perceived as threatening, but it conveyed only helplessness.

"Aluf Rotelmann was right, he did go to the embassy and ask to use the code room."

"And did he call her?"

"He called her."

"So what did he say to her?"

"He didn't say anything. He just asked her to pick up his uniform from the laundry."

"His uniform from the laundry? Could that be a code?"

"'The first condition for encoding is the co-ordination in advance of an inverse function between the users,'" the adjutant quoted from the intelligence manual. He did not mean to be rude, so he quickly clarified: "We know they could not have co-ordinated a code in advance because this conversation was the first time they had ever communicated with one another."

"So what does it mean?"

"I don't know. She did actually try talking to him about the abduction, but he interrupted her and said they'd talk about it when he returned to the Unit."

"And when is he returning?"

"He didn't say."

"So we have nothing?" Zorro said in disbelief.

"We have nothing," Oren repeated.

Zorro fell silent. Aluf Rotelmann had to travel to Jerusalem after the Prime Minister summoned photographers to document an "urgent security consultation" about the abduction in Paris.

"He left the embassy?"

"Who?"

"Abadi, that's who."

"Yes, he left right after the conversation."

"Where to?"

"I don't know. It's not like we can have him followed there."

"And Segen Talmor? Did she collect his laundry?"

"We don't know," the adjutant said.

"And why not?" Zorro said. "It's not like you can't follow her there."

Chapter 33

Ming's second-in-command sat inside Breizh café. He Xiangu was named after the only goddess among eight gods, and while her mythological namesake had been immortalised after she had eaten powder from a jar carried to her by angels, He Xiangu knew all too well that she herself was mortal. She ordered sparkling water and a salad.

She had chosen a spot with her back to the wall, facing the front, as was her regular habit. Through the glass door she could see her bodyguard switching posts on the pavement outside, and she observed him casting discreet glances at the elegant women coming and going from the surrounding boutiques. The character of the neighbourhood surprised her. Breizh café was located in the heart of the Jewish quarter, but so far she had seen no-one she thought looked like a Jew. She certainly hadn't seen anyone who resembled the only Jew she cared about at the moment, Unit 8200 soldier Vladislav Yerminski, otherwise known as Yermi.

She had brought seventeen men with her. Yesterday it had seemed excessive for the mission – monitoring the operational squad. But now that the mission had gone south, her commando unit felt cripplingly small. She had ordered ten men to search every hotel and hostel, a task that required prodigiously more manpower. Three men she allocated to a surveillance mission in front of the Israeli embassy, and three more she had sent to the El Al terminal at Charles de Gaulle airport.

Now there was no-one left to send to help Erlang Shen. She had thought about ordering him to leave those two losers alone and bolt, but Ming did not like loose ends. There was no telling what damage the two could still cause.

They had already damaged her standing within the organisation, this much she knew. Her employer had built a brilliant empire from the shadows and had chosen to remain there, a whisper behind the rumour. Members of the organisation delivered, or the odds were high that they would not live to learn from their failures.

She studied the location of the execution on her screen. There could be a plausible explanation for their decision not to continue to the safe house; for instance, they might somehow have found out they had screwed up the mission and were afraid to carry on with the plan. But there could also be another – not entirely plausible – explanation: that the Israelis had been handling them from the start.

Giving Erlang Shen the green light to execute a clean-up operation eliminated the need to investigate why the two had aborted the original plan. And there were other benefits: releasing Erlang Shen to the task of tracking down Yerminski would burn the French police's only lead from the morning's action. Oh, and it would also send a clear-cut message to the Israelis that she was not playing games.

She considered the possible disadvantages of authorising the operation, and reached the conclusion that the damage would be minimal: the French police would suffer another insult, which might lead them to increase their efforts, but that nuisance would be negligible. What could they do? Erect more barriers? Stop more South East Asians for random security checks?

In fact, the very opposite would probably happen. Taking out the assassins from the morning would be viewed by the French police as validation for not interfering too much with what would seem like a gang's revenge killing. There was nothing people from that field liked more. It calmed the T.V. viewers, made them believe that the criminals were being punished without society's intervention, like a divine decision.

You can relax, my dear bourgeois, she said to herself and pressed the button, giving the green light. The order made its way to Erlang Shen, across the river. Perfect timing: at that moment, her salad arrived at the table.

Chapter 34

Oriana opened the door and found ten soldiers waiting for her. She tried to understand why all of the section's investigators were huddled in Rachel's room at this time of day, and recalled that in the morning, before she had learned of the appointment of a permanent head of section, she had summoned all the soldiers for a pep talk during the shift change. Rachel must have forgotten to cancel.

Anyway, Abadi wanted an answer within an hour. She took a deep breath. "I'm sorry about the delay. We're in special investigation mode, all regular tasks are cancelled. Please, sit anywhere, even on the floor, take out your devices and log into the page Rachel is going to open for us. Rachel, I need a case number and an operation name."

Rachel looked at her commander, slack-jawed, but quickly came to her senses. "The running number is 54082866, Commander," she said, and logged it into the file. "The generated code names currently start with "L". The options are 'Lingering Fog', 'Long Night' or 'Last Straw'."

"They all kind of work," one of the soldiers said, and the others laughed. Since most of them were by now sitting on the floor looking up at her, she felt as though she was a new teacher on the first day of school. They did indeed look like children, and since she was in fact no older than they, she wondered if that was how she came across in their eyes as well.

"In honour of the work still ahead of us, under the command of the new head of section, Aluf Mishne Zeev Abadi, Operation 54082866 will be named 'Long Night'," she said, and wrote the name on the whiteboard. "Questions?"

There were no questions.

"This morning, at 10 a.m., as you must have heard on the news, an Israeli passenger named Yaniv Meidan was abducted from Charles de Gaulle airport in Paris. The event corresponds with an alert that appeared on The Most Wanted list about the intention to abduct a soldier from the Intelligence Corps in Paris, but Yaniv Meidan had no connection to the corps. Intelligence-gathering Operation Long Night, grade 7 precedence and top-secret clearance, is designed to examine whether the kidnappers intended to abduct a different Israeli and took Meidan accidentally. The purpose of the investigation is to find out whether there was a soldier from Unit 8200 on the flight who arrived in Paris and may be unaware of the threat to him. Questions so far?"

The first to raise his hand was Tomer, the newest, most junior investigator in the section, who looked more like a soldier from the technology unit than a security investigator in Special Section. "Is this an overt investigation?"

Excellent question. Just what Oriana needed right now – to reveal Abadi's request in front of the entire Intelligence Corps, not to mention Zorro.

"No, at this stage this is a covert investigation. We keep the noise to a minimum so we don't attract the kidnappers' attention," Oriana lied through her teeth, and went on before follow-up questions could be raised. "We have the names of thirty-three Israelis who were on that plane. We need to cross-check them against the personnel database to see if any of them belong to the unit. If there are no hits, it means the kidnappers were targeting a non-Israeli passenger from a different flight to the same terminal. If you get a hit, you log it into the secure page and call me immediately."

"The regular service database or the general database?" Alma, a languorous blonde who looked half-asleep, asked apprehensively. Someone behind her grumbled, "What do you think?"

"You check the database that includes reserve soldiers, but limit the search to those who were discharged less than five years ago," Oriana said. There was not much intelligence value in old information from 8200; the unit and its operational field were changed beyond recognition. "Pay close attention. For some we don't have first names, and all the spelling is in English, so we'll have to try different versions of names."

There were no questions. "You're ten and we have thirty-three names. Who can guess how many names each of you will get? Let's go. Rachel will divide you into groups. Bring me an answer, fast."

An answer of "no hits" would be welcome, Oriana thought. I don't need a commander who's pleased with himself on his first day.

Chapter 35

At last, Zhulong saw the river.

It took them longer to reach it than he had calculated. Twice they saw police patrols and had to change direction. When they were already very close, they crisscrossed the national library complex and could not find the stairs leading to the banks of the Seine.

His subordinate suspected nothing. Even now, standing in front of the bridge, waiting for orders. Oddly, it was Zhulong who hesitated. He gazed at the river, as if the answer would appear in the water.

He had imagined a narrow yet powerful river; he had imagined ancient steps descending sharply to a deserted bank where two or three Parisian beggars would be slouching about, dazed by alcohol, minding their own business. He had imagined a massive stone bridge crowded with the noisy traffic of vehicles. He had imagined what he had wanted to find.

Instead, he found a very long footbridge, modern, built of wood, designed in the shape of rising and falling waves. Under the bridge a wide river ran sluggishly, many *bateaux mouches* steaming up and down it. The riverbanks were also crowded – tourists, hikers, couples.

He could see no beggars, but in the middle of the bridge stood a pedlar dressed in rags. The pedlar sent flying into the sky laser toys that drew a greenish line in their flight before looping back into his hand. Enthralled children gathered around him, demanding a toy from their parents at the top of their lungs.

Clearly, you could not dispose of someone on this bridge.

He considered going down to the riverbank, but at that exact moment he saw two policemen patrolling on bicycles and had to look for another solution. Across the bridge was a large park; surely he could find a corner there in which to recover his dignity, as well as that of the organisation.

He started walking over the bridge, his subordinate trailing mutely behind him. The odd wavy design of the deck made for a slow pace. After two minutes of walking, they started going up again, and they found themselves directly above the middle of the river. From up close, he observed that the pedlar was Chinese like them, and even looked familiar. The children's excited shrieks blended with the whistles of the soaring toys, and Zhulong felt such a heaviness in his chest that it was a struggle to breathe.

Turning in his tracks, he rushed back in the direction of the national library buildings, towards the bank from which they had come, and a few moments later, once his brain had caught up with his feelings, he broke into a run. He heard the abbreviated yelp of his young colleague, but he did not care.

The small laser toys spun in the sky above him, splashing their menacing abstract art above his head. By now he was very close to the road, and the angle of the slope changed again; with giant strides he climbed towards the edge of the bridge, like a messenger in Chinese mythology ascending towards the palaces of the gods.

He heard the sharp whistle, looked up and saw the green object flying towards his neck at a dazzling speed; only then was the explosion heard. As his head was severed by the blast, a flame burst out, sketching, in the last instant of his life, the mythological creature after whom he was named, the dragon with the human face.

Chapter 36

Abadi pulled back the curtain and let the sunlight flood the room that had once been his. The bed was narrower than he had remembered, the desk smaller. Stacked on the shelves were his comics, which he would probably reread at some point, perhaps after retirement.

The view from the window had not changed. Three windsurfers were competing across the artificial lake, and beyond the lake he saw the other architectural whimsies this city had known over the years – cauliflower-shaped buildings, a residential tower built like a steeple, a fire station in neon blue, and in front of these, opposite the small synagogue, right beside the last station of métro line 8, stood the Créteil-Préfecture shopping centre, once the biggest in Europe.

"No nostalgia. No nostalgia. No no-stal-gia," he repeated to himself, maybe out of doubt, perhaps out of sorrow.

On the street below, two police cars were parked, their engines idling. That had not been a rare sight in his childhood either: Créteil, the huge suburb south-east of Paris where he grew up, was a violent place even before its current swell of anti-Semitic incidents. A group of teenagers defiantly surrounded the policemen, who remained in their vehicles. The kids soon got bored and dispersed.

"Do you prefer to start with crescent briks with egg or triangle briks with mashed potato and harissa?" his mother called from the kitchen. She had already updated him on the family news, including the wedding of his niece who had married an Ashkenazi, "but a very nice man", as she always said when trying to alleviate the misfortune of all those poor people who had not been born Tunisian Jews.

The table was set. The artichoke, marmuma and méchouia salads were very spicy, which forced him to temper them with tirshi, in which the carrots and turnips were seasoned with nothing but kosher salt and lemon. From the aromas he could tell that the main course was couscous boulettes, and he asked himself whether he would be able to meet the challenge of such a meal. As a kid, he never had such problems.

His mother joined him at the table, carrying two different trays of briks, her usual solution to food dilemmas. He started with the classic brik. The egg was almost poached, trapped inside the thin shell. He ate carefully, from the centre out, scooping up the bursting yolk with the fried pastry.

"I can't find the old-fashioned brik sheets here anymore, they're too thick, almost like filo. They say the Jews here no longer know what brik is, they make Chinese eggrolls with it, or something like that. I got these from the Arab around the corner, he imports them from Tunisia."

"I did feel that they're thinner," he said with his mouth full. "And where's the harissa from? It's spicier than usual."

"I made it myself. The kosher harissa is bland now, and the Arab only stocks tins." He moved on to the second tray, in which the brik was folded into a perfect triangle and filled with coarsely mashed potato, flakes of tuna, parsley and something else he could not identify. He could not stop eating from the tray, and anyway he was not about to insult his mother on what was too rare a visit.

"*Maman*, what are those tiny, salty pieces inside? It isn't capers."

"No, *ya omri*, it's bottarga. The real thing, the fish seller brings it from Italy especially for me. They don't even have this kind in Tunisia."

"That reminds me, I brought you something," he said and took out of his bag of seedless grapes, fresh moist dates and a kilo of cucumbers.

"*Bel'Hout ââlik*," she blessed him, "we can't get any of this here.

Nothing is better than the fruit and vegetables from Israel, it fills me with joy. I'm so sorry we don't live there. Sometimes I miss the time we spent there."

"When you were there, you missed being here."

"No, no, it wasn't like that," his mother said, hastily rewriting family history. "It's just that after what they did to your grandfather I could not continue living there."

He fell silent. She changed the subject. "Your father apologises for not being here, he has a meeting in town he could not reschedule."

The excuse was so implausible, it begged further discussion. His father was eighty years old and had not boarded the métro to Paris in months, if not years.

"He's still angry with me?"

His mother shifted uncomfortably in her chair, and out of embarrassment took the last brik for herself.

"It's difficult for him, what you did, with the publicity and all that," she said at last. "'What the devil were you doing in that galley?'"

Quoting Molière was a habit of hers. Abadi had transferred out of the French education system at the age of eleven, and had never fully integrated into the Israeli system. He had never mastered the art of literary allusions.

"What is it with you and this Ashkenazi leftist thing? Would these people testify in court for your trial?" she said. "You might have thought about the impact on your father. The Jewish newspapers here dedicated entire pages to it, and some called you a traitor. In the synagogue they moved your father to a pew at the back. It has not been easy." She shivered, as if seeking to dispel the impression her words made. "But it will soon pass. I'm bringing the couscous."

"I'll help you," he said, but she refused to let him near the kitchen. He called after her, in an attempt to lift her spirits, "I've gone back to the army, *Maman*."

She stopped in her tracks and returned to the table, excited. "The Israeli army? Tzahal?"

"No, *Maman*, the Venezuelan army. Of course Tzahal."

"And they agreed?"

"They're the ones who asked," he said without elaborating. There was no point in upsetting his mother with descriptions of how things worked in Tzahal, or in organisations in general.

"I'm so happy!" she exclaimed. "I knew that it all had to be a misunderstanding. It's a great honour for us that you're such a high-ranking officer in Tzahal. I'll call your father right after this. He'll be so happy. He keeps complaining that the army is weak and doesn't know how to handle the Arabs."

"And what does he propose?" Abadi said, mainly to cheer himself up, because he knew all too well what the answer would be.

"He always says we need much more force, that we're too soft on them," his mother said. Both knew that his father's suggestions were more specific.

"And does he already have a number in mind, so I can report it to general headquarters? What, we kill three million, six million, twenty million Arabs? How many does he suggest?"

"You can laugh all you want," his mother reprimanded him. When she was angry, she looked even younger than usual. "We grew up with the Arabs, your father and I, we know who they are and how to talk to them."

Then she froze, as if remembering something important. "The couscous! I left the soup for the couscous on the burner," she cried and rushed back to the kitchen.

"*Maman*, can I use the telephone? I need to call Israel."

"Does it have to do with the army?"

"It has to do with the army."

"It would be a great honour for our telephone," she called.

Chapter 37

She came out of the Saint-Augustin métro and crossed the boulevard without waiting for the pedestrian sign to change. A driver honked with rage, but she did not turn her head. Her blonde hair was concealed under the hood of her black sweatshirt, and, because of her height, it was easy to mistake her for a man.

She walked until she reached boulevard Haussmann, number 89, where she was swallowed into the lobby of a building with the obscure logo "V.T.B. Bank". She went to the cashpoint to check her bank balance from the branch in Moscow.

The same news awaited her here, as clear and unequivocal as in the text she had received: four hundred euros had been transferred to her account an hour ago. She wanted to withdraw the money – the only effective way to combat the distrust that still surged inside her. The machine thought for fewer than thirty seconds before discharging the bills.

Four hundred euros; it was by far the easiest money she had made since arriving in Paris.

Light-headed, she left the bank and read the instructions on her mobile once more. She had to act quickly if she wanted the second half of the payment.

She crossed boulevard Haussmann in the direction from which she had come, again without waiting for the pedestrian signal to turn, and walked quickly to Le Printemps department store. Despite her best efforts, she went in through the wrong entrance, and after a nervous search approached the information desk, where she was given a map and directions to the neighbouring building through the overpass. Hordes of tourists were browsing around her, many speaking Russian.

Finally she reached the correct building and approached her objective, the special stewards' stand. A handsome, diffident young man listened offhandedly to her request and asked for her I.D. She handed him a student card. He opened the cabinet under the desk and a moment later claimed they had nothing under that name. It was the price one paid in this city for wearing a tracksuit. At her insistence they looked again, and the coveted bag turned up; it was bigger than she had expected. In accordance with the plan, there were two boxes inside, each tied with a silk bow and bearing the reassuring stamp "paid".

Ignoring the steward's offer to call her a taxi, she turned towards the side exit. Within four minutes she found herself standing in front of the monumental facade of the Gare Saint Lazare. She dashed down the stairs to the train station's basement and found the lockers on the right.

Number 703 was a small locker on the right-hand wall. She punched in the code and the door opened. The gun gleamed at her from inside like a jewel. "The world's deadliest semi-automatic", the instructions she had received stated. It was lighter than she had expected, and had a shiny gold-plated handle. She hid it at the bottom of the department store bag, and then picked up the manila envelope awaiting her in the locker. It contained a white, unmarked magnetic card in a cardboard keycard holder from Le Grand Hôtel. In neat handwriting was the information: room number 5508, guest name Vladislav Yerminski.

It was 4.58 p.m., Monday, April 16.

Chapter 38

Aluf Rotelmann was in a sombre mood, as he always was when he returned from the office in Jerusalem. Zorro tried to think of a way to lift his commander's spirits, but like everything else he had tried today, it did not go well.

"It's possible that it's a coincidence, that there's no connection between these things," he eventually said.

Aluf Rotelmann stared at him with a blank expression. "It's possible. It's possible there's no connection. It's also possible that everything will just work out on its own, that someone from the future will travel here in a time machine and fix all the damage you people have caused."

The adjutant wanted to protest.

"I chose the two of you as my confidants," Aluf Rotelmann said. "Besides the Prime Minister, ten people know about this threat to our intelligence sources, and I chose you two to lead the mission on my behalf. Perhaps the most sensitive mission I've had since my appointment, and I chose you to execute it. It's impossible to tackle this type of danger through the usual channels with so many threats from inside and out. And here we have it, when it finally happens, it turns out you're completely unprepared. You're on the ropes and you have no idea what hit you."

"We've managed in the meantime to gather the basic facts," his adjutant said cautiously.

"So what are the basic facts?" Rotelmann's voice was as cold as a slaughterhouse.

Oren lowered his gaze and read off the page: "Sgan Aluf Shlomo Tiriani was in charge of information security in Unit 8200 for six years. When the decision to establish Special Section was made, following the conclusions of the investigation committee it was only his title that changed, and he was appointed head of Special Section. But formally, something did change, because from that moment he was subordinate to the command of the Vice Chief of Defence Staff, in accordance with the decision to make the new section autonomous."

"And when did she join?" Aluf Rotelmann said.

"They'd worked together for a year, but she was appointed even before Tiriani got the job. The Vice Chief of Defence Staff chose her based on her commanders' reviews, and of course on the basis of all the cases she'd cracked. The Unit 8200 commander approved her appointment to Special Section's deputy, and we received a copy of the appointment letter."

"And you didn't bother showing it to me? It seemed no more than a boring letter to you?"

"It wasn't important at the time," the adjutant said. "We hadn't been asked to build the operation yet. I didn't even know Tiriani and we never talked about that section. It was one appointment letter out of dozens we received."

"When was Tiriani thrown out and why?"

"Two days ago Sgan Aluf Shlomo Tiriani was summoned to the office of the Vice Chief of Defence Staff. Military policemen came to pick him up from Special Section in their vehicle, and Tiriani did not have time to notify anyone, not even us."

"And then?"

"A special military police investigator was waiting for him there, and in the presence of the Vice Chief of Defence Staff, he informed Tiriani that he was suspected of embezzlement and of conduct unbecoming to an officer. It seems that Tiriani had changed his address in the administrative department, reporting that he had moved to Kiryat Shmona. On those grounds, he was entitled to monthly reimbursements for rent and for a hotel room in Tel Aviv on weekends. In reality, the apartment in Kiryat Shmona belongs to his brother, and he himself continued to live in exactly the same apartment in the outskirts of Tel Aviv."

"Well, so what? He's the only person in Tzahal to con the housing department?"

"No, but the Vice Chief of Defence Staff informed him that owing to his sensitive role, these offences, which had been going on for three years, were unforgivable. He gave him a choice: immediate discharge while keeping his pension or standing trial."

"And he chose the discharge."

"Yes, he went straight to the induction base from there, and underwent a quick release of funds process. He was told that he couldn't talk to anyone about this, no matter how high-ranking, because the investigation was ongoing and it could be regarded as obstruction of justice."

"Yeah, sure."

"Segen Oriana Talmor was appointed temporary stand-in. This morning, as in less than twenty-four hours later, the Vice Chief of Defence Staff notified the Unit 8200 commander that, from now on, the role of head of Special Section would be carried out by an officer with the rank of aluf mishne or above, and he decided to appoint Aluf Mishne Zeev Abadi, who was about to be released from service following his testimony in favour of the conscientious objectors."

"That, we remember, thank you. How did he talk to the commander of 8200? That guy hasn't returned my calls from this morning."

"We don't know exactly. He left the States yesterday, we're not sure on which flight. He could still be in the air."

"And how is it that Abadi just happens to be in Paris right now?" Aluf Rotelmann said.

"It's his discharge holiday. He was granted approval to travel to the CeBit Europe Fair."

"Meaning, he was on that same flight."

"Yes," Oren said submissively. "He was on that flight. He was the first person who noticed Yaniv Meidan's friends huddling together, he's the one who called the embassy's military attaché, and they sent over the representative of the Israeli police."

Aluf Rotelmann looked at them with eyes full of pity: "How did Zorro put it? 'It's possible that it's all just a coincidence.'"

Chapter 39

Tomer sprinted from the administrative building of Unit 8200 to his commander's office in a mad run, or at least that was her impression given his rapid panting when he knocked on the door. Oriana noticed that, at any rate, he was more flustered.

"I think I've got it," he finally managed to say, and handed her the printed personnel card.

Oriana studied the form. Among the flight records Abadi had dictated to her appeared a passenger by the name of V. Yerminski. In the active personnel files of Unit 8200, Tomer had turned up a soldier by the rank and name of Rav Turai Vladislav Yerminski. He had been enlisted to the unit two years earlier based on his proficiency in Russian, attended a course at Intelligence Training Base 15, and in his first year was stationed at a front-line listening post in the Golan Heights with security clearance.

And then, four months ago, he was transferred to the El Dorado department in the Central 8200 base in the Negev desert.

Oriana's heart stopped. If she had to estimate the potential damage caused by the abduction of a soldier from Unit 8200 according to the secrets he had been exposed to, the abduction of a soldier from El Dorado was the worst-case scenario.

"Maybe it isn't him?" she said in a hopeful tone that sounded rather pathetic even to her. "It isn't a common surname, but it's possible that somewhere in Israel there's another person by that name. We have to check with the base if he's there."

"No need," Tomer said.

"Why?"

"Because I've already asked the administrative department if they happen to have an up-to-date report on him, and they do. The base reported that he was granted a special ten-day leave that began yesterday."

"That doesn't prove it's him."

"The leave included permission to travel overseas. On the overseas leave form, the base is required to state the travel destination."

"Don't tell me . . . "

"They wrote that he was going to Paris," Tomer said.

"Under what circumstances does an active soldier get a special ten-day leave?" Oriana wondered.

Tomer had to admit that he was not sure. "On the base's form they had to give a number to indicate the reason for the leave. They put down '05'."

"Rachel!" Oriana shouted. Rachel reported at the door as if shot from a cannon.

"Yes, Commander?"

"Please check what reason for leave number 05 means on the administrative forms."

"I don't have to check, Commander, everyone knows that. Leave 05 is an authorisation for wedding leave."

"Why would a soldier need ten days to attend a wedding?"

"It's not just to attend a wedding, Commander. Attending a wedding only gets you a one-day leave. Leave 05 is if the soldier himself is getting married. It's a wedding holiday. The soldier who's getting married brings the relevant forms and is automatically entitled to ten days off. His commander can't object. Same goes for women in the ranks." Rachel sounded like someone who had spent many hours memorising military leave orders.

Silence prevailed while Oriana absorbed the information. Rachel did not dare return to her post. It was Tomer who finally broke the silence.

"But what does that have to do with an overseas travel authorisation?"

"If the soldier is getting married abroad – for instance, in Cyprus – then he also receives permission to travel overseas," Rachel recited the orders.

"We're talking about a soldier of Unit 8200 who's serving in a department that has a top-secret purple clearance," Oriana said. "Are soldiers like him even allowed out of the country?"

"Depends where to," Rachel said. "There's a whole list of countries they're not allowed to travel to up to five years after their discharge from the unit. He can't travel to Russia, for example, but … "

"But he can to France." Oriana completed the sentence for Rachel.

"But if he's getting married in France, he's allowed to travel to France," Rachel confirmed.

"And if he's kidnapped in France, what do we do? Explain it to me, since you seem to have answers for everything today. What do you do when he's kidnapped in France?"

"What's the problem?" Rachel said. "Abadi's there, isn't he?"

"That's a load of nonsense, Rachel. So what if he's there? He's not James Bond, he's Abadi. Get me El Dorado's network intelligence officer on the secure line."

Chapter 40

Her instructions were to wait in front of Le Grand Hôtel until the opportunity to slip in unnoticed presented itself.

There was no good reason to take such precautions. The gun was at the bottom of the bag. She was wearing a tracksuit, like many tourists in Paris. The giant shopping bag completed the appearance of a foreign guest at a large hotel. But it would be a severe setback to lose the second payment of four hundred euros just because of a bored security guard asking to see her guest card.

After a few minutes a taxi pulled up to the entrance and a family of blondes like her got out, all carrying impressively large shopping bags. She crossed the street in time to blend in with the family while the doorman held open the door. The security guard stared in their direction before returning to his own affairs.

She followed the family to the lifts, waited while they entered one, then summoned another. Alone in the lift, she pressed the button to the second-floor convention centre, "Salon Opéra".

The floor was deserted. She admired the heavy curtains, the marble sculptures, the crystal chandeliers and other objects that could have been pilfered from one of Catherine the Great's palaces. She pulled herself together and made sure no-one was following her to the ladies' cloakroom, which turned out to be nearly as lavish as the convention hall itself. Once there, she checked there was no-one in the cubicles.

Pulling back the hood of her tracksuit top, she let her hair tumble over her shoulders like a golden house of cards. She set the Printemps bag on the marble floor and took out the gun, which was even more beautiful in the flattering lighting. She laid the two boxes from the department store on the marble counter around the sinks, and began to undress.

Naked, she looked at herself in the mirror and succumbed to the temptation to take a picture. But she had no-one to send the picture to since she had no interest in getting entangled in a relationship at this stage of her life. When she saved up enough money for an apartment, she would start thinking about who was worthy of sharing such a gift.

The smaller box contained a pair of red stilettos. The thought that she would get to keep them after it was all over made her almost as happy as the payment. In the larger box she found a red hotel uniform. She put her tracksuit and her trainers into the boxes and the boxes into the large shopping bag.

She stood in front of the mirror in her elegant uniform and practised drawing the pistol. She took out her mobile to take another selfie. With all due respect to the strict instructions, it would be a shame if none of her friends got to see her like this, glamorous in red in the city of lights. She chose some filters, wrote in Russian "Just another boring day at the office", and waited for the image to upload to Instagram. She got three "Likes" from her friends even before she had closed the app and turned off her phone. She put the pistol into the bag, opened the door and strutted towards the lifts to get the most important "Like" of the day.

Chapter 41

Rachel put through El Dorado's network intelligence officer, but warned Oriana that he was refusing to talk.

"This is a secure line," Oriana said.

"Maybe the line's secure, but as far as I'm concerned, you're not," he said without concealing the disdain in his voice. On Oriana's computer, the officer's profile details read "Segen Eitan". Dropping surnames was a new trend in the unit, yet another attempt by the the Intelligence Corps desk jockeys to emulate elite combat soldiers, and Lieutentant Eitan was no different.

"I don't understand," Oriana lied.

"I don't have to answer your questions. If the head of southern command orders me to talk to you, I will, but even then you'll have to come here," Segen Eitan said.

"A soldier in your department, Rav Turai Vladislav Yerminski, has gone missing during a trip abroad, and we believe that his life is in danger. We don't have time for this kind of power game."

"This is not a power game. This is a matter of national security."

"And it's precisely because of national security that I do, in fact, have to know his exact location in Paris. I have to understand what he does in El Dorado, and I have to speak to his friends in the department. So tell me, Eitan. What's it going to be? The security of your ego or the security of your country?"

"I'm not even going to confirm the existence of such a department, and I'm certainly not going to authorise you to speak to Yermi's friends," he said calmly.

From his voice she knew he had the complete backing of someone above him, perhaps the base's Chief Network Intelligence

Officer or perhaps the man above him, the head of southern command. Above or below, people whose country entrusted them with the secrets of others supposed that they belonged to a superior race. The extreme caution with which the unit was required to protect intelligence sources played into the hands of swollen-headed, obnoxious officers. She switched tactics.

"Your soldier left for Paris without leaving contact details. His disappearance corresponds with an alert on The Most Wanted, and you should have been aware of that. Do you need me to connect the dots for you, or can you do that by yourself?"

"You can try to intimidate me. It might work for the Special Section in other places, but it won't work with us. Go back to threatening your pot-smoking soldiers in Tel Aviv and stay out of things that are above your clearance level."

"Nothing is above my clearance level. Log in to your computer and take a look."

"I have no intention of wasting a single moment on you," he said, and hung up.

Her soldiers tried to avoid her gaze. She needed to send some of them home, if only so there would be someone to open the section the next morning. But under the present circumstances, she could not afford to let a single one of them go. Eventually she sent Rachel home. Rachel had opened the section early that morning and Oriana knew that she did not like to be on the base after dark.

Left with ten soldiers, she divided them into teams of three and kept Tomer under her direct command, perhaps to give him positive reinforcement for successfully locating Yerminski in the database. She gave him her computer and within a second he had opened a new file named "Team Oriana".

The other soldiers placed a rapid succession of calls to every person listed on Vladislav Yerminski's recruitment file. She was hoping to get some results before her conversation with Abadi, but the initial information they gathered was disappointing. Yerminski's parents did not answer their phone, and no other family members were listed.

"Well, it's understandable," Alma said, overcoming her usual lethargy.

"Why is it understandable?" Oriana said.

"What do you mean? Their son's getting married. Seems obvious to me that they went to Paris with him. Not to mention that he's an only child. If I got married right now, my mum would come with me, even to Timbuktu."

It was obvious. Oriana was surprised she had not thought of it herself.

"They weren't on the flight with him," she said. "Yermi and his parents have the same surname, and the list included only people who travelled on their own. So we know that they didn't go with him."

"Then maybe they flew in before him, or maybe they took a later flight today. At any rate, they aren't picking up their telephone," Alma said with a shrug.

In the absence of other family members, they tried the references on Yerminski's file, all teachers from his secondary school in Ashdod. They all recalled him very well, spoke about his remarkable academic achievements, but none of them could say whom he might be marrying. Even back then everyone called him Yermi, because he hated the name Vladislav and his surname was too complicated.

Julie, the only investigator who knew French, also came back empty-handed: marriage application registries were confidential in Paris, which meant they were not published online.

"Shouldn't it be public information who he's marrying?" Oriana said. "Isn't there something like that? Like in the movies, I'd be able to know and go to the registry office or the church, and I'd be able to object because he's actually married to me, or because he's knocked me up or something?"

"Yes, there's that, but the privacy laws in France ban the digital distribution of personal details," Julie said in an attempt to defend the principles of her former homeland. "The list hangs outside the *mairie.* You can read it there. But even then you would have to know which *mairie*, because every arrondissement has its own."

"How many arrondissements could there be?" Oriana said, and immediately regretted it because Julie looked at her as if she was not worthy of the officer rank Tzahal had awarded her.

"Twenty," she said. "But he might be getting married in a suburb, because people say they're getting married in Paris even if, actually, the marriage is in the *mairie* of some suburb way outside the *périphérique.* There are large Jewish populations in the 9th, 16th and 17th, but most Jews live in the suburbs. The bride could be from a few cities – Sarcelles, Créteil or Vincennes – and if she's rich then she'll have many other options. If someone wanted to run around all those *mairies*, they'd need at least three days."

Yermi's appearances in the government databases were few and far between, and predictable: a driver's licence awarded after his first test, an application for a passport after his final exams in secondary school, and at one point he had left the country for South America. The mailing address was his parents' apartment in Ashdod.

Her social media investigators, among the best in the Intelligence Corps, narrowed in on that South American trip without result. Yerminski did not have an account on any social network. He appeared in other people's Facebook albums and Instagram accounts, usually those of girls, his blue eyes slipping away from the camera, his long fingers holding a drink or a slice of watermelon. They sent messages and located mobile numbers and even got some replies. None of the girls in the photographs had kept in touch with him, none of them knew who he was marrying, and none could recall a French female tourist from that trip.

Only close friends remained. She assigned Boris, the most experienced samal in the section to the task. He was the only native

Russian speaker. Special Section had a chronic shortage of foreign-language speakers because the unit's technology and intelligence centres took priority. After his course, Boris had been stationed as an intelligence signaller up north. One night, after three months of wearisome listening shifts, he had broken a chair over the network intelligence officer's shoulders and, after a stint in prison, had turned up in her section.

Boris was a disciplined soldier, nonetheless, a thorough researcher who never took special notice of her. Other soldiers either blindly worshipped Oriana or were scared to death of her, but according to the irregular updates Rachel made sure to present to her commander, Boris never talked about Oriana behind her back.

Which is why she was surprised when he suddenly looked up from the other end of the room and raised his voice. "We're dicking around," he said.

"No, we're not. We're trying to save a soldier who's an abduction target." She really had no time for a tug of war.

"No, no we're not," Boris said. "We're sitting in the heart of a technological empire and you're sending me to make calls to the abduction target's pals. And you're allowing his commander to kick you down the stairs over the telephone. You could have gone around his entire fucking department. You could have drafted an urgent order, to route all his text messages sent from Paris this morning from the moment he was kidnapped. You could have asked the police for the soldier's telephone records, for movements in his bank account . . . You could have asked the building next door to screen every telephone call in every hotel across France. With the push of a button you could have redirected to this section every e-mail ever sent that even mentioned Vladislav Yerminski. It isn't such a common name. You could have had every soldier in this unit on his feet – thousands of soldiers, tens of thousands of robots and millions of antennae. But instead, you're making us ask favours on the telephone from people who don't understand what's so urgent about a repeat background check of someone they barely remember. So, we're dicking around."

Oriana agreed with him. But she could hardly come out and say so. Abadi had ordered a covert investigation, not that she knew why. As the manager, how could she explain that she was not really managing anything, that she too was a mere pawn in an invisible power game that could shift any second?

"Instructions from the unit commander," she lied through her teeth, once again. "We're playing a game of chess, here, against an unknown enemy that seems to have managed to penetrate the manpower structure of one of the unit's most secret departments. It's only natural that the commander prefers we operate alone."

She hated herself for the cheap adulation, the inflation of the enemy, the self-aggrandisement and also the chess metaphor. All of it made her sick – but all of it worked. Boris nodded and went back to making calls. She nodded and gathered the skimpy material they had collected. She knew it would not be enough for Abadi to locate Rav Turai Yerminski in the city of lights, but it was all she had, and with that he would need to go to war, and with that he would have to win. She took a few jamming instruments out of the safe and ran towards the laundry shed.

Chapter 42

The name of the game was "hot potato", and they were the best pair of players in Paris, i.e. in France, i.e. in the world.

They started playing together against the rest of the world during their studies at the prestigious École Nationale d'Administration, where the French Republic trains its loyal civil servants. A lot of water had flowed down the Seine since then. Today, one of them was the minister of the interior, and the other was head of the counter-intelligence agency, which operated under the minister of the interior's jurisdiction. On their path to the lavish chambers in which they now sat, they had overcome many obstacles, crushed enemies and dodged investigations and lawsuits, scandals and nosy journalists.

They had their eyes set on the Élysée, which they could see from the windows of the minister's chambers. And the closer they got to their target, the more frequently they had to play the game. In fact, they passed another hot potato almost every day now, tossing it as far as they could from the minister.

One brief meeting was usually enough to settle the identity of the victim. They always planned their moves in a one-on-one meeting, and the meetings never appeared in the appointment books managed by their secretaries. The first secret of succeeding in the game was never to leave your tracks.

The minister's chambers occupied the top floor of the Hôtel de Beauveau, named after the Marquis who had acquired it for his mistress in 1768. The Marquis' son, the Prince de Beauvau, brought a young, orphaned African girl back from his travels and shared the home with her after his father's death. He was one of very few noblemen to remain unscathed during the Revolution – an omen perhaps of the building's political immunity.

For decades, the State had tried to take over the property, succeeding only in the middle of the nineteenth century, after which it served as the headquarters of every French intelligence service, immediately below the minister's chambers. The minister's capabilities for spying on citizens were unrivalled in the Western world, and the law granted him powers that would make the President of the United States envious.

The various units of the intelligence services were spread across every building in place Beauvau, which were connnected underground by passages, and the secrets flowed accordingly – who was writing to whom, who was sleeping with whom, who was paying whom. This mighty machine operated without judicial oversight, without, in fact, any oversight at all. Theoretically, it was designed to maintain civilian security. In reality, it worked night and day to bolster the minister's position.

The centre of the empire presided over by the head of the counter-intelligence agency was a giant underground structure on boulevard Mortier in the east of the city, because the historical buildings in place Beauvau were deemed unfit to support the necessary computers. At any given moment, more than a billion items were recorded and decrypted within the structure on boulevard Mortier: telephone calls, text messages, video calls, e-mails. The unit was the only one of its kind in the Western world that collected more information on its own citizens than on the rest of the world's population combined. There was no heating in the building, because the computers emitted more than enough energy to warm it.

The minister himself never issued a formal request to spy on his political enemies. Years ago, a scandal broke out when it was revealed that President Mitterrand had ordered the tapping of the phone of a famous actress who had caught his eye in her role as a

Bond girl. Ever since then, French politicians had been careful not to get too close to the listening unit, and, officially, the minister never visited it.

Nor did he need to; that's why he had appointed his good friend from his university days as its commander, and if they happened to meet every day, sometimes twice a day, those were simply private meetings between old friends.

"We have to keep this away from me," the minister said, half an eye on the Élysée Palace.

"We don't yet know for certain this is not a criminal matter," the head of counter-intelligence replied. "Can't we claim it's just another gang war, the Chinese mafia for example?"

"Anything's possible," his friend said. The ministers always liked options that were open to any interpretation. "But run-of-the-mill criminals don't murder with microdrones that even our department has never seen before." He could not suppress the admiration in his voice.

"And why is a senior Israeli officer suddenly here? Who is he?"

The head of counter-intelligence took out his mobile and read off the screen: "Colonel Zeev Abadi, former deputy commander of Unit 8200 in the Israeli Intelligence Corps, commanded the unit's training course at the Intelligence Academy, founded the unit's big data centre and, until recently, as I mentioned, served as deputy commander. He led their work with the N.S.A. after the Snowden leaks."

"So he's no longer in post?"

"We can't be clear about that. A year ago he testified in support of the unit's conscientious objectors in a military trial, and shortly after that the news of his retirement was published. On the other hand, he's certainly acting as though he's still on the job. He's the one who discovered the hidden camera in Charles de Gaulle."

"Who's leading the investigation from our end?"

"Commissaire Léger, from major crimes. He has responsibility at Charles de Gaulle as a temporary replacement."

"So he belongs to the Préfecture de Police de Paris?"

"He belongs to Paris."

There was no need to say more, because everything was understood. A double homicide in the very centre of Paris, on the bridge over the Seine leading to the national library, was a humiliation for France. The minister must not be connected to the affair in any way, which was why his security services could not be connected to it.

It was clear that the scandal and indeed also its investigation would prove a national humiliation. You could not expect the French police to crack such a case, with a mysterious Chinese commando unit on one side and Israel's Unit 8200 on the other. It was better to roll the two cases into one and sacrifice a police commissaire who had already been involved in an unsatisfactory investigation since the morning.

The head of the counter-intelligence agency picked up his mobile once more. Another hot potato was being passed.

Chapter 43

As Oriana prepared to leave the section at a run, Tomer did not dare ask his commander if he could join her. In her absence, he was head of "Team Oriana"; it should have been a source of pride, but the more he looked at the results of his work on her computer, the gloomier he felt.

In the course at the Intelligence Academy he was taught to focus, in each investigation, on no more than three open questions at one time. He had many more than three, but first he tried to do it by the book. Why would China, or any Chinese, have an interest in Rav Turai Yerminski?

How had they located him, when his digital footprint gave no indication that he served in the Intelligence Corps?

How could they have known that he was travelling to Paris and when?

Soon enough he had twenty questions. He was supposed to answer each one and move on to writing the case's probable scenario, but he could not come up with even one answer, and every scenario seemed improbable.

So he proceeded to search for the answer to the question that actually interested him: did Oriana have a boyfriend?

It was not the first time he had tried to glean information about his commander's personal life. Her enigmatic beauty was in perfect sync with her secretive nature, which is why his attempts to know more about her had always failed. Nor did her computer come with much personal information: her user window was locked and the shared folders included only military documents. He had located her browser cache, but the history was empty, in accordance with the guidelines and as befitting an outstanding officer of information security.

The photo album contained only one file, a headshot of Oriana in uniform, probably the picture she used for official documents. She was so beautiful he did not dare meet her eyes, even if, obviously, the siren on the screen could not actually stare back, just like he felt she did not actually see him when he moved around her in real life.

In this state of distraction he clicked 'Save' on the photograph, and confirmed when asked if he was certain. A split second later he recalled in horror that he had logged into her computer with his own username. In terror, he clicked 'Cancel', but the computer had already registered the command and begun downloading the image.

Tomer's mind scrambled for excuses while he waited for the chaos he remembered from his course on security protocol to unfold – screen lockdown due to unauthorised entry, the sounding of an alarm and an instant video recording of the suspect on the central system. But, astonishingly, none of these happened. Neither the alarm nor the video was activated, the screen remained lit, and in fact the file downloaded in the normal way to his own user folder as if it had not been copied from another user via a shared computer.

He looked at the screen, struggling to understand what had just happened. His confidence was so shaken by the inexplicable non-event that the relief he felt at being spared an investigation, not to mention the terrible humiliation, did not help. Like every soldier in Special Section, he had come into the course computer savvy, and all the skills he had put to use over the past months only deepened his current confusion.

The person he was supposed to approach with such questions was his commander, but even in his state of extreme infatuation,

Tomer realised he shouldn't push his luck. The only senior figure around at the moment was Boris, who was in the throes of exasperating conversations in Russian with Rav Turai Yerminski's friends from his previous base. And besides, he might infer that the section rookie's hypothetical question was not so hypothetical.

There was a computer whizz who had served with him on the course, who, once they arrived in the unit, had been assigned to the technology department. Tomer located him in the internal system and called him on the secure line.

"I have a stupid question about material from the course, Yossi," Tomer said.

"I'm not sure I still remember the material from the course." Yossi's voice was friendly, but also cautious.

"It's about the alarm that's triggered after the entry of an unauthorised user," Tomer continued with as casual a tone as he could muster. "Do you remember under what circumstances that doesn't happen? I mean, what could explain a user downloading another user's file on a shared computer and the alarm not going off?"

"There's no way that could happen, you don't need me for that," Yossi said. "Everyone knows the situation you're describing is impossible."

"When you have eliminated the impossible, whatever remains, however improbable, must be the truth."

"Is that a quote from the course book?"

"Either that or from Sherlock Holmes, I'm not sure," Tomer said. "What I'm asking you is what kind of bug would lead to the situation I described?" There was no way this was a bug, he knew that much. "Maybe it's some kind of computer glitch ..."

The statement was stupid enough to be a risk, but it was sure to elicit a response. Yossi, Tomer recalled, was reliably literal in his thinking.

His friend considered for a moment. "Then it has nothing to do with the computer," he said. "It's the Intelligence Corps' central system … Way above some specific terminal. The central server acts like a proxy for all its users, c'mon that's basic, so it would be the central server triggering the alarm."

"Free as ever with the technobabble," Tomer said, desperately trying to maintain a lighthearted tone as he weighed Yossi's confirmation of his fear. "So if the central server is only a default proxy, right, then the person who controls it can decide whether to protect a specific computer in the system – or not?"

This time there was a longer silence, at the end of which his interlocutor sounded less confident and more concerned. "I suppose, theoretically, yes, it's possible. A certain user could be disconnected from the system, and their computer, their actual machine, could be infiltrated. If this has happened to you, we have to report it, like, right away. I mean, like, now."

"No, no, what are you talking about, you don't understand," Tomer said, his manner overly cheerful. "It's 100 per cent theoretical, I'm preparing a test for new soldiers and I wanted to stage a similar scenario, to check if they'd know how to react."

"You moron, you really scared me," his friend said with undisguised relief. "You have nothing better to waste your time on? What were you planning to do, ask the Chief of Intelligence to disconnect a user from the main proxy just because you feel like scaring some new soldiers? You're stationed in an important section, stop messing around."

Meanwhile, Oriana's computer had switched to sleep mode, and on the screen before him the official Unit 8200 screensaver appeared. Below the Intelligence Corps symbol, warnings flashed, one after another, from the information security department. Biblical verses, Buddhist sayings? His eyes traced one of them: "Deceitful men shall not live out half their days; But I will trust in You."

"You're absolutely right," Tomer said and hung up. He gazed around him helplessly. Oriana had not returned yet; two more unresolved items to be added to the list of open questions she had asked him to draft. Someone in the top echelons of intelligence had ordered the installation of a rootkit to monitor her computer. Who? And why?

Chapter 44

In Paris, Commissaire Léger considered calling it a day, going home, then taking two sleeping pills.

He hated Roissy. He hated bodiless murders. He hated investigations that were dumped on him outside his administrative scope of responsibility. And today he learned that he also hated hotel greeters in red uniforms, hidden security cameras and Israeli investigators. He was supposed to monitor the work of the forensic teams on the construction site. He was supposed to launch a criminal investigation into the leaking of the security camera footage to the Israeli media. He was supposed to supervise the gathering of initial findings from the victim's body, once they actually had a body. He was supposed to provide the juge d'instruction with hourly updates on his progress on all these fronts.

Nonetheless, he called his driver and stretched out on the back seat. If he had hoped to sleep the whole way home, he soon discovered that was not going to happen; high-pitched voices and piercing sirens emerged from the police radios in the car.

"What is it, what happened?" he asked the driver.

"A double homicide on the Passerelle Simone de Beauvoir, Commissaire, in front of the new national library. A double assassination apparently from above: whoever did it used a drone."

"In which arrondissement is that?"

"The bridge probably belongs to the 12th, Commissaire. But it still hasn't been established that they're getting the investigation. Maybe it'll go to the border police, since they were Chinese."

"Who were Chinese?"

"The victims and the killer, Commissaire. He used microdrones that hone in on the victims. That's what the news reports said."

"Turn up the volume," Léger said. His voice was hoarse, almost frantic, and he had to point at the radio so the driver would understand.

The reporters' voices, almost hysterical now, emerged from the speakers. The eyewitnesses repeated that it was "like a scene from a movie", but none could explain what they actually saw. "It's unbelievable that such a thing could happen in the middle of Paris," the broadcaster said. "We have Paris' Préfet de police on the line. I assume you're very busy right now, so thank you for agreeing to talk to us."

"It's my public duty. I'm grateful for the opportunity to speak here, and to assure the public that we're committed more than ever to protecting the peace and the security of the capital's residents."

"What peace and what security?" the broadcaster wanted to know. "Microdrones operated by an assassin who is still at large, in a double homicide in the heart of Paris, that's peace and security?"

"It's a serious crime. I've assured the *maire* that the assassin will soon be apprehended. This is a case of underworld figures settling scores, a war between international criminals which has no connection to France."

"So you're optimistic?"

"I'm a bearer of good news today," the Préfet said. "The murder has already been solved. We've linked this assassination to the abduction of an Israeli passenger who landed in Charles de Gaulle airport this morning, a criminal pattern characteristic of drug deals. One of the victims fell into the river and is still missing, but the second victim has been identified as the perpetrator of the abduction at Charles de Gaulle airport. As I said, underworld figures squaring accounts. We will soon locate the assassin, and it is our intention to dismantle this criminal organisation."

"So we can expect an arrest?"

"Now that the murder has been solved, the rest is only a matter of time and perseverance," the Préfet said. "The case has been assigned to the head of the special team investigating this morning's abduction, Commissaire Léger of the Paris police, an officer with vast experience. I have every confidence that he will complete his investigation with exemplary expedition."

"Turn it off, turn it off!" Léger shouted at the driver.

The driver pulled over to the side of the road, uncertain how to proceed. He turned off the radio but did not dare switch off the siren, which kept wailing. Léger looked through the window, bemused, registering expressions of surprise and curiosity on the faces of passing drivers. He tried to sit upright, but a shooting pain in his back momentarily paralysed him. He also felt a vague pressure in his chest – an impending panic attack or a heart attack? One way or another, his body was telling him what his enemies had long known: he was finished. He could not handle the pressure of the present because, from head to toe, he was made of yesterdays.

The forces that controlled the present had put him in an impossible position. He had been publicly assigned an investigation that had now been labelled a success when it was certain to be a failure. He had been asked to solve "with exemplary expedition" a drug case that had nothing to do with drugs. He had been instructed to come up with criminal findings that matched a gang war, which effectively put an end to any attempt to involve the only authority that could actually handle this case – the counter-intelligence agency. He had also been publicly described as an officer "with vast experience", which meant a perfect candidate to force into early retirement when the magnitude of the failure eventually surfaced.

The only way to save face was to play this game in the opposite direction. He needed to show, just as publicly, that this spiralling chaos had nothing to do with the Paris police and everything to do with power games within the world of espionage.

There was only one spy who might be willing to play those games with him. Admittedly, he was a spy in the service of another country, but as far as Léger was concerned, that was a minor detail.

"Give me the police radio," he said to the driver. In some strange way he felt his strength returning, and even his headache had gone. He might be finished, but he had every intention of putting on one final show.

Chapter 45

Oriana climbed the wooden ladder to reach the high folding table. Plastic-wrapped bundles of washed uniforms filled the space, giving off a sharp smell of industrial detergent. She lay on her back, her head cushioned by two packs of Dacron uniforms.

She looked at the black telephone and willed it to ring, as if she were reliving her teenage years. When is he going to pick up the phone and call me?

To the delight of the quartermasters, she announced that the laundry service was closing early due to a security inspection. Once she was alone, she scattered the jamming instruments around the facility, more for her personal sense of security than to prevent tapping, which usually took place hundreds of kilometres from the target. She intended to have as brief a conversation as possible. Two words would be enough: Vladislav Yerminski.

She could not imagine how Abadi would be able to locate the soldier without any information on his whereabouts. Should he search wedding halls, the Eiffel Tower or the *mairies*? Where would Rav Turai Yerminski be, an intelligence soldier gone off to get married without suspecting that waiting for him in the city of his dreams was a deadly Chinese commando team accompanied by a glamorous blonde, a honeytrap who had demonstrated her fatal power of attraction that morning?

Would he prove more resilient than Yaniv Meidan? Do men try their luck with every blonde they meet, even when they're about to get married? She could not say. She did not really want to think about it, which is probably why, as if through sheer telepathy, the telephone rang.

"Hello, Oriana," Abadi said, and for the first time, she noticed his voice, soft and soothing like the sea.

"One of our men actually was on the flight," she said. "His full name is Vladislav Yerminski, known as Yermi. He belongs to the gold mines' department in the south."

There was such a long silence, Oriana feared for a moment that he had not caught the reference.

"I was afraid that might be the case," he finally said.

Oriana said nothing.

"Do we know where this soldier is staying?"

"No. It's a special leave. He wasn't required to fill in an overseas travel form, and he didn't."

"Why did he get a special leave in Paris?"

"It seems he recently met a girl from France, and they decided to get married. I guess the wedding's in Paris. The base had no choice but to approve the trip."

"Who is the girl?"

"We don't know."

"Does he have friends who might know the bride? A name even?"

"We have called all his associates and no-one knows. There's barely anything on him on the internet. He has not submitted any application to any governmental agency in the past two years, and all there is on him in the state's databases is the issuing of an I.D. card at sixteen and a driver's licence at seventeen and a half. His address in the census registration is his parents' house in Ashdod, and they aren't answering the telephone. He doesn't have a criminal record, he never filed a lawsuit, and was never sued."

"Do we know what he's doing in that department? I thought they didn't have grechkos over there."

"No-one uses that word anymore, Abadi," Oriana said and burst into surprised laughter. "It's like saying 'shiksa' or 'goy'." She was relieved to hear Abadi laughing as well.

"Grechkos" had been a nickname for Russian-speaking radiomen in the unit. Back in the period when the unit listened in on Nasser's Soviet advisors in Egypt. It was definitely a pejorative term, named after some anti-semitic Russian, and it implied a certain suspicion towards Russian immigrants who had yet to prove their loyalty to the State of Israel. Grechkos were not allowed to serve in El Dorado or any other sensitive department.

"Anyway, you're right, there are no Russian-speakers in that department. He must know some other language."

"Which language?"

"We don't know."

"We do know," Abadi replied. "You know it yourself. It's the only way the facts connect."

Oriana became contemplative. She thought she could hear his peaceful, deep breaths on the other end of the line.

"You can't be sure," she said, finally.

"I'm pretty sure. His base won't confirm it for you?"

"No. The department's network intelligence officer explained to me with unbelievable arrogance that the department is above our clearance, and that he'd talk to me only at the head of southern command's authorisation, and then only face to face."

"He might get what he's asking for sooner than he thinks," Abadi said, in the same nonchalant voice. Oriana laughed.

"Why are you laughing?"

"You really are playing the hot-headed Mizrahi Jew for me, Abadi," she said.

He thought she was a much better conversationalist, natural and breezy as if she had known him since childhood, her voice playing scales of intimacy that he would not have been able to replicate even after years of practice. Compared to her he felt too cautious, too alert, too sharp, like a wanted man deliberating whether to turn himself in. He tried to conjure up the memory of her laughter but his brain rang instead with the sound of the new volume of *Military Ethics Law* as it had thudded on his desk.

"... all prejudicial conduct between a Tzahal commander and his or her subordinate shall be punished at the discretion of the military court and shall lead to immediate dismissal before trial."

The rule book. In the corner of his mind was the niggling thought that he had missed something important.

"What were we talking about a moment ago?"

"That we won't get the head of command's authorisation to enter the base." Her voice resumed its matter-of-fact precision, leading him to wonder if he had imagined it all. He sat on his childhood bed and pressed the telephone into his ear.

"Before that. What you said before we talked about the department."

"That we don't know where Vladislav Yerminski is staying in Paris."

"And what else?"

"That he got a special leave to get married in Paris. And that we don't know who the bride is."

"There was something else, something you said we didn't know."

"How he got to that base?"

"No." It was driving him crazy. Dutifully, she repeated each detail: "We couldn't find any close friends. His referees barely know anything about him. His parents aren't answering our calls. He has almost no internet presence. He has no criminal record, no court records, he hasn't submitted any applications to the governmental databases ..."

"That's it."

"That's it? That he has not submitted any applications to the governmental databases in the past two years?"

"Yes."

"What's so unusual about that? I haven't submitted any either."

"That's because you aren't getting married. Neither is he, apparently. If he really was travelling to Paris to get married, he would need a birth certificate, a single-status certification, a population registry extract. He didn't submit any applications, because, like you, he didn't need those forms, he didn't in fact go to Paris to get married."

"But the base approved his trip, he must have brought them some kind of authorisation."

"I don't know what the protocol is, I'm not even sure there is a strict protocol. Maybe it's enough to show text messages in French from a loving girlfriend. But it doesn't matter. Stop looking for a bride, there is no bride."

"So what are we looking for?" Oriana said. She sounded nervous, and he regretted being the cause of it.

"We are looking for the real reason he went to Paris," Abadi said. "When we find out what that is, we'll understand everything. With a little luck, he'll still be alive."

Chapter 46

His bodyguards had changed once again the procedures for exiting the Prime Minister's building. He liked this military atmosphere around him, the bulletproof vest designed for him, the ride to the bunker at the Ministry of Defence, the motorcycles and the concealed weapons and the close shielding of his body and this suspended moment, waiting for the signal to proceed.

He was engulfed by the usual entourage – consultants and the Chief of Staff, assistants and the Military Secretary, and always someone who asked to ride in the car with him on the pretext of a private update on something important; but he always refused because there was nothing like being alone, just him and two young, silent, armed security men, an ideal setting in which to mull over his next move in the political jungle.

It was also a rare opportunity to be outside, really outside the walls, bathed in an orange sunset over the hills of Jerusalem, caressed by a pleasant, almost cool breeze. "Air," he said, and the whole entourage nodded enthusiastically: air.

Across the road, on the pavement opposite the government compound, the psychologists' protest was taking place for the third consecutive day. He could hear them shouting his name, to the rhythm of some stupid rhyme. When his convoy passed by them in a howl of engines and sirens, he saw a few of the signs: "Who's the Mental Case Here?", "Social Welfare, Not Corporate Welfare!", "Where's the Money?", "A Normal Country Needs Sane Mental Health Services".

For many years he had been leading this nation as their Prime Minister, and one thing still surprised him anew, each day, this obsessive desire to be a "normal country". Speeches by the opposition, newspaper articles, Supreme Court verdicts and heated monologues on Facebook all included a melodramatic outcry with these words: a normal country.

Only once in his life had he seen a normal country.

It was during a family holiday in Tuscany, just before his eighteenth birthday. His father was in low spirits, made lower still by the rain and a grim atmosphere throughout the trip. Nothing helped – not the varieties of pasta they ate, the luxuries of the house they rented, the quality of the Chianti they drank, the impressive expertise of the tour guide they had booked.

And then they visited Siena, and during a tour of the magnificent Palazzo Pubblico, his father suddenly came alive. It happened in the council room, in front of the famous mural "The Allegory of Good and Bad Government". Introducing the painter Ambrogio Lorenzetti's early Renaissance masterpiece, the guide explained that the artist sought to juxtapose the dark forces of religious government ("Here to your right, the tyrant with the horns and the six vices of humanity") with a good and just government ("On the wall to your left, the chosen ruler, dressed in white") that bestows upon the people peace and other blessings.

Then the guide pointed at the third wall, a peaceful rural scene, and told them that the painting depicted the positive outcomes of good government. "Here we see the city and the country, and all its residents prospering in their trades and living peacefully. All due to moral virtues. That's what the painting really means."

It was cold and he just wanted the tour to end, but then he suddenly heard his father awaken and say, "That's not all the painting says."

The guide said something polite along the lines of "Of course, each person can see different things in it," but there was no stopping his father, who strode up to the wall and pointed at the upper part of the mural. "The meaning of the painting has to do with the figure hovering above it, which some art aficionados ignore," he said with his measured, didactic tone, pointing at the figure of a bare-breasted angel hovering above the landscape of Siena. "Her name appears here in Latin, above her: 'Securitas' – security. It's thanks to security that this region prospers, without security this democracy would not exist, it's the key to good government, and it's as true today as it was for fourteenth-century Tuscany."

He had since visited Siena a dozen times, including with his university supervisor and even with the Prime Minister of Italy, and every person who accompanied him always failed to notice the figure until he drew their attention to it. Just as everyone around him here missed it today. Psychologists, social workers, tycoons, the poor, the religious, the secular, Ashkenazis, Mizrahis, rock, paper, scissors, a normal country, a normal country, a normal country.

There were tribal conflicts and class conflicts and ideological conflicts and financial conflicts and religious conflicts; there were a million small conflicts in this country as everywhere, and all these conflicts ignored the vital need for security.

As far as he was concerned, the personal attacks against him were also just a distraction from the real, major conflict, the one that would go on forever, the Jewish–Arab conflict, which the world made sure to call the Israeli–Palestinian conflict, as if reducing it to its current phase would transform this eternal war into a problem with a solution. All the rest – from the protests of the Ethiopian immigrants to the inquiry into whether they had travelled to Monaco for his wife to get her hair done – all the rest were distractions intended to prevent him from performing his historical role.

In the meantime, the convoy had reached the Ministry of Defence in Tel Aviv, and the driver manoeuvred the large vehicle into the special lift. The soldiers saluted when the entourage entered the building. "Tell Aluf Rotelmann I'm here," he told the duty officer.

Chapter 47

She waited for Boris to finish his conversation in loud Russian, his umpteenth attempt to get one of Rav Turai Yerminski's friends talking. The other soldiers in the section were waiting too, since they did not actually have anything else to do. What she saw in front of her when she opened the door, still panting from her efforts to put the bundles of uniforms back in place and return to the section, were people mostly pretending to be busy.

For some reason Tomer had returned to his own computer station. She entered the file from her computer, swiftly going through the few scenarios he had outlined, all based on the elusive bride and the assumption that Yerminski had travelled to Paris for the purpose of getting married. How could she have been so stupid?

"The border police returned our call, but the officer there wants to talk only to you," Alma said.

"Get me the officer," Oriana said. She could have dialled herself, but she had already learned that, in the organisational universe in which she operated, refraining from such ceremonies led to a decline in status, including in the eyes of those performing the ceremonies. And indeed, Alma immediately nodded. "No, no, no, you get her on the line first, and then I'll pass her on," she scolded the police officer who was presumably fighting just as determinedly for her commander's status on the other end of the line.

"Why did you switch places?" Oriana asked Tomer while the territorial squabble continued over the phone.

"There's a proxy error on your computer, so it seems safer to write it on mine," he said.

"Why would you run a proxy check on my computer?"

"I always run a proxy check before entering data. On my own computer too," he stuttered.

"She's on the line," Alma said.

"But how do you run a proxy check without connecting to the central system?" Oriana said.

"She's starting to get annoyed," Alma warned.

Oriana picked up the phone.

"With regard to the query you left us earlier," the representative of the border police said with a flat and bored voice, "the soldier's parents aren't listed in the database of recent exit records."

"So they're in Israel? Are you sure of that?" Oriana asked. There was nothing surprising about that – if Abadi was right about the wedding.

"I'm sure they're not listed in the database of recent exit records," the officer said. "I'm not familiar with the details of the case. These people could have boarded a yacht and gone to Cyprus, they could have paid cross-border smugglers in Sinai, they could have hopped on a private jet and landed on some other island. But they did not leave from Ben Gurion airport en route to Paris, or to anywhere else."

"I understand. Just one more question."

"Shoot."

"I want to know who went through passport control with him. I mean, who passed through the same counter, a minute before and a minute after."

"It doesn't work like that. If he passed through the biometric counter, then we'll have the exact minute, but if he passed through a regular counter, the passengers aren't listed according to the order in which they reached the counter, but according to when they scanned their boarding pass before entering the duty-free area. I don't know who stood in front of him or behind him, I can only try to find a record of everyone who passed through all the counters at the same time."

"And that is according to the exact time?"

"I don't have each and every minute, it's recorded alphabetically every five minutes."

"How many people is that?" Oriana said. She had not travelled abroad in the past two and a half years, and this conversation was stirring within her a fierce desire to leave everything behind and drive straight to Ben Gurion airport.

"Depends on how busy it was in the airport. That early in the morning, during low season, I'd guess about a hundred passengers."

I'll take anything I can get to occupy ten soldiers with nothing to do, Oriana thought, and said, "I'm giving you my secure e-mail. How soon can it be ready?"

"It'll take about two days," the officer said reluctantly.

"Let's settle for tomorrow morning," Oriana said, unwittingly imitating her commander.

Chapter 48

"*Maman*, I have to go," Abadi said. While he had been on the telephone, she had set eight different types of desserts on the table.

"But I made you *makroudh*," she protested. As a child he had been crazy about the traditional pastries made of semolina and dates and soaked in hot honey, but when his parents returned to France he parted company with the *makroudh* as well, and was unwilling to fall in love with it anew. But since he did not have the heart to disappoint his mother, on every visit he had to devour a dozen *makroudh*.

"I'll take them with me, *Maman*. I'm sorry, but I have to go to Roissy. I have to meet someone there before he takes off."

"Does it have to do with Tzahal?" his mother asked hopefully.

"It absolutely has to do with Tzahal."

"In that case I'm very happy. May God bless our soldiers with strength, health and luck," she said and started preparing plastic boxes.

Rav Turai Vladislav Yerminski was certainly going to need every possible blessing, Abadi thought. Along with the *makroudh* she hurriedly packed the rest of the desserts, and he left his parents' house with a bulging Carrefour bag.

"Are you staying here for a while? Will you come back to visit?" she said as he stood near the door.

"I don't know, *Maman*," he said. "I managed to steal a couple of days to be here, I was supposed to be starting my new job."

"In the army."

"In the army."

"It isn't a new job, it's a life mission. You're going to help the People of Israel fight its enemies."

Maybe, he thought as he ran down the staircase, maybe he had re-enlisted in order to help the People of Israel. He had not thought about it that way. He most of all thought it would astonish all his enemies in the unit, and that was a good enough reason to say yes. He stood outside the building and tried to remember where he had parked the rental car.

The two police cars in front of the gate awoke from their slumber, and four plainclothes policemen surrounded him.

"Colonel Abadi? Colonel Zeev Abadi?"

"That's me."

"You are suspected of leaking criminal investigation materials. If you could come with us, Commissaire Léger is waiting for you."

He looked up, to make sure his mother was not watching from the window, and got into the car. The driver turned on an ear-splitting siren and drove off. During the ride to the French police headquarters, Abadi cradled his mother's semolina pastries on his lap.

Chapter 49

Two of her soldiers had done a pre-army volunteer service year, so they were older than the others. As was Boris, since he had joined the unit through the preparatory programme. Oriana was twenty-two. No matter how she played with the numbers, the average age in the room hovered around twenty, which was not something that would normally bother her, but today she would have been glad to have had at least one researcher on her team who knew something about life.

"How many of you have been to Paris?" she said when they were gathered around her. Three out of the ten soldiers raised their hands, including Alma. Five had been to South America, two to Australia and, quite surprisingly, two had travelled to China before enlisting. None had been to Jordan or Egypt or any other Arabic-speaking territory. She herself had visited Paris once, not that she shared that fact with them. Instead, she said, "Shall we start?" And they started.

Boris chose Tomer as the data co-ordinator, not an obvious choice, and one that Oriana interpreted as an olive branch. Alma volunteered to take the minutes and hooked her computer to the giant screen. The others sat on the floor in a circle, pushing back tables and cabinets. Oriana sat on the floor with them, taking advantage of her rank to grab the only spot where she could lean against the wall. Her team was full of good intent, but young and inexperienced. The chances of saving Rav Turai Yerminski seemed to grow more slender by the minute.

Boris arranged his notes like a news presenter before a dramatic address to the nation, took a deep breath, and started reading.

"So, first we checked with the consular services of the Ministry of Foreign Affairs, and they confirmed the claim of the new head of section, Aluf Mishne Zeev Abadi, that one cannot get married in France without a birth certificate and/or a population registry extract issued in Israel and approved with a special stamp in the three months preceding the wedding.

"We double-checked with the Ministry of Interior, and they confirmed that the missing soldier had not submitted any special requests to the authorities since joining the army.

"So, formally, this raises a clear suspicion that Rav Turai Yerminski travelled to France under false pretences. Based on this, we believe we should be able to launch an open investigation and submit a request to the head of southern command to question witnesses in the El Dorado department."

"He'll never let us in," Alma said. "He'll say it's a disciplinary offence, and that it's none of our business. The most he'll authorise is an interrogation of the unit welfare officer who approved his trip to France. We will not be questioning a single El Dorado soldier, we will not be allowed into the department, let alone into the soldier's quarters. He'll say it's a matter for the military police, not for us."

"It may be only a disciplinary offence," Boris said, "but given the circumstances and the high sensitivity of the department he serves in, it has all the earmarks of a security offence."

"The head of southern command has noted your request. He will address your request in accordance with the priorities of the unit," Alma recited sarcastically. "We don't stand a chance this way. Either it has to do with the Chinese commando unit that kidnapped the Israeli at Charles de Gaulle airport this morning, and then it *is* our business, or it has nothing to do with it, and then it's his commander's business."

"Does anyone need a reason to go to Paris?" Julie said, with an exaggerated Gallic shrug. "And maybe he did actually meet someone and follow her to France, and said he's travelling to get married just to get an overseas leave approval."

This was perfectly logical, and Oriana was normally one to encourage debates in the section. But this was the wrong time for exercises in direct democracy, so she quickly intervened.

"Boris, do we know anything new about Vladislav Yerminski that we didn't know before?"

"We know a lot," he said, offended that no-one had taken stock of all the calls he made.

"And can any of it be useful?"

"Since we don't know what we're looking for, we can't know what might be useful," Boris said.

"Try me," Oriana said. Boris sighed and returned to his papers.

"Born twenty-one years ago in Ashdod, to parents who emigrated separately from the U.S.S.R. His father, who had been an engineer, was hired as a technician at E.L.T.A., a subsidiary of the Israel Aerospace Industries in Ashdod, and worked there until he was laid off into early retirement two years ago. His mother, who had been an accountant in Moscow, became a bookkeeper in the municipal education department."

You could guess from Boris' tone what he thought about the way the Yerminskis had been greeted upon their arrival in Israel, or what he thought about his own parents' immigration experience.

"Did his mother show up at work yesterday as usual?"

"No. Yesterday she left for a week's holiday."

"Does Yermi have a hobby?"

"His parents' dream was for him to become a professional chess player, and his father used to drive him to a prestigious chess class in town every evening. When Yermi was twelve, he joined a chess club in Tel Aviv, and his father took him back and forth almost every day. At some point during *khativat beynaiym*, around the age of thirteen or fourteen, Yermi rebelled and he has not played chess since. Even in the long night shifts at his old base up north, when the other soldier on shift begged him to play, Yermi always refused."

It was not hard to imagine how much work it had taken to gather these pieces of information. For a team lacking actual experience in complex covert investigations, they were doing a pretty good job. She dreaded the moment when she'd have to tell Boris that in everything he had gathered there was not a single useful fragment.

"Is there anything in his youth connecting him to France?"

"On the contrary. When he started learning languages, his teacher recommended French and arranged private lessons with one of the teachers, but it did not appeal to him."

Oriana picked up on this possible lead.

"What do you mean 'started to learn languages'?"

"After the chess insanity, he went through a period of teaching himself languages. First Slavic languages, then Italian and then German. It went on until the ninth grade, when he got over that obsession and, following the advice of one of the teachers who spoke to me, he agreed to focus on one language and study it in depth."

"And which language was that?"

"Chinese," Boris said. A dim note of victory accompanied his statement. "From the age of fourteen on, Yerminski studied only Chinese. Since there wasn't a Chinese option in his school, he studied it by himself online, and his father drove him to the exam at a secondary school in Rishon LeZion."

"What exam?"

"The matriculation exam. Only ten students majored in Chinese, and he was one of them. I spoke to the exam department at the Ministry of Education, and they all remember him over there. He got a perfect score, and even corrected a spelling mistake on their form. They say he knew Chinese better than the examiner."

"*You know it yourself. It's the only way the facts connect,*" Abadi had told her. She tried to hold on to the facts, but they kept slipping through her fingers like ice cubes, melting and disappearing one after the other. The soldiers continued to sit in their circle around her, waiting for instructions. But Oriana remained silent.

It was 6.25 p.m., Monday, April 16.

Chapter 50

If we were to observe rue Rabelais from high above, analysing the data from that evening, we would easily spot Chico, marching in clumsy yet brisk steps towards the embassy. His red hair betrays him, as does the barcode on his I.D. badge, the unique signal of his mobile even when it is switched off, the discrete signal emitted by his remote car key as he locks his vehicle.

But, most obviously, the way he walks betrays him. Had he been walking along a completely different street, in a different city and in a different country, military and private intelligence agencies would still be able to identify him by his walk.

So what of it, Chico would probably ask, I have nothing to hide, let them follow me if they want. But Chico doesn't ask, because in the back of his mind he's aware of the reality and he doesn't dwell on it. Trying to undermine the algorithms would be a Sisyphean task and he determines that it's not worth his effort. At the moment, he's busy lumbering ahead, presenting his badge to the officers, who salute him and open the gate. The officers don't log Chico's name because he has a permanent entry permit, a small gesture that both saves him time and permits him the illusion, at least, of freedom and privacy.

A tiny street like Rabelais produces more than a million data items every hour, each one of them documented, transferred, backed up, catalogued, classified and analysed. Not only Chico's entrance to the street, but every telephone call from the Israeli embassy, every e-mail sent from the office building, each credit card transaction at the corner kiosk and each licence plate from each passing car. A million data items an hour, and those who held the puppet strings were demanding a billion more.

In the back of his mind Chico is aware of all this, and ignores it. So when he spots the embassy's head of security, who has just stepped outside the building for a smoke, he walks briskly over to him and says, "They found him. They're taking him to Léger at police headquarters. He was at his mother's, in a Jewish suburb in the south-east."

"Who, this Abadi character?"

"Aluf Mishne Abadi, to you."

"Aluf Mishne, my ass. I knew from the beginning he was up to something. What are they going to do with him?"

"I don't know," Chico said. "But they were eager to get their hands on him. I was afraid they'd want to arrest me too, but they're only looking for him."

"He's still sticking to his lunatic theory that they intended to kidnap a different Israeli?"

"I think so. He got the list from El Al's security officer without my knowledge."

"And he left the code room here a moment after making the call, also without your knowledge."

"It's not my job to handle these things. It's your job," Chico said.

As if awaking from a dream, the embassy's security officer tossed away his cigarette and said, "We're not supposed to talk about this outside." The two walked towards the embassy.

In the office building opposite, in the space rented out just three hours earlier, the Chinese radio operator drew the antenna back inside, removed the Trimble monitor and once again read the sentences that flashed on the automatic translation screen. He could not understand exactly what had been said at the entrance to the Israeli embassy, but he understood enough to press the button on the radio they had left him.

In the giant pool of Hôtel Molitor, He Xiangu was working on her strokes, which were as precise as they had been when she was very young.

Her form looked perfect. Kick, pull, breathe. Kick, pull, breathe. He Xiangu was determined to honour her pool time, under water she could detach from the world. Persuaded that there was nothing harder than butterfly, she sliced through the surface more forcefully, the smooth line of her body dispelling any trace of effort. Leap after leap, breath after breath, she counted and moved forward.

It was a breathtakingly beautiful fifty-metre pool, listed in the registry of Paris' historical monuments but He Xiangu's eye was on the white tile at the end of the lane and her turn – she was determined to achieve a personal best.

However, when she touched the wall just before the twenty-third lap, she saw her bodyguard standing above her, signalling her with the radio she had entrusted to him.

"Leader of Team Three thinks he has something," he said, and handed her a towel. He Xiangu kicked the water in a fury and pulled herself out of the pool. She rejected the towel and tried to understand, dripping and shivering, the meaning of the recording.

Speaker A: They found him. They take light to police down. He was at mother his, at Jewish suburb south-east.

Speaker B: Who? The Abadi this?

Speaker A: It is for you, Colonel Abadi.

Speaker B: He was in my ass, I knew from beginning above something. What will they do to it?"

Speaker A: I do not know, but they were complete hot to his hand. I fear they arrest, but they only looking for him.

Speaker B: Is he still glue to crackers idea? Maybe want different Israeli?

Speaker A: I see yes. He got list from officer Hallal without I knowing.

Speaker B: Minute after call left treasure room here you without knowledge too.

Speaker A: It is not my profession to knob these things. It is your profession.
Speaker B: We are not apparent talk this outside.

This was certainly important, she had no doubt, but it was also incomprehensible. It probably was not the best idea to base an operative mission – or any kind of mission – on an automatic translation algorithm. "What treasure room? What crackers? Who's arresting whom?" she typed. The reply quickly followed: "It is not clear at the moment."

"And who is Colonel Abadi?" she typed, and the team replied that there was someone by that name in the central system's file, but he was not supposed to be active, so they would have to double-check.

She sighed in despair. As always in situations like these, she asked herself where Erlang Shen was, and recalled that she had sent him to take care of the stupid blonde who had seduced the wrong Israeli.

"When's the backup arriving from London?"

"They're supposed to land in ten minutes," the team leader texted back.

"Do they have any Hebrew translators with them?"

"Yes, Commander, two."

"Drive them straight to the team by the embassy and have them listen to the recording. How soon can I expect a normal translation?"

"A little under an hour," the leader of Team Three estimated.

He Xiangu confirmed and handed the radio back to the bodyguard before jumping into the pool. Kick, pull, breathe. Her strokes now seemed far less precise and far more nervous.

Chapter 51

Oriana switched to Tomer's computer. The open questions he had spent the past two hours toiling over had changed, and were now displayed on the big board in the middle of the section.

Had Rav Turai Yerminski travelled to Paris of his own free will?

Was he the real abduction target of the Chinese commando unit this morning?

Is his disappearance connected to his service in Unit 8200's El Dorado department?

Her instinct was to answer yes to all of them, and to focus on the next question: how can we find the soldier before the Chinese do?

She would have liked to tackle that question on her own, to stay alone in the section, just her and the investigator at the actual scene of the crime, who only happened to be her commander, just her and Abadi and maybe Rachel, who could come in the morning with bagels. That's what she loved most about this job, that she could crack any case on her own.

But she had grown used to managing others. She had grown used to managing their times, determining their priorities, defining their targets, sharing her deliberations with them, she encouraged and guided and motivated and demonstrated and reprimanded and warned and taught and did so many other things that at times she asked herself whether all these efforts were really worth it. And it was in moments like these that she wanted to work alone, alone with Abadi, and maybe Rachel.

She thought about sending some of the soldiers home, but none of them wanted to miss participating in a real investigation, the first in Special Section since they had joined it. She split them into teams with designated telephone tasks: tracking down neighbours, the parents' neighbours, relatives, Chinese teachers, friends yet to be found. They all opened the conversation with the vague phrase, "We're contacting you from the army," which was not untrue. While they were not met with any refusals to co-operate, they did not glean any information that might shed light on Vladislav Yerminski's reason for being in Paris.

Boris' team went back to the soldiers who had served with him, this time with a completely different set of questions. Questions about love and a possible bride were set aside for the more exotic: did he ever talk about China? Did you ever hear him speak Chinese on the telephone? Did he ever speak about Chinese friends? And above all, did he ever exhibit odd behaviour?

"Commander, do you want to add anything?" Tomer asked hesitantly and pointed at the board. She awoke from her thoughts and stared at the three open questions he had drafted. She had a million more. She also wanted to ask him why he and Rachel called her Commander, and how he had discovered that her computer was unsecured. Instead, she asked loudly, "Who wants pizza? I'm going to the mall."

They called out their orders. Three soldiers wanted black olives, two green, one mushroom, and one pineapple, which was vetoed by the others. Oriana patiently let the squabble run its course. The tradition of bringing in take-away during investigations pre-dated her appointment as commander, and granted her temporary respite from running the section's kindergarten, where the question of toppings always triggered heated discussion.

"O.K., so it's settled, three olive and three mushroom?" Oriana said. By now she understood that soldiers only compromised when under threat of a mushroom pizza. And indeed, Alma immediately protested and within less than a minute had organised a list far more detailed than the Chief of Intelligence's Most Wanted list, including exotic requests such as half pineapple and corn and half strawberry and extra mozzarella.

"Should I come with you?" Tomer said. Oriana would have relished some time alone, but she realised she would need help with the pizza boxes, not to mention the order. "Come on," she said, and led him to her car.

They were waiting for her a little after the memorial wall, just before the turn: a police car and a civilian jeep. The policemen signalled to her to pull over, but it was the two men in civilian dress who approached once she had lowered the window.

"Segen Oriana Talmor?"

"Who wants to know?"

"We're from the General Security Agency. We'd like a brief word."

They were both a bit older than the Shabak men she knew. One was plump and wore a *kippah.* The other was not exceedingly thin, but still they looked like Laurel and Hardy, maybe because both were wearing black from head to toe.

"I need to get food for my soldiers, they're on an urgent mission."

"It'll take less than fifteen minutes. You can leave your vehicle here and we'll drive you back."

"I can't answer any of your questions without the authorisation of the head of Unit 8200."

"We haven't been able to locate him, but we have the authorisation of the Chief of Intelligence, so I assume it's O.K."

Oriana assumed the same; there was no point in being clever, and she had no time to waste. She handed Tomer the list of pizzas and sent him on his way.

"It won't really take fifteen minutes," she said when he insisted on waiting. Taking her service revolver from the glove compartment, she took a last look at her beloved jungle of antennae and got into the jeep.

Chapter 52

A single *makroudh*, bathed in honey-soaked solitude, remained on the desk in Commissaire Léger's office. It was too hot. Every so often Léger got up to turn the knob of the radiator to the left or right, without apparent conviction. Abadi could not tell whether his host was actually trying to lower the heat or to break up the predictability of the questioning.

It was one of those meetings in which both sides assume the same tired and predictable roles, but neither is at liberty to forgo the ceremony and get straight to the point. Abadi was being interrogated under caution on suspicion of leaking investigation materials, and his passport had been confiscated. Refusing to answer the questions, he admitted only to being an Israeli military officer on holiday.

To the commissaire's left sat a police officer at a small desk, typing out Léger's predictable questions and Abadi's no less predictable responses. On the wall above him hung a giant whiteboard with the victims' details and time of death. The names of Meidan, one Chinese corpse and one Chinese missing person on the bridge were scribbled in compact handwriting at the top of the board, presumably to leave room for future victims.

"It seems you don't appreciate the gravity of your actions," Léger declared for the umpteenth time.

"These are not my actions, Commissaire."

"Leaking material from an ongoing case is a serious criminal offence in France."

"I had nothing to do with it."

"Whoever gave that footage to an Israeli television channel, the juge d'instruction has instructed me to locate and prosecute him."

"Commissaire, I explained to you twenty minutes ago, the urgent task right now is not to identify the leaker but to locate the next Israeli who's going to be kidnapped. I gave you every detail I have about Vladislav Yerminski, and you refuse to update me on the measures you've taken to find him, if indeed you have taken any at all."

"I don't have to update you on anything. The chutzpah of you people is simply unbelievable."

"Chutzpah is a national trait in Israel, a little like elegance in France."

"Are you making fun of me?"

"Not one bit! But you have to help me track down Vladislav Yerminski in one of the city's hotels before you find his body in your river."

Abadi walked over to the window, standing with his back to Léger. The river flowed peacefully below, transporting ducks, *bateaux mouches* and balloons that had strayed from some birthday party.

"The representative of the Israeli police is the one who needs to transfer that request to us," Léger said. "You have no status here, apart from that of a suspect in a criminal investigation."

"I have no need for any status. I'm simply a tourist."

"A tourist who happens to serve in a sensitive intelligence unit of the Israeli army."

"I'm just a security officer, a type of policeman."

"For a type of policeman you're certainly mentioned a lot on the internet."

"Trust me, Commissaire, if we don't make any headway with this conversation, you'll be making headlines yourself on the internet soon enough."

Léger fell silent. "That's all for today," he said at last to the stenographer, who saluted him and quickly left the office.

Chapter 53

"What we need to understand right off is that we're on the same side," the first Shabak officer said. He held the door open to let Oriana in first, a gesture that was both clumsy and insincere.

They took her to a meeting room on the convention floor of a big business hotel, on Herzliya beach. No-one addressed her during the journey, so she made use of the time to resume her as yet unsuccessful telepathic efforts; but she had no-one to turn to. Abadi was too far away, or too busy, or was refusing to heed her mental calls. Her father had always had time for her when she needed him, and she looked up at the sky, the presumed location from which he watched over her. This situation would not have made sense to him in the army that he knew.

"Of course we're on the same side," she said.

The room was small and ugly. In the corner stood a coffee station with a water cooler, an enormous wooden box with an absurd selection of teas, and cheap Argaliot biscuits. The window overlooked the sea. Laurel and Hardy sat at the far side of the table and Oriana sat in front of them. Shabak Officer Laurel had three pens in the pocket of his shirt, an odd look for someone in intelligence. Maybe the pens were his version of Officer Hardy's *kippah*, more a declaration of faith than practice: when I do the interrogating, the suspect always ends up signing the confession. That's why I have three pens. Throughout the entire meeting he used none of them. They did not take minutes, and Oriana assumed that everything was being recorded.

"And because we're on the same side, it's important to emphasise that this is not an investigation, you're not suspected of anything, heaven forbid. We were asked to question you about a certain matter. The request was transferred from the Chief of Intelligence's office to the head of the Shabak's office. According to protocol, the head of Unit 8200's office was also informed, he's simply out of the country at the moment."

"According to the protocols you're supposed to inform the direct commander of the soldier you're investigating, by which I mean the new head of Special Section, Aluf Mishne Zeev Abadi."

"Aluf Mishne Zeev Abadi will be assuming his new position at midnight," Laurel said. "Right now you're the head of Special Section, at least for the next four hours. I promise that if this investigation continues past midnight, we'll formally update Abadi."

"I thought this wasn't an investigation."

"It isn't." The first Shabak officer stepped into his role. "We thought you could help us solve a riddle."

"What riddle?"

"How do you explain your excessive loyalty towards Abadi?"

As an investigator, the best advice she could give people was simple: never confess in an investigation. For some reason, her parents insisted on giving her other, less useful advice, such as never water your lawn during the hot hours of the day. If she ever had kids, she would offer them the real thing, the truly useful pieces of advice, starting with that one, never confess in an investigation. Because an investigator is not really after the truth, and he lacks the tools to verify the authenticity of the subject's statements. All he wants at that specific moment is to check whether the subject in front of him fits the profile. There will be many opportunities to confess, my sweet child, and this ain't one of them.

Besides, she did not know how to answer that question. She ventured, "I don't understand any of the words in that sentence. What riddle? Is the Shabak trying to compete with the Psychoanalytic Association, and now you're researching motivation? What's up with you calling him 'Abadi'? Are you such pals that you leave out his rank? And if you aren't, would you disrespect Aluf Mishne Abadi like that if he had an Ashkenazi surname? And if you are friends, isn't there a conflict of interest in your being here, investigating something that has to do with him? And above all, what exactly is 'excessive loyalty'? If, say, you don't cheat on your wife, would she consider that excessive loyalty?"

Laurel took the reins, perhaps because his friend was flushed and breathing erratically.

"Segen Oriana Talmor, we all know that the best tactic for an interrogation subject is for her to turn the tables and answer the question with a question. We're not belittling your intelligence and your achievements as an investigator, so don't insult ours. You were asked a simple question, and you understand the question very well."

"No, I don't understand the question."

"According to our records, you haven't worked with Aluf Mishne Zeev Abadi in the past. Have you ever met in a personal capacity?"

"Neither personal nor professional. I have never met him, and until today, I had never spoken to him."

"He was a character witness in your unit's conscientious objectors' trial."

"Our paths never crossed."

"He's quite famous in Unit 8200 as someone who chose to defend those who betrayed the unit's values."

"He's quite famous for a lot of things. There are at least three investigation tactics named after him. And yes, he's also known for choosing to testify on behalf of the 8200 objectors, to everyone's surprise. What does that have to do with me? I was not in 8200 then."

"True, you were in the military police investigations unit, but you had a part in it, since you were responsible for locating the source of the leak."

"It was a side investigation in the case, something not very important. A soldier leaked documents to the papers, you guys investigated for an entire year and couldn't track the leaker. The Chief of Defence Staff decided to transfer the case from the Shabak to the military police and it was assigned to me. It had nothing to do with Abadi and I did not investigate him."

"Aluf Mishne Zeev Abadi was a character witness in the trial."

"Could be. I testified in much earlier stages of the trial. I never met Aluf Mishne Zeev Abadi, and I didn't place much significance on the matter of the defence witnesses, let alone character witnesses. Didn't think anything of it."

"But Aluf Mishne Abadi had some thoughts about you, even if he did not identify you by name. In his testimony he expressed his opinion that the investigating officer pursued the defendant, and I quote, 'with great talent but equal ruthlessness'."

"I didn't know that. That's the first I've heard of it. I'm honoured."

"He also raised doubts about your ethics, when he enquired how you were able to track down the defendant where so many experienced investigators had failed. He suspected that your success relied on questionable or even illegal investigation techniques."

"Just jealous, I guess."

"You didn't know that's what Aluf Mishne Abadi thought of your work?"

"No, not until this moment."

"How did you really track down the defendant, and did you use unethical investigation techniques?"

"Nice try. I never revealed how I got to her and I'm certainly not going to tell you two. I did not use unethical investigation techniques, if that isn't obvious."

"So since you've never spoken to Aluf Mishne Zeev Abadi before, and in the only intelligence case you were both involved in you were on opposite sides, how can you explain your excessive loyalty?"

"My answer hasn't changed. He was appointed my commander and my loyalty to him is self-evident, regardless of his opinions. It isn't *excessive* loyalty. I can't believe you dragged me here in the middle of an important operation to talk about a case that was closed more than a year ago."

The first investigator had meanwhile regained his composure and seemed ready to resume his role.

"It reminds me of a key phrase I read once: 'Who will guard the guards?' It's a profound question."

"Indeed," Oriana said. She did not know whether to laugh or cry.

"Because this is what we're talking about here."

"Maybe. But, at least in the books I've read, when a person asks that question, he usually means that he's the one who should be guarding the guards, so I'm not sure we can agree on that one."

"O.K., I'm glad we've clarified that," he said with a tone of finality, and the two got up. Oriana remained seated. There was no point in pretending the investigation was over when it had not even begun. And it arrived soon enough. "Actually, there's one other small thing, unrelated to our previous discussion," the second investigator said, and they sat back down.

Chapter 54

In an undefined, almost imperceptible way, something in the atmosphere in Commissaire Léger's office had changed. Abadi thought that the room might be less hot. Léger had finished his explanation about the chief of police's public announcement, the non-existent drug deal and the hundreds of police officers working their way through the *Quartier Asiatique* with photographs of the assassin from the bridge, so far without any result.

Abadi responded mostly with questions, as was his way, and Léger answered to the best of his ability. There were more than six thousand registered hotels in Paris, he said, not to mention the unregistered hotels. No credit card with the name of Yerminski was registered on Airbnb or similarly regulated websites, but dozens of apartments were probably for rent off the books. The hotels were legally obliged to transfer their lists of foreign guests to police headquarters, but the database did not update in real-time, and the collection was conducted every night at midnight. As a result, if Yerminski checked into a hotel in Paris under his real name, it would take five hours for his location to appear in the database.

Abadi stood up and looked out of the window, down at the river. The sun had begun to set behind the Eiffel Tower, but it was still full daylight. Hundreds of people were scurrying towards the St Michel métro, anxious to leave the city before rush hour. Yerminski could be anywhere – in Paris, outside Paris, in some hotel, in some apartment, in the Bois de Boulogne, in the Bois de Vincennes, in a public garden, in a church, in a department store, pacing the streets, sleeping on a bench, staying with an Israeli friend, riding the métro back and forth, strolling along the river, drifting in the river. Anywhere.

"We'll have to go with my method," Abadi said, his gaze boring into Léger's eyes.

The commissaire did not raise any objection. "And what's your method?"

"There's no point continuing to search for the assassin from the bridge. He's not in the *Quartier Asiatique* and he's not a pedlar, so we have no way of knowing where to look for him."

"And you think we can locate this Yerminski?"

"Maybe not, but we have to try. You must have officers in this building who specialise in hotel theft, who know the hotel security officers. We need to ask for their help."

"And what will my people do in the meantime?"

"They need to find the girl," Abadi said. "The Chinese may be looking for Yerminski right now, but they're also busy covering their tracks. They took out the two assassins from this morning, and they'll definitely be going after the blonde they used as their honeytrap."

"She isn't necessarily blonde, mind you."

"It doesn't matter. The footage is sharp, and hundreds of thousands of people watched it. Even if she's totally changed her appearance, someone will have recognised her by the way she walks, her features, height, a certain gesture. The hotline must be busy by now."

"More than two thousand calls, as we speak. One identified his ex-girlfriend, parents who're sure it's their missing daughter, all types of perverts calling in, we're flooded with calls. We can barely make our way out of this mess."

"Who's we? Two people?"

"I have a team of three experienced investigators on it, they're steadily screening the calls."

"Then I suggest that whoever's looking for the Chinese assassin in the *Quartier Asiatique* come back here so we can at least screen the calls faster."

"*Cherchez la femme,*" Léger said.

"Look for the woman while she's still alive," Abadi corrected him.

"And what will you do in the meantime, Colonel? If you don't mind me asking."

"I need to go back to Charles de Gaulle airport to return my rental car."

"Of course. If only everyone were as strict in matters of law and consumer responsibilities as you are. But your car has already been returned to the rental company. We towed it here from Créteil after we had it searched."

"Without a warrant?"

"The juge d'instruction gave me a warrant without batting an eyelid when he heard it was you."

"I'm flattered. In that case, I'll take the train to Charles de Gaulle."

"To rent another car? I'm not sure they'll be too excited."

"No, I have another meeting I am already late for. I'll be back in two hours. Update me on my mobile if there are any developments."

"As far as I'm concerned, the only development is that you're going to Charles de Gaulle."

"Don't worry, I'm not leaving France before you find Yerminski."

"I'll keep your passport here," Léger said. He reached for the last *makroudh*, as if to bag a final victory before surrendering.

Chapter 55

Wasim got off the métro at Père Lachaise and waited on the platform for the passengers to disperse, to be sure he was not being followed.

He was wearing a blue Adidas Olympique de Marseille tracksuit. He did not like soccer, but the outfit garnered a certain respect among the Moroccans in the neighbourhood to which he was heading. It was also convenient, because the tracksuit had many pockets, and he needed them all. He stuffed the hash – two kilos in small bags – in the pockets of his tracksuit bottoms.

The two mobiles were in the pockets of his jacket, the real one in his right-hand pocket, and the one for clients in his left. The upper pocket of the jacket contained the brains of his communications mechanism: a day-by-day pillbox, the kind favoured by old people, in which he had arranged fourteen different S.I.M. cards. Changing the S.I.M. every hour meant he had fourteen different numbers, each "new" mobile with the contact numbers and meetings relevant to that hour. The other mobile was permanently switched off. He turned it on once every two hours to check which of his customers had called.

While it guaranteed the police would have a hard time tracking him, it did not guarantee that he would not get his ass kicked by the Moroccans that night. In the inner pocket of his trousers, the one sealed with a double zip, he kept the blade he had brought with him all the way from his tribe in Afghanistan. The blade folded into a carved wooden handle decorated with flowers Wasim could not name. Nor could he read the Dari verse etched into the handle, but he knew it by heart: "With God's will may my blow be fatal."

In his back pocket he had a list of the night's rounds, every client with their own set location. The first was a theatre producer who had ordered large quantities for an actor who refused to go on stage without it. After that he had four more runs in the Left Bank, then the students in the 13th arrondissement, followed by the cool gays in the Marais, and the concierge of a big hotel near the Champs-Élysées.

The last client of the evening was the strange girl from the fountain at the Pompidou Centre, the one who had agreed to carry out the mission for the Chinese in the airport that morning. Her fee was eighty grams of pot, but she was now demanding double. Since the Afghans he knew only dealt with hash, he was forced to venture outside the confines of Paris and into the Moroccan neighbourhood.

The platform slowly emptied and the final remaining passengers walked up the stairs and disappeared. Only an old Chinese pedlar, struggling to drag a cartful of products, waited with him for the next train. Wasim quickly changed the S.I.M. card in his active mobile and sent his contact a text saying he would be at the scheduled drop-off within twenty minutes. New passengers started pouring through, and after two minutes another train arrived. He boarded it, hopped down onto the platform the moment he heard the buzzer signalling the closing of the doors, took a quick look to see that no-one had got off with him, and jumped back onto the train, causing the emergency system to reopen the safety partitions. The passengers in the carriage averted their eyes.

At Gallieni, the last stop, he waited until everyone else had got off the train. For that neighbourhood, there certainly were a lot of young white people; they had probably all come to buy pot. He preferred to walk slowly behind them, and a single-file line soon formed on the narrow pavement. Wasim did not notice any police presence. The Chinese pedlar was lumbering in the line, but Wasim did not give him a second glance.

After about five minutes, groups of four to five teenagers started appearing around them, each time pulling out of the line one buyer, who then accompanied them to complete the deal. As usual, every customer was forced to circle the block several times until the deal had been made. No-one approached Wasim, and less than ten minutes later, he was walking alone. The old pedlar had disappeared.

He reached the end of the road, an area misleadingly nicknamed "the Woods". Wasim was mystified as to how a place without a single tree could have such a name. It was a huge dirt field, surrounded by bleak low-rises occupied mostly by immigrants. Burned-out cars and remnants of playground equipment were scattered about. Some of the boys scaled the piles of debris to watch what was going on while the teenagers stood around on the rooftops. Some were mere kids.

All at once, a group of about a dozen teens appeared in front of him, blocking his way. Some were black and some were Arab; Wasim was neither. Unlike them, he had already passed the age of criminal responsibility under French law and suddenly felt too old for such games. But it was too late to back down.

Out of nowhere, four unleashed pit bulls sidled up beside him, as quiet as a graveyard. Behind the group, two tall guys with keffiyehs covering their faces got out of one of the abandoned cars. They approached him with measured steps. Wasim leaned against the rusty fence and tried to project similar bravado. "You're the Afghani?" one of them asked. Wasim nodded and gave them his contact's name.

They led him in circles around the neighbourhood before they arrived, twenty useless minutes later, in the main multi-storey car park. There they took him to the freight lift and rode down to basement level three. All the lights were out, either smashed or because they had found a way to turn them off at the mains. They remained standing by the steel door without saying a word.

Car lights flashed in the distance, and they signalled him to approach. Heading for the car, he gripped the handle of his blade with his right hand.

The transaction itself went quickly and smoothly. The digital scale stood on the asphalt in front of the car lights. He put down the hash, and a black hand gathered it, placing a bag of pot on the scale. The smell was auspicious. The figure jumped to 1.5 kilos. There was no point in arguing and, anyway, the deal reflected current market forces. Once he had picked up the bag, the car lights went out.

Half-blinded, he tried to find his way back to the entrance. Three or four car engines started behind him, their lights off, and thirty seconds later it was just him and the silence. His hands were outstretched as he fumbled from one parked car to the next. His eyes slowly adjusting to the darkness, he finally spotted the green light of the lift door. Relieved, he stepped confidently towards its flickering light.

He realised his mistake too late. Someone was standing in front of him with a helmet and night-vision goggles, like in an expensive video game. The man pointed a very long gun at him, and then a red light flashed, illuminating the Chinese pedlar's cart. Without knowing why, Wasim understood straight away that he was going to die.

Chapter 56

The Military Secretary stood in front of the giant *National Geographic* map of the world that hung in his office, talking on the secure telephone. The political advisor was sitting on the couch behind him, nervously awaiting the results of the conversation.

"The Prime Minister told me he was not worried at all," the Military Secretary said. It was a complete lie; the Prime Minister never shared his feelings with him. In fact, the Prime Minister kept him on a need-to-know basis, and what he needed to know was always information the secretary could have obtained from other sources. But he liked to tell his interlocutors that the Prime Minister told him this or that, in the hope of creating at least an appearance of information exchanged. "He told me he was not worried" – the implied question being, "So what did he tell you?"

Aluf Rotelmann's calm voice came through on the line, "I'm happy to hear that." A silence lingered. The Military Secretary knew that his pretence convinced no-one, and certainly not someone with the I.Q. attributed to Aluf Rotelmann. But one could settle for persuading people with low I.Q.s and still make a career out of it; which is why he brought the conversation to an end and immediately called Zorro, Aluf Rotelmann's deputy. He began by saying, "Aluf Rotelmann told me you have already been updated on everything." From there he could navigate easily.

He spoke once more with the military attaché at the Israeli embassy in Paris, who was too far away to grasp the intricacies of the balance of power in Jerusalem, and only then called the Prime Minister, who was in his car en route from the Ministry of Defence. The exchange took less than two minutes, but still enabled him to save face in front of the advisor, who was doing his best to seem not to be listening. Only after this entire rigmarole did he allow himself to turn to him and say what he had planned to say from the beginning: "Everything's under control."

"Famous last words," the advisor said. "How is everything under control? How is it under control when we aren't on top of a single scenario in this affair, when we didn't create it and we're not going to be the ones who end it? If it ever ends."

"It'll end soon," the Military Secretary said. But would it?

"Define 'soon,'" the advisor persisted. "Uncle Saul is arriving next Sunday. The Boss wants this affair behind him well before then."

"The Boss" was the Prime Minister's uninspiring code name. "Uncle Saul" was the code name of his primary donor, Saul Wenger, a Swiss billionaire who had amassed his fortune from casinos and cable T.V. He came to Israel once a year, and each time the Prime Minister's Office suspended all activities to make sure that the visit was a success.

"I believe this affair will be behind us by tonight," the secretary said, more hopeful than confident.

"And what does Aluf Rotelmann believe?"

"My assessment is based on conversations with Aluf Rotelmann and others. By the time Uncle Saul lands, this affair will have dropped off the radar and the Prime Minister will be able to focus on other things. Don't forget we have a great Tzahal tour planned for Uncle Saul, a visit to the Hatzerim airbase, conversations with pilots, we'll give him a large printed photograph of him sat next to a fighter jet as a souvenir; they print and frame it on the spot."

"The Prime Minister has not approved that tour itinerary yet," the advisor said. "But there's still time for that. What we need to focus on at the moment is making this affair go away. Have you talked to the head of 8200?"

"No-one has talked to him, but from my understanding, he's expected to land in a few hours."

"How is it possible that he has not been in touch since the kidnapping this morning?"

"I don't know where he is," the secretary admitted. "He left San Francisco yesterday, but his office said he won't be back until tonight."

The advisor became quiet, and his gaze travelled across the map of the world on the wall.

Chapter 57

He Xiangu heard her mobile beeping while she was in the shower. Erlang Shen? Had he found the blonde? It could not be Team Two, because the translators had yet to arrive at the building in front of the embassy. Whoever the message was from, they would have to wait.

She let the water wash away the chlorine from the pool. She increased the flow of cold water and steadily turned down the warm. She closed her eyes and tried not to think about anything, not about her status in the organisation, the failure of the abduction or the question marks that only multiplied the more she tried to repair the damage she had already caused. Most of all, she tried not to think about Ming's possible reaction. Her mobile beeped again.

Her bodyguard turned away when she walked naked to the table. He was sitting in the armchair facing the front door, his pistol drawn, and she turned her back to him as she disconnected the mobile from its charger. She typed the code for reading texts, but not before checking in the mirror to be sure the bodyguard was sneaking glances at her as often as he ought to. As she became increasingly aware of her body, she closed her eyes, the better to focus on the screen once she opened them again.

The message was from Team Four. It took her a moment to remember what Team Four's mandate was and where it would now be reporting from. In fact, she nearly forgot that at noon she had sent three of her *xiake* to keep watch at the El Al desk at Charles de Gaulle airport. It was possible that Yerminski would decide to return to Israel.

"Team Four to Commander. Report from El Al check-in zone for Israel. A man caught on Team Two's cameras this afternoon entering and exiting the Israeli embassy in Paris (documented as John Doe 24), has arrived here. According to Team Two's recent report, which is still in stages of decryption and translation, it appears that John Doe 24 is the chief investigating officer of Israeli intelligence's Unit 8200, Colonel Zeev Abadi. Video attached."

He Xiangu pressed play. The video was only seconds long. John Doe 24 was seen in profile, probably from a camera concealed in a briefcase. He was documented presenting a card and entering El Al's security zone. He was tall and muscular, with feline grace, and would have looked like a million other secret soldiers around the world if not for his face, which counterbalanced the ordinary efficiency of his body. There was a strange harmony to his features, in which the thin lips, strong nose and scarred chin gave way to a wistful, slightly amused gaze, like that of certain cats.

Once his entrance had been approved by the security guard, John Doe 24 turned his head and his eyes swept the area, locking for a split second on the agent carrying the hidden camera, who interrupted the taping and walked away as a bird abandons a tree when a cat approaches the trunk.

The second message was not at all reassuring.

"Team Four to Commander. Colonel Zeev Abadi (former John Doe 24) met in the security zone a heavy-set man with silver hair, who has yet to be documented, and will be known from now on as John Doe 38. The two spoke for approximately two minutes, and from their body language it appears that John Doe 38 is higher in rank. It is therefore possible that John Doe 38 is Abadi's direct commander – head of Israeli intelligence's Unit 8200. It should further be noted that the flight to Israel was due to depart in less than forty minutes and that the check-in area was already officially closed, but El Al crewmen personally escorted John Doe 38 and opened a check-in desk for him. Before leaving, John Doe 38 handed Colonel Abadi a

small package wrapped in tinfoil. Colonel Zeev Abadi left immediately upon receiving the package, while John Doe 38 approached the check-in desk. We were unable to document the encounter, and the operative of Team Four was detained for questioning by French policemen at the request of El Al security when he got too close to the barrier. He was released after his passport had been checked, and will be sent back to the homeland on the next flight. A xiake *from Team Four was sent to follow Colonel Abadi upon his departure from the terminal, whereas the team leader has remained at his post, and awaits further instruction."*

When He Xiangu started school, her grandfather gave her a kaleidoscope. It was a traditional Chinese kaleidoscope, with black silhouettes on a yellow and red background. She was scared to death by the strange object, and tried for more than two hours to understand how the colourful shapes could refract into so many symmetrical, unrelated parts. Finally, overcome with rage, she stomped on the gift, which broke, and the glass shards lost their visual coherence.

Now she felt her mind turning into that broken kaleidoscope. She tried to make sense of the message she had read and grant it some kind of logic, but it only caused the riddle to refract into ever more vibrantly coloured shapes, which were related in a symmetrical yet unpredictable way, adhering to a pattern she could not grasp.

She felt her legs, still wet, buckling under her and stumbled back in the direction of the armchair, falling into the lap of the bodyguard, who did not protest. She read the message a second and third time, replaying the surveillance footage to hone in on the last shot and dive into the laughing eyes of John Doe 24. Was this Abadi, the one referred to as the senior investigating officer of the Israeli unit, the same Abadi mentioned in the recording that the translators were trying to decipher this very moment?

Until this point, she had believed she was the one who had initiated the operation. She was the one who had planned the abduction, the one who had authorised all the operative details, the one who had set the rules of the game. But had she been a pawn all along, manipulated into believing the initiative was hers? Was the soldier Yerminski not the targeted victim but the bait? Were the Israelis convened in some other hotel, as if in a parallel universe, watching her as she watched them, playing tricks on her, laughing the deeper she dug her grave? Who was the bird here? And who the cat?

She felt her bodyguard harden beneath her. She arched her back, her limber body a question mark furling into its own exclamation point. Her literary namesake in the Chinese classics aroused her husband, Ximen Qing, by feeding him an overdose of herbal aphrodisiacs until he lost his mind. He Xiangu was so enraged, she could have easily killed someone, but she decided she would be better off relaxing through an activity that only came close to death.

Placing her mobile underneath her, she rubbed against the tense young man, back and forth, sprinkling him with water, foam from the hotel soaps, honey from between her legs, memories of an interrupted meditation. He moaned and the heavy gun slid from his hand and landed on the carpet. Her legs carried her weight up and down to the rhythm of his breathing against her back. From the floor, the screen flashed one last time before switching off, and she saw Colonel Abadi's playful gaze challenging her before being swallowed into the darkness of the room.

Chapter 58

"Air, fire, water and earth." When she had a hard time concentrating, Oriana would quickly recite Maimonides' four elements. "Air, fire, water and earth." Her father would sometimes try to throw her off by reciting Plato's order of the elements, but she never got confused: air, fire, water and earth.

Air.

In the silence that fell over the meeting room, Oriana could hear the grunting of the air-conditioner. It was on the highest setting, not only in accordance with a man's tendency to freeze every woman in his midst, but also – or so she assumed – in order to drown out the possible hissing of hidden recording devices.

Shabak agent Hardy was the one who had asked the real question they had brought her in for.

"We really do have only one last matter. Earlier today, Segen Oriana Talmor, you went to the laundry service of the 8200 headquarters. In fact, you went there twice, one hour between each visit. The first time, according to the quartermasters' testimony, you conducted an unsecure phone conversation with Aluf Mishne Abadi. What were you doing there the second time?"

"Aluf Mishne Abadi asked me to pick up his uniform," Oriana said, "so I went over there. I did not know it was forbidden by Aluf Rotelmann."

"That was the first visit," Laurel corrected her. "The question is not what you did there the first time, but what you did on the second occasion, when there were no quartermasters there."

Fire.

Even as a young girl she had found it easy to understand the vast advantage of the tribes who had discovered fire, to imagine the fear in the eyes of their enemies, those who witnessed for the first time people carrying torches and flaming arrows. That's how she felt as an intelligence officer, because discovering secret information was as terrorising as fire in the Stone Age. I listened in on your telephone calls. I know things about you and you don't even know what they are.

Now she was on the other side, which was also familiar to her. When Shabak agents see you creeping at night between village houses in the Galilee towards the nearest forest, they know you're gay. When the credit card company statistician sees you've purchased, for the first time, an enhanced moisturising cream and a coconut snack bar, they can guess you're pregnant even before you yourself know. What did Laurel and Hardy know about her, and what could they guess?

"The first time I went to the laundry service I noticed that the telephone was not secure, so I ran an information security check. And yes, I discharged the soldiers, per security protocol."

"Shortly after the soldiers left the laundry service under your instructions, strong magnetic activity, electronic transmission-blocking, was registered in the unit," Laurel said slowly. "It seems that someone over there had activated jamming devices to block remote bugging. That isn't an information security check. That's an application of electronic warfare, and you need to explain what could justify it."

"Help us help you," Hardy said.

"You knew very well there was an unsecure telephone there, you didn't find out about it on your first visit. We need to understand what reason you could have had to activate electronic warfare equipment when you went back there an hour later. Give us a reasonable answer, and this affair will be behind us."

Water.

"Can I first have a glass of water?" Oriana said, trying to force a smile into her voice. Hardy got up and walked to the coffee station at the entrance. How odd that the Greeks did not include time within the context of elements. Was Einstein really the first to make the connection? She promised herself she would look into it the moment she got out of there, if she was still allowed to check things online.

Yes, water. An important stalling element, even though Hardy returned with a jug and cups with relative speed. Once again her mind wandered to Einstein's genius instead of rapidly coming up with a reason that could justify her use of jamming devices, apart from the obvious one, that she already knew the second time that she was about to divulge classified information on a landline, and all this for what, all this for Abadi the silver fox, the leftist who trashed her on the witness stand.

Her thoughts trailed off in every direction. Wake up, Oriana, wake up, focus, what was the fourth element?

"We're waiting for an answer, Segen Talmor," Laurel said.

Earth.

Earth, of course; dust, in the language of Judaism, and Rabbi Moses Cordovero even explained why dust came last, but at the moment she could not remember the reason. There was a lot of dust in front of her right now, from the windows overlooking the beaches of Herzliya. She drank from her cup of water and her gaze wandered to two girls on the beach, undressing despite the evening breeze and taking photographs of themselves in bikinis against the sunset. A terrific example of open source intelligence. How many girls around the globe had taken photographs in bikinis against the sunset? A hundred million? A billion? Did humanity need another photograph of a girl in a bathing suit? Was there truly an infinite demand from men for photographs of girls in bikinis? It certainly seemed to be the case, since even Oriana had at one point been tempted to send one to a man – until at the last minute she came to her senses and deleted the evidence from her folder.

All at once her thoughts focused. She saw, with complete clarity in her mind's eye, her computer folder, and suddenly understood how Tomer could have known her computer had been hacked. She also realised what she would say. She put down the glass of water and looked them, one after the other, straight in the eye.

"I'm still not sure it's any of your business, but I'm in the middle of a complex operation and I don't have time to waste on pointless arguments. So I'm answering your question even though I don't have to. In short, between my first and second visit to the laundry service, evidence was found indicating that my intelligence terminal in the system had been hacked, and was not protected by the proxy server. I subsequently took a series of defensive measures, one of them being the placement of jamming equipment in hot spots around the base, including the laundry shed. I can give you my terminal number and you can check it yourselves."

Now it was their turn to try to conceal their surprise, and they were very bad at it. Oriana read aloud the terminal number from her mobile as slowly as possible. They did not write it down because they knew that at that very moment someone on the other side of the wall was hurrying off to verify her claim, and they also instinctively understood that it was true, and that she was slipping between their fingers.

"How is that possible?" Hardy finally said. "All terminals are protected by the main server."

"I believe that takes us back to your earlier question, '*quis custodiet ipsos custodes?*'"

"What was that?"

"Who will guard the guards," she said.

Chapter 59

Georges Lucas arrived at Le Grand Hôtel two minutes before his evening shift, as he had done every working day for the past twenty years. He shook the hand of his colleague from the morning shift, who as usual was in a hurry to make it to the R.E.R. before rush hour. They had been working together for more than a decade, and had never exchanged more than brisk pleasantries during shift rotation.

The security room was a presidential suite that had been converted into a surveillance centre. On all four walls hung the screens of the dozens of cameras scattered around the hotel, though no-one actually monitored them in the hotel itself anymore; that was the job of global headquarters, which hired employees for that purpose from less expensive countries than France. Lucas set his rucksack down on the bed, which would be used by the employee who would replace him at midnight. He took out his reading glasses and a bottle of mineral water before turning to the main computer.

He went through the list of messages. A warning had been sent from the chain's American headquarters regarding a con artist posing as an Italian duke who had already managed to pull one over on three of the chain's hotels in Brussels, Hong Kong and Buenos Aires. There was also a query from another of the chain's Paris hotels about an English guest who had stayed at Le Grand Hôtel in the past and was arousing suspicion by having, among other things, ordered since yesterday twenty-four bottles of champagne from room service.

In the hotel itself quite a few incidents had been registered in the course of the morning shift, which was generally the most troubled:

a couple from Australia forgot their baby at reception when they checked into their room after a 24-hour flight, then squabbled over who would go back down to get him; a guest from Spain was injured in a car accident while photographing the Arc de Triomphe; and a guest from Germany insisted that an expensive ring had been stolen from her nightstand, even though the sensor logs clearly showed that the door to her room had not been opened since she entered it the previous evening.

Three messages awaited from Paris police headquarters. The first reported the early release from jail of a burglar who specialised in hotel room thefts, targeting the large chains; the second warned of road blocks in the Opéra district next week due to a movie shoot; the third was about the abduction of an Israeli passenger from Charles de Gaulle airport that morning, who had booked a room in a business hotel near the CeBit Fair in south Paris.

Lucas checked the reservations from Israel. A hundred and fourteen new guests had checked into the hotel today, and three of those rooms had been booked from Israel. An additional Israeli guest showed up at reception without a reservation, standard behaviour when Lucas had first started working in the hotel industry, but which nowadays was regarded as suspicious. The guest's name sounded Russian – a red flag for any hotel in the city of lights.

There was no particular reason for linking the guest with the abduction that had taken place in the airport that morning, but just as hotel guests came to find excitement in the French capital, Lucas always held out hope that one of them would interrupt the boredom of his job. Picking up the house telephone, he asked reception for the passport photograph and credit card of Yerminski, the guest with no reservation.

Chapter 60

In another historic Parisian hotel, He Xiangu stood up and stared at Tarzan. At first she did not recognise him because he was very young in the photo, but there was no mistaking those muscles. Wearing a white bathing suit he flashed his teeth at the camera.

"Why do they have a poster of Tarzan in this conference room?" she said.

"The hotel conference rooms are named after him," the leader of Team Three said. "I mean, not after Tarzan, but after the actor who played him in the movies, Johnny Weissmuller."

"But why?" He Xiangu persisted. From the corner of the table, one of the older men raised his hand. It was the French translator who had been brought in half an hour earlier to assist the translators from Hebrew.

"It says here that the swimming pool at Hôtel Molitor was inaugurated in 1929 by the Olympic champion Johnny Weissmuller, who later became famous as the actor who played Tarzan," he said. "He broke a record here."

He Xiangu's nostrils flared with indignation. She wanted to get back into the pool to challenge the dead man's record. Instead she said, "Tarzan would have killed the Israeli by now while you're still standing here waiting for him to appear," and she returned to reading the transcripts.

However, her people had done a fine job summoning a French translator to clarify obscure points from the intercepted conversation and cross-referencing the main database to provide the background. It was not their fault that they were still a long way away from an adequate explanation.

Speaker A: They found him. They will take him to the light at police headquarters. He was at his mother's, in a Jewish suburb south-east of Paris.
Speaker B: You mean this Abadi?
Speaker A: I correct you, Colonel Abadi.
Speaker B: [Swearing] I knew from beginning he was up to something. What will they do to him?
Speaker A: I do not know, but they were anxious to find him. I was afraid they would want to arrest me too, but they were only after him.
Speaker B: He still believes they intended to abduct a different Israeli?
Speaker A: I think so. He got the list from the El Al security officer without my knowledge.
Speaker B: You also did not know he would leave the code room in the Israeli embassy in Paris a minute after making a call.
Speaker A: It is not my job to handle these sorts of things. It is your job.
Speaker B: We are not supposed to talk about this outside the embassy.

"I don't understand where they're taking him," she said. "What is 'the light'?"

The French translator rushed to reply. "We believe the word '*léger*' in the recording is not the French word for 'light', because it doesn't add up with the rest of the sentence, and there's no reason why the Israelis would suddenly use a regular French word in the middle of a Hebrew conversation. It's more likely to be someone's name. *Léger*."

The team leader loaded a photograph onto the screen. "Given the context, it's clear to us that they're talking about this man, Commissaire Jules Léger, the senior criminal investigator in charge, according to the French press, of solving the abduction that took place at the airport this morning."

"And where is he? Where is this police headquarters they're talking about?"

"The police here have many buildings and many headquarters," the team leader said, "but from what we have found out, the department headed by Léger is located in the historic building on the Île de la Cité, in the centre of Paris. The formal address is 36 quai des Orfèvres, but it's a giant building with many entrances and underground passages, including from the adjacent courthouse and even the church next to it, which is called Sainte-Chapelle."

"So Colonel Abadi, who was meeting the Head of Unit 8200 at the airport a short time ago, is now on his way to that building?"

"That's what we deduce from the conversation," the team leader said cautiously.

He Xiangu requested an update from the leader of the team at the airport.

The reply confirmed Team Two's findings. "John Doe 24, currently identified as Colonel Zeev Abadi, left the terminal with a tinfoil-wrapped package on his way to the taxi stand. A police car pulled over next to him and he entered the vehicle without protest. The squad car left in the direction of Paris with its siren on, and the Team Four *xiake* in charge of surveillance lost John Doe 24's trail."

If so, complete confirmation. The head of Unit 8200's Special Section suspected that the Chinese commandos had wanted to kidnap a different Israeli that morning, and it stood to reason that by now he knew the name of the correct Israeli. He might even know how to locate Vladislav Yerminski. And to help him succeed in the very mission that she, He Xiangu, had been bungling since this morning, he had managed to enlist the French police.

How? Why? It was not very important. He Xiangu recalled an ancient lullaby, "The mouse was so confused, he went to the cat for love." But who was feeling confused here other than her? Not

Colonel Abadi, it seemed. She looked at the map and the photographs of the police headquarters, which were next to the river. It was obvious by now that any attempt to reach Abadi was doomed. She read the transcripts of the conversation again.

"What's this thing with his mother?" she said.

"It seems that his mother lives in a Paris suburb," the translator told her.

"So we can get to her?"

"Yes," the team leader said confidently. "There are fewer than ten people by the name of Abadi in that area. But I'm not sure she knows anything."

"She will certainly know how to contact her son," He Xiangu replied with a blank expression. "I have heard that Mediterranean men are very attached to their mothers."

Chapter 61

Erlang Shen breathed in the night air. Standing on the roof of the building in Saint-Ouen, he gazed wide-eyed across the skyline towards Belleville in the distance, a war zone in every respect, an enclave of madness within the French capital. There was considerable commotion on the neighbours' rooftops and it spread to the look-outs posted across the many balconies. Below, small groups gathered along the paths connecting the buildings, wandering in a seemingly aimless manner, but in fact marking territory like military patrols. Erlang Shen was not sure he understood the scene he had stumbled upon, but he knew he needed to remove himself from it as swiftly as possible.

He arranged the two bodies in the only lit corner of the roof. He had brought the body of Wasim, the man who had recruited the blonde, using the freight lift from the parking garage. The second body belonged to a black teenager who had the misfortune of manning a look-out post on the same roof. He was young, perhaps only fourteen. A large plastic container with home-cooked food lay next to the chair in which his body now lay. Erlang Shen reckoned it was a meal prepared for him by his mother.

He took the strange knife he had found in Wasim's pocket, turned the boy over and thrust it into his back, if not to mislead the police investigators, then at least to throw off the gangs just long enough to make himself scarce before they gave chase. He took out his camera and photographed the bodies and the contents of Wasim's many pockets for the report.

He liked Commander He Xiangu, but he would have no alternative but to describe the chain of blunders that had led to this situation. Not only had the man employed by the squad turned out to be a drug dealer, but he, Erlang Shen, Ming's own *xiake*, had been sent to complete internal damage control independent of the mission to capture Vladislav Yerminski. It was a task whose only objective was to conceal the extent of the incompetence with which this operation had been managed. No, he would have no choice but to file a detailed report directly to Ming.

But first he had to complete the mission on which he had been sent.

He studied Wasim's delivery list. He was supposed to be relieved of the largest amount at the end of his route, at a stop described as "the funny fountain". The rate was not mentioned. He was struck by this anomaly, but needed further confirmation.

He arranged the S.I.M. cards and the two mobiles on the floor. As he expected, access to the devices was protected by fingerprint scanners. He took the mobile closer to Wasim's lifeless hand and pressed his dead thumb against the activation button until the main screen appeared.

He located the texts at the third attempt. The S.I.M. cards were no doubt switched at fixed times and the text messages were sent that morning, around the same time as the botched abduction.

"Did it go well?"

"Is everything O.K.?"

"Call me as soon as you can."

"Call, I have a big, grade A gift for you."

The reply arrived an hour later. "It was horrible. A lot more dangerous than you said. I'll be waiting for you at the fountain at midnight. Don't you dare come without at least double the amount."

The time stamp corresponded with Wasim's last scheduled delivery. Perhaps he had taken the organisation's money for himself and was planning to pay the bait he recruited in weed. The sheer unprofessionalism of this business made his skin crawl.

He did not know what fountain they were talking about. He

searched for the word "*fontaine*" in the S.I.M. card and found a saved location on the maps app. Zooming in on the point with the star, he arrived at Fontaine Stravinsky. The app explained that the fountain's design had been inspired by Stravinsky's ballet "The Rite of Spring", and that its spirit aligned with the adjacent music centre and the museum of modern art in the nearby Pompidou Centre. Whimsical, but not for much longer.

Chapter 62

Taxis were waiting outside the hotel. Her driver said he was hoping for a tourist who wanted to go to the holy sites in Jerusalem, or at least a fare that would be substantial enough to justify the wait, but if a sweet girl like her needed to get to Glilot, then fine, he was willing to do a *mitzvah*.

Oriana did not reply. She wondered what Abadi was doing, and whether her soldiers had left her any pizza.

It had been a narrow escape. She had left the Shabak's agents too puzzled to keep their vague promise to return her to the base, too baffled to order her to report her next steps. Oddly, she did not feel relieved but frustrated. Who was she supposed to report this to, the head of Unit 8200? To Abadi? Excessive loyalty, indeed! She would inform the head of 8200's bureau chief, whom she knew personally. She had no contact with Abadi anyhow.

The Mediterranean music on the radio switched to commercials, and then to the nine o'clock news. The broadcast opened with the Paris airport abduction.

"The search for Yaniv Meidan continues . . . Israeli sources close to the investigation say it was a drug deal gone sour."

Oriana wondered whether all the news she heard was fabricated, or whether the truth was missing only from the news that she happened to know something about.

The taxi trailed along a traffic jam in front of the large interchange in Herzliya, part of it caused by middle-class suburbians driving home from work in Tel Aviv, part of it by officers from her beloved 8200 base driving to the pubs downtown after their shifts.

The broadcast moved on to the Iranian threat, and then elaborated on the dangers of illegal immigration.

"Tzahal is investigating another case of arson attacks by settlers on homes of Palestinians in Samaria . . . In Tel Aviv roads will be blocked tonight due to the light rail construction . . . In Jaffa a teacher from the bilingual school was attacked by a masked assailant." In the foreign news segment, the presenter detailed a series of anti-Semitic incidents that had taken place that week across Europe. Swastikas were spray-painted in a Jewish cemetery in Belgium, and in Strasbourg a Jew wearing a *kippah* was attacked on his way back from synagogue. "Europe is not a good place to be a Jew," the driver observed.

They reached the turn. Oriana asked to be dropped off by the memorial, since she did not want the guards seeing her arriving in a taxi. The driver pulled over and refused to take her money, which made her regret that she had not been more friendly in conversation. Before walking towards the guard post, she took a long look at the lit jungle of antennae, trying to draw strength from them, or at least magic inspiration.

Chapter 63

At Le Flamboire in Paris, He Xiangu finished ordering the chef's signature dish, beef ribs *à la Flamboire.* The impudent waiter tried to talk her out of it, claiming it was a dish meant to be shared by two, and recommended the faux-filet Chateaubriand instead. He Xiangu never understood why people ordered filet, and certainly was not going to settle for a cut whose only saving grace was that it resembled filet. She liked meat that bit back.

Mesmerised, she stared at the flames that rose from the giant grill. And then her mobile beeped. One message. Two messages. Three messages. By what miracle had these messages landed before her dish arrived at the table? She decided it was a sign from the gods that she would come out stronger from this wretched operation.

The first message was a confirmation request from the leader of Team Four asking to send back to the homeland the agent who had been detained by the French police next to the El Al area. She considered sending her bodyguard with him on the flight, before one of her enemies in the organisation caught wind of the versatile uses she made of him. But she was still in need of distraction tonight, and he was the ideal candidate – approachable, discreet and obedient.

The second message was from the leader of Team One, the biggest team: by 8.00 p.m. they had checked 70 per cent of the cheap hotels in Paris, and the soldier Yerminski was not staying at any one of them. He estimated they would have finished checking all the lower-grade hotels in the next two hours, and would then move on to the mid-level ones.

Grim tidings. She was about to send him a harsh reply, but opened the third message before responding.

To: Commander
From: Leader of Team Two
Urgency: Immediate

Att. message transmitted 20:03, Paris police radio network. Decrypted: listener no. 56. Edited: translator no. 3;

The 9th arrondissement police station seeks instruction from Commissaire Léger pursuant to a phone message from the security officer at Le Grand Hôtel on Scribe Street regarding a suspicious guest. The security officer has been collaborating with our station for many years, we believe his warnings have a high level of credibility. The guest in question, one Vladislav Yerminski, is an Israeli who did not present a credit card upon check-in, and who may have entered France on the same El Al flight from which missing person Yaniv Meidan was abducted this morning. According to the hotel's electronic sensors, the guest is still in his room, but is not answering his door or phone. The deputy officer at the station asks whether he should send a squad car to look into the matter, or whether the investigations department will handle the query directly. Out.

It was almost too good to be true. She checked the location of Erlang Shen, the only one she could truly count on, and saw that he had reported finishing handling the man and was moving on to the blonde bait. She hesitated for a moment, but time was of the essence and she did not have the luxury of choosing the best people for the task. As often happened at critical moments in the organisation, waiting for the best could lead to the worst outcome. She quickly typed:

To: Leader of Team Three
cc: Leader of Team Two

From: Commander

Urgency: Immediate

Leader of Team Three to send all available warriors to Le Grand Hôtel. If necessary, he is authorised to second xiake *from Teams One and Two to assist. The objective is to locate the reel. If it is not found in the target's luggage, the target must be brought to Le Bourget airport for questioning per earlier instructions. If circumstances prevent such action, the target is to be eliminated; prior authorisation will not be required. Leader of Team Three to confirm mission completion.*

Her ribs arrived at the table, done to fat-dripping perfection. The gods, in their infinite wisdom, must have chosen to shower her with luck, prosperity and success.

Chapter 64

The police car sped along the hard shoulder of the *autoroute* to Paris' Porte de la Chapelle, where it was forced to slow down due to the traffic in both lanes. The driver finally managed to enter the city courtesy of the wailing siren, and turned into boulevard Malesherbes. At the instruction of the senior officer who sat next to him, he turned off the siren after entering the city, and now the car was crawling along the dim boulevard. Throughout the ride, in the back seat, Abadi did not raise his head once.

He was immersed in the marvel his commander had given him, a new kind of smartphone with tracking capabilities, the brainchild of 8200's technology centre. Code-named "Navran", the communication device was the fastest he had experienced and it came with its own encryption system. The video was sharp and stable even in the dimmed light of the car.

But most important of all, the device operated on its own network, it was independent from Aman's central proxy server and Rotelmann's nosy intelligence operators. Navran 001 was represented by a blue dot now showing the head of 8200 taking off from Charles de Gaulle. He would be unreachable for at least four more hours before angry orders from above might force him to halt the investigations of his new, unpredictable head of Special Section to whom he'd given Navran 008.

Oriana's device, Navran 012, had not been connected to the network. He typed her name into the search field. The Navran located her civilian mobile number in the unit's database and ran a trace. Her phone had been switched off for the past hour and its last cellular signal, sixteen minutes ago, had been sent from the hotel strip on the coast of Herzliya. He asked himself what she could have been doing in a hotel. He didn't have an answer.

Outside, it started to drizzle, causing the windows of the police car to fog up. He opened the window closest to him and breathed in the air. Lonely pedestrians rushed along the boulevard in every direction. How was it that his first investigation upon returning to service in Tzahal was taking place in Paris, a city which he had never seen as a new beginning for anything? The car slowly turned left and he noticed the Madeleine church. Which girl had he kissed on its steps? Which woman had he deceived in one of those buildings? Everything would be so much simpler if he could walk the streets of this city without constantly hearing echoes of his past steps and glimpsing ghosts over his shoulder.

The police radio suddenly came to life.

"The Commissaire is asking how soon you'll be bringing him in."

The sergeant held the microphone and did a quick calculation. "Half an hour at the outside."

"So hurry up. All kinds of developments here."

Abadi opened his eyes. He felt a familiar pressure in his chest, as if in preparation for unwelcome news.

"What developments? Tell him I want to talk to Léger," he said, leaning forward, ready to snatch the radio in the event of a refusal. But the sergeant complied.

"The client is asking what developments. He wants to speak to the Commissaire."

Two minutes passed in radio silence. The darkness that had engulfed the ride suddenly lifted when the car catapulted, as if from a cannon's dim mouth, into place de la Concorde, which twinkled with thousands of bright, buoyant lights. Abadi's eyes were fixed on the silent radio.

The Peugeot was travelling along the Jardin des Tuileries when the driver's mobile rang. He glanced at the screen and, without saying a word, passed the telephone to Abadi.

"Colonel Abadi, so kind of you to take an interest, I thought you'd forgotten about us."

Abadi tried to guess from Léger's voice what new information might have come in. The Frenchman sounded alert, almost cheerful, but Abadi kept his response as matter-of-fact as possible. "Commissaire, if there have been any new developments, I hope you'll share them with me?"

"And why not, Colonel? After all, you have always disclosed your own information to me, haven't you?" It was not a question, and Abadi did not answer it.

"Very well," the Frenchman said, tiring of his own game. "What do you want to hear first, the bad news or the really bad news?"

"Whichever you prefer, Commissaire."

"Then first of all, officially, we have two more corpses linked to the case. The second Chinese commando was found in the river, near my office in fact, behind Notre-Dame. And you'll be happy to know that the sewage treatment plant called, and the body of your countryman, Yaniv Meidan, may have been found. Boudin says the corpse is in reasonable condition and should be easy to identify."

The news was hardly pressing and Abadi sensed more was to come. "That would be a matter for the representative of the Israeli police," he said. "But if there are any additional developments, then—"

"Indeed there are," Léger said, interrupting him, and he tried to contain the sudden excitement in his voice. "It's possible that we have found your other Israeli, Vladislav Yerminski. That's to say . . . we haven't actually found him because he isn't answering his telephone, but we have theoretically located him."

"Where?" Abadi sat upright in his seat. The exhaustion he had felt only moments previously was gone. He focused on the commissaire's voice as if he could alter the policeman's answer through willpower.

"Le Grand Hôtel," he said. "It's an exclusive hotel and we didn't even think to search it. Yerminski checked in early this afternoon, and the indications are that he is still in his room, though he's not answering the door."

"Commissaire, please, I ask you, send police cars over there at once."

"We are not even allowed to approach him, I checked with the juge d'instruction. To our knowledge, your man has not committed any offence. I have asked the hotel security officer to knock on his door, and if he still doesn't answer, to try entering with his master key under the pretence of concern for a guest. But we're not permitted to be there."

"I am allowed," Abadi said, and it was his turn for animation. "Commissaire, this is extremely important."

Léger sounded almost grateful. "Well, Colonel, of course, if you felt that you wanted to drop in on this historic landmark hotel," he said, "there would be nothing I could do to stop you."

For the first time, Abadi sensed a note of genuine warmth from the Frenchman and he met him in the silence between them over the radio. "Commissaire, I have been released after an official arrest by the French police and I think I'd like to be taken to my hotel," he said. "I've heard good reports about the one on rue Scribe."

"You are absolutely correct, Colonel. I believe I have heard them too." Léger hung up, and almost immediately his voice could be heard across the radio again.

"Take him to Le Grand Hôtel, rue Scribe. You're accompanying him inside, but only unofficially. You have authorisation to turn on the sirens."

Apparently the driver had been waiting for the order, because he instantly made a wild U-turn, and the car was swallowed into the courtyard of the Louvre with blasting sirens and screeching wheels.

"Where's rue Scribe?" Abadi said.

"Near the Opéra," the sergeant said, as if he never imagined that a person with a colonel's rank would ask such a simple question.

"Where the phantom from 'The Phantom of the Opera' lives, if you've seen the musical."

"I haven't," Abadi said, trying to expel the dark thoughts that enshrouded him. "Please tell me it has a happy ending."

"What's a happy ending?" the sergeant asked. "From my experience, one person's happy ending is another's sad."

Before Abadi could reply, the driver took a left turn against the traffic into place de l'Opéra and came to a screeching halt by the entrance to the hotel.

"After you, Colonel Abadi," the sergeant said.

Chapter 65

The huge desk was made of a massive piece of pine that only the very best craftsmen would know how to fashion. It had electrical sockets elegantly concealed on every side. Those present rushed to charge their mobiles. The Prime Minister's Military Secretary was not sure which was the best seat at the table, but as the room filled up, he finally sat down with his back to the door.

At the last minute, the meeting had been relocated from the Prime Minister's office in Tel Aviv to the Minister of Defence's office next door, perhaps due to the number of participants who kept pouring in. Among those in uniform, he recognised Aluf Rotelmann, the Tzahal spokesperson, the head of the Mamram Centre of Computing and Information Systems, and the head of the technology department. All these men were accompanied by their assistants, bureau chiefs and secretaries. In addition to the Military Secretary, all four strategic advisors from the Prime Minister's office were present, as well as the official spokesperson who was accompanied by the Ministry of Defence's spokesperson. The Prime Minister himself had as usual sent a message that he would be late and that they could start without him.

A man more naïve than the Military Secretary might think that he had been summoned to an urgent meeting to bring all parties up to date on the abduction in Paris. But he knew who he was dealing with. And indeed, once the lights had been dimmed, it turned out that the Tzahal spokesperson's presentation was to be about the billionaire Saul Wenger's forthcoming visit to Israel and his tour of Tzahal.

"We've planned three different visits for him, after the last plan –" and here the Tzahal spokesperson shot a glance at the Military Secretary – "was deemed unfit."

The Military Secretary took care not to respond even with so much as a glance, and concentrated on taking notes. Men take note of a man who takes notes, anyone who had ever tried to survive in a bureaucratic organisation knew that, especially someone who had been serving as Military Secretary in one of the most conflict-ridden periods in the history of the general headquarters.

And so the Military Secretary jotted down the suggested itinerary for the guest. The first stop would be to the induction centre, and include "heartfelt encounters", as per the Tzahal spokesperson's prophetic definition; the second stop would be to the Hatzerim airbase, a suggestion that was copied and pasted from the itinerary he himself had submitted; and the third day would focus on the future technology of Tzahal, and include visits to the three top-secret bases: the Mamram Centre of Computing and Information Systems, the Computer Service Directorate, and the Technology Centre of Unit 8200 of the Intelligence Corps.

The Military Secretary continued writing. When he had finished, the Chief of the Intelligence Corps, Aluf Rotelmann, was the first to respond.

"I don't think we can authorise a visit, as big a supporter of Israel as the guest may be, to a Unit 8200 base."

"We'll settle the details between us tomorrow," the Prime Minister's Chief of Staff said. "I just wanted to clarify that his next gift is for Tzahal technology, so it's important that we show him what we're doing."

Aluf Rotelmann's voice sounded distant, almost aloof. "His next gift, like his previous gifts, is for the politicians. Only a fraction of his philanthropic efforts, which are of course admirable, goes to Tzahal. I suggest we be very cautious."

The Chief of Staff was indeed cautious, as he proved right away. "It's precisely for that reason that I've asked the Ministry of Defence's legal advisor to join us today." And sure enough, the Military Secretary spotted the lawyer – whose nickname in the corridors of power was "the steam iron" thanks to his ability to straighten out any matter – seating himself at the head of the table.

True to his image, "the steam iron" accepted the floor with a display of reserve. "I would first like to say that I'm here in an unofficial capacity, since there's no need for legal advice in the matter you're dealing with. The Prime Minister, who, as you know, also serves as Minister of Defence at the moment, asked me through his Chief of Staff to provide a little background, which is indeed required, judging by the question that was just raised here."

So many words, the Military Secretary thought, so many words and such a hollow legal introduction, essentially void of meaning, and yet the echo it created conveyed an unambiguous message. When had the law started permeating every facet of the military? When had lawyers started being summoned to staff meetings at headquarters? He could not remember when, since today it seemed so natural.

"What I would advise here, if I were asked to advise – and as I said, that's far from being the case – is to apply sound and just discretion. Let us remember an important legal principle under Israeli law, the 'Buzaglo Test': one law for a respectable citizen and the same law for Buzaglo. Put another way, if a poor Mizrahi Jew like Buzaglo has rights, a billionaire friend of the Prime Minister shares those same rights."

"I don't have to tell you about Uncle Saul's staggering contribution to the nation, to the economy and to Tzahal in particular," said the office's political advisor, who sat at one corner of the table.

"It would be cynical, verging on a hypocrisy that contradicts the values of our country and would certainly not hold up to legal scrutiny, to discriminate against Herr Saul Wenger on the basis of his political opinions, which are nothing if not enthusiastic towards Zionism and the State of Israel," the legal advisor concluded. "I thank you for listening, and hope my words were understood in the spirit in which they were intended."

Was there some other way to understand his words? The Chief of Intelligence was being asked, in effect, to comply with the office's demands, even if it meant closing his eyes, covering his ears, and perhaps holding his nose.

The lawyer got up to leave without waiting for a response. Rotelmann did not react. He was immersed in the messages on his secure mobile, typing away with growing irritation. It was impossible not to think about the drama being played out in Paris. The Military Secretary badly wanted to be updated, but he could not think of a way to pose the question elegantly in such a broad forum.

The Tzahal spokesperson sat quietly and seemed to be waiting for something. And indeed, the door opened once again, and the Prime Minister entered the room. How convenient, the Military Secretary wrote in his notebook, how convenient – officially, he had not witnessed any discussion regarding the renowned benefactor's visit. "Hello, everyone, don't get up," the Prime Minister said briefly, and grabbed the chair that had just become available at the head of the table. "You've worked out everything without me and I can leave, yes?"

Affected chortles rose from all around the table. The Chief of Staff cleared his throat. "We've built an excellent itinerary with the help of the Tzahal spokesperson and the rest of the participants here, Mr Prime Minister. We have only a few technical details to finalise tomorrow, but it's clear that it's going to be a very successful visit."

"Excellent, excellent," the Prime Minister said and changed the subject, as if Saul Wenger's visit was not his top priority. "And what about this affair in Paris, will that have a successful ending too?"

His gaze travelled from one participant to the next, until it came to the Military Secretary.

"Our best men are working on it, Prime Minister. God willing, it will end successfully, absolutely."

The political advisor intervened with an amused tone. "And if God is not willing?"

"Then in that eventuality I don't know," the Military Secretary said with a serious expression. "You can't achieve any success if God does not will it."

Aluf Rotelmann looked up from his telephone screen and, facing the Prime Minister, replied, "We're confident we'll wrap up this matter tonight."

The Prime Minister nodded, giving the impression of someone trying to think of a joke to lighten the mood. Failing to pinpoint one, he got up and took leave of the participants with a round of handshakes.

It was 9.40 p.m., Monday, April 16.

Chapter 66

It's one of the best-known experiments in psychology.

The premise is simple: people are invited to watch a video of students playing basketball, and are asked to count the number of passes made by the players in white shirts. About halfway through the recording, which lasts less than a minute, a gorilla enters the court (or rather, a student in a gorilla costume), stands in the middle of the screen, faces the camera and thumps its chest before departing the frame.

Supposedly impossible to miss. But in the original experiment, more than half the participants did not notice the gorilla because they were focused solely on their counting. When they were shown the video a second time and the gorilla was pointed out to them, they found their omission hard to believe, and some even accused the researchers of switching the videos. Abadi was familiar with the experiment, which had come to be known as "the Invisible Gorilla" and he had participated in a replication of the experiment in his intelligence officers' training course. Nevertheless, here in the lobby of Le Grand Hôtel, he had almost missed the gorilla.

The premise here was simple as well: the lobby was huge, absolutely enormous. Abadi ignored the reproving stares of those around him as he ran across the width of the ground floor to reception; the two policemen charged with accompanying him struggled to keep up. He had identified the hotel security men at their posts around the lobby, and in larger numbers than he would have expected: three in uniform at the entrance, a fourth near the service lift and a fifth by the lift for the disabled. Two security men stood inside the lift area to the left, their plain clothes doing little to disguise them. The main entrance doors and lift access points were beyond the sight line of the staff on reception, which probably explained the whole excessive security set-up, he thought.

With a firmer grasp of the surroundings he understood their particular security challenges: studded with entrances and exits, the lobby of Le Grand Hôtel was in effect a lavish hub, its opulent concourses connecting the place de l'Opéra, rue Auber, rue Scribe and boulevard des Capucines. A separate entrance from the street led to the hotel restaurant, its famed name displayed on a half-concealed sign, "Café de la Paix". And as he reached reception, he noticed yet another entrance, revolving glass doors onto boulevard des Capucines.

A long line of guests stood before the reception desk, but at the sight of Abadi and his coterie of uniformed policemen, they dispersed. In haste, the duty manager ushered the men aside. Dreadful things went on in hotels, especially in the more luxurious ones; and the crucial thing was to keep the guests in a cloud of insouciance. Abadi met the manager's hauteur with impatience, and briefly considered tossing him back to his perch behind reception; instead he restrained himself and let the officers do the talking.

As he listened, he took note of all the lobby's competing sounds: the clinking scales of crystal from the restaurant; the printing of a credit card transaction slip; the clicking of high heels on cold tiles as a redhead in a dramatic evening gown glided by on her way to the cocktail bar. He listened as the duty manager explained that the head security officer had just gone up to the room of the guest in question, and they must wait for his return. Abadi absorbed the voices, his mind defragmenting the clatter. And the gorilla passed.

He heard it first. He heard the gorilla tapping.

Against the general commotion, a tack-tack-tack-tack-tack. A tapping, but a different kind of tapping from the heels, more cumbersome, heavier, more erratic. Abadi identified the sound a split second before his eyes followed the noise to its source: a heavy suitcase rolling down the marble staircase, tack-tack-tack-tack-tack, wheels rolling then slamming against each polished step.

Abadi always carried his suitcase like a man, or at least like a man with a sense of tradition. There was something undignified about the sound of a rolling suitcase, certainly on a city street, but more particularly in a hotel lobby. A person rolling a suitcase draws attention to the fact of his arrival, he's a newcomer at the threshold of comfort. Or worse: he's just leaving it, abandoning the gardens of delight and returning to the humdrum of life.

Abadi's gaze shifted from the suitcase to its owner, a young man, thin and meticulously dressed, and there seemed to be no reason for him to roll his case down the stairs instead of using one of the lifts. And he was in a tremendous hurry. It was only when the man reached the bottom of the staircase and turned into the lobby, avoiding reception on his way to the exit, that Abadi's mind finally caught up with his senses, and he realised *this* man was Chinese. Chinese and wearing a black business suit. Chinese, in a black business suit, and someone who had – this suddenly became clear – quite a few friends here in the lobby, all young South East Asian men in black suits who looked like replicas of that morning's commando team.

The lobby was suddenly awash with them: one standing by the entrance to the restaurant, pretending to peruse the menu; another by the lift area, next to the front entrance; two more sitting in armchairs next to the bar, opposite each other, so their combined fields of vision encompassed the room. And a young Asian man in a black suit was now standing by the revolving doors opening onto boulevard des Capucines. Abadi could not tell what was more unusual about him, the fact that he stood against the wall, behind the security man, or that he was wearing dark sunglasses.

Profiling. Was there any act more typical of security officers around the world? Abadi swiftly calculated the odds. In a city visited by tens of millions of visitors each year, were six Chinese tourists in a single hotel lobby so out of the ordinary? And during a week in which Paris was hosting a large, international tech convention, was it so strange that these six should be businessmen in black suits? Abadi heard the policemen behind him asking for the room number, and he heard the manager's response: "5508, but let's just wait for him a little longer, the security officer will probably be back in a minute to update us." Abadi heard this but his mind was now totally immersed in the rhythm of the scene.

And no bad thing, because suddenly the rhythm broke. The two men seated in the lobby got up and walked towards the main exit to rue Scribe. The third man who had been reading the menu with such interest now marched through the restaurant; to an exit on rue Auber. The man standing by the lift area ran towards the main exit and disappeared from Abadi's sight, while the fifth man, in sunglasses, pushed the heavy revolving doors, shoving one wing so that he was inside the drum while the next opened for a person behind him. The gesture was clearly intended for his friend with the suitcase, passing now, rapidly, behind the uniformed officers and in front of Abadi, who needed, swiftly, to make a decision.

The gorilla experiment proves the limitations of memory and the illusion of eyewitness testimony, but it also reveals the extreme way in which human intuition corrects itself. From the moment the subjects' attention was drawn to the existence of the gorilla they developed an obsession with the ape, and in subsequent viewings focused on it alone. Abadi's gaze wandered back intuitively, almost involuntarily, from the young man who passed him to the suitcase which had stirred his thoughts in the first place. Blackish and heavy to the point of bursting at the seams, it was rather tatty compared to the streamlined elegance of the person rolling it. And then Abadi noticed the side handle. Wound around it, a white barcode sticker indicated a flight number with which he was very familiar: LY 319.

"STOP!"

Had he uttered the command himself before he lunged, or had the French police officers shouted it when they turned and saw him tackle a seemingly innocent hotel guest? It didn't matter because as soon as the young man looked back and saw Abadi, he dropped the suitcase and made towards his friend, who pushed through the revolving doors and disappeared into the boulevard.

The doors continued to turn, opening another wing into the lobby, but Abadi reached it a second too late. Protected by the glass partition, the man smiled back and made one final shove towards freedom.

Instinctively, Abadi reached up towards the control panel located in the door beam above his head and pulled the emergency brake with all his strength. The door stopped, and the screech of its brake cut through the lobby, bringing everyone in it to a halt. The officers grabbed Abadi abruptly from behind, restraining their visitor before he committed yet another faux-pas that would require paperwork, but his quarry had been trapped, and was flailing only centimetres from the street outside.

"That's the Israeli's suitcase," Abadi managed to say, surprised by his own coherence, struggling to wrest himself free of his chaperones. "It has the El Al flight sticker on it. Look!" Apprised of their mistake, the officers loosened their grip while the Chinese man continued to plead for help to his friends outside.

A second later, the glass shattered. A torrent of blood covered the door and the suspect slowly collapsed in front of their eyes. "On the ground!" Abadi shouted in French to those in the vicinity. "Down on the ground, now!" And the lobby obliged, including the accompanying officers.

He estimated he had fewer than two minutes before the hotel was swarming with the type of police presence that would be a great deal more rigorous than his two chaperones. "The guy was shot from outside with a silencer," he whispered to the sergeant. "Wait for back-up," he added, and started crawling towards the lifts.

"Where are you going, Colonel?" the officer hissed from under his arm as he lay on the floor. "To see what's waiting for me in room 5508," he said.

Chapter 67

Oriana hovered above Paris. She knew it was Paris because she could see the Eiffel Tower below, and Abadi waving to her. She landed softly beside him, like Tinker Bell. She wore a short, peach-coloured dress but she was not cold; it was a beautiful day with as blue a sky as only a dream might conjure. She asked Abadi if they weren't supposed to be in uniform. Abadi said no. He was wearing a three-piece suit but he had fins on his feet; he told her they were going to be diving into the Seine to find Rav Turai Yerminski's body, and that she was dressed perfectly for the mission.

Many people stood around them eating pineapple pizza: women in crinoline dresses and a firefighter's marching band and Chinese men in black business suits prowling behind them. Abadi held Oriana's hand and led her along the river, rushing ahead while everyone else walked behind them, the marching band playing "La Marseillaise". They turned onto the bridge, and when they reached the middle, the weather suddenly changed, the sky turned grey with many black clouds, and the band stopped playing.

The Chinese group followed them onto the bridge, but when she turned back to look at them they had disappeared, and in their place stood Zorro. He was wearing a Tzahal uniform with a black Zorro mask, and he was also riding Zorro's black horse and whipping the marching band players with a long black whip. The horse ran amok and in the mayhem Oriana somehow got separated from Abadi. She cried out to him, "Abadi, Abadi," and tried asking him what to do and where to go but it was too complicated and she could not understand him and then he was swallowed into the crowd.

Now she was shivering in the cold in the middle of the bridge and Zorro tried pushing her over the parapet into the water, so she climbed onto the rail by herself and tried not to look down. She slipped and grabbed the steel beam at the bottom of the bridge; her strength was steadily dwindling and she thought that now was the time to wake up and for the dream to end, but she did not wake up, she could hear Tomer saying, "I'm not waking her up," and Boris saying, "I'm certainly not waking her up," and Alma saying, "If Rachel was here she would have woken her up already," and then she fell into the Seine, and only at the very last moment, because her body had collided with the water, did she wake up with a start and look around her.

"We didn't want to wake you," Tomer said. "You fell asleep, Commander," Alma said. Only Boris was cool-headed and direct. "We woke you up because there was a call from the office. You need to go see the commander a.s.a.p."

"Which commander?" Oriana asked in confusion. She did not understand how Abadi already had an office.

"The Unit 8200 commander," Alma said softly. "They called from the office of the head of 8200."

That was more likely. Oriana stood up and stretched.

"How long was I asleep?" she said.

"A few minutes," Tomer said.

"An hour and a half," Boris said.

"And how much pizza did I eat?" she asked, staring at the empty box on her desk.

"Barely one slice," Alma said, and Boris said, "Three slices, Commander."

Oriana picked up her beret and left. It was already dark outside and the jungle of antennae glowed in all its splendour, as beautiful as a small sun. She covered the distance to the command building in a sprint, mostly because she was cold in her thin army shirt, but perhaps also to compensate for the pizza she had eaten. She picked up her pace the closer she got, and when she leaped from the dark trail into the square in front of the command building, the rookie on duty shot up and quickly saluted, knocking over his weapon which was perched against his chair.

Oriana did not feel the need to reprimand him and returned his salute. She pushed open the heavy doors, and in front of her, engraved on the wall above the lift in golden letters, appeared the biblical motto of Unit 8200: "But if the watchman see the sword come, and blow not the trumpet, and the people be not warned; if the sword come, and take any person from among them – he is taken away in his iniquity; but his blood will I require at the watchman's hand."

But what if the watchman does not realise that what he's seeing is a sword? Oriana thought. And what if the watchman blows the trumpet and is summoned to the Shabak for questioning because he was interrupting an afternoon nap? What if it wasn't clear who posed a greater danger, the sword or the watchman? Then what, whose blood should be required in that case? She pressed the lift button, then changed her mind and started up the stairs.

Chapter 68

Four thousand kilometres away, Abadi ran through the endless corridors of Le Grand Hôtel. In such an urban warfare setting, he was supposed to advance slowly and methodically, from one corner to the next, until he reached Yerminski's room, relying on his colleagues' covering fire before moving into a new position. But he was unarmed and did not have any colleagues, so he simply ran all the way to room 5508.

The door was closed, and a "Do Not Disturb" sign hung from the doorknob. Abadi had every intention of disturbing. He took out the Navran and directed it at the room. The radar's sensors detected, pressed against the opposite side of the door, a large object, registering the temperature given off by a human body.

Not good.

Ear-splitting police sirens blared outside. If that was Rav Turai Vladislav Yerminski's body on the other side of the door, Abadi preferred to examine it before the French police raided the place. The hotel door lock system used an encrypted key card. The Navran had no trouble deciphering the series of characters, a 32-bit key. The lock system made a cheerful sound and the door opened.

Had there been an earthquake, the room might have been in a state of less disarray than its current one. Signs of a struggle were visible in every corner of the ransacked room. The bed was a mess and the mattress torn up. The T.V. was shattered, along with the vase and the fruit bowl, and the drawers wrenched from the dresser. The minibar was wide open, its contents scattered across the rug. Some of the bottles were broken, and the liquid had left a dark, wet line along the carpet, which merged in the middle with the blood that oozed out of the body leaning against the door.

It was the body of an approximately sixty-year-old man, wearing a blazer similar to those worn by the security men he had seen in the lobby, the hotel logo embroidered on the upper pocket. Georges Lucas will not be giving tips to the local police station anymore. Abadi checked for vital signs and was not surprised when he did not find any, seeing that the man in charge of security at Le Grand Hôtel had been shot point-blank between the eyes with an automatic weapon. His hand still clutched the master key card that had allowed him to enter the room.

Abadi assumed the shooter had waited inside, then pulled the trigger after making sure it was not the Israeli. But where was the Israeli? If the Chinese had taken him from the room, why stay in the hotel? Their hasty retreat made it rather clear they had not planned on assassinating the security manager. And if they did not have Rav Turai Yerminski, and they were waiting in the room in the hope of capturing him, then who had him?

From the corridor he heard the sound of running footsteps and orders in French. The officers were presumably advancing from corner to corner as in the manual, which gave Abadi about thirty seconds. Scanning the room, he came across only more destruction. Yermi was not hiding under the bed, and there were no signs that he had even been there at all. The footsteps in the hallway were getting closer.

"*Vite, une ambulance!*" Abadi yelled in the direction of the hallway. An ambulance would not be much use, but neither would shooting at someone who had just yelled for an ambulance. Four men in black uniforms carrying submachine guns entered the room. Behind them, and affecting insouciance, Commissaire Léger provided the rearguard. A swift professional glance took in the body, the name tag, and the blood on Abadi's shirt.

"Whatever you're thinking, Commissaire, I arrived too late to save him," Abadi said without looking up. "But we can still save Vladislav Yerminski. He's our key." Without turning his head, Abadi waved his arm behind him in the direction of the room. "Judging from this, I think we're close."

"I don't hold out much hope for our chances," Léger said, stepping aside for the forensic technicians. He recognised the faces of his antagonists from the previous round at the airport, and nodded with exaggerated deference as they passed. "Tell me, what do you think they were looking for?" he said.

"The truth is that I don't know, Commissaire."

"The truth is that you maybe don't know but you do have your suspicions, Colonel. Would you mind sharing them? Oh and anything else you may have found in this mess. Please excuse my men while they perform a quick search, just to be sure . . . My apologies."

Two policemen reached for Abadi's pockets, their arms under his own. "I haven't found anything," he said, his patience now gone, "and I doubt if the Chinese kidnapped Yerminski and hung around to perform this search," he said. "We saw the commando unit bolting from the hotel. They had Yerminski's suitcase, but they didn't have Yerminski."

Léger watched Abadi shrug the officers away and heard the snap of silk as he straightened his jacket. He opted for reconciliation.

"We have a very neat crime scene here, it's a space we know well, unlike at Charles de Gaulle There is a lot of physical evidence, and there are cameras," he said, adding as much for himself as for Abadi, "I'd like to see the minister's spokesmen stick to their claim that this is a drugs deal now! We have two more dead, and another Israeli kidnapped in a military-style operation, complete with guns, silencers and a sniper rifle."

"I'm glad you're happy, Commissaire," Abadi said, but he himself had not been mollified. "Since Yerminski is not suspected of any crime in France, the Israeli security services would like to take official possession of his suitcase."

"Corporal Yerminski's suitcase will remain in our custody, Colonel." The older man smiled as he spoke, his eyes fixed on Abadi's. I might have tried the same, he thought. More finesse, perhaps. But the same.

"Yes, it contained some very interesting hacking equipment, and of course you would know more than me about such things, but I'm told it's all quite standard and is most unlikely to be the reason for the kind of mayhem we see here."

Léger looked around, drawing the intelligence officer's gaze, along with his own, to the scene of destruction. "Oh, and it contained some clothes, too, so we'll find you a clean shirt. It seems that both you and young Vladislav are close in height and size."

Abadi complied. He undid the buttons on his bloodstained shirt and took it off as Léger left the room. Before long, the commissaire returned with Yerminski's suitcase from which he pulled a navy blue shirt with bright contrasting trim. He offered it to Abadi with care, and in complete silence, as if in expiation.

Chapter 69

The advisors sat in the chambers of the Prime Minister's Office and waited. Two were on the sofa, two more waited in chairs by the desk, the Prime Minister's Chief of Staff waited in the guest armchair, and only the Military Secretary waited standing up. They did not know how long they were supposed to wait, since none of them was sure the Prime Minister would show up at the late debriefing meeting he himself had summoned.

The ringing of a telephone cut through the silent vigil.

There were four telephones on the Prime Minister's desk. The white phone, a Tadiran Coral D.K.T.-2320, was connected to the secure switchboard and was for direct calls from the Minister of Defence and senior Tzahal personnel. Next to it was a black telephone, a Nortel M.3904, which was connected to the regular switchboard in the Prime Minister's Office and was for internal office calls and transferring screened external calls. The grey phone, a Telrad 79-100-0000, was for the Prime Minister's private calls. And next to it stood the red telephone.

The red phone was made in Taiwan, a Uniphone U.D.-F1016. It had been purchased a year ago in Office Depot by the Prime Minister's communications advisor, who was next to the Military Secretary on the sofa. The advisor had summoned a photographer from the Government Press Office to record a meeting presided over by the Prime Minister on the eve of Operation Cast Lead, and had wanted a red phone to appear in the photograph, thinking it would contribute to the deterrent effect.

But when the engineering department was asked urgently to install the red phone in the office, it turned out it did not comply with the switchboard's technical standards. The advisor left the red telephone unconnected on the Prime Minister's desk, and so it appeared in the photograph published in every newspaper, right between the Prime Minister and his Chief of Staff, a red telephone imbued with meaning but without a cable. And it had been standing there ever since, next to the other telephones.

The ringing stopped, then immediately started again. The shout of the office's night secretary was heard through the door. "Avraham, it's for you guys, pick up! The white one."

Avraham, the Chief of Staff, approached the white phone. "It's for you," he said to the Military Secretary, who glowered at him.

The Chief Military Censor was on the line. She had been given an odd instruction by the Prime Minister's office, via the Chief of Staff, to keep an eye out for and suppress impending news of the killing of a Chinese tourist in Paris. The censor asked what she was supposed to do with such an order. The Military Secretary considered admitting that he had no idea, but said he would enquire and get back to her.

"Did any of you ask to censor news about the killing of a Chinese tourist in Paris?" he asked no-one in particular, but glancing suspiciously at the communications advisor. To his surprise, the political advisor raised his hand.

"That's what this meeting is about," he said. "I didn't want anything published before we made a decision about what we're going to do." The Military Secretary wanted to ask what business was it of his, but instead he explained to him, with elaborate patience, that military censorship could in no way block a foreign news item that had been appearing on every website around the world over the last few minutes.

"Then maybe they should make clear that any item referring to the involvement of an Israeli in the killing has to go through our censorship."

"We'd only be raising the editors' suspicion about Israeli

involvement in the story, which for the time being has no connection to this morning's kidnapping story," the Military Secretary said. "It's running now in the foreign news as a brief item. If the Military Censor sends them such a message, every editor will immediately look for an Israeli connection. This isn't a good time of the day to raise this kind of ruckus. The T.V. channels are getting ready for the evening news editions and the papers haven't sent tomorrow's front page to press yet. We have to maintain media silence for at least another hour, and then everyone will be off to bed anyway."

The political advisor shrugged. "Whatever you think," he said with ill-disguised contempt. Reaching for the white phone again, the Military Secretary called the Chief Censor and explained it was a misunderstanding, and that she could ignore the instruction. There seemed to have been a blunder when the original message was sent.

Deep down he knew that was not true. A blunder described a deviation from expected behaviour, whereas everything that had taken place in the Prime Minister's Office was consistent with its normative behaviour. What the Prime Minister's men thought had nothing to do with what they said. What they said had nothing to do with what they did.

"All in all, we accomplished our goal," the political advisor said. "We've made it clear to the armed forces that we're on top of this thing, that we're running it, and that they can't make decisions without us surprising them." Everyone nodded.

Chapter 70

The head of Unit 8200 was not in his chambers. Oriana's friend the bureau chief was the only one waiting for her in the office, and for some reason she was in civilian clothes. Was the dress from Zara? Banana Republic? Topshop? Oriana, who would have given a lot for a shower and a change of clothing, lay on the sofa and stared at her with open envy.

"How do you get authorisation for civvies here? On the second flight of stairs I realised I've been sweating in this stinking uniform since this morning's meeting. Can I have the uniform exemption they gave you, like, just for tonight?"

"Can I have the body they gave you, like, just for tonight?" the bureau chief said. "Trust me, if I looked like you, I wouldn't mind being in uniform 24/7."

They had met at an advanced training course for intelligence officers and been friends ever since. It was a cautious, somewhat shallow friendship, the kind with a potential that would never be fulfilled. Oriana had not forgotten that her friend from the office failed to give her a heads up that a new commander was about to be assigned to Special Section.

"I'm sorry I could not tell you about Abadi," the bureau chief said, as if reading her thoughts.

"Nonsense, don't worry about it," Oriana said.

"I guess I was afraid you'd file a complaint, like you threatened to do to Oren this morning."

Oriana was not sure her friend was joking. "What, you've already heard about that?"

"There isn't an office in the Intelligence Corps that hasn't been buzzing with the story," the bureau chief said. "When the officers returned to their departments from that meeting it was all they could talk about."

"It's a shame they didn't talk about how Aluf Rotelmann has become tired of the autonomous behaviour of 8200."

"Who even cares about him?" the bureau chief said. This time, Oriana was sure she was not joking. "The unit commander certainly doesn't."

"Where is he?" Oriana asked. "I was told to report a.s.a.p."

"He's landing at Ben Gurion in two hours, that's why I'm in civvies, I'm picking him up. But here, you have a love letter from him. Three letters, actually, which is more than I got from him today." She handed her three envelopes, each bearing a Tzahal sticker with a barcode, "For Segen Oriana Talmor, Top Secret – To Recipient Only".

The first envelope contained a copy of a Tzahal temporary change of station order. Twelve soldiers from the criminal investigation division of the Military Police were to report at 23:30 to the 8200 headquarters for temporary placement in Special Section. Her name appeared on the order as their new commander.

"What am I supposed to do with twelve military policemen?" Oriana asked.

"I've been working on that order for the past two hours," the bureau chief said. "Don't tell me it was a waste of time. I have the criminal investigation division's authorisation – you wouldn't believe the logistics involved. Every administrative department was already closed and we had to involve the Vice Chief of Defence Staff."

"I'm sick of having only the Vice Chief of Defence Staff intervening on my behalf," Oriana said. "It's so humiliating. Why can't I get backing straight from the Chief of Defence Staff?"

"Maybe Tzahal's Chief of Defence Staff doesn't want to be involved in these internal wars. So he's putting the raid on his deputy."

"What raid?"

"Open the next envelope."

The second envelope contained a unit operation order, in which the head of 8200 defined her as the person in charge of Operation Long Night, a surprise inspection of southern base of Unit 8200 which included the gathering of every document related to Rav Turai Vladislav Yerminski and the seizing of any evidence that could help locate him in the French capital. The order had a complicated line code: 23:55APR16F8200HSPS01:00APR17NHSCCSBNIC001.

Oriana rapidly deciphered the figures. The order would be effective at 23:55, turn into an open investigation, and copies of the order would be sent to the head of southern command, the commander of the southern base, and the Chief Network Intelligence Officer. The time of the raid was set for 01:00. The head of 8200 assigned the H.S.P. – the head of Special Section – as commander of the operation.

"Will Aluf Mishne Abadi be back by one in the morning to command the raid?"

"How could he be back? He has to stay in Paris, it's a huge mess over there."

"But the operation commander is specified here as the head of Special Section."

"That's why the time of the order is five minutes to midnight, dummy. How did you ever get to be outstanding cadet of the course? Everything in that order is valid until 23:55, meaning exactly five minutes before you stop being the head of Special Section. You're the one who's raiding the southern base, not Abadi."

Oriana looked again at the line code. 23:55APR16F8200HSPS 01:00APR17NHSCCSBNIC001. Indeed, there was no room for error: today, April 16 at 23:55, the head of 8200 would appoint the head of Special Section to command the inspection raid on April 17 at 01:00, an hour and five minutes after the order came into effect.

Like most officers at the 8200 headquarters, Oriana had never been to the southern base, and certainly did not have the necessary experience to search for something that someone would want to hide there. It was possible that the investigation was too urgent to postpone the raid until Abadi returned; it was also possible that the failure of the investigation was so predictable that they preferred to pin it on a junior officer.

"How am I supposed to get there, with my Fiat 500? All those military police are going to get there with their cars?"

"Open the third envelope."

Chapter 71

Subsequently, when Commissaire Léger was invited to lecture at the École Nationale Supérieure de Police about the most dramatic night the major crimes division had known under his watch, he would make sure to leave out these next two critical hours. The cadets would look at him with sparkling eyes, yearning to hear the secrets of his success. Capitalising on a surplus of slides and the general excitement his presence evoked, it would not be difficult to conceal this link in the chain of events.

He would say, for instance: "At this stage, 21:00 French time, we had a total of five bodies, one Israeli, one French and three Chinese. You must remember that the other Israeli, Vladislav Yerminski, was still defined as a missing person and we had no way of knowing at that point whether he was dead or alive. We certainly did not know that we would see many more victims, and that the event would eventually earn the macabre name by which it's known today, 'The Night of a Dozen Bodies'. But what we did know by then was enough for me to achieve a major breakthrough at exactly midnight, with help, of course, from our Israeli colleague, Colonel Zeev Abadi.

"The coveted breakthrough might seem to you, in hindsight, logical and predictable. But you mustn't forget that at 22:00 we were confronted with a new murder scene, in the low-rises of "the Woods" on the outskirts of Paris. It would have been only natural for us to be thrown off by the perpetrators, and fail to connect our case with the discovery of the bodies of two drug dealers. And yet, despite all the seemingly unrelated crime scenes throughout this entire affair, we caught the misdirection, and by midnight we knew who we were really after."

Even after he became more confident, presenting his full version at the Command Course for the sixth or seventh time, the commissaire was honest, straight and gave credit where it was due. "In theory, the new information that reached the investigators at Le Grand Hôtel should have thrown us off. And indeed, it threw me off. I was sitting in the security room at Le Grand Hôtel when I got the detailed reports from the new crime scene near Belleville. It all seemed obvious, and I put two and two together. That was a mistake, but I did not realise that. I remember that, throughout those two critical hours, Colonel Abadi completely ignored the reports arriving from the scene, insisting on reviewing the hotel footage over and over again, typing away on his strange telephone, turning his back on our rampage as if it had nothing to do with the case."

When he delivered his presentation in the early years, this would be the point when Léger delivered his punchline. But with time, as he gained experience, he would develop the technique of a seasoned lecturer, waiting for the raised hand of one of the alert police cadets, who would ask if the commissaire had found an explanation for the Israeli's behaviour.

"Yes, indeed, young man, today I have an explanation for that," Léger would then reply in a booming voice before his audience. "Later on, I happened to watch a documentary series about Easter Island, famous around the world for the Moai statues scattered across its coast, those mysterious giant heads. The narrator asked why the statues were all positioned facing the island, with their backs to the ocean. And the answer was that the heads were looking at the inhabitants to alleviate their fears, and turned their backs to the dangers coming from the sea, since, according to their mythology, the gods do not have to see the evil spirits to know their intentions."

Léger would let the last sentence linger in the room for a while. He would sip from his water before stating what he considered obvious. "And that's how I realised, at exactly midnight, that Colonel Abadi was like a messenger from the gods who had come to save us from our mistakes. He looked away from the information we wanted to communicate to him because he did not need it, because at that point he had already worked out the identity of the forces facing us and the diabolical strategies they intended to pursue."

Chapter 72

Beyond the city limits, the night sky cleared. Oriana filled her lungs with the cold, sweet air, as if storing oxygen.

Abadi's instructions were to organise the convoy between the main car park at the Tzrifin base, from which the vehicles were to be gathered, and the Yad Mordechai intersection, from which the convoy would enter the Negev desert and the south district's command zone. Summoning everyone to the point of departure made the most sense, but Oriana did not know anyone there and the very thought of all the required permits exhausted her.

She scheduled the pick-up point in the middle, at the entrance to the naval base in Ashdod, where she had cracked one of her first cases, a string of thefts from shipping containers. She was not superstitious, but for such a crazy mission she preferred a place in which fortune had once smiled upon her. She was not anticipating many smiles at the southern base when they burst in.

She stood on the small hill, staring at the surprisingly modernist lighthouse, painted in cheerful red and white checkers. The beam it projected every six seconds imbued it with a childish and soothing charm, casting golden hues on the many boats that waited to be unloaded at the gates of the port, all laden with the goods and dreams of other people.

She heard the jeep door slam behind her and Rachel's heavy footsteps. Her favourite soldier reached the hilltop short of breath and sat at her feet, gazing out in the direction of the sea like her commander.

"I'm sorry I woke you up," Oriana said. She wasn't really sorry. In fact, from the moment she opened that third envelope the unit commander had left her, her first thought was to send a car to Rachel's house and bring her back to the base, because Oriana was not sure she would manage the preparations without her.

The envelope contained permits for military equipment. The first form instructed Segen Talmor to report immediately to the unit's technology centre "to receive special personal equipment for operative purposes". The detail field contained one line: "Navran 012".

Rachel was still sleepy when she arrived at the section, but the form woke her up. "You're going to get a Navran, Commander? That's the hottest accessory in Tzahal, only thirty people have it. It's like getting a Birkin bag, or a modified Kalashnikov. No-one knows how to get one."

"Then why did I?"

"I guess Abadi needs to be with you during this raid he organised for us." Thanks to the early wake-up call, signs of Rachel's affection towards her new commander had disappeared from her voice.

"How is he going to be with me during the raid?"

"That's what this device does, Commander. You initiate a conversation and you'll be in video contact the whole time. You install the Navran on your shoulder and he can see and hear everything you see and hear. It's like Peter Pan's Tinker Bell. When you want him to, he appears on your shoulder, and it also works the other way around."

"I don't need anyone on my shoulder," Oriana said.

"Maybe he needs you on his?" Rachel said.

Oriana instinctively shrugged. Rachel removed two more forms from the envelope. The first ordered Segen Talmor to report immediately to the main garage to receive "vehicles for the operation as determined by the competent authority". The second form instructed her to report to the duty officer at the centre for security information in order to receive an Eagle 24 drone. "The officer is requested to bring form no. 1004 with her", someone had pencilled in. Oriana could not wrap her head around reporting simultaneously to three different places, but Rachel reassured her.

"You get the Navran from technology, and I'll take care of the rest, Commander," she said; and so it was.

Now she lay at Oriana's feet and tried to nap by the sea. A deceptive tranquillity engulfed them both.

"Why here?" Rachel asked.

"I cracked my first case here. I had a bogus container parked down there, you can see the spot by the blue crane. I waited for the thieves to exit the naval base in their Mack truck to steal the cargo. And after forty-eight hours they showed – four turais and the samal who drove. They broke the secured seal by shooting at it with their M.-16s . . . The samal would be able to explain the missing ammo the next day by saying he'd taken the truck to the night shooting range."

"But how could you arrest them from here? They must have seen you when you ran down."

"I wasn't up here, Rachel. I was inside the container. And they got one hell of a shock."

Rachel looked at her commander, bewildered.

"When are they getting here?" Oriana said.

"They'll be here in thirty minutes," Rachel mumbled.

"All of them?"

"Our soldiers will arrive first; they finished signing out their weapons and jeeps at the Ashdod intersection. Boris will arrive last with the listening vehicle, since he's the only one with the appropriate licence. The military police will arrive with their sirens on in half an hour. Alma drove straight to the air intelligence at Beersheba and will work on the tapes from the drone. She and Boris are co-ordinated."

"How many people is that altogether?"

"Including the jeep they gave you, you're leading a convoy of forty-five people." Oriana fell silent. "I'm sorry to say this, Commander, but it's insane."

"It's completely insane," Oriana agreed, "but these are Abadi's instructions."

"What does he want you to do with all these people?"

"I don't know. He was supposed to explain that by now, but he isn't on the Navran and he isn't answering my calls."

"Where could he be, the motherfucker?" Rachel said, directing her question at the sea.

Chapter 73

From above, place de l'Opéra looked like a birthday cake crawling with ants. People hurried into the métro or out of the métro or to dodge the métro-goers. Everyone was running in every direction. Those left standing were tourists trying to take perfectly angled photographs of avenue de l'Opéra while angry drivers drove around them blaring their horns. Abadi looked down from the balcony of Rav Turai Yerminski's hotel room while Léger yelled contradictory instructions to the two unfortunate officers dangling and twisting between heaven and earth.

The climbing rope was thin but proved strong enough. The buckles, loops, and draws were all professional, and even when Léger tugged on it to haul both his men back up onto the balcony, the rope remained steady and secure. That was not the problem.

The problem was that from the moment the two officers tried to re-enact Yerminski's abduction, one playing the presumed kidnapper and the other his Israeli victim, it set off a flurry of flashes from cameras and mobiles from the square below, and within fifteen seconds drivers were stopping to gawk at the spectacle and passersby were pointing up in wonder. Tourists, drivers, passengers emerging from the métro, employees in the office building opposite, opera-goers, hotel guests on adjacent balconies – everyone feasted their eyes on the re-enactment of the abduction, and it was not surprising that more than one person called the police.

"There's no way that's what happened," Abadi said to Léger while the latter was busy complimenting his men on their performance.

"A climbing rope is strong enough for a commando to descend with his victim on his back," Léger protested.

"Indeed. But even the best secret agent in the world could not kidnap someone that way without being noticed. The Opéra is one of the most photographed buildings in Paris. It's completely implausible."

Commissaire Léger gave Abadi a meaningful look.

"Don't look at me like that," Abadi said.

"I can't help it," Léger said. "This is the kind of situation you learn about in elementary school. In the morning a man disappears inside a lift and you tell me it can't be. Then in the evening you're the one who's saying that a man disappeared inside a locked hotel room, and I'm the one telling you it cannot be."

"In what elementary school do they teach about that?" Abadi said, genuinely curious.

"What's important here is the reversal of roles. Let me enjoy my little revenge and admit that even as your man Meidan was not swallowed by a closed lift but got out of it on a different floor, your man Yerminski did not disappear inside a closed room, but left it through the window."

"Commissaire, I'm inviting you to check with dispatch how many civilians have called the police over the last minute to report this re-enactment, authentic and professional as it might have been. I wager more than ten." The investigator standing next to the Commissaire nodded almost imperceptibly, pointing at his screen. "And I have no problem if you want to ask an officer to climb out of the window every hour throughout the day, not just during the evening rush hour," Abadi said. "There has to be another explanation."

"But there is no other explanation!" Léger was exasperated. "You watched the footage yourself, you saw the findings."

"When the only explanation to a problem makes no sense, it's a sign that an element is missing in the definition of the problem," Abadi said peaceably. "Anyway, that's what they teach at the elementary school I went to."

"Then let's go over the definition of the problem again," Léger said, sighing with the resignation of a parent who is tired of denying the whims of a particularly difficult child.

They walked the length of the hotel's marathon hallways. Room service trays lay on the floor outside the rooms, empty champagne bottles, shoes awaiting polishing, now and then an empty designer shopping bag – mute testament to the fact that the world would keep spinning even without Vladislav Yerminski. They took the lift down to the security room, which had been temporarily converted into Léger's headquarters. For people whose boss had just been shot on the job, the security staff functioned rather impressively. The morning shift manager was summoned as liaison, and at Léger's request presented the updated findings. Léger's technicians had already connected the giant screen on the wall, and one could not help but be reminded of the footage from the airport. Once again flickering images, once again an attempt to interpret what you see by what you cannot see. Sometimes Abadi missed the era before digital evidence, the time when the story relied on the human factor alone: the memory of the witness, the pathologist's report, the police officer's rigorous work, the investigator's experience and the inflated sense of self-confidence of all these combined.

"The software identified seven accomplices to the kidnapping, all with South East Asian features," the morning security officer said in a weary voice and started presenting the photographs on the screen. "They were seen on the external cameras gathering in the place de l'Opéra at 21:00, clearly pointing in the direction of the victim's room." The photographic layout had already been edited, as if for presentation in court. All that was missing was background music.

"According to the system, the abductee was in the room at the time. The six assailants entered the hotel via four different entrances. The cameras caught them positioned across the ground floor by the doors; three then went up to Yerminski's floor, two by lift, one using the stairs."

"Isn't the software supposed to report any unusual movements?" Abadi said.

"At this point it did not report any unusual movements on the cameras because they had done nothing unusual. They came into the hotel separately, and even if the whole group had walked in together through the same entrance, I doubt the software would have reported it. But a report *was* triggered when three of them arrived at his floor and stood in front of his room. They were seen knocking on his door for a whole minute. Then, at 21:13, the software reported abnormal activity in front of room 5508."

Every time someone entered the lens' field of view, it took the cameras between a second and a second and a half to focus, which turned the footage into a jumble of mysterious flashes and made things harder for the identification software. But the results were nevertheless conclusive, clear and irrefutable.

21:14 – three Chinese men are seen trying different cards until they manage to open the door. The "Do Not Disturb" sign on the handle is clearly visible.

21:18 – two Chinese men are seen leaving the room and walking towards the stairs. They take up positions across the lobby with the others.

21:20 – Georges Lucas, the hotel security officer, crosses the same hallway in the direction of the room.

21:21 – Lucas arrives at the room. He appears to take stock of the "Do Not Disturb" sign, but decides to knock on the door. He knocks, on and off, for thirty seconds.

21:23 – Lucas unlocks the door with his security key. He leaves the door open.

21:24 – the door is slammed shut from the inside.

21:27 – the third perpetrator comes out of the room with Vladislav Yerminski's suitcase. He pulls it down the hallway towards the stairs.

21:29 – dispersed across the lobby, the commandos initiate a retreat through the different exits, except for one who remains by the revolving door.

21:30 – Colonel Abadi notices the man with the suitcase.

"As you can see for yourself, they did not take him out of the room through the door. The suitcase has been examined. I told you that there were some interesting things inside it, from Israeli military equipment to the shirt you're now wearing, but trust me, it did not contain a body," Léger said triumphantly.

"It seems clear to me: the three overpower the Israeli, lower him from the balcony into the hands of their partners below, two return to the lobby and the third stays in the room to gather the Israeli's belongings in the suitcase. Then, following my instructions over the telephone, Lucas knocks on the door and the Chinese man still in the room shoots him the moment he enters. That's what happened, that's the only possibility."

"That's the only possibility if Yerminski was in the room," Abadi said.

"He was in the room the entire evening. The system knows when a guest leaves, that's what enables the hotel to know when to clean certain rooms and when not to, for instance."

"How does the system know? Are there cameras in the rooms? Sensors?"

"It can tell by the magnetic card. You can't turn on the electricity in the room without the guest inserting his magnetic card into the electronic wall slot. When you take the card out of the slot, the system registers that the guest is no longer in the room. According to the system, Yerminski was in his room during the entire kidnapping, the whole evening, in fact."

"What keeps him from leaving the room without removing the card?"

"You can't. When the door opens and the card is still in the slot, the lock sensors flicker to remind the guest to take the card."

"And what if the guest ignores it?"

"Why would he ignore it?" Léger said, drawing a blank in his own mind.

"Because right now he's being kidnapped so he isn't really thinking about whether he left the card in the room."

The morning shift manager sounded exhausted, but still maintained a polite tone. "It's impossible, because we've gone over every camera on this floor from the moment the Chinese entered the hotel, at 21:02. Yerminski was nowhere in sight. Had they taken him through the door, we would have seen them with him on one of the cameras. All they took from this room was the suitcase."

"What if they kidnapped him an hour earlier? Two hours earlier?"

"Then why would they come back, why break into the room again? Just so that you could prove that your theory is better?" Léger was angry.

"I don't know," Abadi said. "But it's the only possibility. Let's quickly look at just the camera in the hallway by the room. It will only take fifteen minutes, and then maybe we'll be calmer afterwards."

"I am perfectly calm." Léger articulated each word with care.

"That's a pity, Commissaire, because in our profession, success requires vigilance against any false sense of ease," Abadi said. He pressed the play button.

Chapter 74

Mme Abadi was watching the evening news on two screens. She watched the news from Israel each evening on the small T.V. set; on the big screen, their normal T.V., she watched the main French station, T.F.1, despite the fact that her favourite presenter, Patrick Poivre d'Arvor, had been replaced almost a decade ago.

She felt the need for two televisions after she gave up trying to discover through the French media what the Israelis were going through during the war in Gaza. She had seen at her neighbour's, her good friend Mme Zerbib, a cable box that picked up the news from Israel, and had asked her son for something similar as a birthday present. He installed the double screen that enabled her to switch from one screen to the other as she chose.

But tonight, with the two sources broadcasting at the same time, she found it hard to follow. While the French edition kept replaying the same images of a terrifying attack on a bridge in Paris, with the commentator somehow linking it to a kidnapping of an Israeli businessman that same morning, the Israeli channel focused on an event at the airport and security footage of an Israeli boy being led to his death, with the event on the bridge portrayed as a response to the Israeli angle of the abduction. A silver-haired commentator whose name Mme Abadi could not remember said in an authoritative tone that there were things he was not at liberty to reveal during the bulletin, but it had been conveyed to him by security sources that Israel could not afford to sit on its hands, a message intended for both the terrorists and the French.

"We have Chinese terrorists now?" she said to her husband. Her husband, who was dozing in his armchair, mumbled that she was talking nonsense and headed for the bedroom. Mme Abadi knew he was angry with himself about their son's visit, and thought it best to wait until tomorrow to raise the subject with him.

While her husband was in the bathroom, she pressed the remote and switched back to the French screen, where they had already moved on to another Chinese killing, this time at a hotel next to the Opéra. Mme Abadi remembered President de Gaulle's warning that "when China wakes up, it will shake the world", but at the time she did not suppose it would involve a series of murders in Paris. She missed de Gaulle, even if towards the end he was not as great a friend of the Jewish state as he had been at the beginning.

She reverted to the Israeli channel, but the young anchorwoman had moved on to the upcoming visit of a Swiss billionaire and the biggest donor of the Israeli Prime Minister, may God bless him and keep him safe. The image on the screen switched to the Prime Minister's wife. Mme Abadi did not care for her as much. The anchorwoman said that the government's legal counsel had decided she would not be prosecuted for some sort of expenditure in Monaco, and a lawyer in the studio explained to the anchorwoman that a witch-hunt was under way against the Prime Minister's wife.

Mme Abadi switched off both screens and began turning off all the lights in the apartment. As she was switching off the kitchen light she took a quick look through the window in the direction of the lake. Below, along the walkway, two Chinese dressed in suits were talking on their mobiles.

It was an odd sight, and an even stranger coincidence; the commune of Créteil may have been inhabited by immigrants from all cultural backgrounds, but it was not blessed with Chinese businessmen. Mme Abadi felt a shiver crawling up her spine and went to sit on the sofa, in the dark living room.

Notifying the police would be ridiculous, that much was clear. She called Mme Zerbib, who never slept though not even the faintest noise ever emerged from her apartment; in that respect she was the ideal neighbour. She picked up after less than two rings. "Good evening, Mme Abadi."

They called each other Mme Abadi and Mme Zerbib even though they had been friends for more than twenty years.

"Good evening, Mme Zerbib. I apologise for bothering you this late."

"You never bother me, Mme Abadi."

"And yet, it's a very un-Catholic hour."

They burst into laughter. It had been a running joke between them ever since Mme Zerbib first heard that French expression.

"I'm just a little worried, because I'm standing by the window and see two people looking at the building, two Chinese, and after today's attacks in Paris, it makes me uneasy."

"That's completely understandable," Mme Zerbib said, but Mme Abadi heard in her voice a certain tone of surprise.

She quickly withdrew. "No, it's truly nonsense, I'm so sorry I called you, it's been a long day. I'll go to bed now."

"Why don't you come over and sleep here?" Mme Zerbib suggested, always quick to take any chance to alleviate her own anxieties. "It might make you feel safer. After all, two Tunisian Jews in their prime, what could Chinese terrorists do to us?"

Mme Abadi laughed politely. In truth, the joke only increased her anxiety.

"Thank you, Mme Zerbib, but my husband's already gone to bed and I've never slept without him, so two Chinese aren't going to make me start now."

After lengthy parting words she dialled her son. She very rarely bothered him, but since he was in Paris, she felt she might as well. There was no answer, and after the fifth ring she reached his voicemail. She did not leave a message.

She went back to the kitchen to make herself some lemon verbena and chamomile tea. While the water was boiling she looked out of the window again. The men were no longer there.

Chapter 75

With its bright colours, its water-spraying creatures, its absurd rotation, the fountain was as twisted as the story behind its construction.

In 1978, the city of Paris commissioned five modern fountains. Only one of them was built. Opened in 1983, its official name was "*La fontaine Stravinsky*", but everyone called it "the Pompidou Centre fountain", or "the colourful fountain". The Swiss sculptor Jean Tinguely was known for his darker works – mostly made in black metal – and after winning the tender he imposed an unexpected condition for delivering the piece: that the city commission sculptures for the fountain from his wife, the artist Niki de Saint Phalle.

The change in the tender's terms entailed a number of adjustments, including disconnecting the fountain from the regular power grid and using very low-power electric motors to avoid electrocuting children. Providing the necessary power for twelve heavy statues to spin on their axes was an engineering challenge. But it was the right thing to do in terms of safety, and eventually everyone was pleased.

Everyone but Erlang Shen.

He exchanged his torn clothes for the green uniform of the city's sanitation workers and ditched his pushcart for a plumber's toolbag. At first, he refused to believe what he had read about the fountain; only after stepping into the water and checking it himself did he realise he would have to come up with a different solution.

The pool was large but not deep. In the bright light of the street lamps it was easy to see that the colourful animals were not screwed into their strange black bases, they were simply placed on top of them, with a low-power cable next to the bases to conduct the necessary power from the motor attached below.

The Firebird. The Elephant. The Mermaid. The Clown's Hat. The Frog. The Heart. The Fox. Death.

All the characters from "The Rite of Spring" spun past Erlang Shen and spat jets of water at him, ruining his meticulous plan.

With only twenty minutes left before the rendezvous the blonde had scheduled with her handler, Erlang Shen stepped out of the pool, picked up his bag and started walking towards the corner supermarket that was still open. He was hoping they had a toaster.

Chapter 76

The blonde was also on Abadi's mind. In fact she visited him three times, like the ghost of Hamlet's father.

First when she was documented entering the hotel with her hair gathered under a hood that hid her face. She was wearing black and nothing stood out about her appearance other than her height and giant shopping bag.

She appeared to him a second time when she was caught in the footage of the camera installed on the hotel convention floor, dressed in a red suit whose colour resembled the one she had been wearing in the El Al security officer's footage.

"*Merde*," Léger called out.

She looked different now, nothing like her appearance when she first entered the hotel. She was as glamorous as a shampoo model, her shining hair flowing over her shoulders, her endless legs marching across the fourth floor's wall-to-wall carpet as if she wanted to check the exact length of a property she had received by divine decree.

And finally a third time, in the hallway leading to Rav Turai Yerminski's room, blurring the camera's focus. Once the image had sharpened, the lens revealed a tall blonde in a short red uniform and matching heels taking out of her bag the ultimate fashion accessory: a long, golden pistol that Abadi instantly identified as the American model of the Desert Eagle, an Israeli semi-automatic. It was so beautiful that no Hollywood movie or computer game could be without it. With that gun in her hand, the blonde looked almost too perfect. She knocked on the door with the golden butt, and when the door opened the camera caught, for a split second, the profile of the poor victim as he saw the barrel in front of him. The blonde went in, closing the door behind her.

According to the camera system's internal clock, she remained in the room for forty-three seconds, not nearly enough time for a methodical search. Was that why the Chinese returned to the scene of the crime? To look for something Yerminski had left behind? He came out of the room first, his hands raised. The blonde must have said something to him, because he suddenly lowered his hands and started walking briskly towards the lifts. He was pale, wearing jeans and a sweater, no jacket. She came out with her weapon drawn, then switched hands and put the pistol in the bag, once again switching hands to keep the gun inside the bag while pointing at Yerminski's back, as if balancing a tray. It looked a bit strange, but not strange enough for the security guards in the lobby to detain her as she left.

While Léger's men barked conflicting orders into the radio and uploaded the kidnapper's blurry face onto the software, Abadi focused on Yerminski. He paced along, baffled but brisk. At such a moment, didn't survival instinct dictate a slow walk, the shuffling of feet, a staged fainting? Some kind of resistance, if only passive? Abadi could not but wonder what these young men were made of. That morning Yaniv Meidan had marched confidently to his death with an incredible level of stupidity, oblivious to the red flags waving above the head of the blonde who led him to the lifts. Fewer than five hours later Rav Turai Yerminski approached different lifts with a similar blindness.

"He took the bait hook, line, sinker, fisherman and island," Léger said.

"Maybe your men will find it easier to look for an island than a fish," Abadi said.

"Not so," Léger said. "I have no doubt we'll find him, only he won't be alive. If the Chinese meant to kill him this morning at the airport, they must certainly be in a hurry now, twelve hours behind schedule."

It was 11.30 p.m., Monday, April 16.

Chapter 77

In Melbourne, Australia, it was 7.30 a.m., but it was hard to tell that in the conference room. On the management floor of all the casino houses owned by the empire that Uncle Saul had founded, as on all the casino floors below it, there were no clocks on the walls, no windows facing out, and even the closed-circuit T.V. screens were set so that the electronic clocks would not appear on them.

Saul Wenger had not chosen the nickname "Uncle Saul", it had been given to him by the Israeli security guards on his first visit to Jerusalem. But he liked it, because it implied generosity, the wisdom of age, perhaps even a certain frisson of darkness. Until then, out of earshot, he had been called "*le Petit Suisse*", a diminutive if ever there was one. But "Uncle Saul" was not really Swiss, and although he was still skin and bone, and was short in height, he was certainly not small anymore, not with a net worth of twenty billion euros.

Other casino moguls might like to say they had been "raised in a poor but loving family". He couldn't say as much. According to his birth certificate, he had been born eighty-three years previously in the dispensary of a camp for displaced persons near Geneva. His father was described as "unknown", his mother, as "G. Wenger", a 23-year-old Alsatian refugee, who had died in labour.

Was she Jewish at all? Was he? The official papers couldn't say. When Saul was three, the Swiss Confederation expelled all foreign refugees, and he was added to a group of Jewish orphans cared for by an American philanthropic organisation. They travelled to Trieste and took one of the last boats to Shanghai, a divided territory where no visa was required. There, in the Restricted Sector for Stateless Refugees, he first learned to count.

By the age of ten, Saul could speak French, Chinese, Japanese and Italian. He could read and would forge papers for other refugees in exchange for food. All the children he knew were in the same horrendous state, near starvation, and none of them had ever known anything else.

This changed dramatically after Pearl Harbor. The U.S. aid workers who helped the refugees and managed the local school were expelled from China, and as they strove to help the children they had left behind, one of them alerted the Swiss consul to the incongruous presence of a Swiss-born child in the Japanese sector. Saul found himself separated from the rest, and within a week he was on board a luxury liner, escorted by the consul's wife, who took it upon herself to bring him back to the land of his birth, perhaps as an excuse to return to safety herself.

The official from the Ministry of the Interior was waiting for them at the border. He thanked the consul's wife for bringing "little Saul" home, caressed his head and explained that a place had been found for him at Le Rosey, a prestigious boarding school nearby. Saul kissed the consul's wife goodbye and was not very surprised to find himself, two hours later, interned in a forced labour camp.

As a result of his age, he was moved within a week to another camp, and then another. In all, he changed camps on seven occasions, until he was put in the care of a foster family on whose farm he laboured for long hours and without pay until the end of the war. So, no, he could not even say he was raised in a poor but loving family.

Could anyone understand this? Saul Wenger sat at the head of the table and looked at his executives, who always looked half asleep in the morning conference, as if 7 a.m. were not the perfect hour to start the day. He often toyed with the idea of firing them all and appointing interns, if only for one quarter, to see if his men were in fact making any contribution to the company's profits. His guess was that they were all dispensable.

He had learned a lot from his childhood years during the war and, most importantly, he had learned to pay attention to details. People were bored by them, and he knew how to take advantage of that: numbers, small print, delivery dates, exchange rates. He was, to this day, a manager of details, and he left it to God and statistics to look after the bigger picture.

For example, he did not himself know any of the hundreds of thousands of employees at his casinos, but could recite from memory each one's salary according to role and seniority. Not a single payroll decision was made without his written authorisation. Wenger believed, until it was proven otherwise, that penny-pinching in the expense department necessarily led to plenitude in the profit department. His employees used to say behind his back that he was willing to lose a million dollars to save a dime; but while he very often saved dimes, he never lost a million dollars.

They reached the third topic on the agenda, a carpet for the new lobby that connected the roulette rooms downstairs. The carpets in all Wenger casinos reflected the branding of the empire as tourist-friendly: illustrations of windmills in Holland, emblems of the monarchy in England, kangaroo prints in the Australian casino, and so on, in seventy-two casinos worldwide generating total profits of twenty million euros a day.

Unlike the floor coverings in most private homes or office buildings, the carpets in Saul's casinos were all loud, juxtaposing colours that clashed with asymmetrical compositions, objects that were definitely challenging to the eye. And indeed, the idea was for the gamblers to look at them as little as possible. Whenever a roulette player tried to take a break from the wheel, he would be met by blinding lights, noisy walls and disconcerting carpets. The difference between a plain blue carpet and a wacky red one could translate into millions of dollars a year. Saul Wenger was not one to underestimate the importance of a carpet.

"I vote for sample four," the C.F.O. said. He was an even bigger idiot than the others. There were eight carpet samples on the table, and Wenger did not even bother looking at number four. His executives pretended to be debating, as with every decision. He chose the loudest carpet, a blue geometric print with broken lines and asymmetric drawings of diagonal lightning bolts, sample two. His executives nodded enthusiastically, including the C.F.O.

The decisions regarding the casino in Australia were not important, it amounted to a mere 2 per cent of his revenue. He had no casinos in Switzerland, where gambling was illegal when he devised his strategy. And he left Las Vegas to the moguls cutting each other's throat there, the Adelsons, Packers, Wynns, all those born "into loving families".

The chief source of the empire's revenues in recent years had been Macau, and that was now under threat. Alas, the carpets in all his casinos there were always red, a lucky colour in South East Asian culture, so his attention to detail concerned itself with more complicated matters.

A beep came from the direction of the screen: the shift manager switched to camera 283, the one directed on the main roulette table. With one glance, Wenger took in the data displayed at the bottom of the screen: it was the fourteenth time in a row the ball had landed on black. Dozens of gamblers crowded next to the table, fighting to place their chips on what seemed to them a sure bet.

Saul had not studied statistics and did not need to: he understood this intuitively, that the wheel had no memory at all, and certainly no desire to split the odds fairly. And that was why he had no sympathy for the pathetic souls downstairs, the ones waiting for the roulette ball to make a "fair" decision and land on red after choosing black so many times.

There never has been justice in this world, and there never would be. And indeed, the ball rolled, rolled, hesitated and hesitated before finally landing on black for the fifteenth time. The only principle guiding the ball was that Uncle Saul had to make more money than all the players together.

They moved on to the last topic on the agenda, his visit to Israel.

Chapter 78

The flashes of the military police car beacons behind her painted red and blue the rear view mirror, the car windows and the surrounding desert. Stretching ahead there was nothing but asphalt, and her jeep swallowed the white road lines underneath it as she drove south. Oriana could have continued like this forever without getting tired, here, in the almost complete darkness of the Negev.

In the back seat, Rachel was sound asleep, wrapped in both their coats. Her lips were pressed against the metal bars of office on Oriana's windproof coat in what looked like an enactment of the *mezuzah* ritual, or perhaps an erotic signalling of hunger. They had not exchanged a word since leaving Ashdod. The silence was as frozen as the desert wind that somehow found its way in through the closed windows. Every now and then a hostile howl was heard in the distance.

On the dashboard, the tiny light of the Navran flickered. The voice came in several seconds before the image.

"This is Abadi."

"This is Segen Oriana Talmor, Commander of the Fourth Army. All I need is a few fighter jets and I'm good to go."

"I considered arranging for you guys to arrive in helicopters," she heard him say.

An image of Abadi on the Navran's screen accompanied the sound of his voice. Even though he was smiling, it did not look as though he was joking.

"It's O.K., I can settle for a convoy of twenty military vehicles, five military police motorcycles and one armoured personnel carrier with scary antennae."

"It has to have scary antennae. If it didn't, we wouldn't need it."

"But why *do* we need it?"

"It's all about branding," Abadi said. He was walking somewhere fancy, and the Navran's lens struggled to focus. "Let's say you arrived in your own little car, unaccompanied. What would happen then? The guard at the gate would detain you for an hour. Then the Chief Network Intelligence Officer, who had already mouthed off to you, would argue about you asking questions, which would take another hour. And then they would answer nothing, or if they did, they would hide things from you. But when you arrive at the gate with dozens of investigators and policemen, a whole convoy of cars, motorcycles and a listening armoured vehicle, they'll find it harder to dismiss you. And we haven't even mentioned the drone hovering above their heads throughout."

O.K. then, branding. Oriana was willing to be persuaded. "So I walk in and start scaring them?"

"They got the order ten minutes ago. They're probably thinking you'll arrive tomorrow morning, accompanied by two or three of your soldiers. If your location on the Navran is correct, you'll be there in less than fifteen minutes. Wait at the turn before the base until 01:00 hours, following the operation's order, organise the convoy as impressively as you can, and drive in as if you're about to break through the gate."

"And after I scare them, what do I do then? I don't even know what to look for. I'm not sure anyone there knows where Vladislav Yerminski is."

"You're looking for something strange. It may be something unexpected, it may be something that's missing, or it may just be something that looks out of place. What it is not is information about this soldier's whereabouts, because no-one knows where he is. He was kidnapped from his hotel from right under my nose."

"How?"

"I'm not sure yet. But it happened with the same honeytrap, the blonde in the red uniform."

"Didn't she throw away the red uniform in the chemical toilets in the terminal?"

"Yes. I guess she had more than one. This time she wasn't even accompanied by the Chinese. She settled for a gun to threaten him with until they'd left the hotel. She got him into a taxi and, according to my poor friend Commissaire Léger, they got out at Saint Lazare. It still isn't clear what they did there and whether they boarded a train."

"You have the kidnapping on video?"

"Only from the hotel cameras. It's a giant mess, no cross-references and the lighting conditions keep changing."

"Send it to me on the Navran. I have an hour to kill here."

"Segen Talmor, you may be commander of the Fourth Army of Special Section, but are you insinuating that you'll spot something that I did not in the pictures of the kidnapping?"

"Aluf Mishne Abadi, you may be my commander now, but allow me to be frank. Yes. In fact, I have the feeling you called just to ask me to take a look at the footage, only you're too embarrassed to ask that of a woman."

"That has nothing to do with it, it's nothing to do with your gender."

"Of course it doesn't, it has nothing to do with my gender, it never has. Well, come on then, send me your blonde, let me decide what has to do with *your* gender and what doesn't."

On the screen, Abadi was seen working the buttons of his Navran. His gaze was now less defiant and his smile more bashful, like that of a child who knows he's done something wrong, even if he hasn't worked out what.

Chapter 79

The payee's address was "13uEbM8unu0ShB4TewXjtqbBv5Mndw-fX6b". No-one knew his name or the country he was in. They knew only, based on the first digit, that it was the account of an individual, and that it was a single-use address for the specific transaction. Once received, Mr or Mrs 13uEbM8unu0ShB4TewXjtqbBv5Mnd-wfX6b would most likely disappear with the payment.

There was nothing remarkable about it, other than the amount: based on the fickle conversion rate of the cryptocurrency, the payment would be in the region of twenty million US dollars.

It is impossible to cancel a payment order in bitcoin. Once the order is given, the payer cannot request a refund. Payment in bitcoin was the closest thing to handing over a suitcase full of cash that modern times had come up with, apart from the fact that the person handing over the suitcase doesn't know who's receiving it.

Some bitcoin payments are transferred to the payee within sixty seconds. Other payments must go through the minimal number of verifications dictated by the system, six confirmations from each of the twenty thousand computers that vet the payments. And then there are payments that must go through multiple verification stages, delaying the payment for a matter of hours.

For this payment, the system had determined the highest number of verification stages possible. There were several reasons for this: first and most obvious, the amount; second, the identity of the payer, a private company registered in China which, contrary to usual practice, authorised payments based on only one digital signature. The payer's wallet address was also confidential, but the system identified his nickname, so short and banal it didn't seem possible its owner had the digital authorisation to transfer millions at the push of a button: Ming.

The computerised system decided that the holder of account number 13uEbM8unu0ShB4TewXjtqbBv5MndwfX6b would have to undergo thirty verification stages before receiving Ming's money. The estimated time of transfer that appeared on the order screen was five hours. Twenty million dollars. A non-refundable order. To an untraceable person.

Chapter 80

At 23:40, a total of five murders were listed on Commissaire Léger's briefing board:

1. Yaniv Meidan, 25 y/o, Israeli citizen, victim of mistaken identity. Murdered 10:50, Terminal 2A, Charles de Gaulle airport. Body found 20:05, Acheres purification facility. Identification confirmed through biometric data from Israel.

2. John Doe, approx. 30 y/o, Chinese origin, presumed commander of abduction squad of victim no. 1, murdered passerelle Simone de Beauvoir 14:40. Body retrieved from Seine, beyond the bridge, fifteen minutes later.

3. John Doe, approx. 24 y/o, Chinese origin, presumed junior member of abduction squad of victim no. 1, murdered same time/place, several body parts recovered from quai de Montebello 20:15.

4. John Doe, approx. 30 y/o, Chinese origin, member of abduction squad of Vladislav Yerminski, trapped by Colonel Abadi main entrance Le Grand Hôtel, murdered by his partners 20:54. Yet to be identified.

5. Georges Lucas, 62 y/o, French citizen, security manager of Le Grand Hôtel. Entered hotel room of Vladimir Yerminski, shot by victim no. 4, 20:46.

Léger himself was feeling like a corpse. Physically, because he was exhausted from a day that would not end, and professionally, since this new discovery at Le Grand Hôtel had brought his career that much closer to its bitter end. Not only had he failed to apprehend the minister's imaginary drugs gang, but another Israeli had been kidnapped from under his nose by the same bait, and in a manner that Léger could not comprehend. If the blonde had snatched the Israeli from his hotel room at 17:20, why would a whole Chinese commando team need to return to the scene of the crime? To pick up a suitcase that contained nothing but basic hacking equipment, some clothing and a few toiletries? And if the Israeli was to be murdered immediately after his abduction, like the first Israeli that morning, why did the blonde take him to the railway station in a taxi instead of killing him at the hotel?

For answers to any of these questions, Léger was dependent on the municipal surveillance system and its identification software, and at this busy time of night the two operators assigned to it could not handle the load. In any case, his technicians had not been able to isolate sharp enough pictures of her in the hotel hallways, and it seemed as though the assassin from the bridge, the Chinese pedlar, had worn a professional latex mask that made it effectively impossible for the software to identify him either. All the passenger lists from all trains leaving Gare Saint Lazare had been checked by the police, but to no avail. Where did the blonde go, was Yerminski still alive, where were all the other Chinese, and who had been in Le Grand Hôtel and what were they doing now? Who were they killing?

The answer was soon forthcoming.

Oddly enough, the credit was due not to an algorithm but a human: Brigadier Muhammad Yousefi, the duty officer of district 93's anti-narcotics task force, recognised in the security footage a Chinese pedlar who matched the description distributed after the killings on the bridge.

"We had a double showdown here, looks like a drug deal gone bust," the officer told him on the telephone with unconcealed pride. "We have two bodies on a roof here in Bagnolet, rue de la Capsulerie, near Gallieni métro. They would appear to have taken each other out over turf, but it seems off to me because one was a lookout for the Moroccan gang and the other was an Afghani shit dealer."

"Shit?" Léger tried to follow. He did not have much time for the jargon of the anti-narcotics task force, whose officers tended to adopt the gang members' slang.

"Hashish, Commissaire. He was a dealer with clients in Paris, there was no reason for the Moroccans to kill him in 'the Woods'."

"What wood? Brigadier, please try to be clear."

"I'm sorry, Commissaire, I'm used to reporting to the task force captains. 'The Woods' is the nickname of rue de la Capsulerie near Gallieni métro, right next to the 20th arrondissement and Belleville. It's the Moroccans' territory. There's no good reason an Afghani dealer would try to sell hash there, it makes no sense."

Léger began to understand the meaning of the report. "You mean you suspect he was killed for some other reason?"

"Yes, Commissaire. There are surveillance cameras all over the area, and I also got the images from the métro security unit. You can clearly see that the Afghani was being followed from Père Lachaise métro long before he arrived at the area. Throughout the ride, and even when he followed the Moroccans' instructions and walked around the compound, you can see a strange man hovering, a Chinese pedlar with a loaded cart."

"And you're sure it's the same one photographed on the bridge? There are thousands of those pedlars in Paris."

"Not in my area, Commissaire. We have no Chinese pedlars here, no-one here's going to buy a postcard of the Arc de Triomphe, or a selfie stick, trust me. That pedlar followed the Afghani dealer, whose name according to the documents on him was Wasim Zeerak, to the building where he was killed. We think the murder did not even happen on the roof, but in the car park below."

"And does the footage show where the pedlar went?"

"Yes it does, Commissaire. He slipped away from the compound but I located him again in the métro footage. He boarded Line 3 again from Gallieni station, changed at Arts et Métiers and got off at Rambuteau."

Léger did not know much about drug investigations, but he knew Paris as well as any officer in the city.

He did not need to look at the map to follow the killer's route and its logic. Changing lines for only one stop would be unusual even for a regular passenger, not to mention someone being hunted by the entire Paris police force. There was only one explanation: he needed to reach his destination as quickly as possible, and even at night the métro was faster than walking between those two particular stations. What Léger could not understand was what was so urgent about getting to Rambuteau, a station that was used by visitors to the Pompidou Centre.

"He doesn't strike me as a lover of modern art," Léger mused aloud.

"Not to mention that the museum is closed at those hours," the brigadier said, stating the obvious, to Léger's annoyance.

Without waiting for the conversation to end, Léger's deputy began to make calls in every direction, and there was soon chaos. Investigators burst in with reports and notes and photographs, technicians stuck red pins all over a map of the city and sirens were heard outside while excitable reports came over the police radio inside. Five minutes later, the briefing board looked different.

6. Wasim Zeerak, 26 y/o, Afghani origin, drug dealer, murdered border of Paris-Bagnolet 18:30, most likely by Chinese assassin from passerelle Simone de Beauvoir. Connection to abductions not yet clear. I.D. confirmed through fingerprints.

7. Sa'id Aboumdane, 14 y/o, member of "the Woods" gang in Bagnolet, murdered shortly after victim no. 6, likely same assassin. No connection to abductions, believed to have interrupted assassin while killing victim no. 6. I.D. confirmed by mother.

Fewer than eight minutes later, a report on another body came in. Its implications were clear – the loss of the single connecting thread.

8. John Doe, approx. 20 y/o, recovered from Seine (Méricourt)

21:25. Analysis of water currents suggests river drowning (area around curve – Tour Eiffel). Body currently unidentifiable due to damage caused by freight ship propellers. Possibility under exploration: body is of second abducted Israeli, Vladislav Yerminski.

Léger felt despair, less at the number of bodies on the board than by the thought of having to inform Colonel Abadi that the target of his search was at the pathology institute on the banks of the Seine. He preferred to call his redheaded Israeli colleague first. The duty officer at the embassy transferred the call to Chico's mobile, and when he answered, Léger had a suspicion that he had been sleeping. "Are you sure it's him?" Chico said.

"We're not sure of anything," Léger said crossly. "The body can't be identified yet, it's too badly damaged."

"Commissaire, we've known each other for years. I'm asking you to update me on any development in this case. It's important."

"There are a lot of developments in this case. I've been continually updating Colonel Abadi."

"I have a lot of respect for Colonel Abadi, but he's not the official representative of the Israeli police in France, in fact, he's not the official representative of any Israeli authority on French territory. I'm asking to be informed of everything, especially information about Vladislav Yerminski, alive or dead. Anything."

Normally, Léger would have hung up in fury. But these were not normal times, and what was the limit to the number of enemies one person could make in a city that had never been known for its camaraderie? He instructed his deputy to update Chico on all developments, and the deputy called Chico a few minutes later, because the on-call pathologist did not wait for the autopsy to send an initial finding: the body of John Doe had been in the water for at least three days.

The officer standing near the board erased victim number 8: the length of time he had spent in the river disqualified him from the case. But then another call came in, and although the report was laconic, it provided answers to all their previous questions: why Rambuteau, where were the Chinese, who was connected to whom. The officer took his marker and added a new line to the board:

8. Corinne Lemarquer, 20 y/o, acting student, deliberate electrocution, The Rite of Spring fountain, place Stravinsky, 4th arrondissement. 23:45. Identification to be confirmed (dental records en route). Possibility under exploration: victim was Chinese commando team's honeytrap.

Having called Chico, the deputy again called the pathology institute, whose staff sounded even snappier than his boss. On an average day in Paris they received perhaps two or three bodies for autopsy. Six bodies was a union matter.

His deputy ended the conversation sharply and collapsed into the chair in front of Léger's desk. He started reading from his notepad in a cold, official voice as if rehearsing for the investigation committee. Always dance like nobody's watching, but report to your superiors as if the entire hearing committee is sitting in front of you.

"Commissaire, the picture is clearer now. Fifteen minutes ago the Chinese assassin murdered a girl who was waiting at the fountain by the Pompidou Centre, next to Rambuteau métro where he was last caught on camera. The tools he used were primitive but deadly. He climbed to the roof of the nearby music centre and used a split extension cord to plug various electrical devices into the outdoor socket – a cup boiler, a toaster and three portable radiant heaters – and dropped them into the fountain. The girl was in contact with the water. She didn't stand a chance."

Léger heard himself asking, "Are we sure she's connected to our story?"

"We're not sure yet, Commissaire," his deputy said, and Léger could not tell if he was mocking or imitating him. "But in the victim's wallet we found used return tickets for Charles de Gaulle, with time stamps that match the morning's abduction, and there were messages on her mobile from one of the numbers belonging to Wasim Zeerak – victim number six. In one of the messages he asks if it all went well, moments after the kidnapping, and then promises the payment, probably the drugs he went to buy for her at the car park where he was murdered, probably by the same killer."

"And of course we have no idea where the pedlar is now, right?"

"We have the images from the métro cameras, I distributed them to all units in the Paris area. The camera network can't help us that much at night, but the software might locate him tomorrow at dawn if he's not holed up indoors somewhere."

How many more people would the pedlar kill before dawn? He had already slaughtered Léger's career. Now he recognised the enormity of the error he had made by turning to the Israelis. Co-operating with Abadi had yielded no results, and the cover story concocted by the Préfet and the Minister about a massive drug deal was receiving unexpected reinforcement. Now he would not be able to explain what he had been wasting his time on tonight. He might as well start drafting his letter of resignation.

He looked out of the generous office windows at the river. To the right, the Eiffel Tower cut through the night sky with a beguiling beam of light. Léger began to suspect that the mysterious Colonel Abadi was somehow responsible, directly or indirectly, for the whole affair from the very start. Would all these murders have happened if Abadi had not come to Paris? Was he really an investigator for a secret Israeli intelligence unit and not the head of a hit squad masquerading as a Chinese commando unit?

This possibility hit him with fearful clarity, as the beacon of the Eiffel Tower appeared in the skies. Like the tower itself, this suspicion was inescapable, unprecedented, improbable, and yet completely real.

Léger called the makeshift investigation room at Le Grand Hôtel. An inspector who sounded younger even than the narcotics task force brigadier picked up. Since when had everyone in this city become so young?

"What's he doing?"

"Who, Commissaire?"

"Colonel Abadi, obviously. What is Colonel Abadi doing?"

"Till now he was on a video call on that weird telephone of his, and now he's typing on it. He keeps watching the security footage of the blonde over and over again. He's not taking any interest in the reports I've been passing to him."

Léger recalled Abadi's response to the first kidnapping: "I don't like blondes . . . and in a short red uniform, no less." Maybe it was wiser for Abadi to ask to see her body instead of watching the footage again.

"He wants to talk to you, Commissaire."

Léger could barely shake himself out of his musings. "Who?"

"Colonel Abadi, Commissaire. He's asking to speak to you. Should I put him through?"

As every night at midnight, the Eiffel Tower performed its light show, delighting the tourists standing under Léger's window. The camera flashes could be seen all along the Seine as Léger grunted his consent and listened with growing astonishment to Abadi.

When Léger looked out of the window again, the Eiffel Tower was still sparkling at him from a distance, erect and defiant, gleaming and unattainable. And that's when it hit him, the glorified commissaire, at one minute past midnight: Abadi was a messenger of the gods who had come to save him from his mistakes.

Chapter 81

Oriana switched off the Navran and glanced at the clock on the dashboard, trying to arrange her thoughts.

"Ten minutes to 01:00, Commander." Rachel's voice was a whisper. "When are you going to give the order?"

"Maybe I should give the order in French," Oriana said, her mind elsewhere, it seemed to Rachel. "'*Soldats de Tzahal, à l'attaque!*' or something like that."

"Why in French?" Rachel said.

"Because Abadi wants me to join him in Paris tonight, that's why. I have to perfect my French."

Rachel was quick to respond. "Commander, can I work from home on some kind of project or other while you're there? Boris will be the acting head of section in your absence and he can be an awful tyrant."

"I have another idea, Rachel. Why don't you register for the officers' course? The tests begin tomorrow."

"Me, Commander? I'm not ready to be an officer."

"Don't talk that kind of nonsense in the interview, samelet. Repeat after me, 'I will make an excellent officer.' Look at me and say it. 'I will make an excellent officer.'"

"I can't, Commander. You're joking, right? I'd rather suffer under Boris for two or three days, or for however long until you and Abadi come back."

"If we come back," Oriana said.

"Why would you say something like that, Commander? Now you're the one uttering nonsense. I mean, is it dangerous? Did Abadi tell you what your mission is there?"

"For the moment he just wants what all men want from me," Oriana said, "and that's for me to help them with another girl."

"It's because you scare them. You have a paralysing beauty," Rachel said.

"I have a what?"

"Paralysing beauty."

"Oh my god, Rachel, where did you get that one from?"

"Tomer explained it to the girls today when you were sleeping."

"Yeah, remind me to deal with Tomer and the shit he pulled today. But I have something else to deal with first."

"First you have something else, Commander, yes," Rachel said, looking ahead through the windscreen.

It was a minute before 01:00. In front of them, fewer than a hundred metres away, was the gate of the southern base, the largest, most powerful intelligence-gathering base in the world, sleepy as a ghost ship in the middle of a black ocean. Oriana drew the radio's microphone to her mouth. "Force 24, this is Eagle. At my command we launch Operation Long Night. My vehicle leads, motorcycles at the rear and sides, and no-one goes in before the drone is above the gates. Acknowledge all."

The voices on the radio were so clear and confident, it was difficult to remember there was a real world out there too, not so far from the secret intelligence base in the heart of the desert, a world in which you did not give kids vehicles and weapons, and you did not let them play a game whose rules no-one really understood:

"Falcon 1, Roger."

"Falcon 2, Roger."

"Falcon 3, Roger."

"Falcon 4, Roger."

"Hawk 1, Roger."

"Hawk 2, Roger."

"Hawk 3, Roger."

Oriana turned on the external speakers. "South base, this is a security inspection by Special Section, 8200 headquarters. Today's password is '584210'. You have one minute to open the gate."

It took ten seconds for four spotlights to light up simultaneously across the access road. Oriana regretted not being on the other side of the gate to witness the scene herself. The gate did not open. A further forty-five seconds passed.

Again, she drew the microphone close to her mouth. "Force 24, commence raid on my order, on 'Three'." She turned off the microphone and switched on the speakers.

"South base, you have ten seconds left. If you do not open the gate, you will be charged with disobeying operation orders."

No response. Oriana turned on the internal microphone. "Force 24, prepare for order. 'One'."

As if from thin air, the drone appeared above them, its engines blaring above the gates.

"Two."

The military police vehicles turned on their sirens, and two motorcycles drove up to her jeep. Rachel squealed in admiration.

"Three."

She hit the accelerator and the military jeep hurtled towards the barrier. After a horrible screeching among the cacophony, the first barrier slid open.

"I will make an excellent officer, I will make an excellent officer," Rachel said in prayer, and the gate to the southern base started to open. The jeep lights illuminated the darkness, and the four, armed soldiers blocking the entrance came into view. In front of them, trying not to blink at the lights, stood a bespectacled segen. Oriana presumed that he was the network intelligence officer who had refused to answer her questions on the telephone.

She stopped the jeep a short distance from the soldiers and jumped out. As she slammed the door, a cold desert wind hit her and banished her doubts.

Chapter 82

Ming waited inside his plane at Frankfurt International airport's private jet terminal. The Boeing 747-8 had been modified for his needs by friends in the Chinese military aircraft industry, but the plane was not listed under his name. And in any case, Ming was not his real name.

Out of precaution, he never flew directly to his destination, and today he instructed the crew, which included two pilots on this long-haul flight, to employ extreme measures beyond those he customarily used to pop surveillance. Over German air space, the acting pilot requested permission for an emergency landing in Frankfurt "due to a mechanical failure in one of the engines", and they were now waiting for the verdict from the mechanics at the V.I.P. wing of the Frankfurt Aviation Service.

There had been no mechanical failure of course. But now Ming could register a new flight plan from Frankfurt to Le Bourget. It was an internal European route governed by the Schengen Agreement and there would be no customs search upon landing in Paris. The weapons hidden behind a fake panel in the bar were well concealed, but he did not want to take unnecessary risks. Not today.

Ming read Erlang Shen's report carefully. "上屋抽梯", determined the *Book of Qi*, which he had established as the guiding set of principles for the Ming organisation: "Lure your enemy onto the roof then take away the ladder." The enemy was definitely on the roof. This was not supposed to happen, certainly not on the roofs of Paris, a dangerous city which promised the sublime but which never delivered.

When he had first received the eight-second audio clip on his mobile, he had understood at once the magnitude of the threat. Only six people knew his telephone number and he trusted them all. But on listening to the file, on hearing his own voice in the recorded conversation, the danger had become clear and present.

The anonymous sender knew about his payments to the high-ranking official in exchange for control of Macau's gambling heart. The sender knew more, and he was demanding a huge sum of money for his silence and the return of the audio file. Ming had originally thought the blackmailer was Chinese, but then the payment number had come through, a long, obscure and anonymous string of characters. Anonymous for most people, but not for Ming, who counted members of the Chinese secret services among his friends.

And so it turned out that behind number 13uEbM8unu0ShB4-TewXjtqbBv5MndwfX6b was an Israeli named Vladislav Yerminski.

"How could an Israeli have hacked into my secure e-mail and phone?" Ming was stunned for all of two brief seconds before reason returned, and he answered his own question. "The tone signals on the file itself should provide that information."

Ming had no wish to pay for his own e-mail correspondence. However, now that He Xiangu had botched the plan, had failed to catch Yerminski and had endangered his best *xiake*, he had no other choice.

He checked the long number again and clicked "Approve payment". He was counting on Erlang Shen to get the money back for him, but first he needed the audio file. And then he needed to make He Xiangu pay for it. Erlang Shen would know what to do.

Chapter 83

To: 8200/US Intelligence Liaison Unit

From: 8200/Head of Special Section, via Navran 008

Priority: Urgent/Top Secret

Clearance: Black

cc: 8200/Commander

cc: 8200/Chief Network Intelligence Officer

cc: 8200/Special Section/Navran 012

1:704-01:00 U.T.C.

Following operation order Long Night presently in system, request transfer to me all electronic correspondence conducted via Le Grand Hôtel Paris' own network within order's defined time-frame.

Network: DHCP wi-fi: legrand inter guests

Time: 10:00–14:00 U.T.C.

This request overrides any other request in or outside the unit.

To: 8200/Head of Research Division

From: 8200/Head of Special Section, via Navran 008

Priority: Urgent/Secret

17:04-01:00 U.T.C.

Following operation order Long Night presently in system, request transfer to Special Section any/all anomalies in data transferences from Paris yesterday at 10:30 to current time. Special attention to deviations from norms: cellular communications, flight bookings, financial transactions, signal mixing, data scraping related to China.

This request overrides any other request in or outside the unit.

To: HATZAV OSINT/Social Networks Department
From: 8200/Head of Special Section, via Navran 008
Priority: Urgent/Secret
17:04-01:00 U.T.C.

Following operation order Long Night presently in system, request transfer to 8200 Special Section any/all social media posts, texts, photographs, location, reviews from Le Grand Hôtel, Paris incl. surroundings, possibly related to abduction described in updated operation order.

Requested location: 48°52'15.1'N 2°19'49.8'E
Requested time: 13:00–17:00 U.T.C.
This request overrides any other request in or outside the unit.

To: 8200/Chief Network Intelligence Officer
From: 8200/Head of Special Section, via Navran 008
Priority: Urgent/Top Secret
17:04-01:00 U.T.C.

Following operation order Long Night presently in system, request transfer to Special Section any/all recent electronic correspondence to & from Corinne Lemarquer, Paris. Mobile: +33-6-4481043; e-mail address unknown.

This request overrides any other request in or outside the unit.

To: 8200/Bureau Chief, HQ
From: 8200/Head of Special Section, via Navran 008
Priority: Immediate/Restricted
cc: 8200/Commander
17:04-01:00 U.T.C.

Request order one plane ticket for deputy head Special Section, Segen Oriana Talmor. Flight: next El Al departing Ben Gurion airport 05.25 for Paris-Charles de Gaulle. Segen Talmor currently leading unit operation, South. Request any/all possible assistance to guarantee arrival, clearance to board. Please confirm upon execution.

Chapter 84

How many traits did he have in common with an investigator like Commissaire Léger? Abadi tried to gauge them. They were both methodical, certainly. Stubborn, absolutely. They were suspicious of their commanders, and of the system at large. As was every good investigator. But as for the most fundamental trait of any investigator in any field – openness to possibilities – Abadi had to acknowledge the fact that his French colleague had nothing but contempt for it.

Abadi tried again. "Commissaire, all I'm asking is that you take a look at this short scene from the kidnapping of Vladislav Yerminski," he said and rewound the clip he had edited.

Like most hotels on such a scale, Le Grand Hôtel had a network of synced cameras, sixty-four, of which sixty-one were in working order. Unlike the El Al camera, the hotel's system operated on time-lapse technology, one image every two seconds. It added to the viewing experience a vague sense of awe, the same feeling of reverence inspired by movies from the early days of film-making.

The real problem was positioning them. There were cameras in every lift but none in the stairwells. Four cameras were installed at the reception desk, but the giant lobby was full of blind spots. And on the convention floor, where the blonde had gone to get dressed, there was not a single camera. Presumably out of respect for business confidentiality.

But the system was synchronised, providing Abadi with the ability to cross-cut footage from the various cameras in a relatively short period of time.

0:00 – The door to Vladislav Yerminski's room is still closed (camera no. 43).

0:02 – The door opens, the image sharpens above Yerminski, who looks to his left and then to his right (cameras no. 42, 43, 44).

0:05 – Yerminski exits the room with his hands raised and stands in the hallway facing the lifts (camera no. 42).

0:09 – The blonde comes out and slams the door behind her. The "Do Not Disturb" sign swings from the impact. In her left hand is a Printemps shopping bag (camera no. 43).

0:15 – Yerminski starts walking towards the lift (cameras no. 40, 42). Behind him the blonde is seen taking a gun out of the bag with her right hand, pointing it at his back and talking to him (camera no. 40).

0:17 – Yerminski lowers his hands and starts running towards the lifts (cameras no. 38, 40).

0:22 – She runs after him. She transfers the gun to her left hand to conceal it in the bag (cameras no. 35, 38).

1:15 – They both run down the hallway and turn left. She's holding the gun inside the bag, switching again to her right hand. She puts her left hand in her pocket (cameras no. 31, 33, 35).

1:23 – They stand in front of the lifts (cameras no. 20, 27).

1:25 – Yerminski presses the lift button (camera no. 20).

1:40 – The doors of the left lift open. There are people inside the lift. They enter, Yerminski first, the blonde immediately following (cameras no. 8, 20).

1:50 – The camera in the lift captures only the upper half of their bodies. They stand among a family, probably Americans. The blonde is close to Yerminski (camera no. 8).

1:57 – The camera in the lift registers her moving the bag. She's now holding the gun at a sharper angle towards the lift ceiling (camera no. 8).

2:03 – They are the last to leave the lift. Yerminski exits before her. She straightens her hand, holding the gun at an upright angle behind him (cameras no. 5, 8).

2:20 – They exit the hotel through the main entrance and run to the taxis, skirting the line of limousines and skipping over a puddle on the way to the opposite side of the street (cameras no. 5, 15).

2:40 – They get into a taxi, he first, then her. She pulls in the bag after settling in her seat and closes the door with her left hand (camera no. 15).

"So, what did we see?" Léger said.

"It's the gun they had in 'The Matrix' movies," his deputy told him.

"That's right," Abadi said. "And in a lot of other movies, not to mention computer games. But that's not what I wanted to draw your attention to."

"Then what is it?" Léger said.

"Commissaire, if you focus on the two clips I just showed you, you'll see for yourself that the blonde girl moves quickly and confidently in her heels, she even runs and skips over puddles on the way to the taxi, while in the airport she struggled to walk in the same heels and got rid of them the moment she could."

"So what does that mean, Colonel, that in the meantime she learned how to walk in heels?"

"No, Commissaire. It means it's not the same girl."

The reaction of Léger's men alternated between cries of surprise and whispers. Léger himself struggled to follow what his Israeli colleague was saying.

"Not the same girl?"

"Not the same girl."

"Just because she can walk in heels in the second video?"

"They look alike, but it isn't the same girl. If you compare the camera angle in the airport lift to the one in the hotel, you'll find that the blonde in the hotel is taller, actually, than the one in the airport, and there's scarcely any facial resemblance. They're both tall, thin, fair-skinned blondes in short red uniforms – that's all they have in common."

"It can't be a coincidence."

"Not at all. It was the leaking of the footage of the first blonde that brought on this copycat."

"I accept what you're saying, Colonel," Léger said in a hesitant tone, "but I assume that as we speak the assassin is busy taking out the second blonde, so it doesn't really help us."

"We can find her before he does," Abadi said. He wanted to add that it was Oriana's discovery, so he added, "Obviously I did not figure this out by myself."

The officers looked at Léger as if Abadi had just credited him with the discovery. Abadi wanted to correct himself and explain about Oriana, but he seemed to have lost his way with words, and just shrugged.

Chapter 85

What did Vladislav Yerminski do in a place like this, day and night? The antennae field was huge, but the base itself was much smaller than Oriana had expected. The pavements were painted green and white, the colours of the Intelligence Corps. Along the pathways were directions to the dining hall, the living quarters, the bunker, directions to everything but the exit from the base, since apparently everyone knew the way out. Six trees swayed in the wind that blew sand through the command square, and around a command poster that stated in red letters: "A RIGHT IS ALSO A DUTY".

The drone continued to hover above their heads, its buzzing growing louder in irregular cycles. The base was full of night sounds that she did not recognise, used as she had been to her kibbutz in the north. Irrigation pipes dripped across a symbolic square of yellowing grass. Crickets chattered from every direction. Every now and then she heard the growl of an old air-conditioner compressor that someone had forgotten to turn off.

They were light years away from Unit 8200 as it was portrayed on the outside, and light years away, in fact, from any technology unit. On the exterior wall of the dining hall was a giant reproduction of Munch's "The Scream".

It wasn't a painting, Oriana discovered, but a mosaic made of thousands of bottle caps. A metal plaque explained that the soldiers on the base had worked on the piece for three months as part of an artistic recycling project sponsored by Coca Cola.

The command board included a guard duty roster and the punishments imposed in the disciplinary trials that week: four hundred shekels for failing to wear a beret, a week's detention for substandard cleaning of the showers.

So what did Vladislav Yerminski do in a place like this, day and night, for a year and a half? Oriana still could not answer that question. The base's exasperating network intelligence officer had decided to exercise his right to file an appeal against the inspection, forcing her to wait forty-five minutes before her people could enter the intelligence bunker.

"The El Dorado department is the most secret place in this country, carrying out the most sensitive intelligence-gathering missions. I strongly protest this inspection and hereby appeal against it," he shouted at her, cleaning his glasses like a nineteenth-century academic. When she took out the Navran to appeal his appeal, he looked at the device like a child robbed of a toy promised to him and him alone.

She assumed the unit 8200 commander would reject the appeal, but nevertheless decided not to wait before logging initial findings. The drone had already located an impressive number of information security offences. The soldiers on the base regularly sent each other private e-mails, text messages and photographs that included geolocation data during their shifts. Over the last twenty-four hours, dozens of posts had been uploaded onto Facebook from the base, more than a hundred photographs onto Instagram, and at least one of the intelligence antennae had been tuned to a sports radio station, most likely the initiative of soldiers who wanted to get updates during their shift. In the meantime, the team raided the offices and living quarters, where there was no-one to object.

"Where's the base commander?" Oriana asked the only administrative officer they could find.

"All administrative officers are at home except for me. I'm the duty officer," he said.

"Even the base commander?"

"Especially the base commander."

According to the manpower structure in the base's administrative department, ten soldiers served in the El Dorado department. Three of them, including Yerminski, were on leave – quite a high proportion for a sensitive department in a closed base. Oriana opened the charts relating to the living quarters and took four of the section's soldiers to raid the missing soldier's room. His bed was made, and a poster of the movie "Ocean's Eleven" hung on the wall behind it. His locker was almost empty. Rachel listed the items:

One set of clean combat uniform.

One service dress windproof jacket.

Four pairs of socks.

Four books in Russian (Boris Akunin, Fandorin series).

Coin pouch.

Paris travel guide in Hebrew from ten years ago, property of the base library.

Pair of keys.

Sennheiser helmet headphones with 0.7 jack.

Civilian I.D. card.

P.O.W. card with dog tag.

Three packs of military wafers.

"*You're looking for something strange. It may be something unexpected, it may be something that's missing, it may just be something that looks out of place*," Oriana thought.

She did not notice anything missing. As for strange, almost everything in that locker looked strange to her. Tomer burst into the room panting, bearing the folders from the administrative department. Yerminski's two roommates served with him in the El Dorado department. One of them, a signaller for English communications named Joe, was on leave outside the base, and the other, a signaller for Arab communications named Shlomo, was presently doing a night shift in the bunker to which she had yet to obtain access.

The folders Tomer carried also contained the rosters of the different departments. For the past three months Vladislav Yerminski had requested his roommate Shlomo as his shift buddy, and they had pulled most night shifts together. Tomer also found Yerminski's overseas leave request, authorised by a unit welfare officer. She had approved his request without interviewing the intended bride, "due to distance". Only one witness confirmed the existence of the upcoming wedding: Yerminski's roommate Shlomo.

Shlomo was Shlomo Cohen, Tomer announced gloomily, and with such a common name there was no point in searching for information on him on the internet. His military record, Tomer reported, included a complaint concerning vandalism of military property, which had resulted in a fine, and two incidents that had led to detentions.

It could be what she was looking for. It could also be, for the time being, coincidental. To find out, she had to interrogate Rav Turai Shlomo Cohen, who was at a safe remove in the sealed-off bunker.

She checked the Navran again; still no authorisation to enter the El Dorado department. "In the meantime let's check Cohen's stuff," she told her soldiers, and they returned to the room. A military policeman picked the lock and Rachel took out the objects and described them while Tomer filled in the report. They did not dig up anything in Russian, and certainly not in Chinese, or anything that linked him to Yerminski. The findings were slim:

One set of service uniform.

One field sweater.

Keys.

Five pairs of socks.

A Bluetooth mobile headset.

A toiletry bag.

A pair of slippers.

A Samsung Android mobile (switched off).

Four packs of halva snacks from combat rations.

A Swiss army penknife.

A copy of *Rich Dad, Poor Dad* from the base library.

"Maybe we can arrest him for stealing halva snacks from military combat rations," the commander of the military police unit said with absolute seriousness.

"In case you haven't noticed," Oriana said, "I can't even get authorisation to question him for aggravated desertion. I don't think halva is going to get us anywhere."

"So you want us to put everything back in his locker?" he said.

The filed articles were still laid out on Yerminski's bed. What was unexpected here, what was missing?

"No, take everything to my jeep. Leave a receipt for confiscated objects registered under Vladislav Yerminski and Shlomo Cohen's names. I'm going to find out what's going on."

She left the living quarters in the direction of the bunker. From a distance she noticed the bespectacled network intelligence officer talking to someone. He seemed familiar, and when she drew closer, she recognised Zorro even before she noticed his stripes. She did not need to ask herself the reason behind the Deputy Chief of Intelligence's presence here in the desert.

Chapter 86

At Hôtel Molitor, Erlang Shen sat at the edge of the pool and waited, stroking the steel handle of his gun. It was an N.P.-30, a masterpiece of the Chinese weapons industry and a special adaptation of the American Colt M.1911. For the purpose of the mission, he had equipped it with a silencer, an American 45 Osprey that doubled the pistol's length and unfortunately compromised its harmonious beauty.

Only three employees were in the lobby at this time of night, a security guard and two receptionists. Access to the pool was symbolically fenced off by a chain bearing an apologetic sign requesting would-be swimmers to respect guests' sleep. Erlang Shen hopped over it easily without being noticed.

Ming's instruction was to spare the bodyguard's life if possible. Under normal circumstances it would have been more than possible, because at night the bodyguard was supposed to guard the boss from the hallway. But despite the hour, the lights in He Xiangu's room were still on, and what little time Erlang Shen had before his next mission of the night was running out.

He tried to guess where the bodyguard would choose to position himself inside the vast room. The four windows and the door to the balcony overlooking the pool presented so many weak spots for the bodyguard. Why did she choose this hotel, and why a suite with a balcony? As this miserable operation played out, Erlang Shen found He Xiangu's conduct an embarrassment.

His telephone vibrated. The two junior *xiake* had positioned themselves outside the apartment in Créteil and requested approval to burst in and carry out the abduction of Mme Abadi. As if the team had not chalked up enough humiliating failures for one day. "Don't make a move before I get there. Confirm message," he typed. They confirmed.

The listening team had already evacuated the building in front of the Israeli embassy, the teams searching for Vladislav Yerminski were ordered to stop, and the back-up forces were instructed to return to their London base immediately. Erlang Shen had only six junior *xiake* at his disposal, not including the commander's personal bodyguard. He calculated that even if they boarded the flight at the last minute, and even if Mme Abadi did not pose an especially difficult challenge, the drive from Paris to Créteil and from there to the airport did not leave him much time.

The lights in the suite were still on, in the living room as well as in the bedroom; she had probably let her bodyguard go and had fallen asleep without turning them off. It was against regulations, but He Xiangu had already demonstrated her blatant disregard of regulations.

Ten more minutes passed. There was no point in waiting longer. Erlang Shen put his gun back in his pocket, ran to the white railing and started to scale the white fence, an Art Deco gem that had survived thanks to preservation laws. For twenty seconds he looked like a swift black cat, and even though his action invited attention, the cat disappeared onto one of the balconies without anyone raising the alarm.

Erlang Shen peered into the living room. He did not see the bodyguard at the most logical lookout post, the side armchair by the door. Nor did he see him anywhere else in the room. The door was closed. As he had supposed, He Xiangu had fallen asleep and her bodyguard was standing in the hallway. Thanks to the silencer, the bodyguard would not suspect a thing and would have no reason for entering the room. He would receive an order from the organisation to leave the hotel and drive to the airport.

Erlang Shen took out long pliers and turned the lock of the

balcony door, which slid silently open. The heating was on full blast, with music emanating from the bedroom. Closing the door behind him, he scanned the room again.

Empty. Hallway empty. Bathroom empty. Everything was empty and lit. He drew his gun and carefully opened the bedroom door. At first, he did not register what he saw.

For a moment he thought He Xiangu was in the throes of a nightmare, her arms flailing in the air, obscure guttural sounds emerging from her throat. But she was not dreaming. Underneath her, buried in the sheets, moaned a much taller figure; it was his arms that were flailing. The bodyguard's gun was on the carpet next to the bed. He Xiangu's swarthy body moved rhythmically against the white sheets, and Erlang Shen noticed a large tattoo of a wolf on her arched lower back. The bodyguard suddenly spotted him beyond the rising shoulder of his commander; he tried to get up, but she pressed him back onto the mattress. Erlang Shen aimed at her tattoo. He almost regretted using his silencer.

Chapter 87

On occasion, people have a sense of foreboding. And when faced with it, they try to set their house in order. Parents call their children. Lovers text each other from afar. Executives ask for the revenue report. People get blood tests, write wills, change the oil in their cars, gaze at the sky in search of a sign.

Abadi had never understood this. He understood the feeling itself, of course, but not the impulse to examine its roots. What good would it do? Nor did he understand people who got up in the middle of the night when they thought they heard a strange noise coming from the living room. If no enemy was lurking in the living room it was best to go back to sleep, and if there was one, getting up to greet him would certainly be the least advisable course of action. Why buy into the idea that knowing the problem necessarily led to its solution?

By now – one hour after he had detailed the intelligence information he requested for an urgent operation authorised by the head of Unit 8200 – hundreds if not thousands of intelligence reports should have coursed his way. In reality, not even a single data report waited in his inbox. The same answer came from every department and unit he enlisted:

N.T.R.

N.T.R.

N.T.R.

N.T.R.

Suppose there was indeed "Nothing To Report"? An implausible supposition given the massive amount of data he had ordered and was there not something eerie about a series of negative, laconic responses sent at the very same time and in the very same form?

Nor could he ignore the fact that forty-five minutes had passed since his deputy requested authorisation to enter El Dorado in the southern bunker without receiving the desired confirmation of the 8200 commander, the one who had ordered this investigation in the first place.

But what good would it do now to make calls, send messages, decipher the dynamics driving the forces fighting high above? Better to focus now on escape routes from the quickly dissolving plan. And the only alternative at his disposal, the only tool that was not confiscated from him in the internal war carried out thousands of kilometres from where he was in Paris, the only man who could help locate Yerminski without requiring the intelligence-gathering services of Aman, was a French commissaire on the brink of retirement, lacking any technological knowledge, who was moments away from getting fired.

Léger listened to Abadi's requests and tried to the best of his abilities to answer them. He focused and focused, and finally it was he, surprisingly alert at this time of night, who articulated a clear and concise answer: the French police had no way of extracting e-mails, text messages or telephone calls from Le Grand Hôtel without an appeal to the counter-intelligence service, which would not rush to their aid. "All the French police can do is French police work," he said in an apologetic tone.

What could Abadi do? He suddenly felt that he had lost his own centre of gravity, that he existed only within the confines of the circumstances.

"*Per angusta ad augusta*," Léger said.

Abadi looked at him with distrust. "What?"

"It's Latin. A quote from Victor Hugo, I think."

"But what does it mean?"

"Through difficulties to great success. It's the motto of the

French secret service. The D.G.S.E., in fact, our version of your Mossad."

"Considering our position, Commissaire, I'd settle for even a small success."

"There may be a tiny success on the way," Léger's deputy interrupted them. "The fraud division's duty officer wants to see us. He says it has to do with Le Grand Hôtel."

The fraud division? Léger feigned a rapid sign of the cross in supplication. "May the saints protect us, the dead serve us. And God help us."

It was 1.00 a.m., Tuesday, April 17.

Chapter 88

Zorro read out the decision from his mobile, as if he was afraid to get even a single word wrong.

"Aluf Rotelmann decided moments ago to accept the appeal of the network intelligence officer of the southern base regarding the need for an inspection by Special Section in the El Dorado department, as defined in operation order Long Night. Aluf Rotelmann appreciates Special Section's excellent work in searching for an explanation for Rav Turai Vladislav Yerminski's absenteeism without leave, yet believes that exposing the section in which he served is unnecessary for the continuation of the investigation."

The white light emanating from the screen lent Zorro's face a melodramatic touch in the darkness that engulfed him, like the victim in Caravaggio's crucifixion paintings. Oriana tried to focus on the message itself, but her thoughts kept wandering to art class. Who is in the centre of the painting, what is the painter trying to express, what does he suggest is about to happen to the figures in his work?

"In order, however, to grant the request of the commander of Unit 8200, if only partially," Zorro kept reading in a hesitant voice, "Aluf Rotelmann has decided to authorise deputy head of Special Section, Segen Oriana Talmor, to briefly question the appellant, the network intelligence officer in charge of the soldier, as well as Rav Turai Yerminski's roommate, who is suspected (based on accumulating findings) of aiding Rav Turai Yerminski in perpetrating his offence. The questioning will take place outside the intelligence bunker, and will focus solely on questions that may shed light on the conduct of the absentee soldier."

Bravo, Maestro, Oriana thought. One could not help but admire the virtuosity of Aluf Rotelmann – with just a few sentences, an investigation of national inquiry commission proportions had been turned into the negligible matter of a disciplinary offence. The El Dorado department's Chinese expert had simply gone absent without official leave, and so, if Rav Turai Shlomo Cohen was his accessory, he was merely a suspect in aiding an offence of absenteeism. Oriana was being portrayed as someone who had swung the entire Special Section into high gear in order to chase down some troubled soldier, and Aluf Rotelmann was generous enough to let her play in the sandbox just a little longer.

On the one hand, she had been granted authorisation to investigate Yerminski's disappearance, but on the other, they had done everything to ensure her investigation would fail. The questioning of Yerminski's roommate had been restricted to a staged interview, in the presence of two hostile advocates – the Deputy Chief of Intelligence on one side, and the network intelligence officer on the other. Without access to the El Dorado department she would have no physical findings, and without findings she would not even know what to ask. Oh, and even if through some kind of miracle she did know what to ask, she would not be allowed to ask it without linking it somehow to the absenteeism offence.

"Let's get this charade over with," she said.

Chapter 89

On landing at Le Bourget airport, Ming got into the limousine that awaited him. He asked the driver to take him to the Gare Saint Lazare.

He was surprised by the bustle at the station at this time of night – hundreds of people swarming in all directions, shops still open, and quite a few policemen patrolling the area – and hurried down to the basement level. Everything was brown marble; the electronic storage compartments to the right of the stairs stood out in their shiny white solitude.

Number 702 was a medium size compartment along the right wall. He typed in the code and the door opened to reveal a plastic bag and, inside it, a strange object, antiquated yet menacing: a magnetic reel.

It was a five-inch audio reel made by the German company Uher, the most prestigious tape recorder brand in the history of espionage, favoured by all intelligence services both east and west of the Berlin Wall, the only audio reel allowed on the space mission to the moon, the only object Chairman Mao, President John F. Kennedy, the Israelis and the Indonesians, James Bond and George Smiley could claim to have in common. And now he had it in common with them.

He took the reel in both hands. Although everything had already gone digital by the time he entered the profession, he still had a vague recollection of the recording technologies of old. He admired the fact that it was a four-track reel with two-way storage capacity, which meant it had between ten to twelve hours of recording power, just as the little bastard Yerminski promised.

Ming tossed the reel into his briefcase and walked out into the lit square. He stood under a modernist sculpture made of dozens of clocks, each showing a different time. On any other day it might have made him laugh, but not today.

Taking out his phone, he checked the dots on the organisation's map. Most of his men were already at the airport, awaiting instruction to retreat via a commercial flight. His own two pilots would be waiting at Le Bourget. Four junior *xiake* had been left in Paris, awaiting the order to aid Erlang Shen. Two additional dots were seen by a lake in Créteil. The red dot marking Erlang Shen had just crossed the 13th arrondissement, heading south. He pressed the conversation button. Erlang Shen answered almost immediately.

"I will reach Créteil in half an hour, Commander. I'm driving within the speed limit to avoid being stopped. I was informed that she had gone to bed. I'll be inside her apartment in less than an hour."

"Don't be afraid to shake her up a little if it helps the conversation with her son," Ming said, and hung up.

Chapter 90

They brought Shlomo to her in the dining hall, as if to signal that she was no longer free to barge into the offices of the seniors on base. The cook was in the middle of early breakfast preparations, and the meal would be waiting for the soldiers when they finished their night shift in the bunker: bread, a slice of hard cheese, runny cottage cheese and an omelette that looked as if it had already been thrown up.

At least she could now cross halva off the list of suspicious items.

Rav Turai Cohen turned out to be a very tall, very thin, very young and very dark-skinned man. He had a sleepy gaze and a frozen expression, his entire person declaring an indifference to life. He sat down on the bench on the other side of the table, as if he and Oriana were about to share breakfast at the end of a shift. Then he removed the beret he seemed to have taken pains to wear, as if realising he was not on trial after all, and placed his iPhone on top of it. He took his military I.D. card out of his shirt pocket and placed it on the table between them, exactly in the middle.

Oriana picked up the I.D. and pretended to read it. For lack of a better option, Zorro and the network intelligence officer also sat down on the bench, one on each side of the soldier. Oriana focused on the card for an extended moment, stretching out the uncomfortable silence.

"You may begin," Zorro said.

She raised her head, looking straight into the eyes of the soldier, who flinched, as if from an electric shock. She was not aiming for anything beyond that, beyond sending a tremor through the ground beneath this staged event, beyond signalling that she had no intention of admitting to failure.

"Are you Shlomo Cohen?"

"Yes."

"Did you make a statement to your welfare officer that your roommate, Rav Turai Vladislav Yerminski, has a French girlfriend whom he's about to marry?"

As she assumed, Cohen had prepared for the question. She let him go on and on about Yermi's power of persuasion and about how he – Shlomo – regretted having believed him and that he just wanted to help, and all Yermi probably wanted was to take a nice break in Paris, but he – Shlomo – did not realise it at the time.

Oriana tuned out during the monologue and did not take notes. When the soldier had finished, she looked up at him again. "Shlomo, what kind of music did Yermi like listening to?"

Cohen reacted with surprise and glanced at the officers flanking him.

"What difference does it make?" the network intelligence officer wanted to know.

Zorro considered intervening, but did not want to entangle himself in an unnecessary war. "If it will help the Special Section, I'm willing to allow the soldier to reply."

"Yermi did not like any kind of music," Cohen said and shrugged to stress his indifference.

"But what did he like listening to? What did he listen to?"

"He didn't listen to anything. He's the only one on the entire base who doesn't have any music on his mobile. When he was a kid his parents made him listen to classical music, and he's hated it ever since. He doesn't like to listen to any kind of music."

"So what did he listen to? The news? Football broadcasts? Other radio shows? Lectures? Podcasts?"

"I'm telling you, nothing. He didn't listen to anything. He liked quiet."

"That's strange, Shlomo. I found Sennheiser headphones in his locker. Are you saying he used them for work during his shifts?"

Zorro leaped up as if bitten by a snake. "That's impossible, Segen Talmor. That's against military regulations."

"Going abroad under false pretence is also against military regulations."

"There could be several explanations for those headphones. Maybe, unbeknownst to his friends, Rav Turai Yerminski listened to music on his iPod or iPhone or whatever it's called."

"They're headphones with a 0.7 jack. They're almost out of production, and used only for very old sound systems, like analogue radio sets. You can't use them for iPhones or iPods or iPads or any other type of 'i-'."

"You can't use that kind of headphone on our regular systems either," the network intelligence officer said hesitantly.

Oriana kept her eyes on the prize. "So you can use them on non-regular systems?"

"We don't have non-regular systems," the network intelligence officer said, digging his grave deeper.

"Does the department have any audio equipment you can plug headphones with a large jack into?"

The network intelligence officer looked at Zorro, who clearly had no idea what to expect. Between the two, the soldier now held his beret, crumpling it between his fingers. Finally he put it back on the table and started playing with his iPhone. Oriana watched him, spellbound. The network intelligence officer finally answered.

"Yermi used analogue back-up equipment, he could understand the Chinese better on it."

"You mean, in violation of information security orders, you let someone bring equipment that enables copy-making into the unit's most secret department? What is it, a tape?"

"It's an Uher reel-to-reel tape recorder, probably thirty years old.

It can't make any copies. Yermi was allowed to transfer the digital material to it once, that's all."

"And who kept track of the cataloguing and safeguarding of those reels?"

"Yermi," the network intelligence officer replied, his shoulders drooping from the weight of his admission.

"Terrific," Oriana said. Her gaze suddenly honed in on Rav Turai Cohen's fingers, which were nimbly scrolling down an endless thread of Instagram photographs.

"One could still argue it isn't necessarily connected," Zorro said.

"One could argue anything. That's precisely what you three are doing here," Oriana said, eyeing Shlomo's telephone.

Zorro lost his composure. "Segen Talmor, your impudence is already well known throughout the entire intelligence department. I'm telling you now, you had better watch it."

"You're absolutely right," Oriana said in a subdued tone. "I need a cigarette. Is smoking allowed here?"

"Of course not!" the network intelligence officer protested in a high-pitched cry.

"Then I'm taking a break, a few minutes outside. I'll be back and we'll wrap up the investigation quickly."

"It's your time. This investigation is over in fifteen minutes whether you use this time for questions or cigarettes," Zorro said.

"Sure," Oriana said. She left the rancid-smelling dining hall and found Rachel waiting for her outside.

"Are you O.K., Commander?" she said. Oriana's fingers unbuttoned the pocket of Rachel's shirt and pulled out her pack of Gauloises.

"I'm fine," Oriana said. "In fact, I finally understand what I'm doing here. I didn't before. The investigation here is almost over."

"So you're celebrating with a cigarette?"

"No, Rachel, I'll celebrate in an entirely different way when we have something to celebrate. I needed a cigarette as an excuse to come out to see you."

"What for?"

"I want you to sneak the things we put in my jeep into section headquarters," Oriana replied. "Take Tomer, maybe Boris too in case we need Russian, get them both in the car and hurry to 8200 headquarters. I'll talk to the duty officer in the encryption department and tell him to expect you. We'll go over the details on the way."

"It's a military jeep, Commander, I can't go above speed limit."

"Why else did Abadi hook us up with hot motorcyclists, Rachel? You'll have an escort all the way to Glilot, don't worry."

"And what about you, Commander?"

"I'll stall them a bit longer, until you're at a safe distance, and then we'll get the hell out of here," Oriana said. "How long is a cigarette break?"

"Four, five minutes, but seven is also not unreasonable," Rachel said while texting. "So that's about how long you have to organise this smuggling," Oriana said. "In four minutes, I'm going back in." Rachel lit her commander's cigarette and ran towards the parking area.

Chapter 91

Erlang Shen surveyed his surroundings with admiration. Créteil had, for many years, been a Communist suburb, and every building in the neighbourhood was a gem of '70s proletarian architecture. Someone here had thought about the workers instead of shoving them into housing blocks with tiny apartments that resembled rabbit cages. Someone here had tried to give the working citizens the feeling that the government cared about them.

The results were disastrous, but that was another story. Across the lake stood tall cauliflower-like buildings, on the right was a narrow tower most likely planned for bachelor pads, and on the left totally wacky buildings evoked psychedelic monsters.

Mme Abadi lived on the top floor of a rather standard building, as much as any orange and white construction can pass for standard. A gate with a keypad lock led to a courtyard and several doors, all of them locked.

"Are you sure she's in there?" Erlang Shen asked for the second time.

"One hundred per cent sure," the pair replied in unison. Erlang Shen had never worked with them before, and the number of blunders in this operation did nothing to reassure him.

"Let's go over it again," he said, and the two took out their surveillance report.

"It's the top apartment on the left, number 35. The surname 'Abadi' is written on the intercom, the mailbox and the door itself," said the taller of the two *xiake*, who had no command authority, but intended that to change as a result of these findings. "Mme Abadi left the building at 18:32 to go to the grocery you see there on the corner. We're sure it was her because she was greeted by name by the man at the store. He offered to have his employee deliver her groceries, but she declined and piled everything into her baskets. I followed her to the entrance of the building, and after she got into the lift I went in to check that she actually went up to the top floor."

"In the meantime I settled on the roof," the other one cut in, loath to let his partner steal all the glory. "I could see her getting out of the lift and entering her apartment with the groceries. She and her husband were talking very loudly, and then I heard the television."

"What were they talking about?"

"I don't know, I don't speak French," he said, and the first *xiake* seized the opportunity to take back the reins.

"Two hours ago I saw the light go on in the bedroom, and it seemed that the husband had gone to bed. It's the window on the far left, with the flowers on the balcony."

Erlang Shen's concern only intensified. "You stayed here all that time and watched the building? What if a neighbour had called the police?"

"At that point I had already joined him downstairs; it looked a lot less suspicious because there were two of us, and we pretended we were talking. And the fact is, the police didn't come. Patrol cars pass here every now and then, and nobody gave us a second glance."

Erlang Shen was about to respond, but the device in his pocket began buzzing. It was a message from Ming, and he read it several times before confirming.

"I have to get back to the city," he said, raising his eyes from the screen. "Something important is going on in Paris. We have no time to waste here. I'm going up, you wait for me here with the car ready."

"Don't you want one of us to help you knock her out?" the first one asked.

Erlang Shen took his gun and loaded the tranquilliser dart. "This would knock out a lioness," Erlang Shen said, "and however much Mme Abadi loves her son, she's still not as strong as a lioness." He approached the door of the apartment building.

Chapter 92

The road to the fraud division was paved with good intentions, and also with seventeenth-century mosaics, medieval stained-glass windows and horrifying guillotines. The Paris Préfecture de Police building was connected through ancient underground passages to the Palais de Justice, the detention centre and the Public Prosecutor's office. Until the relocation of all employees to a new, ultra-modern location in the suburbs, this network of buildings occupied a quarter of the entire grounds of Île de La Cité, and Commissaire Léger now scurried between them.

"Where the hell is it?" he asked his deputy when they inadvertently arrived at the passageway ascending to the island's royal chapel, the Sainte-Chapelle.

Abadi had visited these places in the past, but without any inkling of the vast dimensions of the underground part closed to the public. Under the Conciergerie building, the prison that had once hosted Marie Antoinette, hundreds of redundant display objects were piled up. Under the chapel were dozens of sculptures of Jesus and the crucifixion. Between all these stood shelves crammed with criminal files, kilometres of paperwork describing crimes committed over centuries.

They now stood at a junction of passages in the middle of the island, a veritable Bermuda Triangle of the justice system. Abadi gathered from Léger that the major crime division was to the south, the other divisions to the east, and the entrance in front of them led to the Court of Appeals. A wooden sign declared that above their heads was the last vestige of the original cross from the

"Mount of Olives" in Jerusalem. He had come a long way over the course of a day only to find himself in the same place, he thought.

"You're on the right track, Commissaire, it's over here," his deputy said, and led them in the opposite direction. They arrived out of breath and befuddled at the offices of the fraud division, which were larger and nicer than those of the major crime division, as if the nation wanted to make clear that it gave higher priority to monitoring the financial system than to saving human lives.

The detective who greeted them was as condescending as a Parisian waiter. He had light grey eyes, and was almost browless. He shook their hands absentmindedly, invited them to take a seat and told them, reading from his screen, "Among the credit card fraud reports today was a complaint relating to Le Grand Hôtel. I saw your request for information, so I called. I don't have many details. A British businessman named Scott Purduie claims that the maximum withdrawal amount, two thousand five hundred euros, was withdrawn from his account today at 14:30 from a cashpoint at the Opéra."

"His card was stolen?"

"No. The money was withdrawn using a mobile, not a credit card. Which means the thief had to know the account number and access password, and he also had to type into the cashpoint the access code sent via text message by the bank."

"And was his mobile stolen?"

Abadi was the one to reply. "Let me guess. The thief was connected to the same wi-fi network as the account holder, and he managed to connect to the phone without stealing it."

"Exactly," the detective confirmed, and looked at Abadi with surprise.

"And this gentleman was staying at Le Grand Hôtel and using the hotel's wi-fi network?"

"He was a guest at Le Grand Hôtel. But because he filed the

complaint with his bank and not with the police. We don't have more details."

"Is it possible that, apart from the money withdrawal, there were other transactions made from his account that he did not initiate?" Abadi said. "Payments, deposits, things like that?"

"Probably," the detective nodded, "but right now he's on his way back to London. The fraud division's only connection to him is through his bank. I can try to find out more tomorrow morning."

"You mean, this morning, in three or four hours."

"Yes. And now, please don't take this the wrong way, but it's late and I have a lot of work to do here," he said.

They returned to the underground maze. Abadi checked his Navran, but there was still no signal from Oriana. He reached for his personal mobile and glanced at the screen.

His mother had called him two hours ago.

He paused under the ancient chapel, his mind searching for a reason why she might have been calling so late. Failing to come up with anything plausible, he called her back. The phone at his parents' house in Créteil rang and rang.

Meanwhile Commissaire Léger and his deputy advanced in what they estimated to be the direction of the major crime division. Abadi looked at his watch. After a moment's hesitation, he dialled his parents' neighbour, Mme Zerbib.

Chapter 93

As she re-entered the dining hall, Oriana felt that something was different. Cohen was still sitting near the network intelligence officer, but Zorro now sat at the edge of the bench. She tried to turn up clues on her way to the table, and saw that Cohen's mobile was still there. When she sat down she saw an additional mobile on the table – sleek, no camera, secure – which she assumed was Zorro's. Whom had he called in the meantime? She did not need to wait long for the answer.

"Segen Talmor, we've decided that you can't write an inspection report about this affair. I spoke to Aluf Rotelmann and we're in agreement that putting these things in writing, let alone distributing them, may compromise our intelligence sources."

What was it that Oriana detected in his voice? It certainly wasn't triumph, but neither was it submissiveness. Zorro spoke with something approaching resignation, like a man leaving a casino after a string of bad hands.

Who was he playing against?

"You could say that about any intelligence report," Oriana said. "Every time you document information, you're placing the person who gave it to you at risk. Our primary goal isn't protecting our sources but benefiting from them."

"Not every source is *our* source." Zorro bit his lip and raised his voice, "You have four more minutes to question the soldier. Then you will deliver your conclusions to me verbally, and I will pass them on."

"I'll have to consult tomorrow with Colonel Abadi," Oriana said, trying in the meantime to make sense of Zorro's statements.

"Abadi isn't going to be head of Special Section tomorrow," Zorro said. "It was a failed experiment. You have three more minutes."

Oriana stood up and walked to the door, as if wanting to be at a safe distance before her final question. "Shlomo, why do you have two mobiles?"

"I don't have two mobiles." Cohen awoke from his lethargy and pointed at the iPhone. "That's my mobile."

"Yes, that's what I thought. So what's a Samsung phone doing in your locker?"

The implication of this revelation hit Zorro first, accompanied by a sense of helplessness and its cousin, injustice. He rose from the table, hesitant, almost swaying, and looked at her as if the lobster he had ordered at a fine restaurant had suddenly started moving on his plate.

The network intelligence officer got up immediately, and set off towards the living quarters, bumping into the cook who had come to ask if he could admit the soldiers, they were starving. Zorro shouted unintelligible instructions towards the bunker while the network intelligence officer doubled back to try and decipher the order of the panicked head of intelligence-gathering as Cohen said, "It-isn't-mine-this-is-my-phone, Yermi-asked-me-to-look-after-his." Oriana did not bother to explain that the Samsung was already on its way to the encryption department of Unit 8200's headquarters, saying only: "We'll meet again, Zorro!"

Chapter 94

Uncle Saul dialled the operator and asked for an outside line.

He had neither a mobile nor a direct line in his office. This decision originally stemmed from his desire to limit expenditure, but as time went by he became aware of all the additional benefits this seclusion afforded him. It was nearly impossible to monitor his phone conversations, and whenever the tax authorities got their hands on a warrant that would enable them to listen in on him, they were forced to record every incoming and outgoing phone call from his empire's global switchboard, thousands of conversations each minute from every hotel room, casino hall and office building in Melbourne, Macau, Atlantic City and Milan – thousands of calls in a melange of languages, all transferred through the same main telephone number, swamping the calls he himself had made.

What was the time in Israel? He did not bother to check. The middle of the night, maybe three or four in the morning. An ideal time to make such an important call, as it ensured a minimum of pleasantries, words of introduction, useless reports and evasive answers.

"Saul Wenger. Did I wake you?"

The political advisor sat up and turned on the bedside lamp. He shot a panicked look at the alarm clock. Fucking four in the morning.

"Can you hear me?"

The political advisor tried to organise his thoughts. Fuck. Fuck, fuck, fuck.

"Did I wake you? Can you hear me?" As if it was possible not to. Uncle Saul had a loud booming voice at all hours and from all places around the globe, a monotonous bass that was accustomed to making demands, regardless of the hour.

"Hello, sir, I'm glad you got back to me. I tried calling you, but the secretary wouldn't put me through."

"What did you want to say? Say it now."

Yeah, right, the political advisor thought. I didn't want to say anything, I only wanted to stall, and at four in the morning that's not so easy.

"I wanted to ask if you received the itinerary for the visit and if you could be kind enough to approve it."

"And what's going on with the *issue*?"

"It has become a little complicated," the advisor said, trying desperately to remember the points he had jotted down for the conversation. He could only remember the first one: "Do not, under any circumstances, talk to Uncle Saul about the kidnapping in Paris."

"So when are you going back to standard procedure?"

Even in his semi-conscious state, confused, suppressing yawns and searching in vain for a pen, the political advisor noticed the phrase Saul Wenger had chosen: "standard procedure". An irresponsible act that had lasted barely three months and was now threatening to hinder seriously the co-operation between Israeli and American intelligence agencies had become "standard procedure", a glorious, long-standing tradition that without warning had been betrayed, with no satisfactory explanation nor adequate compensation.

"I'm confident, sir, that the Prime Minister would be glad to elaborate on all the available options when you meet here in person."

"I have no need for all the available options. The option we already settled on is good enough for me."

"It's difficult to explain over the telephone," the advisor said. "That's why a conversation in person would not only be more pleasant but also more productive."

"I'd like to believe that," Wenger said and hung up. It was his classic closing gambit, explicit enough to raise concern, ambiguous enough to stir confusion. And he truly did want to believe it, despite having already guessed that things were much worse than he'd been told. He had bet on Israel's Prime Minister long before he was elected, and this alliance had delivered immense benefits throughout the years. But past results were no guarantee of future success, and no-one understood that better than he did.

Chapter 95

It was raining again, torrents upon torrents, and Abadi found himself wiping the windscreen of Commissaire Léger's car, polishing away the steam and peeking through the transparent circle he had created, like he used to do when his father drove him at dawn to Hebrew class.

And just as he had done then, Abadi looked out of the window with both hope and sorrow. Thousands of kilometres away, on the shores of the Mediterranean, the antennae of Unit 8200 had probably by now deciphered millions of correspondences pertaining to the disappearance of Rav Turai Yerminski, and the technology section's mysterious algorithms were churning out keywords, geographic locations and cross-references. There, in the familiar unit to which he had been summoned back, someone could by now determine who Yerminski had spoken to since landing in Paris, someone would be able to explain the connection between him and the blonde kidnapper, and the connection between her and the Chinese commando team, and who here had kidnapped whom.

Whereas in Paris, cut off from his deputy, ostracised by his commanders and without access to known means of local intelligence, he was forced to peer out of a car window and lend his trust to sources that had as little to do with cutting-edge intelligence as one could imagine: a taxi driver and a concierge.

"We'll find him," Léger said, reading his colleague's grim thoughts. "The taxi driver's testimony was unequivocal."

The testimony had come when hope was already lost, after a long night in which hundreds of police officers approached everyone working a night shift near Saint Lazare – the taxi drivers, the prostitutes, the transport service drivers, the waiters in the 24-hour restaurants – with one simple question: "Have you seen the man in this photograph?" No-one had seen Yerminski, and his face had not been caught on any one of the many cameras of the city's public transport surveillance system.

Finally they arrived at the taxi rank in place de la République, from where the night dispatcher reported that, earlier in the evening, one of the drivers had joked on the radio system that he had just driven a blonde who looked like a million dollars, and that neither she nor her partner had left a tip. The other drivers on the radio wanted to hear more details, but all he could add was that the girl was wearing a red suit.

The driver finished his shift and went home to sleep. A team of investigators knocked on his door at one in the morning, waking up his wife. Having drunk a strong cup of coffee and checked his meter, the driver was able to confirm that the photograph was indeed of the guy he had driven with the blonde. He had picked them up at Saint Lazare and dropped them off at place de l'Odéon.

Boulevard Saint-Germain was now awash with the blue lights of police vehicles, and buses filled with police jammed the intersection, their commanders waiting for the signal to let the forces out.

The Odéon intersection was bigger than Abadi had remembered. Two main arteries crossed at the Odéon, boulevard Saint-Germain-des-Prés from east to west and rue de Seine from the river up to the Jardin du Luxembourg. From a distance, at the end of the southward rise, the French flag waved above the Senate building. Everything was still lit: the cinemas, two cafés, the display windows of stores and, in the middle, next to the stairs ascending from the métro, the statue of Danton surrounded by his loyal followers, calling out his desperate address on the eve of the Revolution, "We must dare, and dare again, and go on daring."

Commissaire Léger stood before his men and looked like someone who could use some daring. "The taxi driver dropped them off here, at the taxi rank in front of this statue. That was eight hours ago. You can see how they were dressed in the photograph we gave you. I'm reminding you that we already have eight fatalities on our hands. You're the ones who can stop this massacre. Go out there, and good luck!"

The police officers rushed out, some to the bourgeois streets ascending to the Luxembourg, others to the alleyways descending to the Seine.

As an orator, Léger certainly did not threaten the eminence of Churchill or Shakespeare's Henry V, but at least his speech had been focused and well reasoned. Abadi listened from the sidelines, struggling to understand the logic behind spreading his troops along the many streets surrounding the intersection. "There are seventeen thousand doormen in Paris who meet the professional definition of concierge," Léger's deputy said, while clinging to Abadi like a leech. "They're unionised nationally, and enjoy free lodging in the buildings they watch over, as well as a salary that includes every possible social benefit. Their duties include emptying the rubbish bins, cleaning the stairwells, summoning the lift technician, operating the central heating and, most of all, serving as unofficial informants for the French police."

It was clearly a favourite topic, and Abadi chose not to interrupt him.

"We don't know anything about this kidnapper," the deputy said. "She may be connected to the Chinese commando team or she may not be. She may be connected to the first blonde, the poor girl we found at the fountain at Pompidou, or she may not be. She may already have killed Yerminski or she may not have.

"But there's one thing we know for sure: she and Yerminski got out of the taxi here, at this intersection, and in a historic area like this, there's a concierge in every building. That's our lead. The patrol officers from the 6th arrondisement know each and every concierge personally, and over the next hour they'll be knocking on every door and waking up every concierge until they find one who can identify her," he announced with almost contagious conviction.

In the meantime, Léger had finished dividing up the teams and entered Le Danton café, which was about to close for the night. Joining him at the bar, Abadi ordered coffee and Léger an omelette. Patiently and wordlessly, they waited.

Chapter 96

Ming looked at the screen. He had known many such nights in which hours were spent waiting for a miracle to appear with dawn, and the miracle never came. He had known downfalls and defeats, had seen his meticulous plans scatter to the winds, had known vicious partings and bitter surprises. And his vast experience of riding the crazy dragon of life had taught him one thing: empires always look invulnerable until the very last moment.

But the last moment always arrives, and always when least expected, invariably in a different guise than in previous last moments. One is granted a brief opportunity to save oneself from ruin, to jump from the roof of the empire to the nearby building, or to the helicopter circling above, or to the narrow, almost invisible opening reserved for those who leave everything behind and make the leap. Ming had seen friends and foe alike swallowed into the bowels of the earth with the empires they had founded, blinded by hubris, deafened by pride. And now he gazed at the screen, powerless, following the transfer order of twenty million dollars making its way towards the enemy lurking behind the obscure number 13uEbM8unu0ShB4TewXjtqbBv5MndwfX6b, and he asked himself whether this was a sign that he should leave Paris, Erlang Shen and the rest of Team Four. Should he make a hasty retreat before the house of cards collapsed on top of him?

He carried on because the alternative to this shame was even greater shame. He could not believe that his millions were making their way to this unexpected blackmailer, a one-man hustler whose operation was about to cost him dearly: in money, *xiake*, and face. He could not believe that his meticulous plan to catch this nobody had failed. "I have fallen victim to my own perfection," Ming said to himself. Team One, with the blonde honeytrap at the El Al arrivals hall, falling for the wrong Israeli's stupid approach; Team Two, on surveillance in front of the station locker being recalled by He Xiangu because she was sure Yerminski had been executed. And now he was chasing his own tail, looking for Yerminski's phone or computer or whatever machine would give him access to the Israeli's bitcoin account.

As if guessing that he was waiting for a clue, the bitcoin software on his mobile sent a push notification to his screen: "Estimated transaction completion time: 55 minutes."

Ming waited for another indication, a more explicit sign. He looked at his mobile. No sign appeared.

Chapter 97

They were close, they were far. The lead soon appeared in the image of the concierge of the building next to the medical school, on the eastern side of the Odéon. But she had seen only the blonde stewardess and not Yerminski, the Israeli who kept slipping through everyone's fingers.

The building was massive and grand, with a classic courtyard complete with small fountain, a bicycle storage shed and a large garbage room, to which the concierge pointed.

She was an older woman, with a slight Spanish or perhaps Portuguese accent, dressed in a heavy red dressing gown and scarf over a sweater, as if allergic to the night air. "I'm completely sure it was the girl from your photograph. She was wearing a red uniform. At first I thought she was going to the tourism company on the third floor. I pressed the buzzer to let her in and returned to the courtyard to feed the cats. And then I saw her, from behind. She didn't go upstairs but walked directly to the garbage room, where she threw something away."

Léger's voice was cold, almost hostile. "What did she throw away? Something big? Something small?"

"I don't know. Could not be very big. She threw it into this skip here, the green one, not the recycling one. She closed the lid and went back outside, and that's when our eyes met."

"And the guy in the other photograph? He was not with her?"

"No, no-one was with her. She went back to the front door, did not even pretend that she wanted to go upstairs or anything. Still, she could at least have said 'hello'. Nothing. She pressed the exit buzzer and opened the gate to the street."

"You weren't curious to see what she threw into the skip?"

"No, of course not. It's none of my business. Could have been drugs or something like that."

"I'd like to think that if you really thought it was drugs you'd call the police."

"With you coming around here all the time, I would not need to call," the concierge replied in a triumphant tone.

In the meantime, the police officers went through the skip. From among the full, tightly sealed bags of rubbish, quiet as pillows, an object was released and hit the stone tiles with a plastic-sounding thud. Police torches shone on the gun with the golden butt.

They were close, they were far. A police officer with surgical gloves picked up the gun by the barrel, standard procedure when collecting weapons as evidence, but she was not sure they were in such a situation.

"What's that?" Léger said.

"It's a toy gun," Abadi replied. "We should have guessed that from the way she held it in the security footage. Something seemed off to me, but I wasn't sure what. That gun is supposed to weigh two kilos, but she passed it from hand to hand and held it at shoulder level as if it weighed nothing at all. Now we know why."

Léger's deputy approached the police officer and took the gun from her to examine it. He studied it at length, as if willing the gun to speak. It did not. The rain kept coming down.

"Why use a toy gun?" he said.

"When typically do you use a toy gun?" Abadi replied with a question.

"When you don't have a real one," the deputy tried. "Or to get a lesser sentence in case you get caught."

"Or when you're filming a movie," Abadi said. "You yourself mentioned it when we first saw the gun in the security footage. You recognised it as the gun from 'The Matrix'. She wasn't really kidnapping him, he knew it was a toy gun. He used her to kidnap himself. It was all a show, like the red uniforms and the blonde herself."

"Then why did she bother to throw the gun away?" Léger wanted to know.

"Some places are difficult to get into with a gun," Abadi replied. It was only a guess, but in their situation a guess was better than nothing. "In some public places they search your bags, and maybe they're on their way to such a place."

"A public place in Paris that's not only open at this hour but also bothers to search your bags?" Léger's deputy scoffed.

The rain kept pelting them. Abadi lifted his eyes to the sky in supplication; the clouds had painted it the white of a flag.

It was 4.30 a.m., Tuesday, April 17.

Chapter 98

Aluf Rotelmann put on his headphones and buttoned his shirt to the top. He was not crazy about video calls, certainly not those that took place before the break of dawn, but it was convenient for his U.S. counterparts across the ocean, so there was little use objecting.

It was 10 p.m. in Washington, and Aluf Rotelmann was hoping his counterparts would be tired and polite, or at least cautious and formal. He checked his messages from Zorro again. "The French have been briefed, our men at the Paris embassy are ready, I'm confident everything will be worked out in the next hour," his deputy had written three minutes ago.

How exactly could one be confident that "everything" would be worked out? The affair might end well, or at least result in a bigger disaster being averted. But that "everything" was about to be worked out?

In light of the harsh test before him, he deviated from his usual tradition and ordered from the secretary on duty coffee befitting the occasion: strong and black, with a lethal amount of sugar. He sipped it while waiting for the encrypted signal to appear on his screen. His plan was simple: if they asked, he would deny everything; if they pressured him, he would play dumb; if they got angry, he would say he had to double-check; if they threatened, he would promise to hand over the results of his investigation.

In the office with him, outside camera range, sat the Prime Minister's Military Secretary and his political advisor. Aluf Rotelmann was no longer sure who knew what. The governing body was under the control of a flesh-eating virus that used the normal immune system – the law, media, military and intelligence agencies – to fool its own organs, to the extent that it had become impossible to distinguish between the healthy body and the virus.

The algorithm activated the transfer encryption. Behind the flickering marks, Aluf Rotelmann detected his interlocutors huddling around the camera. He recognised the Cyber Warfare Commander of the U.S. army, who was also head of the N.S.A., the Under Secretary of Defence for intelligence, and the head of National Intelligence, a stubborn old general who for years had publicly disdained co-operation with the Israeli intelligence community.

"Any news?" the political advisor rasped from across the room.

"Shut your mouth," Aluf Rotelmann replied. The conferencing system beeped and he looked straight into the camera. It did not occur to him to smile.

Chapter 99

The gate was at the corner of the alley to the right. It was bolted, and a sign warned in four different languages that it was the entrance to a private courtyard. This is misleading, the patrol officer explained to Léger's team. He was nervous, sometimes saluting at the end of a sentence, and Léger's shouts did not have a reassuring effect.

But even if he stuttered and blushed, the information he offered was solid. This historic alleyway, which ran from rue Saint André des Arts towards the Odéon intersection and was called "La cour du Commerce-Saint-André", was his beat, and he patrolled it three times a day. It was generally packed with tourists: they came for the many souvenir shops and to Café Procope, the oldest café in Paris if not the entire world. The Three Musketeers fought in this alleyway, and a section of the original cobblestone had survived here ever since.

But hidden to the right, beyond a bend, was the entrance to "La cour de Rohan", a series of historic courtyards surrounded by two distinguished buildings. One of the buildings housed the Giacometti Foundation – "he was a famous artist," the officer added – and the other building belonged to the city of Paris, which used it to house foreign guests. Commissaire Léger raised his head to offer the younger man a blank stare.

"The sign is misleading. The courtyards are public property and the gate has to stay unlocked during the day because the schools are open, the Du Jardinet primary school and Fénelon secondary school. But outside school hours they are allowed to lock the gate."

"Explain to us again who you think lives upstairs," Léger interrupted him. His deputy kept pressing the intercom buttons in a futile attempt to summon the concierge.

"It's not a matter of what I think," the officer protested, his face more flushed than before. "It's a matter of what I know. There's a models' apartment up there. I believe that at first the city rented it to models only during the fashion shows, but now they live there all the time. They're all tall and thin, walking on these impossible cobbles on insane heels, there's no mistaking them. I don't know how many live there, but I can say for certain that there are a lot of them, mostly blondes. So when my captain asked me if I happened to know . . ."

"Got it, thank you," Léger interrupted him again. "In a few moments, you'll show us where it is exactly."

"My name is Brigadier Jacques Martinon," the officer said. He was not so confused as to miss out on his moment of glory. Léger suddenly noticed a young bespectacled man in a suit. He was listening to the conversation and keenly taking notes in a leather-bound notepad. Racking his brain, he miraculously remembered, a split second before losing his temper, that it was the juge d'instruction appointed by the justice department.

"What's he doing here?" his whispered to his deputy.

"I called him, Commissaire," the deputy said. "We have to follow the rules, so they don't come accusing us tomorrow. I also called the Israeli police attaché, but he didn't want to come. He asked only that I update him if we actually find the Israeli soldier in the apartment."

"And the juge d'instruction wanted to come, I see."

"Yes, and he also said not to start without him. Said he lived nearby."

Léger did not like people meddling in his business, checking if he was dotting his 'i's and crossing his 't's, and he certainly did not like people who could afford to live in Saint-Germain-des-Prés.

But this was not the time to mull over his likes and dislikes, so he approached the young man and requested authorisation to break into the building.

As he had feared, the judge set about detailing his objections. The police were allowed to break into a private house this late at night only, he reminded the commissaire, if there was probable cause to believe that an act of terrorism could be prevented. Léger swore on all he held dear that there was indeed probable cause, since there were already eight bodies, and the man they were searching for was an Israeli spy, and if that was not probable cause enough, well Léger did not know what probable cause was.

"Let's first break into the building. I'll think of something by the time you reach the apartment," the juge d'instruction said, trying to save both his dignity and the outcome of the investigation.

Léger nodded to his deputy, and less than a minute later two policemen opened the historical gate with impressive breaching tools. The force piled into the courtyard, and Brigadier Martinon, leading them safely into the second courtyard, pointed at a red steel door. "Here. Fourth floor."

This time yet more serious tools were required. From a window in the building next door, shutters were thrown open and a neighbour peeked out from above, retreated, and banged the shutters to again. Much less visible in the dark, two young Chinese men in dark suits lay on the roof of the adjacent École du Jardinet, patiently following Leger's every move.

The red door yielded to a welding torch, and the officers lined up single-file, waiting for the order. Léger turned to the juge d'instruction.

"Maybe we should send in only women officers," the younger man muttered.

The Commissaire did not value advice at such moments, not from someone who lived on the Left Bank.

"There's nothing in the regulations requiring us to favour female police officers even if there are only women in that apartment," he said.

"There will be a lot of undressed young women in that apartment. We're breaking in at an illegal hour based on a warrant I issued to you by authority of emergency regulations that have absolutely nothing to do with this apartment. Even if the officers behave impeccably, which you cannot guarantee, it's still asking for trouble. And let's not forget that the owner of this agency managed to rent them an apartment in one of the most expensive neighbourhoods in the city, in a historic building reserved exclusively for foreign dignitaries. He sounds to me like a man who does not want for connections," the judge said, sharing his concerns with the Commissaire.

Before surrendering, Léger brought in a third party.

"What does Abadi say?" he asked his deputy.

"He isn't here. Said it's a waste of time."

"Why?"

"He thinks Yerminski has to be somewhere he can blend in or hide, otherwise he would have stayed at the hotel."

"Isn't a models' apartment the best possible hiding place? Who could ever find this place?"

"Well, we did," the deputy observed. "He said that there was no point in his waiting, and that he's going to look somewhere else."

"Where?"

"He didn't say."

"He has no authority to conduct a search without us," Léger said.

"He has no authority whatsoever," the juge d'instruction reminded him. "And yet somehow things seem to happen the way he wants."

Chapter 100

Abadi ran along the abandoned street, looking up at lit windows, into passing cars, listening for unexpected sounds. Every restaurant and café he passed was dark and locked. The market on rue de Buci was deserted, and in the square in front of the church of Saint-Germain-des-Prés two homeless men and four dogs were sprawled out. Rue de Seine, rue Mazarine, rue Dauphine, rue Bonaparte – during the day, these streets were unpleasantly crowded, but it was as if he were in a ghost town.

Obviously the model could have brought Yerminski to a more lively area – the Champs-Élysées, Belleville, Pigalle, Montmartre. Abadi did not know how Yerminski had reached her, or what he had offered in exchange for her help. But he knew now she lived in this area. It was perhaps the only area she was familiar with in Paris. So when Yerminski asked if there was anywhere they could hide, she took him in a taxi here, far from the Chinese, and they went to a place he could blend in, far from the killers.

The sky began to clear, and soon the rain stopped and a chill set in. Abadi picked up his pace, partly to beat the forces of evil and partly to keep himself warm. Turning into rue Jacob, he approached his favourite spot in Paris, place de Furstenberg. The green doors of the abbey were still locked, the red doors of the wine bar next to it closed. It was as if the city were sealed off to him.

He kept walking, left onto rue Saint-Benoît, and then it happened. A small crowd huddled on the pavement, not far from the entrance to Café de Flore. Women in skimpy dresses, men in ripped jeans, a Mercedes parked on the pavement, two goons with baseball caps guarding the stairs. The partygoers were calling it a night.

A discreet sign: Le Montana. The entrance was almost pitch black, and Abadi would have ignored it were it not for the large group coming out at that very moment.

There was no point in trying to sweet-talk the bouncers. In Paris or New York, Tel Aviv or Beijing, a man of Abadi's age could enter such a club only if accompanied by the right people. The young group at the exit were the right people: granted access to Le Montana once, they could go back in again.

They were too large a group for him to have that kind of conversation with them. He waited for them to start going their various ways, and that took longer in Paris than anywhere else. The men seemed eager to get into the Mercedes and leave, but not to leave their female companions near the club alone, not even for ten seconds. They stood and waited for the girls to finish swapping farewell kisses and wishing each other all good things. Moments later their Uber rides showed up, hastening the goodbyes.

Finally the group broke up. Some walked to their own cars, others had a driver waiting. Four of them remained on the pavement by the entrance, one guy and three girls. Out of the limited options at Abadi's disposal, the only reasonable means of persuasion was to play on their emotions. These people did not want for money and violence would take too much time.

"*Vous l'avez vue peut-être? Une fille toute en rouge, blonde. Elle se sent mal et voudrait que je la sorte de là.*"

He deliberately skipped an introduction, did not bother with explanations, and despite making sure to inject a healthy amount of worry in his voice, he refrained from dramatic gestures. He had appeared out of the blue, a man relatively old for this time and place, but with a plausible and promising story, the first test of acceptance.

"I saw someone matching that description, she was on the dance floor the whole time. Looked perfectly fine to me," said one of the girls, who was wearing a dress of fleeting transparency.

"Was there a guy with her, about her age, blue eyes, jeans and a T-shirt?"

"He's not with her anymore," she said. "She's on the big dance floor alone. He's sitting in the quiet bar, downing shots. He's the one who doesn't seem to feel too well."

"That could explain why she'd call me to help," Abadi said.

"What's your connection to them?" the man asked. He looked burned out from exhaustion perhaps, or maybe from a brutal comedown, but his suspicion was still aroused.

"She texted me that she needed help, but now I realise that she meant she needed help with him. I'll just take him home."

"Are you a friend of his? Why not call an ambulance?"

Common mistake, asking two questions in a row. Abadi ignored the first and answered the second. "That's what I said. But she said he's afraid they'll do blood tests, and he's taken a lot of drugs tonight. I told her the medics wouldn't call the police, but he's still afraid it'll get registered in some system."

"And she's absolutely right," the girl in the sheer dress said.

The guy apparently felt that the decision had been made and, in the way of most men, he quickly joined the winning side despite his reservations. "You have to go get him out now, they're closing in an hour and the bouncers will call the police if he's too messed up to stand."

Abadi looked at him adoringly. "You're right, of course. But how will I get in this late? It'll look suspicious to the bouncers."

"I can get you in," the girl said, who, as far as Abadi could tell, was not the guy's girlfriend, but was not entirely not his girlfriend either. And indeed, as she had probably been hoping, the guy immediately signalled the seriousness of his intentions, at least for the next few hours.

"We'll all go in, it'll look more natural, as if we just went outside to say goodbye to our friends and now we're going back in to dance." Abadi nodded enthusiastically, and they approached the entrance.

The bouncers searched their bags and hardly looked at Abadi, who, with these girls, could have made it past a velvet rope just about anywhere.

The corridor was dark. Red-covered speakers along the walls boomed trance music, as befitted the hour, which became louder as they descended the stairs. Heavy doors led to the main hall where dozens of people still danced ecstatically. Abadi followed the man as he made his way among the dancers, and felt the girl grab on to his waist behind him. Reaching the side of the D.J. stand, they passed underneath the elevated stage to a steel lid on the floor, like a submarine hatch. The man lifted the lid and led them down a set of spiral iron stairs to the lower level.

It was the quiet floor, if Abadi understood the concept correctly. People were dancing to the sound of music selected by them and that only they could hear, thanks to designer wireless headphones. Many others were sprawled on the floor, sitting against the walls in the area that served as a bar. Flashes of colour from rotating laser spotlights swept the darkness, and it was nearly impossible to detect the long counter and the high stools lined up against it.

An empty whisky glass had been left halfway down the bar.

"He was sitting here. Seems he's gone." The man pointed, and said with surprising sincerity, "I wish you luck."

"Good luck," the girls chorused, and the first one even gave Abadi a farewell peck on the lips. The three went back up the spiral staircase, and Abadi heard the hatch open and shut behind them, the music from the floor above flooding the space for a few seconds.

Chapter 101

The soldier brought Oriana on time to the terminal at Ben Gurion airport, courtesy of his motorbike with its impressive police lights and siren, but then she was held for twenty minutes at security. "I'm sorry, you're B.C.L.ed", the shift manager told her.

"I'm what?"

"You are Border Control-listed. You're registered with border security as someone who can't leave Israel without a permit."

"I know, but I have a permit, it's stamped into my passport."

"Where was your passport in custody? I don't recognise this stamp."

"Unit 8200 Headquarters in Glilot."

"So someone there entered a request in the system to hold you here."

The check-in for her flight was due to close in ten minutes. Oriana shrugged and went to the 24/7 department store. She bought some clothes and a book. When she returned to the El Al security counter, a tat aluf in full uniform was waiting for her.

"Good evening, Commander," Oriana said.

"Good morning, Segen Talmor. You did a good job there."

He was smiling, but reserved. His eyes betrayed weariness, his white hair conveying a sense of old-order authority. He probably had not spoken directly to a junior officer in a number of years, and she decided that false modesty would be the wrong attitude to adopt. "Thank you, Commander," she said.

"I have another job for you," the tat aluf said with minimal fuss. "I need the audio reel that Rav Turai Yerminski took with him to Paris." It was more a plea than an order.

"I'll try my best to assist Aluf Mishne Abadi in the search for him, Commander," she said.

"Aluf Mishne Abadi may be close, but we think the reel may already have been delivered."

"To whom?"

"Someone called Ming."

She wasn't sure how to respond. From what Abadi had told her, she knew the mission would be difficult, and she expected very little background information. But this was close to a blank slate. No intel. Nothing.

"Oh, I almost forgot," said the commander, as he reached for a small suitcase waiting on the counter. "I've brought you some clothes. It's raining in Paris, and your Tzahal uniform would not be the best undercover disguise in the history of Israeli Intelligence."

"I've already bought some," she said, still confused by the exchange.

"Yes, but the leather jacket here contains Rav Turai Yerminski's phone. Thanks to you, it has been unlocked by the technological department. I have sent the password together with some other interesting information to your Navran."

"Does it contain Ming's exact location?"

"Regrettably not, Segen Talmor. Machines are as yet unable to do our jobs. Enjoy it while it lasts." He sounded even more like a man who belonged to the past.

"Commander, what is my mission, precisely?" She was careful not to cross too many lines.

"I need this reel, Segen Talmor. Unit 8200's special relationship with U.S. Intelligence depends on it. Aluf Mishne Abadi will probably meet you at Charles de Gaulle airport, but if he's otherwise occupied, you will need to work on this alone."

Once again, she could not shake off the feeling that failure was so inevitable that the commander preferred to pin it on a junior officer and save his good friend Abadi in the process. She did not reply. The commander shook her hand, as if awarding her a medal, and signalled to somebody behind her.

"This El Al security agent will take you to your flight now. Take-off is in ten minutes. Good luck."

Oriana had a window seat. The pilot instructed the cabin crew to prepare for departure – doors to automatic – and the flight attendant promised breakfast and a duty-free cart. Dawn had broken outside, and as the plane took off she could make out cars glinting in the early light, the outlines of houses, the semblance of normality. She wore her new leather jacket – probably bought by her friend the bureau chief – and began to read the transcripts from the Samsung that Rav Turai Yerminski had left behind.

Chapter 102

I, the undersigned, Philippe du Monticole, Juge d'Instruction of the Court Administration Paris-6 Branch, hereby instruct the following addendum be made to criminal case "76029649656 – The French Republic vs John Does", such document to serve as an integral part of the investigation case under my supervision.

Background

Whereas from the time of the first crime in this case, the abduction and presumed murder of Israeli citizen Yaniv Meidan, the number of victims has grown at an alarming rate,

And whereas the rigorous investigation by the police commissaire in charge of the case, Commissaire Jules Léger, has linked the series of killings perpetrated in the city over the past twenty-four hours to the attempts of a foreign commando unit, apparently Chinese, to abduct a different Israeli tourist named Vladislav Yerminski,

And whereas Yerminski was abducted from his room at Le Grand Hôtel at 17:20 today, the commissaire posits, based on intelligence from an Israeli source, that Yerminski staged his own abduction with the aid of a model or actress whose services he hired.

And whereas the information transferred to me by the fraud investigation division indicates that Yerminski hacked into the bank account of another guest at the hotel, and abused it,

And whereas tracking down Yerminski would substantially advance the investigation, be he the victim, who might then draw in the killers, or an accomplice to the crime, and could then lead us to his partners,

And whereas today at 04:20, approximately eighteen hours after the first crime, Commissaire Léger reported to me, via a telephone call from his deputy, that he had obtained the first solid lead in the case,

And whereas, when I arrived within thirty minutes at the location – the locked gate at la cour de Rohan in the 6th arrondissement of Paris – Commissaire Léger requested that I issue a search warrant for the apartment in which, it is presumed, Yerminski's accomplice to the staged abduction resides.

Decision

This case was defined by the Préfet de la Police as conspiracy to commit drug trafficking. In accordance with the law, I cannot issue warrants for night searches for standard cases such as drug-related crimes because a police invasion into a private apartment at night must be based on probable cause of perpetrating an act of terrorism.

However, based on evidence, Commissaire Léger has suggested that this is in fact an espionage affair, and I have indeed found these killings to be more characteristic of military activity than gang wars. Therefore, and out of a desire to prevent further loss of life and indeed the loss of innocent lives, I have granted the police request and issued the warrant.

Once it came to my attention that the apartment housed not only the model or actress whose services Yerminski allegedly hired but many other young women, I sanctioned the operation on condition that only women officers enter the apartment, in order to minimise any possible complaints by the female tenants, all of whom may have no involvement whatsoever in the criminal aspects of this case.

I signed the warrant at 05:10, after which the police effected entry into the apartment.

Result

Vladislav Yerminski was not in the apartment. No weapons were found in the apartment apart from self-defence pepper sprays. The officers recovered an illegal amount (forty grams) of marijuana in addition to a variety of stimulants, including twenty grams of M.D.M.A. pills, and approximately three hundred Ritalin L.A. 40 mg pills.

Upon the reviewing of documents, it was revealed that the apartment was intended to accommodate four models employed by the Paris Top Models agency, which received the apartment with certain benefits from the city of Paris. In fact, thirty-two young women were discovered on the premises, the majority without a European Union work permit. All of the apartment tenants hold foreign citizenship, most from Russia or elsewhere in Eastern Europe.

It appears the models authorised to live in the apartment charged rent from the foreign models not in possession of legal work permits in exchange for residence in the apartment. It arose from the investigation that such practice is common in the industry, and that the models also arranged private jobs for each other without reporting to the agencies employing them.

Questioning of the only French-speaking model in the apartment revealed that the model or actress who "abducted" Vladislav Yerminski from his hotel room, known to her friend only by her first name, Ekaterina, had responded to a job advertisement in a Russian-language online work forum popular among models. The forum post was new. It concerned location work for the filming of a video installation, and listed requirements such as specific hair colour, height and measurements, all of which matched Ekaterina's. She received a positive response and left the apartment at 15:10. Ekaterina's friends had no further details concerning her whereabouts or the job.

Instructions

1. I have instructed Commissaire Léger urgently to locate Ekaterina using the mobile number which her friends provided to the officers. I have issued an information request warrant to this end.

2. I have decided, in light of the grounds for the warrant, not to submit the incriminating evidence found in the apartment at the time of the search.

3. Commissaire Léger's hostility has led me to question whether he is the correct officer to lead this investigation, and I have summoned him to an inquiry meeting at my office at 10:00.

Chapter 103

So close and yet so far. Had Yerminski vanished again? Abadi searched for him amid the partygoers who were dancing and drinking, snorting and vomiting, but he was nowhere to be found.

A drink or at least some water was definitely required. Abadi sat on the stool vacated by Yerminski and waited; there was no barman. Through the darkness he deciphered a set of instructions displayed on the counter. He pressed the button in front of him and spoke into the microphone. Within a minute, a *Perrier rondelle* arrived on the conveyor belt, *kaiten sushi*-style, complete with a mobile payment system. The world was increasingly resembling 8200, probably much to the joy of Yerminski who, Abadi suspected, had no doubt paid for his drinks with credentials belonging to another guest from Le Grand Hôtel.

He reached in his pocket and pulled out the Navran – no good – then searched for his normal mobile. Approaching its time-out, the payment terminal flashed its "Help" screen. "If a connection is unavailable or if you're out of battery, you are invited to use our secure wi-fi booths in the vicinity of the bathrooms."

Secure wi-fi booths in the vicinity of the bathrooms, sure, that would be somewhere Yerminski might feel comfortable. Abadi followed the signs. A door opened to the bathrooms, which turned out to be huge and full of people. The space was very dark, very gender-neutral, and very open. Ingenious lighting made up for the lack of walls. At the end a dozen large cubicles with saloon doors were marked with a wi-fi icon. Only one of them was open and Abadi spotted a charging station with wi-fi router inside the cubicle, near the door.

Four of the cubicles were occupied by more than one person, but in the last a woman's long legs terminated in red stilettos. Abadi looked around. People were coming and going from their own worlds, lost in the music that flowed through their earbuds. He kicked open the door.

The blonde stood up slowly, a queen from her throne. She was the honeytrap from Le Grand Hôtel alright, still in the same red uniform, and she towered over him in her high heels, displaying the same insouciance now as in the surveillance tapes. She held something in her hand, which Abadi was quick to see was her mobile, its cable dangling from the wi-fi router.

"Rav Turai Vladislav Yerminski?" Abadi said.

The man before him looked even younger than in the video, and was certainly thinner and paler. It was maybe the overhead lighting, maybe the alcohol coursing through his veins or perhaps stress was taking its toll. He remained sitting on the toilet lid and glowered at Abadi.

"And you are? I expected a fully armed escort in Tzahal uniform, not a playboy wearing my own shirt."

Abadi had forgotten the switch in the hotel and suppressed a smile. "I am Aluf Mishne Zeev Abadi, head of Special Section of your unit. I need you to come with me."

Yerminski got up slowly, helped by the Russian model who appeared to be more in control than either of the two men present. She disconnected her mobile and looked at her companion, awaiting his decision. Yermi shot his hands up in mock surrender, and then, in weary resignation, lowered them. His shoulders trembled. "I'll let you keep my shirt," he said, "but the only place I'll come with you now is the bar."

It was 5.45 a.m., Tuesday, April 17.

Chapter 104

Mme Abadi again offered the police officers coffee and again they politely declined. There were three of them, two female officers and a policeman, and none of them had ever seen anything like it before.

"We've never seen anything like this before," the senior officer said. They had been there for thirty minutes and had made not an inch of progress – surveying the room repeatedly, studying their papers and the balcony. They were used to investigating home burglaries, taking a few photographs and notes, and then asking the victim to come down to the police station to file an official complaint for insurance purposes. Almost all of Mme Abadi's neighbours had been through it in recent years.

"Maybe you could tell us again what you reported to the police when you made the call?" one of the female officers suggested, adding, "Tell us in your own words."

Mme Abadi sighed. Did she have any other words? She considered switching to Arabic in protest, but the reverence she held for those in uniform prevented her from doing so. "It's all rather simple, really. Last night, just before I went to bed—"

"Do you remember what time that was?" the officer interrupted her.

"After the eleven o'clock news had finished," Mme Abadi replied patiently. "I turned off the kitchen lights and then, through the window, I saw two Chinese men standing on the path, looking up at my apartment. It scared me, because on the news they had just mentioned there had been an attack in Paris by Chinese terrorists. I called my son to ask what I should do, but he didn't answer. So I called Mme Zerbib."

"Who's Mme Zerbib?" the other female officer said.

"She's the neighbour on my floor. She never sleeps."

"She already explained that," the first female officer said.

"I've already explained that," Mme Abadi concurred. "In fact, I've already explained everything to you. Mme Zerbib said it did sound a bit frightening and suggested that we come and spend the night at her apartment. But my husband was already asleep and in the meantime the two Chinese had disappeared, so I said no need and went to bed."

"And then what happened?"

"My son called me back, having seen that I'd tried to reach him, but by then I'd already turned off my telephone. I always turn off the telephone at night. So he called Mme Zerbib, and Mme Zerbib knocked on my door to tell me that my son wanted me to wake up my husband and that the two of us needed to go and sleep at Mme Zerbib's apartment."

"When was that?" the first female officer said. They had some kind of obsession with the timeline. Mme Abadi made an effort to be patient.

"At two in the morning, less than two hours after I'd tried to call him. My son always returns my calls as soon as he can."

"And what did you do?"

"I did what my son said, of course. I woke up my husband and we went to sleep in Mme Zerbib's guest room. She was very nice, and even left us water on the nightstand, like I do in my house. And then this happened."

The officers looked at each other and went into the bedroom again. The window facing the balcony was shattered. The closet was riddled with bullet holes, nine-millimetre. But the strangest detail was a syringe filled with a purple substance, most likely shot from a tranquilliser gun, jammed into the pillow Mme Abadi would have slept on.

"When did you discover all this?"

"I heard the noise in the night, but I was scared to leave Mme Zerbib's apartment. She and I came over here an hour ago, and I called the police station right away."

They fell silent, and she added with cautious defiance, "Good thing I listened to my son."

The senior officer nodded. "Mme Abadi, I think we'd like to talk to your son," he said.

"Many people would!" she replied, and this time one could not miss the pride in her voice.

Chapter 105

Cursing Europe and the French in particular, Ming exited the building and went back to his limousine. It took him a moment to recognise his own black car among the others.

This was the largest business terminal in Europe, if not in the entire world; it was also among the most expensive. At the executive area of Le Bourget airport, north of Paris, the exclusive business terminal for private planes, black limousines pulled over, one after the other, and the people who stepped out of them were those whose time was valuable enough to meet the club's criteria: C.E.O.s of corporations, movie stars, Russian oligarchs, incognito heads of states, the average spoiled billionaire. No more than ten minutes passed from the moment they arrived at the building and the time their planes took off.

And yet Ming couldn't get the respect to which he was entitled. He shouted at the clerk and asked to see the duty manager, who turned out to be an even more impertinent woman. Both refused categorically to approve his flight, and when he resorted to threats, the manager even called the tower in front of him to make sure air traffic control understood that his request for take-off had not been approved.

Eight hours. According to irritating French labour laws that was the compulsory time for pilots to rest after an intercontinental flight. Because his pilots had landed here from Macau via Frankfurt at 4 a.m., less than four hours previously, they would not be cleared to fly again before noon. He could fly the Boeing himself with his own pilot's licence, but he would still be required to hire a second pilot. Ming had offered the manager a bribe which she had declined, her only suggestion being that he hire a French pilot from a list approved by the airport.

Ming kicked his driver, who didn't open the door fast enough. Inside the limousine, he plugged a secure modem into the console, which he then connected to a frequency mixer and to his mobile, a customised model the Xiaomi company had manufactured especially for him. He checked his messages.

Ming read the surveillance report carefully. The only good thing He Xiangu had achieved before her death was to put a tail on Commissaire Léger, and it was clear that the French would lead them directly to Yerminski. "隔岸观火," the organisation's book advised: "Watch the fires burning across the river." Commissaire Léger was probably exhausted. Colonel Abadi was probably exhausted. Now was the time.

Maybe the French airport staff were right, and his pilots were also exhausted. There was no point in fighting their laws, Ming realised, and there was nothing to gain from waiting with the precious Uher reel till noon. He sent an order to Erlang Shen, gathered his encryption devices and went back to the terminal to register his flight plan according to the rules. This time, his driver was quick to open the door.

Chapter 106

Sometimes a certain word – "betrayal", "money", "parents" – ignited within him an agitation bordering on pure rage, and then his eyes would become so bright that all one could see in his pale features were his fleshy red lips, moist from alcohol and sweat, which he bit and parted and twisted, then pursed and sucked in again and again, a heated argument with Yermi's inner demons that Abadi read and tried to fend off without being able to speak their language.

They sat on the high stools, oblivious to the people dancing around them in silence, loyal only to their soundproof headphones, deaf to the theories concocted by a soldier of Unit 8200 during his many endless night shifts, blind to the tragedy unfurling around them.

"They've moved to after-party music," the blonde updated them, and soon she was back on the dance floor. Yermi would look at her from time to time, between the whisky shots he ordered at an alarming rate.

It wasn't a confession, and certainly not a step-by-step reconstruction. Abadi was careful to keep him going while not encouraging the rant, if only to be able to report that he genuinely tried to bring him back to Israel safe and sound.

"On Independence Day they organised a ceremony at the southern base, and invited all these successful 8200 veterans to speak," Yermi said. "There was the guy that invented instant messaging, and the one who leads the secure communications sector, and the one who owns the patent for dynamic search, all of them now multimillionaires. And all these people – " his hands reached up towards the imaginary stage and the microphones and the generals and finally back to himself at the end of the hall – "all these people who get awarded medals and invited to light a ceremonial torch on Mount Herzl and lecture at expensive universities and sit on all kinds of boards and give advice to presidents and ring the stock market bell, what did they do that was so different from what I did?"

"What did they do that was so different?" Abadi repeated, feigning horror. But he couldn't deny that Yermi was right, that Unit 8200 was a club for the children of a tiny elite who took advantage of its secrets for their own good and greed.

"I did just what they did!" Yermi squealed ecstatically, like a child who had managed to trip up his parents with an especially silly riddle. "I didn't do anything different! They served in Unit 8200 and were exposed to interesting information which they sold abroad. The fact that it was technological information and not intelligence, and that instead of selling it for bitcoins they did it through a start-up exit, makes no difference. It's the same thing. The same thing, apart from the fact that I live in the projects with my parents who don't speak Hebrew and can't just pick up the telephone and call a buddy who knows a guy in a venture capital fund. So I managed by myself, that's all."

They were getting somewhere at last. "What do you mean, 'managed by myself'?" Abadi said. "It just happened one night?"

"No, it took me a lot of nights to work it out", Yermi said, swallowing another shot. "When I first got to El Dorado, I didn't ask myself any questions. I'd translate this Chinese guy's entire conversations, e-mails, text messages, everything. I listened to him night after night. But after a while it was clear to me that he had nothing to do with nuclear equipment, or with Iran. He was in charge of the regulation of Macau's casinos, and he took bribes from a cartel of the big casino groups there. So one night I just got bored with this long list of payments, and I summarised it, something like 'Subject discusses bribe' details."

Abadi could guess what was coming next. "The next morning, I was woken up by the senior network officer. He was furious and he ordered me to pick up and translate the entire thing, directly from the raw intelligence feed. I was not to skip anything, and certainly not the casino stuff. And suddenly Macau began to appear on The Most Wanted list. That was so ridiculous, but by now I understood what was going on, and my boredom was cured."

Occasionally the blonde came to dance around his stool, and Yermi would stroke her back and caress her hair as if she were his older sister, and she would lean into him with her lips hovering above his, then straighten up and take out her mobile, snap a selfie of the two of them and show him the image, before returning again to the silent dance floor.

"Boredom is a powerful engine, rather underestimated," he resumed. "When people look for a motive, they always talk about money, or love, or ego, or God. But if they examined what was really behind the most infamous crimes, they'd discover boredom as the number one motive. Think about it, you're trying to kill time, which is absurd, because everyone knows that it's time that eventually kills you at its own pace. Try to imagine a night shift in front of machines transmitting endless quantities of information. You're waiting for someone to say something important. Night after night, day after day, your entire army service. It's surprising there aren't more cases like mine."

There *are* a lot of cases like yours, that's why they called me back, thought Abadi. He couldn't say that, or anything else that sounded forgiving. He needed to rattle the boy's cage.

"Boredom is a nice explanation, but save it for the judges. Everything you did, from the very beginning, you did for money."

Yermi's rambling became more specific, almost coherent.

"Money, yes. You know, the problem with blackmail is that generally you don't know how much money to demand. Is ten million too much or too little? How about two million, or thirty million? I was lucky. I had all the bribes neatly recorded, so I knew exactly how much money was involved. I asked for half, twenty million dollars, I thought that was fair enough. The Macau guy said they'd pay but they wanted the recording, so I had to find a way to get a tape."

"Where is the reel?" Abadi asked, trying hard not to sound too interested in the answer. Since reading Oriana's report about the Uher, the priorities of his mission had changed dramatically.

That was the moment the Russian blonde chose to frolick in front of them.

"I don't know and I don't care," Yermi replied after kissing her softly on the lips. "I used the hotel's cable box to receive confirmation the payment had been made, and then we left and took the reel to Gare Saint Lazare as agreed. I trashed the room before Ekaterina arrived, to give the impression she had found the reel before kidnapping me."

Ekaterina again. Abadi watched her dancing, intrigued, and tried his luck. "It's not too late, Yermi. It's not too late. Come with me, the plane lands in an hour and the flight back to Israel leaves at 8 a.m., we'll just about make it."

Yermi turned the force of his glare on Abadi, his eyelids rising slowly, as if undressing his interviewer. He smiled at first, his eyes squinting, amusement dancing in his pupils, and then he burst into laughter, high-pitched, wild and full of contempt. Mad. The sound reverberated between the silent dancers, permeating the dark room.

Only after a fit of coughing could Yermi look at him and reply, "In time for what, Abadi? We'll make it just in time for the newspaper headlines about the arrest of the biggest traitor in Israeli history, a gag order, rumours on WhatsApp and a show trial. Flash grenades thrown at my parents' building." Yermi was silent for a moment. "I mean, aren't you the guy who went through all this himself? And for a far lesser betrayal? We'll make it back just in time for what, exactly?"

Abadi didn't skip a beat. "We'll make it back in time for the headquarters' investigation into what happened at the southern base, and to them you'll simply be a by-product of something a lot more serious," Abadi said with almost sincere optimism. "I can't promise that you won't stand trial, but no-one has any interest in making this affair bigger than it is."

"No-one has any interest, Abadi? Is there anything but interests in this affair? The only question is what's my interest, that's all."

"And what *is* your interest?" Abadi said.

He was made to wait for the answer because the blonde was once again all over Yermi, posing for a selfie – two, three, ten pictures. Yermi nodded at her and she backed away. There were fewer dancers on the floor by now, even though the absence of morning light could have kept them going forever. He downed the rest of his whisky before withdrawing his gaze from Ekaterina.

"My interest is that you call the French police and tell them I want to turn myself in," he said in a matter-of-fact, surprisingly mature tone.

"Israel's going to ask for extradition."

"Don't be so naïve, Abadi, Israel won't demand an extradition, they can't even hint at what I did in any official document. If I come with you, they'll throw me into some secret prison and make me disappear. If I go to the French, they'll arrest me on a few petty charges, like the hotel thing, and after making a fuss they'll release me. Forty-eight hours and I'll be out. I had to stick around for something, but now I'm ready."

"If you're talking about the bitcoin payment, we have your phone," Abadi said, and looked into Yerminski's bright eyes. The soldier seemed surprised for a moment, but quickly came to his senses.

"A regrettable development, Abadi, but Shlomo is not my only partner in crime. Call the French police. If you don't, I'll just go out and find the nearest police station," he said and swallowed another shot.

Create the illusion of intimacy with the subject, check.
Retrace the crime with the subject, check.
Present the subject with the options available to him, check.
Stress the severity of the subject's situation, double-check.
Abadi took out his mobile and searched for Léger's number.

Chapter 107

Aluf Rotelmann jogged along the trails of the Hayarkon Park, listening to the morning news. The newscaster was explaining, in his familiar authoritative tone, that the body of Yaniv Meidan had been identified, and that the French police were still investigating the circumstances of his murder. It was not a lie, even if it was not news. What had happened – or at any rate, what they believed had happened – still could not be explained to the public. Returning his earphones to his pocket, Aluf Rotelmann exchanged glances with his two jogging companions, and they picked up their pace and started running in the direction of the lake.

The men were his age. One was his neighbour from the same street in Ramat HaSharon, an affluent suburb north of Tel Aviv, and their children were in the same class at school. He was the chair of the board of a major food company founded by his grandfather. The other was a friend from the army; they had been together on the officers' course and had not parted ways since. A little-known Knesset member, he still found a seat on the Foreign Affairs and Defence Committee.

Both were members of the council for the appointment of Aluf Rotelmann to Chief of General Staff.

The council did not really exist, not in the exact sense of the word. But it worked tirelessly behind the scenes of reality, in that same twilight zone where the truly important decisions are made, in closed messaging conversations, in nightly telephone calls and over morning jogs and formal dinners, and it oversaw inner-circle appointments, budget priorities and the appearance and disappearance of news reports – the twilight zone in which legitimacy is created.

They had in their circle an advertising wizard and a T.V. pundit and a famous lawyer – they were eight in total. All men, they had known each other for years, and in order to survive they had to ensure that one of them climbed as high as possible up the ladder of power. Among the group, Aluf Rotelmann was the likeliest bet even for avowed non-gamblers.

They stopped at their usual spot, beyond the bridge.

"When will the news break?" the Knesset member asked.

"It may not break," Aluf Rotelmann said. "We may find a really good official explanation and everyone will eat it up."

"Even the Americans?"

"No," Aluf Rotelmann conceded. "I got the impression yesterday that they already know what's going on. Obviously the head of 8200 did not like the fact that the Prime Minister's office is transferring U.S. intelligence to someone unauthorised. Maybe the Americans worked out for themselves that there's no nuclear business between Iran and Chinese businessmen in Macau, or maybe they didn't. But they know now that we requested their data from Macau just to help the Prime Minister's main donor."

"What are they going to do?"

"Nothing, I hope. If it remains a criminal matter and doesn't attract any international interest, the Americans will keep a low profile too. It's one thing that we deceived them, but it'll be a whole different problem if it blows up and everyone knows we deceived them."

"We can't take that risk," Aluf Rotelmann's neighbour said, and his military friend agreed.

"We can't take that risk. Even if it passes quietly now, it could blow up five years from now, just when you're planning your move to politics. You can't be involved in this."

"I'm already involved in this. I reported it to them yesterday."

"You told them what you thought was true. That's it. From now on, you stay out of it. The government will not be able to appoint a

Commander in Chief of Tzahal who duped American intelligence. Let your deputy get involved, that guy, what's his name?"

"Zorro? He's an imbecile," Aluf Rotelmann said with regret. "There's no way they'll buy that he was capable of driving a scam of this magnitude."

"What about that Moroccan? The one the head of 8200 rammed down your throat when you weren't looking?"

"He's not Moroccan, he's Tunisian," Aluf Rotelmann said. "But the problem is, he was personally appointed by the Vice Chief of Defence Staff."

"We'll deal with the Vice Chief of Defence Staff later," the Knesset member said.

Aluf Rotelmann said nothing for a long while. Finally he nodded his agreement, and they resumed their jog.

Chapter 108

The juge d'instruction was waiting, quite evidently, for Commissaire Léger to ask one of his officers to drive him home. Léger was waiting, just as plainly, for some kind of miracle.

They were standing on the curb of the boulevard Saint-Germain, looking at the police buses start their engines and drive away from the scene. The corner café was dark. The statue of Danton was mute. Only the billboards in the intersection were lit, brimming with promises. A jeans ad encouraged him to always be himself. Léger was more inclined to be someone else, but no-one was lining up to trade places with him.

He was about to instruct one of his officers to take the judge home when he saw his deputy running towards him from across the intersection, grasping his mobile as if it were the Olympic torch.

"Commissaire, Commissaire," he called out from the middle of the street, panting heavily. "Commissaire, it's Abadi."

Léger was not sure that that was the name he wanted to hear just now. "What does he want?"

"He's found the missing soldier. He says the soldier wants to turn himself in."

"Turn himself in to Abadi?"

"Turn himself in to us," the deputy said breathlessly.

"Where are they?" the judge said, whereas Léger did not dare to ask for details, fearful the magic might disappear once confronted with reality.

"In a club on rue Saint-Benoît, not two minutes from here. What should I tell him?"

"That we're coming," Léger said, suddenly true to himself.

Chapter 109

Oriana woke up in a panic, and several moments passed before she understood where she was and why. The bright lights in the airplane had been switched on, and the flight attendant announced over the loudspeaker that the plane would be landing at Charles de Gaulle airport in approximately half an hour, and the passengers were invited to make their final arrangements.

She looked again at her notes, feeling lost. The name of the man Yerminski had tried to blackmail was Ming, that much was clear from the e-mails on his phone. Yerminski had added a Chinese mobile number to the requests of 8200 from the N.S.A. feed, so that was probably Ming's personal number, from which these conversations were recorded. Yerminski landed with the infamous Uher reel, and the Chinese commando team had tried to kidnap him and search his suitcase. But where was the reel now, and where was Ming? The only answer from Central to her query was that in the past twenty-four hours no passenger with this phone number had flown from Macau to Paris, and no plane registered to anyone called Ming had landed in Paris.

She tried to concoct a plan B but couldn't find one that made sense. Through the window she could see only gloomy skies. She closed her eyes again.

Chapter 110

The Navran buzzed, and Abadi looked at the screen in despair. "Will you accept a call from Commissaire Léger?" it asked. He felt like refusing the call. It did not help that Yerminski's alcohol-drenched gaze bordered on the amused.

But what could he do?

As if to confirm that it was all over, Yerminski slid off the bar stool and went to stand next to the blonde model who was alone on the dance floor. The police sirens had scared off the last few partygoers, and Abadi assumed that the floor above was deserted as well. Every now and then he heard noises emerging from the silence, perhaps club employees folding equipment, maybe stragglers seeking out a corner for one last snort.

Abadi looked at the insistent Navran, then at Yerminski saying goodbye to the blonde in rapid Russian, then again at the screen. He pressed the green button.

"We're here in the basement," Abadi said. "There's a hatch on the floor next to the D.J. stand."

"I'm not even going to try to figure out what a D.J. stand looks like," Léger said. "Tell your soldier to come up with his hands raised. The juge d'instruction will present him with the arrest warrant and we'll take him to police headquarters. You can come with me if you like."

Léger's voice was higher than usual, excited, almost elated. Abadi registered this as he noticed other details: the odd noises around him, the blonde moving slowly in the direction of the toilets, the wireless sound system and laser lights being switched off.

Yerminski looked at him inquisitively, and Abadi repeated the order given by the Frenchman, pointing at the ladder. Yerminski shook Abadi's hand theatrically and walked towards the ladder.

It all happened at two parallel speeds, the slow pace of Yerminski's steps on the silent dance floor and the fast pace of fate whose steps were harder to predict. Abadi waited several moments at the bar, making sure that Yerminski was indeed climbing the ladder. Once he had heard the hatch open and the police ordering Yerminski to hold out his wrists for handcuffs, he got off the stool and ran towards the door through which Ekaterina had disappeared.

The door to the toilets was on the right, but Abadi did not believe she had gone there, just as he did not believe she had been taking photographs while draping herself all over Yerminski. He believed Yerminski had installed his Bitcoin key on her phone, with the account number and password, and that he had decided to turn himself in to the French only when he was sure the money from the Chinese had been transferred.

On the left was a door marked "Employees Only". Abadi pushed it open to find emergency stairs leading up to the street, and could hear the brisk tapping of high heels ascending. One of the things blondes learn faster than others is the location of the emergency staircase in nightclubs.

Abadi took the stairs two at a time and within thirty seconds was right behind her. She kept moving towards her goal – heavy emergency doors bearing a sign that warned of penalties for improper use. Did fleeing an Israeli intelligence officer qualify as proper use? Ekaterina must have thought so. Flinging her heels in his direction – the spikes could certainly kill – she took advantage of the few seconds it won her to push open the right-hand door with all her might.

The two parallel speeds collided with violence. Bullets from an automatic weapon whistled above Abadi's head, and he evaded the crossfire only because Ekaterina did not. Her red uniform was drenched in blood by the time her body fell onto Abadi.

There was no point hoping she could be saved. As the assailants fled, he opened the little purse the model had carried, and found her mobile and a canister of pepper spray. He put them in his pocket before calling Léger.

Chapter 111

Commissaire Léger had been on his feet for the past twenty-four hours. His day had begun with a routine complaint in an area that was not, strictly speaking, under his jurisdiction, and continued, with rollercoaster speed, to a lethal criminal event of shocking proportions. He had almost fallen asleep at the helm, and yet, even in his state of utter exhaustion, physical and mental, the instant he heard the shots fired from the rear of the club, he understood he had to act. Although what he wanted to do was drop to the floor and lie flat, or check on Abadi, he summoned what little strength he had left to shout to his deputy, "Take Yerminski to the car. Now! Get him out of here! Now!"

Yerminski, incredibly pale, handcuffed and surrounded by police officers, was being subjected to a lecture by the juge d'instruction. Breaking into the circle, Léger's deputy instructed the officers to take him to police headquarters in the nearest squad car. The judge asked if what he had heard were gunshots and the deputy confirmed that it was so; Yerminski mumbled something, and Léger's mobile rang. Abadi was on the line.

"Get Yerminski out of here. It's the Chinese commando unit, they've just shot the blonde. Send some men to the club's rear exit."

"We're removing Yerminski from the scene," Léger said. "The squad car is taking him to police headquarters right now. Where are the commandos?"

"I don't know. I think they're scattered throughout the area, maybe looking for Yerminski, or for me."

Out of the corner of his eye Léger saw the juge d'instruction get into the car with Yerminski and the car pull away, sirens wailing.

To his surprise, his deputy had thought to surround the car with four police motorcycles.

"That's odd, I thought I let the motorcyclists go two hours ago," he mumbled.

"What did you say?" Abadi said. But Léger did not have time to answer. He stared with astonishment as the motorcyclists, riding down boulevard Saint-Germain, drew their weapons and sprayed the back seat of the car with four, ten, twenty bullets. The driver hit the brakes, and the car skidded in the direction of the métro station, smashing into the railing.

The biker on the right drove up to the side window closest to him, which was completely shattered, and fired one more bullet into the car, right where the police had placed the key witness from Israel, Corporal Vladislav Yerminski. Like the Horsemen of the Apocalypse, the four bikers fell into line along the boulevard before one turned off in a different direction at the St Michel intersection, a pirouette from hell.

It was 9.18 a.m., Tuesday, April 17.

Chapter 112

Abadi looked around him in the darkness. He tried focusing on possible escape routes, hidden exits, unpredictable solutions. Outside-the-box thinking, as especially conventional people called it.

He was on death row. Not just because the Chinese were after Yerminski's telephone – otherwise Abadi would have hurled it in the presumed direction of the assassins – and not just because they might accurately suspect that Yerminski had talked to him. They wanted to add him to their list of victims because his death would be a nice decoration on their greeting card to Israeli intelligence, and to Israel in general.

The emergency exit door still stood ajar to reveal a typical Parisian courtyard, three trees, a bin room, and the doors of neighbouring buildings. There was no sign of the assassins, but Abadi was sure they were out there.

One option was simply to wait for a special unit of French police to organise his extraction from this basement. As someone who had followed the intelligence reports on the French forces' response to terrorist attacks in Paris, Abadi was not eager to rely on them. And besides, from what he had heard in the background of his call with Léger, Yerminski's death had dealt the final blow to the commissaire's performance and he was the only one who knew where Abadi was right now.

Where was he, indeed? He took out the Navran and switched it to mapping mode. The location mapping put him, as he had assumed, on rue Saint-Benoît. It even indicated that he was one floor below street level, but it did not display further access routes to the rear exit apart from the stairs that had yielded the body of the blonde. He switched the device to X-ray mode. It did not detect any human presence in the courtyard itself, but several windows, roofs and balconies faced that courtyard; from how many convenient hiding places could a sniper hit him the moment he tried to leave? Dozens, at least. And this man had already proven that opportunity alone was sufficient.

There was no choice but to go back and try the club's main entrance, which faced rue Saint-Benoît, in the hope that the number of officers there would allow him to emerge without being shot. Running down the stairs and across the hallway, he found himself standing once again in front of three doors: the door to the toilets to the right, the kitchen door and, to the left, the door leading back to the bar.

He turned left. Before he had pushed open the door, the Navran started to vibrate. Three green dots flashed on the screen. He held the Navran closer to the door and tried to decipher the findings. Three people in a line across the bar, the middle one leaning against the stool on which Abadi himself had sat only minutes ago. It was impossible to know if the red line near the dots signalled sub-machine guns, sniper rifles or R.P.G.s, but the men were definitely armed, and their weapons had been used less than a minute ago.

He tried to understand the commando unit's strange formation, and assumed that, as in the ambush of the model, they were going for crossfire – a method so non-Israeli in its extravagance that Abadi had never undergone training against it. The Navran ran a series of encrypted data, enabling Abadi to gain a better understanding of the squad's positioning: the weapons were heat-seekers, some kind of Chinese advancement the Navran could not trace in the database. The reason for the lights having been turned off downstairs was much clearer now. They could dispense with sight and let the weapons – and Abadi's body heat – do the work for them.

Entering an ambush was one of the most foolish things an experienced soldier could do, unless he was doing it with full awareness and forethought; then it was considered a brilliant tactic, albeit insane. The advantage of insane moves was that they were not measured by the size of the enemy forces, but by the level of fear gripping you. Abadi took a deep, relaxing breath.

He found the bottles resting in a giant fridge in the kitchenette. He chose carefully, forgoing the beer in favour of a dozen bottles of Perrier. He remembered to put aside the Navran while drenching himself in litres of ice-cold sparkling water. He waited thirty seconds for his body temperature to stabilise, then crawled along the conveyor belt designed to transport drinks to the customers at the bar.

The dance floor, which had been so quiet when dozens of people had taken to it with their headphones, now shook from the force of the sirens and shouts penetrating the hatch. Abadi conjured up the counter's structure to estimate the location of the middle shooter; he had no choice but to handle him first and then hope for the best. He saw him from the side, dressed in the dark rags of a pedlar, wearing goggles and equipped with electronic earmuffs, his right eye pressed against the thermal sights of his weapon.

Abadi crawled, dripping freezing water. When he was within arm's reach, he took out of his right pocket a can he had found in the fridge. Twisting the metal base, he waited a minute for the calcium oxide to combine with the water and create a "Hot When You Want!" Nescafé, as the label promised.

When he had counted to sixty, Abadi opened the can and hurled it like a hand grenade in the direction of the door at which the guns were aimed. Heavy fire immediately opened from three directions. He leaped towards the shooter closest to him, pulling off his goggles with one hand and using his other to temporarily blind him with the dead model's pepper spray. The Chinese pedlar jerked forward in pain, and Abadi kicked him from behind, sending the body shrouded in black rags toppling towards the bullet-riddled door. Another volley instantly sounded, and Erlang Shen's body twitched in the air this way and that before finally striking the floor like a rock.

On the counter, right next to where Erlang Shen had stood only moments ago, Abadi found a gun. He recognised the Chinese N.P.-30 but had no time to use it: the two other shooters, confused and blinded by the firefight, aimed their automatic weapons at him, tracing his rising body heat.

He leaped under the bar while their sophisticated tracking systems locked on their own body heat at the same time. The barrages were as rich and dense as a swarm of bees. The two Chinese had shot at least eight bullets at each other before collapsing. Shells flew in every direction and Abadi felt a burning in his right shoulder. He tried crawling back inside on his left elbow, but his body refused to comply and his mind was spinning on its axis. At least that's how it felt before darkness descended.

Chapter 113

Avoiding the line of fellow passengers waiting for their luggage, Oriana took her carry-on suitcase and went straight to passport control. She switched on her Navran while the queue for non-E.U. passport-holders moved at a snail's pace, only to learn that her commander was not waiting for her at the airport. Careful not to pique the curiosity of the French police or gadget-loving Israeli passengers she checked the map again. No matter how much she pinched the screen, zooming in and out, the blue dot indicated his location was a nightclub on the Left Bank.

Oriana had not really expected that her boss would be joining her in the hopeless search for a Chinese person called Ming and an unmarked magnetic reel and yet she still felt a pang of disappointment. What was he doing at a club when she had complied with his request and had flown all the way to the city of lights?

The officer held her passport above the biometric scanner and asked the purpose of her visit to France. "Looking for someone," she said, distracted. "If you can't find him, I'll be here tomorrow too," the officer mentioned with a flourish of hope, but at her contempt-filled gaze he returned to his cautious formality.

She found herself in the arrivals hall of Terminal 2A, about which she had read so many reports over the course of this long day, and she went straight to the information desk. A sceptical clerk listened to her speech and showed her the way to the executive Aéroports de Paris counter on the departures level. By the time she stepped up to the desk, where two Charles de Gaulle airport receptionists in pale blue uniforms were busy discussing the previous day's drama, she had composed her story.

"*Bonjour, excusez-moi,*" she began, then quickly switched to English. "I'm the flight attendant for a private flight to Macau, but I can't find the correct terminal and I'm worried I'm going to be late. The flight is for a Chinese V.I.P., his name is Ming."

"I don't see any flight to Macau listed here," the first stewardess said, clicking on her computer terminal. Her voice was friendly, although her demeanour registered disapproval at such unprofessionalism. "Where is the refuel? At which airport?"

"I'm afraid I don't know," Oriana admitted.

"Do you know which company chartered the plane? Who called you?"

"I don't think it's through a company. My only contact is Mr Ming himself," Oriana said.

"If it's his own plane, it won't be here," said the receptionist, who seemed relieved to be able to pass the problem to someone else. "The take-off would be from the private terminal of Le Bourget. Let me check there." Her fingers moved much more calmly now, as if in a piano recital. And the answer appeared almost immediately.

"I apologise. There is a direct flight to Macau registered and it is, yes, a private plane, but the name of the owner is not Ming. I'm not allowed to say more."

Oriana implored with her eyes, and the woman behind the desk gave in to a small compromise. "Let me check if they asked to hire a flight attendant. Your name might be on the request."

There are two chances for that, Oriana thought, and two chances only: slim and none.

But the French attendant made a very French sound, something like "*Ah voilà, là, là, là,*" and then turned to face Oriana, all smiles. "O.K., it's a small misunderstanding. Your Mister Ming is not the owner of the plane, he is the pilot. They registered him an hour ago, and he was probably asked to bring a flight attendant. It happens all the time. I see he has also requested another pilot, so it fits. You're good."

"I'm good?" asked Oriana.

"You're good to go. Take the special *navette* to the executive area of Le Bourget, there's one downstairs which leaves in four minutes and you'll be there in fifteen minutes. Your plane is parked on F.B.O. 05, you'll see the signs in front of the bus stop. And you're lucky. You're not late because the second pilot has yet to arrive."

She turned to her colleague, her voice dropping in register for the exchange of the shared confidence, "*C'est Menard.*"

"*Le chaud lapin,*" laughed the second woman.

Oriana wasn't sure of the translation. "Hot rabbit"? And she looked at the women.

The helpful stewardess was quick to explain. "You'll have to watch out for his wandering hands, particularly if he calls you to the cockpit. He has a reputation."

"Thanks for the heads-up, I'll be careful," Oriana said. "So, the special bus, downstairs?"

"Yes, the *navette*, it's exit number 12. And have your badge ready when entering the departures zone, security is very tight now. We had a strange kidnapping here yesterday, so the security people are a bit edgy."

"I can see why," Oriana said. She took the carry-on suitcase that the Unit 8200 commander had given her and proceeded to exit number 12, ready to meet Mr Ming.

Chapter 114

It was 7 p.m. in Melbourne. Uncle Saul's flight was scheduled to take off in five hours, and he made use of the time to go over the numbers again and again, making sure his financial controller had not neglected any area in his forecast.

The staff who would accompany him had gone home to prepare for the long journey and say goodbye to their families, perhaps even get some sleep. With age, he had come to need less and less; in any case, sleep had always seemed to him a waste of time, contributing nothing to the bottom line and doing nothing to loosen the noose tightening around his neck.

The bottom line was remarkably clear, and unfortunately he had found no errors in the reports. His share in the casinos in Macau was a mere 10 per cent of the total gambling activity in the city but constituted 48 per cent of his global revenue. If the Chinese were going to pull him off the gravy train, he would have to double the number of casinos outside China in order not to go bankrupt.

He already had the biggest market share in Canada, France, Holland and Russia. Las Vegas was too competitive. And while his investments in Eastern Europe were highly profitable, there simply was not enough money there to justify such a massive investment.

His people had suggested Spain, a country of compulsive gamblers, with the highest number of significant lottery enterprises in the world and a clear lack of casinos relative to the demand. Very close to North Africa, and less intimidating than Monaco. According to the proposal they drafted, a city of a dozen hotels and a thirty-billion-dollar casino could earn them back their initial investment within four years, if their terms were met.

During the past decade, three entrepreneurs had tried building a new gambling city in Spain, and each time the regulator had thwarted the project at the last minute. His offer would depend on the approval of no fewer than ten public officials, including the Director General of the Ministry of Health, who had had the audacity to refuse granting a special exemption to smoke in the casinos.

Each time a gambler went outside for a cigarette break, Uncle Saul lost seventy dollars. Which is why it did not happen – in each of his casinos a gambler could smoke his lungs out if they so desired.

Saul Wenger took a notepad and wrote down the names of the Spanish officials who stood between him and his project. His meeting with the Israeli Prime Minister was scheduled for tomorrow evening, at a big philanthropic gala at which he would announce the establishment of a fund to provide grants for single soldiers in Tzahal and a yearly trip for combat soldiers to the death camps in Poland. Saul Wenger believed there was no such thing as a free meal, and his philanthropic dinners were no exception.

Chapter 115

The *navette* to Le Bourget was full of pilots, flight attendants, flight engineers, medics, all types of air crews and all nationalities, some in full uniform and some not, some speaking French and some not, all with one visible point in common: a security tag with picture and electronic barcode, probably issued by the airport.

Oriana clipped her investigator card to her left pocket, as if she was in Glilot. It wouldn't get her past security, but it reassured casual onlookers with its authority: a logo; a photograph; the correct year; and foreign characters. She listened to the conversations around her to pick up the right intonations, accent and vibe.

The bus travelled through charming small towns. As it approached Le Bourget the surroundings changed rapidly to include commercial centres, storage facilities and chain hotels. The streets bore the names of pilots and heroes, and when the bus turned from rue Antoine de Saint Exupéry to avenue du 8 Mai 1945, the driver signalled to her that this was her stop.

Six people got off with her at the stop in front of the executive terminal, a large building connecting several concrete hangars. The four wearing flight uniforms crossed the road and went directly to the security booth for departures marked F.B.O. 01–20. The two others hurried to the main entrance.

Oriana went to the departures entrance, walking slowly to observe the routine. As she had suspected, the identity check was performed by the traveller scanning his or her badge while the security personnel concentrated on the X-ray detector screen. No human eyes were on the identity of the person going through X-ray: if the badge had the barcode and if it hadn't been reported in the system as stolen, the scan produced a short, happy sound, and that was it.

Oriana fought the urge to alert the guards to the shortcomings of their method. It was strange to be on the other side, but it worked just the same, the only difference being that she was about to exploit the holes she identified in security instead of fixing them. To enter F.B.O. 05 and board Ming's plane, all she needed was someone's badge, and she needed the person who owned the badge to be incapable of reporting its disappearance.

Black limousines arrived, stopped and left in an incessant ballet of opulence and comfort. The sky had grown bright, ready to host the intercontinental journey of yet another triumphant casino mogul. Now was the final chance to stop that from happening, otherwise Oriana risked imminent failure. She checked her Navran. Abadi had not called, and according to his location was still dancing or drinking or both. "Screw him," she said out loud. She took a deep breath, filling her lungs with the cold air, and charged towards the main entrance.

The main Aéroports de Paris desk appeared to be exactly like its counterpart at Charles de Gaulle, but the two receptionists were more formal, and their body language conveyed severity, if not outright hostility. It suited Oriana just fine.

"*Bonjour*, Monsieur Ming wants to know where on earth that pilot of yours, Menard, is? Monsieur Ming's patience has limits, you realise?" she opened without any other introduction, her fingertips drumming a beat of feigned tension on the counter. The younger receptionist tried to decipher Oriana's badge, but her older colleague did not bother.

"*Ah oui, vraiment?*" she said, the exasperation in her voice growing more pronounced as she warmed to her subject. "Let me tell you something, *Madame*, I am fed up with your *Monsieur* Ming and I pity you for having to work for such an odious man. Despite the short notice, Capitaine Menard has just arrived, almost on time, in fact. He's currently making his final preparations before departure, as he is entitled to do."

Final preparations, then, like on the El Al flight. What a strange choice of words, thought Oriana. Her response was cold. "Monsieur Ming saw crew members entering the terminal in civilian clothing. He wanted me to make sure your pilot Menard will be in full uniform."

"Does your Monsieur Ming want to tell me how to do my job? Some pilots change into their uniforms at the last minute – they get them straight from the crew laundry upstairs – and this is the way we have done it for more than a hundred years now."

Not another laundry facility, Oriana thought. She thanked the receptionist and proceeded to the exit on the left, ostensibly making her way to the hangars. When she was certain she could no longer be seen from the desk, she walked rapidly to the door bearing a green sign, ESCALIER DE SECOURS. The staircase was wide and well lit, and on the second floor Oriana found what she was looking for, a detailed emergency plan of the building. She studied it for a minute, and then pushed the exit door.

The laundry service was supposed to be at the end of the corridor on the right, beyond the bathrooms and the cafeteria. She found the door closed. No-one answered her knock.

She retraced her steps along the same corridor, and as she was about to try her luck in the crowded cafeteria, a pilot in full uniform and an impressive peaked cap left the showers and turned in her direction.

"Are you searching for something, Mademoiselle?" he said, very obviously looking at her breasts.

He was big, with a fake smile, a fake tan, fake teeth and probably fake hair, but his security badge certainly looked real.

"I'm looking for a way to kill twenty minutes before my flight, Capitaine . . . –" she stopped and held his badge between her fingers, reading his name – "Capitaine Menard. Do you know if there's a bar here somewhere?" He looked so satisfied with himself she almost laughed.

"*Mais* Mademoiselle, even if I don't have twenty minutes before my flight, I'm sure you'll be able to help me forget prior engagements." He looked hastily around before continuing, "I'm afraid we don't have a bar and the cafeteria is overrun. I could offer you a drink in a modest but discreet office down this corridor?" Without waiting for an answer, he took her by the shoulder and walked her towards the laundry. "I have the entry code. It's very clean in here, it's where we pilots collect our uniforms before we take to the skies."

Oriana did not need to flirt back because Menard was already punching numbers into the keypad. He opened the door to let her through, and she let her suitcase trail at arm's length behind her as she passed, creating distance should he attempt to jump her from behind.

French laundries were certainly different from the facilities with which she was familiar. A bright, natural light filtered through huge windows that had replaced the original rooftop, and the uniforms had been hung according to colour, from bright white to black and gold. A deep leather sofa and a square table filled with airline magazines completed the look of an interior waiting more for design photographers than for crew members with dirty laundry. Behind a counter there was a huge washing machine, which enhanced the pre-war nostalgia.

She heard him close the door behind them and as he tried to seize her from behind she managed to turn and face him. "I think I have changed my mind," she said, taking a step back.

"*Ah non, petite salope*," he said breathing into her face as his hands grabbed her by the hair. He continued to mutter, "*petite salope, petite salope*" as he pushed her face-down on the counter.

At the end of the day, what Oriana really loved about krav maga, the self-defence technique taught at Tzahal, was its absolute simplicity. No Japanese etiquette, no Thai greetings, no Chinese complexity, no American dogma. The one key concept was "היעילות רצף", "effectiveness continuity". And effective it was, as her first kick smashed his right kneecap.

"When a woman says she has changed her mind, it means she has changed her mind," Oriana said by way of simple explanation as Menard screamed in pain, grimacing in disbelief at his folded leg.

Krav maga is all about continuity; only a combination of moves produces true effectiveness. What good would an overweight victim with a broken knee do her, even if he did get the message? Oriana formed a shell with the palm of her left hand and slapped the side of his head as rapidly as she could, sending compacted air into the inner canal of his left ear. Menard's body jolted as it might under an electric shock and he collapsed on the counter. She kicked his huge rear, sending him over to the other side. Then jumped over the counter to slam his right ear.

Blackout: the pinnacle of krav maga's effectiveness continuity. Oriana tore off his security badge and rapidly checked the room. She wouldn't need much time, but she still preferred to delay the alarm. In a drawer she found a printed "*Fermeture exceptionelle*" sign, the least exceptional apology in French commerce, and hung it on the door. The keypad for the electronic lock had a neat post-it near it, conveniently displaying the password. Oriana entered it and changed the combination.

Only then did she go and choose a uniform from the racks of clean laundry. A red uniform would probably suit Monsieur Ming's preferences, which is why she chose an immaculate white.

It was 11.05 a.m., Tuesday, April 17.

Chapter 116

The Military Secretary tried to gauge his interlocutor's level of anger by standard diplomatic codes. First, there was the simple fact that upon arrival at the U.S. embassy he had been subjected to every humiliating security check possible despite his rank. Second, he had been held in the security department's waiting room in the basement for twenty minutes before they called him. Third, despite the hour, there was no lunch waiting for him, not even an offer of coffee, and had he sipped from the water served to him in the flimsy plastic cup he would have discovered it to be tepid – which would have been perfectly fine if the room were in a dim, ancient castle in Burgundy, but on the coast of Tel Aviv it was not the ideal temperature for any refreshment.

In England you could scold an employee while strolling leisurely through St James's Park; a British gentleman would feed the ducks and express restrained dismay. In France there would probably be furious shouts, but at least the wine would be the proper temperature. In Italy he would have been served food. And in Germany, no Israeli military man would have been summoned for a reprimand, not even in this case.

"Do you know how you cure a plague?" the American said.

The Military Secretary tried to shake off the wave of self-pity that had overcome him, and failed to rally the social skills required for the mission on which he had been sent.

"I have no idea, Commander," he admitted. He did not know how he was supposed to address him. By his name? Director? General? Lieutenant General? His interlocutor's title was a formidable enough distraction – DIR.N.S.A., Director of the National Security Agency, concurrently serving as Chief of the Central Security Service and as Commander of U.S. Cyber Command.

"The classic mistake in the event of a plague is to concentrate on people who already have it," the Director of the National Security Agency said. "What you need to do is examine people who should have contracted it but did not."

The Military Secretary nodded enthusiastically while trying to understand the allegory. "That sounds wise," he said eventually.

"What isn't wise is not realising there is a plague."

"There is no plague," the Military Secretary said. He started to divine where all this was heading.

"Over the past twenty-four hours we've been witnessing the unfolding of an espionage affair in Paris that might hinder our work protocols due to a mistake made here, in the southern base of Unit 8200, a mistake that apparently had not been investigated until this very moment," the general said. The Israeli had to fight the sudden and terrible thirst that overcame him and not reach for the glass of water in front of him.

"General, I can assure you that this grave oversight has been investigated and we know exactly what happened."

"So what did happen?" the American general asked in an almost conciliatory tone.

"The soldier in this event, a problematic young man who should not have been drafted to a unit like 8200 and who certainly should not have been transferred to a sensitive department like El Dorado, was exposed to valuable intelligence which gave him the idea to extort payment from one of the officials the department listened in on, a regulator in Macau who was taking bribes from a Chinese crime organisation."

"This intelligence came from our end, right?"

"That is correct, sir."

"So it was not only valuable intelligence but valuable U.S.

intelligence. There was no supervision of what this soldier could listen in on?"

"The systems were not properly in place," the Military Secretary said, careful to stick to the text that Aluf Rotelmann had sent him that morning. "The head of 8200 has already removed the head of Special Section from his post, Lieutenant Colonel Shlomo Tiriani, because he was in charge of supervision, and we may have to remove his replacement, Colonel Zeev Abadi, as well. The two messed up, there's no question about it."

The Military Secretary tried desperately to concentrate on his interlocutor's shiny medals so as to avoid his unblinking glare. The reply came immediately.

"This is yet another issue, I must say. The Commander of 8200, a unit we've had an excellent working relationship with for decades, had replaced the previous head of Special Section and appointed in his place Colonel Zeev Abadi, who arrived in Paris just in time to prevent this soldier of yours from causing unbelievable damage to American intelligence. We're under the impression that his superiors, including you and the Prime Minister's office, did not really aid him in any way."

If so, the power struggle was clear. The head of 8200 was backed not only by Tzahal's Vice Chief of Defence Staff but also had the support of American intelligence, if not someone even higher up in Washington D.C. To "aid in any way" the Commander of 8200, the Prime Minister's Office would have to return to the rebel unit the control of intelligence and its independence.

The Military Secretary failed to find a reasonable escape route. The choice was either to stop or come up against a wall.

"We've all learned from this affair. I'm convinced that Aluf Rotelmann and the Prime Minister's Office will draw the necessary conclusions."

But that was not enough for the DIR.N.S.A.

"Perhaps you could explain why Unit 8200 was listening through us to a Chinese official in charge of Macau?"

It was the question the Military Secretary had been waiting for since the meeting began. There were two possible answers. The first was direct. For example, "You need to understand, General, that our Prime Minister has an important benefactor in Switzerland who's interested in those kinds of things, like who is bribing whom to win the tenders for the blackjack and roulette tables, and so on. And that's why the Prime Minister asked Aluf Rotelmann to help, and it was working perfectly fine. In fact, you would never have heard about it if it weren't for some bored soldier who did not understand why he was being asked to translate conversations in Chinese that had nothing to do with the Iranian nuclear programme. And during those long nights in the desert, alone with an unsupervised recording device, it occurred to him that he too could take advantage of the U.S. intelligence machine to get rich. So he decided to blackmail the Macau official. And who here can blame him? Isn't that the entrepreneurial spirit America wishes to encourage?"

But the Military Secretary opted for the second answer, and stuck to Aluf Rotelmann's text.

"General, we were in possession of information that led us to believe that the Chinese official, alongside his formal role as the regulator in Macau, was involved in brokering deals for nuclear equipment for the Iranians. This information turned out to be false. Israel obviously has no interest in intelligence about casinos."

"Obviously," the Director of the N.S.A. said with a blank expression. The Military Secretary reached for the water and tried to drink without choking.

Chapter 117

Oriana stood by the statue, a white stone monument representing a nude goddess in flight, and observed the tarmac.

She had passed through security without any problem and had been directed to F.B.O. 05. Each plane taxied to the runway from its own fixed base, and the largest of them was allocated to Ming. His plane was not big; it was huge. It was certainly on a larger scale than the El Al aircraft that had brought her here that morning.

How was she supposed to find Yerminski's reel in this behemoth? This was a job better suited for the Mossad, who would have planned the operation in detail for weeks; they would also have sent forty people, minimum. But the Mossad was controlled directly by the Prime Minister's Office, and the commander of 8200 apparently preferred to solve his unit's little internal problem in-house.

The only in-house solution seemed to be to send her into the lion's den, because time and again her Navran informed her that her direct commander, owner of Navran 008 – surely he was vexed to be one digit too many – had no intention of helping her: his location had been updated from a nightclub on the Left Bank to a hotel near Notre-Dame.

She searched the device for more helpful information. According to its database, the plane was a 747-8, the biggest Boeing ever made, it could seat 467 passengers and only seven planes of this model had been customised for private clients. The interiors were designed by different independent contractors, but the plans had to be sent to Boeing for approval. Oriana guessed this mandatory correspondence was the source of the Navran's information and asked herself how many of the world's secret services had intercepted the documents.

She studied the customised aircrafts one by one, uncertain how many people were on the plane with Ming, waiting for Capitaine Menard. The airstair was in place, the front door open and she could make out general movement in the cockpit.

She opened the suitcase and took out the leather jacket, placing Yermi's Samsung in the external pocket, at the ready. She then took out all her identity papers, including her Israeli passport, and buried them among the daffodils surrounding the statue she had been leaning against. *L'Oiseau Blanc*, "The White Bird", had been dedicated to two French pilots who had taken off from Le Bourget in 1927 in an attempt to cross the Atlantic Ocean and who had disappeared without trace. Oriana read the original dedication etched in the stone above her as she patted the soil into place. "In honour of those who tried," the plaque said. When Charles Lindbergh successfully crossed the ocean in the opposite direction, the dedication had been amended to read "In honour of those who tried, and the one who succeeded."

In honour of those who tried, and the one who succeeded, as simple as that. The victor had bulldozed himself into the dedication, depriving the two unfortunate men who had preceded him of their small consolatory gesture. Winner takes all.

Oriana looked at the nude goddess, then looked at the plane. She took hold of her suitcase and crossed the tarmac towards the airstair.

When she was about halfway up, two men in dark suits and sunglasses stepped out of the aircraft and onto the upper podium, blocking her access. She continued to climb nonchalantly, and when she was in front of them, greeted them in exuberant English.

"Hello, this is your captain speaking! Let's get this bird up and off to Macau, shall we?"

The men did not move. A deep voice called out from behind them, "Who the hell are you?"

It belonged to a tall middle-aged Chinese man in a blue suit who was leaning on the cockpit door. Without sunglasses he squinted as he approached, looking at her as though she were a menu.

"I'm Capitaine Menard, the co-pilot you requested. And where is the first pilot, Captain Ming, may I ask?"

The man was now very close, shouldering through the space between the two gatekeepers. "I am Captain Ming."

"No," Oriana said. "You're not Ming."

"Excuse me?"

"You heard me. You're not Ming. Ming has a light musical voice and his English accent is much better than yours."

The three men exchanged glances. The question in their eyes was clear and it was the man from the cockpit who voiced it.

"You mean to say Ming spoke to you?"

"Oh, we're on excellent speaking terms," replied Oriana. She preferred convoluted wording to the truth – which was along the lines of "On my flight here I listened to his phone conversations, you know, the ones that had been recorded against all regulations by an Israeli soldier."

The man in the middle looked lost. "There must be some misunderstanding, Captain Menard. You see, I don't think Ming would ever let a woman fly his airplane. He would not have approved it."

"Then let's ask him, shall we?" Oriana said with forced joviality. "In the meantime, I'll get on with the mandatory pre-flight check."

"I've already done the system checks," the false Ming said, surprised. So, he was one of the regular pilots, she thought. The two men in sunglasses descended the airstair, which suggested they were the bodyguards. Was the real Ming in his limo? It gave her, what, six minutes?

"Oh, but I run a complete check, more than just the system," Oriana said, forcing her way inside. "The cabin, the doors, the air masks, so many things to check, so little time. I'll begin with the rear door."

He followed her, undecided, while she entered the plane and tried to understand what she was seeing. Fortunately, the radio in the cockpit fired call after call, and he vanished inside, closing the secure door behind him. She was alone.

She recognised the plane's layout immediately, with its unique design of several customised planes in one. There was a huge bedroom, then an austere conference room, and beyond that four suites, each including a bed, shelves and a curtain but no windows; a master bathroom followed, with a standard bathroom after that, and then, at the end of the aisle, there was an open bar in red and black, complete with a karaoke machine and four pinball machines.

Oriana checked the file containing the original plans. It belonged to client number 5 of the seven private buyers. The plane had first been customised by a specialist company near Seattle, then modified by an anonymous contractor in China, and subsequently sent to Hamburg for completion before coming back to Washington for approval by Boeing Jets.

The plane looked remarkably like the approved plans – the colours, the furniture, the space. The only part that looked slightly different was the drinks bar: in the pictures sent to Boeing, the bottles were placed on four long shelves behind the counter. On the plane itself, Oriana saw in front of her three shelves only.

She switched the Navran to X-ray mode and approached the wall. The missing shelf had been replaced by a long white panel that was in keeping with the surrounding decor – but was also hiding an entire weapons arsenal according to the Navran. She searched for the opening mechanism and found it under a heavy bottle of Cognac.

Oriana heard footsteps on the airstair and imagined Ming and his bodyguards closing in. She clicked on the hidden button and the panel glided open to reveal several weapons, including two of her favourite rifles: an M.16 exactly like the one her father had used as his service gun, and a brand-new Kalashnikov she felt immediately attracted to, if only because she had never come across this particular model previously.

She scanned the rifle with the Navran, which gave her an instant read-out: A.K.-15K, a special version of the Kalashnikov that used 7.62 × 39mm cartridges. Oriana found a box of cartridges in the cache. And below it, in a plastic bag from an Israeli supermarket chain, was the Uher reel.

The lights went out.

For a moment she thought that maybe she had activated some kind of remote function, but then the doors began to close and she heard the airstair move away. The engine roared.

Oriana buried Yerminski's magnetic reel in her suitcase. By now the doors were sealed, and she could feel the wheels setting the plane in motion when the internal speaker system above her suddenly came alive. This time it was undeniably the voice of Ming.

"*Bonjour*, Captain Menard! So nice of you to join us, especially in view of the urgent message we received from the control tower saying you had experienced some serious health problems."

That would teach her a lesson. She should have killed the bastard, but it was too late to think about that now. If (a) she emerged from this mission alive, then (b) the next time she found herself neck-deep she'd be sure to remember the cost of her soft heart.

Ming's joyful announcement didn't leave her much hope of (a).

"You'll be happy to learn it is already noon so our original flight plan to Macau has now been approved. When we get there, you and I will have a serious conversation in the comfort of my regular place of work, or at least in the basement. We can have a little chat once we're in the air, but first let me taxi this magnificent eagle to the runway so I can engage the autopilot. I suppose you might like to say something at this juncture, but unfortunately passengers are required to keep quiet during take-off."

Oriana opened the cartridge box and began to load the A.K.-15K. It had the same mechanism as her beloved Kalatch at Glilot, but this one was brand new and short-barrelled. She was curious to try the 39mm bullets, because she had heard so much about their effectiveness from Tzahal veterans who had faced their fire in Lebanon. Sadly, if she were to use them now, she probably wouldn't live to tell them about her experience.

The plane turned left, beginning its short journey to the runway. Oriana could hear the flaps open. She lay down on the floor, pointing the muzzle in the direction of the cockpit and lined her finger along the trigger box, resting her thumbnail on the safety lock. Only when she felt the position was assumed and that opening fire was within reach in less than two seconds did she switch her Navran to telephone mode.

The ringing went on for several seconds before Ming picked up.

"You clever little bitch. Of course, your friend the blackmailer gave you the number for this phone. What are you? American? Israeli?"

"Russian, in fact," Oriana said, affecting nonchalance. "*Skól'ko let, skól'ko zim!* Long time no see! President Putin would like to extend his deepest apologies for the troubles Yerminski has caused you. Let's put this behind us. *Vsevo nailychshevo!*"

Ming hesitated for only a moment.

"You *are* a clever bitch and of course you're lying. It will be diverting to find creative ways to check your nationality. We'll see if your Russian is still as polite in an hour or so. In the meantime it seems we have clearance for take-off. Stand by, two minutes to go."

"I have a question for you about that take-off."

"You have a question, clever bitch? You appear to know all the answers without any help from me."

"Don't get too fond of me too quickly, Ming, our relationship is going to end very soon."

"Oh yes, you're so good at telephone conversations. We'll see soon enough which of us gets attached. Now what was your question?"

"How much does a plane like this cost? We're talking what, one hundred million dollars? 120 million?"

"Are you trying to wind me up? A plane like this costs 350 million, and mine cost much more. I paid more than five hundred million dollars."

Oriana began to understand Yerminski better.

"Well, that's a pity, Ming. You see, the moment we reach our cruising altitude, I intend to try out the superb Kalashnikov I found here in the bar. I've never used 39mm ammunition before, certainly not through a plane window, but I'm told the results can be quite severe."

"What? You're bluffing."

"I thought you might say that. Your people told me that you wouldn't allow a woman to fly your plane, so how about allowing her to blow it up in mid-air? Of course, we'll all die . . . but at least I'll have tried out a short-barrel A.K.-15K, one of our national treasures."

"Listen, you fucking little cunt . . . "

"Tsk, tsk, what kind of talk is that, Ming? Russian women believe in gender equality. Do you want me to prove my rapid-fire skills while we're on the ground? At the bottles here on the shelves, say? Or would you prefer it if I shot a single bullet at the cockpit door, to give you a nice little souvenir of our meeting?"

She heard the tower calling the plane on the cockpit radio.

"Time is running out. You have a choice. Do you want your bitcoins back or do you want to go down with your plane, Ming? That was my question."

Ming sounded faint. "How can I get my twenty million back?"

"You will have noticed the payment has been successfully transferred, but it has not left the wallet. The bitcoins have not been spent. Russia awaits proof of your goodwill. First of all you need to tell the tower that you're taxying back to F.B.O. 05 because a passenger on board is ill. Tell them to send an ambulance."

He hesitated. She heard the tower call him on the radio, and for a moment he was silent. Then she heard him say he had to postpone take-off and return to base.

"Good. Now, for the payment . . . President Putin gives you his word that if I return safely to Moscow with the reel you'll receive your money within a week, directly from Yerminski's private key. Don't change your phone number, and don't try to cross me."

The giant Boeing taxied back to F.B.O. 05 and the airport ambulance when it arrived was a little red and white van, its vintage lines almost reassuring. The plane's wings quivered and the engine died. Oriana got up, unloaded the rifle and put it in her suitcase. Short-barrel guns were cool.

"Tell your men to open the rear door after the airstairs have docked, Ming, and in five minutes you can request a new take-off. Don't be tempted to hang around here. You do remember the last rule of your organisation, don't you? You quoted it in several e-mails."

Ming watched on his screen as the aircraft stairs aligned to adjust to the rear door, allowing two paramedics to carry the Russian operator and her suitcase from his pride and joy. She was a clever bitch and on a good day he would have opened fire on the ambulance that drove her away, but this had not been a good day. "三十六计，走为上计" he said, quoting to himself the final rule from the *Book of Qi.* "Of the thirty-six stratagems, fleeing is best."

Chapter 118

The name of the game was "Avert and Divert", and they were the best two players in Paris, i.e. in France, i.e. in the world.

The minister stood on a stool next to the police car at the Odéon intersection, waiting for the cue to go live. His media advisor checked the monitor again and issued instructions to the T.V. crew. The make-up artist touched up the shadows under his eyes, the lighting technician adjusted the spotlight, and the cameraman shifted angles to achieve the most flattering frame possible. It was a cinematic production under the guise of a news report, and all major T.V. channels and websites were expected to open with it.

Behind the cameras, outside the frame, the head of counter-intelligence went over the statement, correcting a word here, a phrase there. The minister needed friends like him in moments like these, when the Élysée suddenly seemed a distant pipe dream.

The lighting and sound checks had been completed. "Seven minutes until air!" the producer called out. The minister stepped off the stool and went over the statement handed to him by his friend.

On the face of it, the event was catastrophic. The Chinese commando unit continued to operate in Paris unabated, under the nose of dozens of police officers. The juge d'instruction had issued dubious warrants, compromising the secrecy of the operation, and had even been injured himself in the shooting. A vital witness had been assassinated apparently after turning himself in to the police, and the main suspect (together with two other commandos) had been taken out by an Israeli intelligence officer before the authorities could even wrap their head around events.

But they had been through worse situations, and this time would be no different. The minister had a deep bass voice and a thick head of hair, and a lot of luck to go with it. He did not need more: even the most clear-cut events could be given a different spin if the story was bold enough, fast enough, had enough edge. People will always prefer stories, improbable as they may be, to everyday reality, even when said reality has taken place before their eyes.

The minister stood in front of his friend and started reading.

"I called Commissaire Léger this morning to thank him personally for the heroic operation to eliminate the criminal organisation threatening to flood France with the largest cache of drugs seized in Paris in the twenty-first century. The commissaire and his men risked their lives in the final, devastating confrontation. Two of them, the Chinese gang leader and his junior partner, as well as a young Israeli of Russian descent, were shot by the armed forces while threatening to seize hostages from the club in which they were hiding. Juge d'instruction, Philippe du Monticole, was injured in the crossfire, having courageously insisted on accompanying the forces during the operation. I would like to take this opportunity to extend my gratitude to Juge du Monticole for his outstanding dedication, and wish him a speedy recovery."

The head of counter-intelligence nodded.

"They'll buy it?" the minister said.

"I thought about adding another paragraph, so they'd have something to argue about with you instead of arguing about the facts."

"Go ahead, surprise me."

How many times had they played this game? How many times had he averted and diverted for his friend the minister, how many times had his friend the minister repaid the favour, how many times had they buried an adversary together, or a potential adversary, or a former adversary, or an imagined adversary? Scores. But they got a kick out of it each time.

He took another piece of paper out of his pocket and read: "I cannot overstate the danger associated with the large-scale trafficking of drugs within the French Republic, as demonstrated by the ruthless crimes perpetrated by the gang which Commissaire Léger and his men dismantled tonight. I personally have no doubt that the fashionable discourse in certain political circles with regard to the legalisation of such drugs is encouraging gangs to overwhelm our country and eliminate their enemies in any way possible. I urge the Président de la République to put an end to this initiative before the next violent crime wave."

The minister looked at his friend with manifest amusement. Employing inflated rhetoric to cover up for a deep failure, the argument was both ridiculous and ingenious. Ridiculous, because it was untrue, irrelevant and illogical. And ingenious, because it was a clear attack on his political enemy in the party, the Speaker of the Senate, and that's all anyone would focus on – journalists, the Twitterati, politicians and taxi drivers.

"Two minutes until air!" the producer called out. The minister straightened his hair and got back up on the stool, looking into the camera lens with an expression of solemn sincerity.

Chapter 119

Abadi returned to consciousness, struggling for breath. Even before he opened his eyes he knew he did not recognise the room from the hundreds he'd slept in over the course of his life – the silence was unfamiliar, the mattress too soft.

He opened his eyes.

"You can't be left alone even for a few hours," Oriana said.

He was lying in a hospital room, then – that much Abadi could gather even through the painkillers. And it was a French hospital – that much he could infer from the sign about patients' rights and the view of Notre-Dame through the window. The woman talking to him was his deputy in Unit 8200's Special Section, Segen Oriana Talmor. That one he knew from the slight twinge in his heart, which hurt even more than the stitches in his shoulder. Why did he have stitches in his shoulder? He strained to remember. Yes, his right arm was bandaged because he had been hit by shrapnel when two Chinese commandos had begun shooting like madmen, and his left arm was attached to a drip probably because it took the French an hour or two to remember to search the area. He had lost blood.

"How did you find me?" he said. He was parched, but he wasn't sure he could reach the water on the bedstand with all these bandages. Oriana was standing on the far side of it, leaning against the wall.

"I was in an ambulance with two extremely handsome French paramedics, and I told them I needed to get to your hotel near Notre-Dame. They couldn't stop laughing. There are better ways to learn that Hotel Dieu is not a hotel but a hospital. It suited them fine and they brought me here."

She wore blue jeans and a leather jacket. Abadi noticed an incongruous aviator hat under her arm and recognised a military strap on her shoulder, with what appeared to be a short-barrel Kalashnikov hanging from it. He was madly in love, and to hell with the new *Military Ethics Law.*

The bells of Notre-Dame started chiming.

"What time is it?" he asked.

"1.00 p.m. exactly. They brought you in two hours ago and immediately gave you Valium. You missed all the glorious press conferences the French police gave."

"Let's hope the casino millionaire doesn't give a press conference in Macau later today. Yerminski gave him the reel and I won't be able to find it now."

"The reel is here, dummy, on your night table. The Macau casino millionaire is someone called Ming. He gave it to me very nicely."

"What? How did you find him?" he said.

"The same way I found that 8200 leaker you protected during trial, Abadi," she said with a matter-of-fact tone that belied the spark in her eyes. "With great talent and equal ruthlessness."

His laughter was swiftly followed by a groan of pain.

"Do you want some water?" she said, pushing off the wall with her foot. "The doctor said that you need to drink a lot." She took a step closer and gently supported his neck while she lifted the glass to his lips. She smelled like flowers and fields, and there wasn't one thing he didn't like about her. He tried to think of something clever to say, although he could as easily remain next to her in complete silence.

"So I suppose the Commander of 8200 is pretty happy now? What are our orders?"

Oriana looked at her Navran and shrugged. "He sent a rather vague operation order to keep the damage to a minimum, whatever that means, and to come back by the end of the week if there was no fallout. But we'll need to stop by a statue at Le Bourget on our way to Charles de Gaulle . . . My passport is buried there."

"O.K. So can you help me get up?"

"You think you're well enough for damage control?"

"No, but we need to go to my mother's for lunch."

Although she had promised herself not to smile at him for at least an entire day, she couldn't help but burst into laughter.

"You're taking me to your mum's?"

"I have to go and visit her. She'll be dying of worry and she won't calm down until she sees me."

"Maybe you should also calm down General Rotelmann, who seems to believe you're an 'immoral, ruthless influence within the unit'?"

"I don't think he's worried about me. At any rate, not as worried as my mother is. He knows there will be many more opportunities to sacrifice me as a scapegoat. I imagine there are dozens of potential Yerminskis in a huge apparatus like 8200, we won't be able to stop them all. So until then, we deserve to rest. Or at least eat some couscous with stuffed artichokes."

Chapter 120

To: Central

From: Police/National Headquarters/Foreign Intelligence

Immediate/Unclassified

The representative of the Israeli police in Europe confirms that another Israeli was killed in a shootout between criminal elements related to the Chinese mafia in the French capital. The casualty is Vladislav Yerminski from Ashdod, a 21-year-old soldier on leave who was previously involved in other crimes in the French capital. The Paris police believe that Yerminski was the abduction target of the Chinese crime cartel that killed high-tech employee Yaniv Meidan in a case of mistaken identity. The French Minister of Interior said this morning at a press conference that the background to the event was a major drug deal, foiled thanks to police alertness, which led to killings within the organisation. A total of twelve criminals have been killed in this affair over the past twenty-four hours, most of them from China, France and Russia, and an unprecedented quantity of Class A drugs was seized.

The commissaire in charge of the investigation, Commissaire Jules Léger, called the embassy this morning to thank the representative of the Israeli police for his co-operation. Yerminski's body will be brought back to Israel for burial after autopsy.

To: All Editorial Boards

From: Military Censor

A sweeping gag order is hereby imposed on the military role of the soldier killed in the drug-related case today while on leave in Paris. It is strictly prohibited to mention or imply the location of his post, his military department or the corps in which he served. The only details authorised for publication are his name, age and hometown. Any other detail from this moment forth, and until further notice, must be submitted to censorship prior to publication.

To: Central

From: Aman/Central Intelligence-Gathering Unit/Intelligence Liaison Unit/Duty Network Intelligence Officer

Priority: Immediate/Top Secret

Clearance level: Purple

The information transferred to us from friendly sources (Code 33) confirms that the assassination of Vladislav Yerminski this morning in Paris, near a nightclub in which a major drug deal was about to transpire, is of a criminal nature and unrelated to his military service in Unit 8200.

It should be noted that yesterday, immediately after the abduction of the civilian Yaniv Meidan in Paris, we relayed that the event was of a criminal nature, contrary to the claims of certain sections in Unit 8200.

To: Aman/EWF – Early Warning Forum

To: Aman Research/Head Divisions

To: Aman/Intelligence-Gathering Command/Head Units

Cc: General Headquarters/Vice Chief of Defence Staff

From: Chief of Intelligence

Priority: Secret/Routine

As of today, the responsibility for communications with foreign liaison departments in the various units will be transferred from me to my deputy, the head of Intelligence-Gathering Command. The shift will enable better co-ordination and better protection of our allies' information security.

Please adjust accordingly.

Chapter 121

Oriana drove carefully, less because of the peculiar traffic laws in Paris than in an attempt to minimise the impact of the bumps on the road, which elicited groans of agony from Abadi every time. The doctor who had signed his release form cautioned that he was still weak and must be brought back to the hospital in the event that he lost consciousness again.

She felt lighthearted and confident, as if the fact of his injury granted her equal status. Every now and then he touched her to point out monuments in a gesture void of authority and consequently rich in meaning. Every so often her hand brushed against him while changing gears. They passed by the Hôtel de Ville, which wasn't a hotel either, Île Saint-Louis, the Jardin des Plantes, the Place de la Bastille and the Bibliothèque Nationale de France.

Between them, in the storage compartment, were two mobiles: Yerminski's green Samsung and Ekaterina's red Nokia into which Yerminski had entered his private key. Oriana was supposed to open his bitcoin account and authorise a new transfer to Ming's account for twenty million dollars. She was sure that her father would have clicked "Send" by now. But would he have been right to do so? Would, for instance, Zorro hand the money back? Would the Prime Minister do it? And would Abadi? He had listened with an impassive face as she told him about "Putin's promise", and had said they would have to talk about it later. She was not sure what he meant. Or maybe she was.

Oriana Talmor felt that it had been a long night. In "effective continuity" she had been a spy in the service of her country, a security officer in the service of her country's spies, a suspected traitor against the nation's interests, an agent provocateur in the service of God knows whom, a seeker of truth and a professional liar; she had been on one side and then on another. On whose side was she now, and on whose side was the unfairly attractive Aluf Mishne Abadi? Twenty million dollars rested between them, in the darkness of the storage compartment.

We're in Paris, Oriana reminded herself, letting go of all other concerns as she did so. We're in Paris, this is happening in a parallel life. He was an officer with a decorated past. She was an officer with a promising future. They drove along the river.

It was 2.40 p.m., Tuesday, April 17.

Glossary of ranks and their equivalents

Israeli rank	British equivalent
Rav Aluf	Commander in Chief
Aluf	general / major general
Tat Aluf	brigadier general
Aluf Mishne	colonel
Sgan Aluf	lieutenant colonel
Rav Seren	major
Seren	captain
Segen	lieutenant
Samal/Samelet	sergeant
Rav Turai	corporal
Turai	private

Israeli title	British equivalent/translation	American equivalent
Rosh HaMateh HaKlalli	Chief of Defence Staff	Chairman of the Joint Chiefs of Staff
Rosh Aman	head of Israeli Defence Intelligence	

Israeli Organisation	English Description
Tzahal	Israel Defence Forces
Aman	Israel Defence Intelligence (military)
the Mossad	Israel's Foreign Intelligence Service
the Shabak	Israel's Internal Security Service

DOV ALFON, brought up in Paris and Tel Aviv, is a former intelligence officer of Unit 8200, the most secretive arm of the Israel Defence Forces. He was editor in chief of Israel's most influential newspaper, *Haaretz*, and chief editor of the leading publishing house Kinneret-Zmora. *A Long Night In Paris*, published in Israel to rave reviews, topped the best seller charts for 24 weeks.

DANIELLA ZAMIR lives in Tel-Aviv, where she works as a literary translator. She obtained her bachelor's degree in literature from Tel Aviv University, and her master's degree in creative writing from City University in London.